GREAT JOB O̶ ...̶en will the next one be coming out? I can̶ ...̶

——

IS THERE GOING TO BE ANOTHER *Cabin* book? I have *I, II,* and *III.* I keep hearing a new one will be coming, but I haven't found it yet. I really love those books. Thanks!

——

WHEN WILL THE FOURTH BOOK be available? Movie possible?

——

THANKS! YOUR BOOKS ARE WONDERFUL. Does this book continue the series and if so will there be any more?

——

I'M AN AVID READER OF YOURS and have already read *Cabin I, II,* and *III.* I was wondering when I could expect the arrival of *Cabin IV.*

——

WHEN WILL YOUR NEXT BOOK BE OUT? Sure enjoyed reading the others. They are just great. I can't put the books down when I start reading them. Will be waiting . . .

I HAVE READ YOUR *Cabin Series I, II, III* and was wondering if the next one has been published. I really enjoyed the first three and am looking forward to the continuation.

— —

I am just wondering when you'll be coming out with the *Cabin IV*. I have read the other ones, and love them. Please hurry! They are wonderful books.

Cabin IV

In Jacob's Shadow

Cabin IV

In Jacob's Shadow

C. J. Henderson

Michael Publishing Company

Michael Publishing
P.O. Box 778
Fairmont, WV 26554

Copyright © 2004 by C. J. Henderson
Photo of author by Warner Photography, Fairmont, West Virginia
Dedication poem by Cecelia Hawkinberry

Library of Congress Control Number 2004108285
ISBN: 0-97102-451-0

First Michael Publishing Printing: June 2004

Printed in the U.S.A

Fairmont Printing Company, Fairmont, West Virginia

To my four wonderful grandchildren,
whose smiles light up my face.
Thank you for your unconditional love,
Ashton, Remington, Logan and Chase.

C. J. HENDERSON WAS RAISED IN THE SMALL TOWN OF Farmington, West Virginia. High points in her early life were long trips to visit family who lived in remote areas of Appalachia. Over time, this environment became as familiar to her as her own modern home, and gradually she was introduced to many families whose homes were scattered miles apart. A typical visit included hours of walking with a group of friends and cousins from house to house, looking for something to do. Because there were no televisions or telephones to keep the girls occupied, the group invented games and told tales. Just as she had observed her father doing for many years, C. J. kept her companions entertained for hours with her stories, in which she combined her own imagination with real-life events that played out in the isolated and poverty-stricken mountain culture.

C. J. married just out of high school and lived on a farm, putting off her longing to write and attend college. She raised two sons, and as they matured, she attended night school at Fairmont State College, and later at Parkersburg Community College. Years later, her position as a land agent for Equitable Gas Company took her to many of the same isolated regions where she had spent time as a child. She found nothing had changed. The impoverished still had no education and remained without electricity, inside plumbing, telephones, television, and other conveniences. This renewed knowledge of their extraordinary lifestyle fueled her desire to create stories about that parallel world of people who live alongside us but remain separate at the same time.

After she resigned from her job with the utility company, C. J. moved to the West Coast and spent three years writing and setting the groundwork for the six novels in The Cabin Series. She then returned to West Virginia and, drawing on her experience as a realtor and as a land acquisition agent, she opened her own real estate company, which she continues to operate. She also continues to devote herself to writing and publishing her novels.

To you, O Lord, I lift up my soul.
O my God, in you I trust.
(PSALM 25: 1–2, NRSV)

THE CONTINUATION OF *THE CABIN SERIES* IS GREATLY encouraged by the response of the many readers who take the time to send e-mails (cj@windingridge.net) and letters, which I receive daily. They inspire me and keep me writing. The comments and ideas of those I hear from are—many times—incorporated into the story line of future novels and make us all a part of the creation.

I'm motivated to continue the series, too, by the many engaging and gracious people that I meet at book signings.

I also want to mention my editor, Valerie Gittings; without her skills and suggestions, *The Cabin Series* may not have been as sought after as it is today.

As always, my family is my main source of strength and support:

Husband, Jack Oliver

Mother, Mabel Henderson

Father, Orval Henderson Sr.

Sons, John Michael, Jr. & Mark Michael

Sisters & Brothers, Fran Henderson,
Harry Henderson, Sr. & Nettie,
Orval Henderson, Jr. & Pam,
Edith Hess & Charles, & Karen Legget & Wayne

Grandchildren, Ashton Michael, Remingtion Michael,
Logan Michael, Chase Martin

Stepchildren, Jack Oliver II, Johnny Oliver & Mandi,
Tamme DeLoskey & Richard

Stepgrandchildren, Taylor DeLoskey, Matthew DeLoskey,
Hunter Oliver, & Abby Oliver

Nephews & Nieces, Lea Robinson & John, Harry Henderson Jr.,
Rick Henderson, Jennifer Chipps & Shawn, Michael Henderson,
Timmy Henderson & Kelly, Chuckie Hess & Cindy,
Pete Cole & Donna, Timmy Spiker, Dean Howerton,
Travis Legget, Terry Sturdivant & Mark,
Sherry Clarke & Chris, Lisa Polis & David

Love of family
The years roll by
You see family grow
You see family cry

Some days are good and some days are bad—
Some days you wish for the people you had

I love them all in a special way
I remember the things they used to say

—Pete Cole

1

*T*HE DARKNESS WAS TOO DEEP FOR HER TO SEE IN THE CONfined place, and the only thing she could hear was the wind as it found its way through the pines, wailing around the mountain, looking to devastate anything in its path. The eeriness of the night was heightened by the occasional call of a wild animal. For the past four years, Patty had enjoyed the fulfillment of her dream of an exciting life in the city. Having been away from her childhood home for such a long time, she'd nearly forgotten the wind's lonely sound and the call of animals echoing just below it.

Sheltered by unfamiliar, rough walls, the girl cowered in the corner, dreading the door's opening and her captor's return. As if her head were filled with cotton, she looked through a haze. *How did I get here? Why don't I remember?* she wondered. A foul odor that she couldn't identify assaulted the cool mountain air. She realized that in spite of the unappetizing stench, her stomach held an empty knot of hunger, and she was thirstier than she'd ever been in her life.

Chilled by the night air, she got to her knees. Cautiously, she crawled around the base of the wall, eventually coming just slightly short of a full circle, about eight feet shy of where she had begun. There she came in contact with an army blanket. Surprised and grateful, she found the edge, unfolded the blanket, and wound it around herself, covering her body from head to toe. Wrapped like a mummy, she sat back against the wall, and tried, unsuccessfully, to make out the objects barely visible in the windowless room.

An unsettling, muffled sound suddenly disturbed the air. The soft, wounded-animal noise was coming from just across the narrow room. Wanting desperately to hide, Patty quickly pulled the rough blanket over her face but could not stop the screams that filled her throat.

Mercifully, a dazzling light filled the room, melting the darkness of Patty's dream, dragging her horror-filled mind slowly back into consciousness.

Tuesday had flipped the light switch on and was rushing across the soft carpet. She sat down on the edge of Patty's bed. Loosened from pins and hairspray, Tuesday's mass of blond hair cascaded around her shoulders.

"It's okay, honey. It's only a nightmare."

Gradually coming up from the depth of a steep, spiraling tunnel, Patty fully awoke to the comforting sound of Tuesday's voice.

"When am I going to stop having these nightmares?" she sobbed.

"Everything's okay," Tuesday soothed.

"I'm so sorry to wake you," Patty said.

"It's alright." Tuesday hugged the girl tightly then released her so she could look into her eyes. She had come to think of Patty as her own child, never once regretting that she and Cliff had adopted her shortly after their marriage.

"Want to talk about it?"

"I've had this same nightmare before. Remember the one about me being locked up in a dark place with the wind howling outside?"

"Yes, I do," Tuesday said. "Did anything new happen? Or can you tell where you were in the dream?"

"No, not at all," Patty said. "My dream ends before I know where I am or who is responsible for—" she sobbed, unable to put words to the horrific scene.

"Take your time, Patty."

"It'd be hilarious if it wasn't so scary." Patty forced a feeble smile through her tears, deeply relieved that what she had just experienced had been only another nightmare.

"We've got to do something about these nightmares," Tuesday said.

"I know. The therapist isn't doing any good. He thinks the dreams are just nerves or maybe hurtful images from my past. He doesn't understand that they're really bits and pieces of my life, past and future."

"I'm afraid he's like most people and has little concept of what your dreams are about."

"You can include me in that group," Patty said. Her bountiful, long eyelashes were wet with tears.

"Maybe another therapist might have had a case like yours and can help."

"Tuesday, that's just wishful thinking. Continuing with therapy is a waste of time and money. Can't you see that? What I need is to find my birth family. They may be just like me. They might be able to help me understand why I have dreams that—days, weeks, months, years later—I find myself walking into, awake, thinking, 'This has already happened,' knowing what everyone is going to do and say."

"Maybe you're right," Tuesday said. "You know I'll do anything I can to help." She paused briefly and then said, "Except of course allow you to travel to the mountain alone."

Choosing to ignore the remark, Patty wrapped her arm through Tuesday's and leaned her head against hers, her dark hair in stark contrast to Tuesday's.

"If only you could. I hate having these horrifying nightmares and knowing that chances are I'm actually going to live them someday."

In one last attempt to get her approval and avoid going against Tuesday and Cliff's wishes, Patty looked Tuesday in the eyes. "I know you and Cliff don't feel it's safe for me to visit the mountain, but I have to go back. That's the only way

I'll ever find my birth family. Annabelle and Aggie must know something! They were the ones tending to my mother when I was born." Patty's eyes filled with fresh tears. "And because Pa never saw to it that we had medical care, the family had to watch as my mother bled to death," Patty said, her voice catching. "Annabelle said that my mother never even got to see me or hold me in her arms."

"Are you sure you've remembered everything that the women have told you about your mother over the years?"

"Yes, I'm sure. Sometimes it's all I think about. Annabelle, especially, always got angry when I mentioned my birth mother. I always thought she felt kind of threatened whenever I wanted to know all about my birth mother, since she'd taken my mother's place in every way that she could under the circumstances. But as I got older, I realized that it was talking to her about my dreams that upset her so much that she'd refuse to talk about my mother."

Patty shrugged. "Tuesday, nothing is going to change until I go to the mountain. Don't you see that Annabelle's actions prove she knows something?"

"I'm not forbidding you from ever returning to your mountain home," Tuesday said. "I'm just asking you to take a few months, and we'll talk about it again."

"Whatever," Patty said.

"You're sounding like your friends now. Anyway, you need to finish with the plastic surgeon. You know he wants to do one final skin graft on your face."

"I know that, but I hate to have to go in the hospital again. I'd thought I would've been finished with all that by now."

"It's no big deal," Tuesday said. "And you knew when we started that it would take more than a couple of hospital stays. The last skin graft didn't take well and he's only going to replace it. After all you've gone through, you can't give up before it's finished!"

"After that," Patty said imploringly, wanting Tuesday's permission, "I'm going to go."

"Let's discuss all this with Cliff," Tuesday said, bringing

him in as a stall tactic. "We have to consider each other when we make such huge decisions."

"Fine. I know he'll see something wrong with my going."

"Patty, we have to decide this together! As a family."

"Whatever." Patty flopped back onto her pillow and pulled the comforter to her chin, causing Tuesday to shift her weight to release the blanket.

"You're not being fair, young lady. We only have your best interests at heart."

Relenting, Patty sat up and threw her arms around Tuesday. "I'm sorry. I don't want to be a brat. I don't know what would have happened to me if not for you. You know that I love you and Cliff. I respect you both, and ever since you've taken me in, I've tried to make you proud, but, Tuesday, no matter what happens, I have to find my birth family."

In the last class of the morning, Patty sat in her usual seat in the second row, next to Ashton, her best friend. Patty had always enjoyed history, but to be learning about witchcraft this semester was terribly distressing. Distressing because with each assignment she found that there were parallels between the stories she had been assigned to read and the events in her nightmares. The class was almost over, and Ashton kept glancing at Patty as she too recognized the parallels. This lesson was on the unsavory ways society dealt with those believed to be involved in witchcraft.

The bell rang and the girls headed to their lockers through hallways filled with laughing, rowdy teenagers. "Patty, that was scary," Ashton said. "The stories where the women were burned at the stake, well, they sound like they were taken straight from your dreams."

"I know," Patty said opening her locker with a bang. "This stuff frightens me, and nobody can really understand unless they've lived it. That's why I want so badly to find my birth family. Maybe they have dreams of the future and the past just like I do."

"I sure don't understand it," Ashton said.

"Last night Tuesday told me that I can't go to the mountain."

"What are you going to do now? I know you were counting, big time, on going."

"I'm going anyway."

Ashton, jostled by a group of freshmen hurrying to lunch, shouldered against Patty, causing her to drop her books. Bending down to help pick up them, Ashton gathered the papers that had slipped from one of the fallen books. "What's this?" she asked, wide-eyed. Ashton held a picture of a young woman tied to a pole, and piled around the base were stacks of wood reaching to the girl's knees. "Patty, did you draw this? It looks like you."

Hastily, Patty took the picture and slipped it back inside her book. "Let's go to lunch."

"I only wanted to know who it's supposed to be."

"Forget it."

"Whatever," Ashton said good-naturedly.

The cafeteria was a den of noisy teenagers, calling out across the room, laughing, grabbing and throwing someone's cap, slamming down their books to hold a seat while standing in the line for food, or just shouting to be heard by those at their table over the clamor in the huge room. Patty and Ashton joined their friends at the usual table. Tiffany was already there with her sister Amber. Almost from the first, the girls had become a tight-knit group, the three quickly accepting Patty and her innocent, unsophisticated ways, which were intriguing to them. Patty trusted her friends and felt free to talk to them about her life on the mountain.

"Now that you can drive, I can't understand why you don't go visit your family on the mountain." Tiffany said. "Are you afraid?"

"Yes, you are," Amber said before Patty could answer. "How cool is that?"

"No, actually, I'm not. I just told Ashton that I'm going. Didn't I, Ashton?"

"Yes," Ashton looked around at the others. "Why not? She has her own car."

"And, anyway, I was never scared to go. I just never wanted to visit someplace I was never very comfortable or happy. Annabelle, the woman who raised me, isn't my real mother, and I have no desire to run into my father or brother."

"Right," said the others, as they began picking at their food.

2

September 5, 2001

The nightmares had become more and more frequent during the last days of summer, and they persisted in earnest as the leaves turned to flaming red, orange, and yellow tinged with little veins of brown.

The others had slipped into the warm comfort of their beds around ten o'clock, but Patty sat at her desk. Covered with schoolbooks and notepads, hers was the typical, cluttered desktop of any ordinary, middleclass schoolgirl. Her doll Summer was propped against the wall at the back of the desk, her skirt fanning out over lifelike legs that rested on the polished surface.

"You know, Summer, sometimes Tuesday worries. She says that I'm too old to have a doll." Gingerly, Patty picked Summer up and straightened her skirt before setting her back on the desk. "She doesn't understand that you're not really a doll, you're family," Patty grinned, "but I won't tell Tuesday that.

"Anyway, I'm ready to go back to the mountain to learn what I can about my family. Maybe my mother was not my only relative besides my father who lived there. I may have cousins, a grandmother, a grandfather, or who-knows-who. Just because my mother died young doesn't mean that her mother, sisters, or cousins are gone too. Maybe I'll find someone who can tell me that I'm not the only one who has these dreams of the past and future. Maybe I'll find out that I'm not an abnormal person or a weirdo."

Patty watched the doll intently for a few minutes, and spoke, "Yes, that's it, Summer. I told you, I know it! These most recent dreams that I've been having are dreams of the olden days." Patty leaned close to the doll; the two looked like conspirators face to face. "The picture that I found in my history book—I must've drawn it while I was asleep. It looks like me. Ashton said so. In the picture the girl's hands are behind her back, tied to a narrow pole. Maybe it's my great, great grandmother or something. I just have to know what all this means. And I'm going to find out!

"Many of the dreams I've been having aren't of events that are going to happen in the future. I'm starting to think they're of my family members' past. Learning about the practice of witch burning in school has helped me begin to understand the dreams."

Patty was quiet again as she considered the doll closely, and then she said, "My final surgery's been done now, and I'm ready to go to the mountain. I don't care if I am taking a risk," she said unconvincingly, looking into the doll's eyes, trying not to remember the most frightening of her dreams.

But they flooded her mind. In one, she was standing alongside a deserted road with brown leaves swirling like funnel clouds at her feet. There was nothing in either direction as far as she could see. In another she was confined in a small, dark place with no food and little water. She shook her head as if trying to shake the vision away.

There were other dreams that she often had, and she had no idea what they predicted. Her father was the center of most of her nightmares. In one, he had begun building a huge house over the foundation of a mansion that had been part of a grand old estate. A man and boy were working there, apparently under her father's instructions. She couldn't identify the two because their faces were lost in murky shadows. The dream conveyed an impression of the great house and its remoteness, but the impact of it was that the building was for Tuesday, Winter Ann, and herself. The man, but not the boy, was in most of the dreams she had of her father, especially during his prison years. The man's personality came across in her dreams; he was callous, rough, and vulgar, so unlike her father, who craftily impressed those who met him as a gentleman.

"Why won't my dreams tell me how my journey to the mountain will end?" She looked at Summer, imploring the doll for a response.

"You're saying maybe they have, aren't you?" Patty asked. Obviously, there must be an answer in her nightmares somewhere.

"Anyway, I can't let dreams that I don't understand frighten me away. I'm going to the mountain and find out who my grandparents are. I'll just let the dreams be a guide to me as I believe that they're supposed to be."

A knock at Patty's door caused her to jump. "Who is it?"

"It's me," Tuesday answered.

"Oh, come in."

"I heard you talking," Tuesday looked around the room as if expecting to see someone other than Patty.

"Oh—" Patty opened her mouth then closed it.

"Who were you talking to?" Tuesday asked.

"I'm alone," Patty sighed. "But I thought I was the only one awake."

Tuesday had let it be known that she was uneasy about Patty's attachment to her doll, but Patty refused to allow it to make a difference. In any other matter, out of love and respect, Patty deferred to Tuesday's authority, but not where it concerned her strange gift, as she had come to think of it.

"I was talking to Summer."

"Oh," was all Tuesday could say.

"Please come in. I want to talk to you."

"Okay, honey." Tuesday stepped inside Patty's room and closed the door.

Patty began, "I'm ready to go to the mountain, Tuesday. Like we've talked before, I just have to find and get to know my family."

"I was hoping that we weren't going to have this discussion again so soon." Tuesday said. "And I have to say, ever since you got the car, I've been dreading this."

"I've worked hard saving for it."

"I know."

"It's time now. I've got to find out who they are."

"I don't think you're ready," Tuesday said. "It's too soon."

"Too soon for what?"

"Oh, I don't know," Tuesday said. "I guess the truth is that I'm not ready. I'm afraid for you to go."

"We've been talking about it since last summer. How ready can you get?" Patty asked and laid a hand on Tuesday's arm. "You know that after what you went through there, you'll never be ready for me to go to the mountain."

"You're right about that," Tuesday took Patty in her arms, determined not to get teary eyed, and hugged her.

"I need to know what my dreams mean. When I was a little girl, they were so much more frightening, and being so immature, I never understood what was going on or the value of them. Anyway, not until I met you. And now I feel that I need to respect my ability and use it whenever I can."

"I see what you're saying. The dreams are invaluable. Look at the way they brought Cliff and me to the conclusion that your father was involved in child trafficking. Just that one instance left no room for doubt about their validity. And we know that your dreams could keep you from danger, if you allow them to."

"You were the first person who ever believed in me. I feel like everyone thinks I'm weird—except for you and Cliff."

Tuesday, having lost the fight against tears, smiled even then at the memory of Patty, the little girl in raggedy feedsack dresses, living on hopes and dreams in the primitive cabin. The first time they'd met, Tuesday had discovered that Patty had spent her tender years frightened by dreams she couldn't understand, having no one in her small world that she could confide in.

"There have to be people who are like me, people in my birth family, I mean."

"No doubt."

"I want your permission to go. May I?"

"I just hate for you to go back there," Tuesday said. "How many times have I told you that I think it's dangerous?"

"Pa's living in the city," Patty said. "And the militia has been disbanded, at least on the mountain above Winding Ridge."

"Well, okay, but only if I go with you," Tuesday said. "I'd like to see Annabelle and Daisy again."

"Tuesday, I don't know how long I'll be gone," Patty said. "Do you really want to leave Winter Ann with Cora that long? I don't think it'd be wise to take her along either. We'd have to be careful where we took her. Remember the awful conditions in the cabin? At bedtime we'd have to get in early having a baby with us. I thought I'd stay at the boarding-house in Winding Ridge, and if you and Winter Ann are with me that means that whatever we're doing, we'll have to stop and head for town and put her to bed. And we can't stay in the cabin; she wouldn't even have a decent bed to sleep in."

Tuesday frowned. "I suppose you're right. Ask Paul Frank to go with you instead."

"No! Paul Frank is busy himself, and I don't know how long I'll be. Anyway, my family may not be people who I'd be proud to introduce Paul Frank to."

"Patty, you'll have to take someone with you. I'm afraid for you to go alone. And I really don't understand why you don't want to ask Paul Frank. You enjoy his company. You had talked about inviting him to your school graduation party."

"Oh, that's so different! Anyway, I want to meet my family first before I go introducing them to other people.

"And sure, I'm still going to ask him to the party. Assuming I get up the nerve." She blushed, the pink flush reaching from her cheeks to her temples. "I can hardly wait. It'll be so much fun to go to a party with him, and maybe it'll make a difference in our relationship. Being with other couples will give us a chance to be in a setting like we're a couple," Patty giggled, "and he'll see how great it is. Oh, I pray that he says yes. If he doesn't, I'll be mortified."

A look of joy and fear showed by turn in Patty's eyes when she talked about Paul Frank and the party, fear because there was Mary Lou to consider. It was obvious to everyone in the Moran household that both girls had a crush on Paul Frank. The problem was that no one knew, or could guess, which girl Paul Frank was interested in—if either one.

"Let's talk about your going to the mountain again later, okay?" Tuesday said. She was relieved when Patty nodded. Tuesday needed time to enlist Cliff's help in the matter.

Two days later, though, on September 7, Patty took off for the mountain alone, determined to find her family and solve the mystery of her dreams. She left a note telling Tuesday and Cliff that she would keep in touch, and for them to please understand and not interfere with her search.

3

September 6, 2001

Annabelle and Daisy busied themselves in their separate chores, Daisy primping for the men she would wait on at the town bar, and Annabelle putting together the afternoon meal, dressed in her usual feedsack dress with her course gray hair knotted and held at the back of her head with half a dozen hair pins.

"Jeb's goin' to put a stop to your workin' in th' bar when he gets wind of it."

"He ain't goin' to find out cause there ain't no one talkin' 'bout it. Th' men like me workin' there, an' they sure ain't goin' to tell th' likes of 'im," Daisy flipped her head back, fanning the shining blue-black hair that complimented her olive skin.

"Ya knowed he stops there on his way home most times, an' ya not knowin' when he's comin', he's goin' to catch ya sooner or later."

Daisy shrugged.

Annabelle picked up the bucket from the floor beside the potbelly stove, and carrying it by one handle and holding it out from her side so it did not bang against her knees, disappeared out the back door.

The sound of the pump handle squeaking in protest as Annabelle drew water caught the attention of the three small children. They abandoned the biscuits that Annabelle had given them to hold them over till supper to play in the water that was sure to spill over, making a tempting puddle of mud.

Before Annabelle could stop them, the children had scooped up the wet dirt and were about to have a mud romp. Quickly, Annabelle abandoned her chore and grabbed Dakota and Kelly Sue by their muddy wrists. She gave Drexel, for whom she had no free hand, a stern look so effective it was as if she'd grabbed him too, stopping him in his tracks as he drew back a palm full of mud, ready to hurl it at Dakota. Dakota wriggled to get free of Annabelle's grip, but by then the whimpering Kelly Sue was no longer interested in slinging mud. By letting go of her, Annabelle was able to gather the three children in front of the pump so she could rinse their muddy hands.

After shooing the relatively clean children back inside the cabin to play their homemade games on the living room floor, Annabelle summoned Daisy and they carried the full bucket of water into the kitchen. She dipped a portion of it into the pot she would peel potatoes in, and she set the remainder on the top surface of the woodburner to heat.

"What 'bout Joe?" Annabelle continued as if she hadn't left the kitchen and their quarreling to go outdoors. "He's goin' to find out, an' ya betta believe he's goin' to tell his pa 'bout it."

"Annabelle! I told ya I'm not goin to worry 'bout it. I'm leavin' th' mountain for good one day. An' I'm tellin' ya, no one's goin' to stop me." Daisy held a mirror in her right hand as she applied makeup, a habit that irked Annabelle mainly because the makeup had been a gift from Tuesday Summers. Generally, though, she was used to Daisy's primping. Even before they'd been forced to travel to the city, Daisy primped when she should've been helping with the chores. At that time she'd owned no makeup, but she'd used the blackened end of a burned farmer's match to darken her eyebrows and pinched her cheeks to make them pink. She continually fussed with her hair, cutting strips of feedsack to tie it back from her face. And she spent much of her time—as Patty had—sitting in the outhouse by the hour, searching through the Sears Roebuck catalogs, dreaming about looking as beautiful as the women who were pictured in them, dressed in the most fashionable clothing.

"You're actin' like those city women, thinkin' ya can do as ya please," Annabelle said. "Mark my words, it just don't work that'a way up here on th' mountain."

"I'm makin' my own money, workin' at th' bar, an' I don't need Jeb to take care of me. He ain't no husband no how, stayin' away most all th' time, an' when he's 'round he has to divide his time between th' two of us. When I've enough money saved, I'm goin' to take my youngins an' go to th' city an' live."

"Yeah," Annabelle snorted. "Who's goin' to take care of a couple of two-year-olds while ya go out an' earn a livin'?"

"Didn't ya learn anythin' when we was in th' city?" Daisy began packing her hand mirror, bottles of makeup, lipsticks, rouge, and eyebrow pencils back into her cosmetic case.

"Th' shelter for abused women's there to help women like us. I'm goin' there, an' they'll help me get started. Other women does it, an' so can I."

Clutching her cosmetic case, Daisy rose from her chair and moved from the kitchen, parting the curtains at the doorway into the living room. Immediately to her right was the bedroom she shared with Annabelle and the man they shared when he was there. She crossed the room, knelt at the side of the four-poster, and stowed her cosmetic case in a chest where she kept her personal items out of the reach of curious children.

Satisfied her possessions were safe, she returned to the living room and bent to kiss her twin boys in turn and pat Sara's daughter, Kelly Sue, on the head. "Where's Sara?" Daisy asked.

"She's out milkin' th' cow an' tendin' th' chickens," Annabelle said.

"Just so she helps ya with th' youngins," Daisy said, and slammed the screen door as she left for her night shift at the bar.

"An' when is it that she hasn't?" Annabelle asked, calling after Daisy as she happily stepped from the back porch.

"I knowed it, Annabelle, an' I don't knowed what I'd do with out th' two of ya helpin," Daisy called back.

The men who frequented the bar favored Daisy more than any barmaid the town had ever seen, and they tipped her well. But most approved of McCallister's treatment of his women—they treated theirs the same way—and didn't think that Daisy would actually act upon her long-time dream of leaving the mountain to live on her own in the city. They all knew women were not capable of taking care of themselves.

As Daisy made her way down the mountain path, she caught up with Tommy Lee Hillberry, who was heading the same direction. He was not moving along very fast as he was carrying quite a load in his arms. He avoided speaking to Daisy as he tried to make room for her to pass by him on the narrow trail, looking as if he wanted to go unnoticed, or at the least unremembered.

"What ya got there?" Daisy asked, wanting to annoy him, refusing to pass right away. Although not really interested in what he was up to, she was not opposed to giving him a hard time, since he and his father, Andy, both were nuisances to the mountain folk and even to the people in town. They were particularly a bother to her at the bar. She had to put up with their getting drunk every day; then she'd have to cut them off from the booze. That always resulted in Daisy and the patrons being forced to listen to the two of them making a ruckus, obnoxiously demanding just one more drink for the road. Rarely did a week go by that Tommy Lee or his father was not thrown into jail for pubic intoxication.

"It ain't none of your business what I got," Tommy Lee spat.

"Looks like bed clothes to me. Where ya takin' 'em? Your cabin's back that-a-way." She pointed toward the overgrown driveway he'd just come from.

"That's my parents' cabin. A man's got to have his own place, an' maybe I have one. Ya don't knowed everythin', an' I told ya, it's none of your business," Tommy Lee said, looking like he'd been caught with his hand in the cookie jar.

He stumbled in his haste to get away from Daisy and her nosy questions—when normally he'd be flirting, happy for her attention—and an army blanket, perched at the very top of the mound of household items stacked precariously in his arms, slid from the heap and landed with a plop at Daisy's feet.

Laughing at him, Daisy scooped up the blanket and set it back on top with its mate. In a huff, Tommy Lee turned and continued his trip down the path.

Having no interest in where Tommy Lee was heading with his load, and not carrying a burden of her own to slow her down, Daisy pushed past him on the narrow path close enough to smell his foul body odor. She held her breath until she got by him, and leaving him lagging farther and farther behind, she hurried toward town.

September 7, 2001

Late the next day, Daisy refused to get out of bed each time Annabelle appeared in the room insisting that she get up, warning that she was tempting fate. Jacob or Joe was sure to catch her in bed at suppertime when she was supposed to be up and about doing her chores, and she'd have a lot of explaining to do then.

Finally Daisy, unable to sleep through Annabelle's constant nagging, rose from the four-poster and dressed. She was agitated at Annabelle and headed for the kitchen with the intention of giving her a hard time. "Ya're determined that I die on this mountain 'stead of goin' to th' city like I'm wantin' to do."

"I'm not stoppin' ya from goin' no where," Annabelle said.

"If I don't get some sleep, how'm I goin' to work an' earn th' money that I need to make th' move to th' city?"

"Your place is here," Annabelle fumed.

"My place is where I want to be," Daisy shouted. "Ya won't even let Joe modernize this place an' make life easier for us. Ya're so stubborn ya can't stand to have life easier. Look at Aunt Aggie, livin' in th' cabin that that militiaman fixed up. She has it easier now, not havin' to chop wood to cook an' keep warm. She don't have to build a fire on a hot day, roastin' herself out'a th' place just so she can eat."

"I'm not havin' no fancy gadgets in here," Annabelle said. "Anyway, I like th' way it is. It's Jeb's call, an' if he wants it changed, he'll do it hisself."

"Forevermore, Annabelle, ya're hopeless."

Just beyond the back door, the girl stood, listening to the women quarreling as she paused on the steps that led to the back porch. Even though Patty had planned for months for her trip to the mountains above Winding Ridge, it had taken everything she had to return to the place where she had been so neglected, suffering starvation much of the time, in addition to sexual abuse from her father.

Unexpectedly, repugnant memories washed over her, ones she had buried deep in blessed forgetfulness. Overcome by them, she realized how they had overshadowed her life in the remote cabin throughout her childhood. The recollection of her father's abuse was too much to bear, and she turned back toward the car.

"Patty, is that ya?" Annabelle crossed the kitchen to the back porch. She had caught sight of the girl from the kitchen window above the woodburning stove just as Patty had turned to leave.

Patty hesitated, then deliberately pushed away the horrid memories, burying them once more. During the past four years, she had replaced them with her new life and had found solace in the doll Tuesday had given her. Right now, Summer was waiting for her, propped in the passenger seat in the car. Pulled by the sound of Annabelle's voice, though, Patty turned once more toward the cabin.

"Look at ya, girl" Annabelle said, hurrying out the back door to greet Patty. "Your face . . . What happened?"

Patty put her hand to her face, as if forgetting the birthmark was gone, and smiled, allowing Annabelle to lead her across the porch. She hardly realized that the area, where the women had previously dumped wash water, had been cleaned up, and the rancid smell she had really never noticed—another facet of her impoverished life—was long gone.

"I didn't knowed ya!" Daisy exclaimed, holding the screen open as they passed, and Annabelle led Patty into the kitchen. "Ya look great. Patty, ya're beautiful." The women were in awe of the startling transformation Patty had undergone. She wore a mint-green, silk blouse, accented by a forest green cardigan, and a pair of nicely fitting jeans. Jeans had become her everyday favorite. She looked very much the city girl.

"Sara, come look," Annabelle said. "It's your sister back. Her birthmark's gone. It's like magic."

"Never thought I'd—" Sara appeared in the kitchen, dressed in blue jeans and a tee shirt. She abruptly stopped talking in mid-sentence. Her mouth agape, she stared at Patty's lovely face, now minus the huge purple birthmark that had once completely covered her left cheek.

"You never thought you'd see me again," Patty finished for Sara, staring herself at Sara's new look. Both girls were pleasantly surprised, as they had never known each other dressed in anything except feedsack dresses.

Joe had always been the best dressed of the lot, with Jeb's castoff city clothes, ill-fitting as they were. With Jeb gone and Joe in charge, Annabelle still refused to give in to change, content with her everyday feedsack dress, but after admiring Daisy in outfits that Tuesday had given her, Joe had seen fit to provide Sara with jeans, blouses, and sweaters. Sara's stylish look, though, stopped at her neck with her homemade haircut, and as usual she wore no makeup.

Hearing the excitement in the woman's voices, the three

children abandoned the game they were playing on the living room floor and came scooting into the kitchen single file, with Drexel in the lead. They raced across the kitchen floor, leaving the tattered doorway curtains in a tangle. Kelly Sue, propelled by a grease spill, skidded into her mother's legs and wrapped her arms tightly around one of them to keep from falling flat on the floor. From between Sara's legs, she peered at the newcomer, astonished at the unfamiliar sight of a beautiful stranger. The toddler realized only two things: Patty's speech was different (it reminded her of her Grandpa Jeb, whom she rarely saw), and she had never seen this person before. Where did she come from?

"Kelly Sue!" Sara admonished. "Don't hang on me. How many times do I have to tell ya?"

As she looked around, Patty's heart pounded, pushing against her chest walls, and she gasped involuntarily, clutching her throat. This scene was an exact replica of one of her dreams.

I absolutely must find out what my dreams mean. I hope they're not telling me to stay away because I'm in danger. Could their purpose be to guide me away from here, to let me know I'm wrong to come? No! That's not it. I'm right to come back to the mountain where my life began! At least, I pray that's the way it is.

Getting her breath back, Patty noted that although there were many changes in Sara and Daisy since she had lived there, the cabin, like Annabelle, was virtually unchanged. The plank floors still had the same poor construction with cracks that exposed the earth below, although the place was somewhat cleaner than she'd remembered it. She was pretty sure that was the result of Daisy's and Annabelle's time in Wheeling, where they had spent months at a shelter for abused women, learning skills to make them employable. They had received instruction on childcare, housekeeping, sewing, and were made ready for other positions that did not require reading and writing. They were taught, too, about the benefits of proper hygiene and the risks of improper sanitation.

Patty happily listened as Annabelle talked about all the happenings in the past four years. She smiled as she watched Annabelle scurry about, taking care of the chores, while the others did her bidding or simply got out of her way. "No changes here," Patty said, laughing, bringing Annabelle to a halt.

"What ya talkin' 'bout, Patty?" Annabelle asked, a hurt look on her face. "I'm keepin' everythin' up just th' way Jeb likes it."

"Oh, Ma, I didn't mean to hurt your feelings. But except for the change in Daisy and Sara, walking around in their new clothes, nothing is any different in this cabin. I know Pa doesn't care to fix up anything, but you'd think Joe would." She raised her eyebrows. "Anyway, there's been so many changes in my life in the past four years, I guess I expected there to be some changes here, too. It's eerie. Like time stood still here on the mountain."

The little ones were unaccustomed to outsiders coming around to visit, but unlike Kelly Sue, hiding behind her mother, Drexel and Dakota had no fear of this gentle stranger. Not the least bit happy about being ignored, they had crept nearer and nearer to Patty, drawn by her soft voice with the unusual cadence. Soon they were vying for her attention, tugging on her pant leg.

"I don't like change. Ya ought to knowed that," Annabelle puffed her chest out.

Patty sighed, ignoring the children, determined to stick to the task at hand.

"Why on earth're ya here?" Annabelle continued to keep half her attention on her chores. "I didn't expect I'd ever see ya again."

"It's my family," Patty said, and because she knew that Annabelle did not want to hear any discussion about her dreams, she didn't go on to say she was desperate to find out their meaning. She simply continued, "I feel I must find out who they are and meet them."

"What do ya mean you're here 'cause of your family?" Annabelle asked. "We're your family. You're a McCallister.

Oh, I knowed ya let Tuesday an' Cliff change your name to Moran, but that ain't right, an your pa ain't goin' to stand for it when he finds out. No way, he ain't goin' to like it one bit. Mark my word, it's goin' to start more trouble than Cliff an' Tuesday's goin' to want."

"I'm talking about my birth mother's people."

"What? Now what on earth brought this on?" Annabelle said.

"Well, if you must know," Patty began reluctantly, knowing full well what Annabelle's reaction would be, "I've been having dreams about future and past events, and I want to find out if I'm the only one who has them."

"You knowed that I don't want to hear 'bout your foolish dreams. An' ya're still comin' to me talkin' 'bout them? Ya knowed folks're goin' to think you're crazy, like th' old woman that lives by th' edge of th' forest."

Unable to ignore the twins anymore, Patty sat on the bench that served as seating at the homemade table, and allowed them to climb on her lap. "Ma," she said, "we're the only ones here. We can talk about it. Stop trying to scare me and make me think that I'm a freak because I can see the future through my dreams."

"Well, don't ya look an' talk city now?" Annabelle said bitterly, not really sure in her own mind of why it offended her so much that Patty had always aspired to leave the mountain. "I hadn't never had a notion of tryin' to make ya think that ya're a freak, an' I ain't goin' to discuss such craziness."

"Annabelle," Daisy said, "why're ya so stubborn? It's obvious this ain't somethin' ya can ignore by hidin' behind your fear. It ain't goin' to hurt ya or anyone else for ya to talk 'bout it."

"I don't want to talk 'bout it," Annabelle said stubbornly.

"I have to go to work, Patty," Daisy said. "Are ya goin' to be here when I get back?"

"Work!" Patty was shocked, knowing that it was unthinkable for mountain women to work outside the home. Actually, it was virtually impossible; there were very few jobs for them. "Where on this time-forsaken mountain would you get a job?"

"At th' town bar," Daisy said proudly.

"Does Pa know?"

"Of course not," Daisy said.

"How're you getting away with it?"

Drexel had climbed on the bench that was attached to the table and pulled at Patty's hair. "Can ya play with me an' my brother?"

"Drexel, if ya don't be good, ya're goin' to have to take your brother an' play in your room," Daisy admonished.

"By th' skin of her nose." Unable to keep her opinion to herself, Annabelle replied to Patty's question.

Daisy ignored Annabelle's remark. "I'm movin' to th' city when I save enough money."

"Tuesday and Cliff offered to help," Patty said. "You can move there. Tuesday will help you get a job, and you won't have to worry about Pa catching you."

"I need to do this myself."

"He's going to catch you!" Patty said, alarmed that Daisy was so bold as to defy Jeb while she still lived in his cabin under his care. And now she was refusing to accept help to get away from him. Patty thought perhaps Daisy was stalling, frightened and unable to make such a huge change in her life.

"He won't catch me."

"You're fooling yourself."

Daisy shrugged.

"Daisy, with no one helping you, moving to the city is not as easy as you may think."

"I knowed that it's not goin' to be easy, but when me an' th' others was taken to th' city when Jeb was in trouble, we was in a shelter for abused women, an' that's where I'm goin' to start."

"That's what they told us they're there for, to help abused women," Sara said.

"I'm guessing that Pa doesn't come around here much now," Patty said. "Otherwise, you would never defy him so openly like you are!"

"He manages to get here now an' then—not very often," Daisy said.

"Then he'll catch you," Patty said matter-of-factly. "And you saw what he did to Tuesday and me, locking us in that damp, rat-infested cellar. He even made you and Annabelle help him. I know you didn't want to do it, but don't you see? Pa making you do it when you didn't want to is abuse in itself."

"He don't abuse me," Annabelle said, "an' I never saw him hurt you'ns neither."

"Ma, I saw Pa hit ya many times. Anytime ya'd say somethin' he didn't like, he slapped ya. That's abuse!" said Sara.

"Ya may not call treatin' us like we was his cattle 'stead of his women abuse, but I do," Daisy said. "Just to work an' earn my own livin' puts me in jeopardy 'cause Jeb wants to own us like we're his property. He don't want us to have no money 'cause then he knows that with our own we'd be able to take care of ourselves. I for one am not goin' to take it anymore."

"We don't need to take care of ourselves," Annabelle said stubbornly, "'cause we have Jeb to do it."

"Ya call *this*," Daisy spread her arms in an arc indicating the interior of the cabin, "takin' care of us? I'm not listenin' to your nonsense. This is no life for any woman. Ever since we was in th' city I learned that there really was somethin' betta out there just like we seen in th' Sears an' Roebuck catalogs. An' ya knowed yourself, even th' folks in Windin' Ridge, only a few miles below us, live ten times betta than us. Any of us can live th' dreams we've always wanted."

Patty untangled herself from the twins and embraced Daisy. "I just want you to be careful until you get away from here and Pa's influence. Saving money is the right way to go about it, if you really won't let Tuesday and Cliff help you."

"Ya'd be surprised at how much money I make in tips, Patty. Anyway, that's why I have to go to work now, but will I see ya tomorrow? I get up late 'cause I get to bed so late."

"Yes, I'll be around for a while. I'm planning on staying at the boardinghouse in Winding Ridge while I'm on the mountain, though."

Daisy hugged Patty good-bye. "Good luck in finding your family. I like th' way ya follow your heart." She kissed the children and was out the door, briskly striding on the path toward town.

"Patty, don't let Daisy put all that nonsense in your head. We're your family, an' I'm your mother. It's best that ya forget lookin' for any others. We're all ya're needin'."

"Ma, Daisy isn't putting anything in my head. You know I've always thought of you as my mother," Patty said, "and you've always treated me as if I were your daughter. If you're threatened by my wanting to find a new family, it's not like that. I want to find my birth family, not a new one, to find out if there are others like me."

"I'm not threatened like ya say," Annabelle said. "I just don't want ya to open up a can of worms."

"What do you mean?" Patty asked.

"Ya knowed what I mean, girl. Don't do this."

"Oh, I'm going to do this," Patty said firmly. "I have to."

4

OZZIE MOATS SAT AT HIS DESK WAITING, AS HE DID MOST afternoons, to watch Daisy strut through town, her luscious blue-black hair swinging around her shoulders as she headed for the bar. She sure was a beauty. Along with his enjoyment of *Playboy,* watching Daisy or Rosily (who had been known as the town tramp for years) pass by his window was what he lived for.

The possibility of McCallister catching Daisy working at the bar was potential for a free-for-all. Everyone knew that McCallister would not tolerate his women coming to town, let alone stand for them fraternizing with the bar's patrons. Certainly, McCallister would have it in for the owner, Humphrey Rudd, for having the audacity to hire her in the first place.

Hump, who was the largest and meanest man in town, acted as his own bouncer. He clearly had no fear of any man, and that included Jacob McCallister. As did many of the men who frequented the bar, Hump had his eye on Daisy for himself. It was obvious that she had no feelings for him other than a natural respect due a boss, and that she felt secure in the knowledge that he would not tolerate any of his customers taking advantage of one of his barmaids.

Hump was a patient man, though; he could wait. She wouldn't be the first bar maid who, after showing no interest in him, turned to him in the end. Most of the girls who worked for him had dreams of making enough money to make a life in the city, and they looked to him for guidance. There was no doubt that Daisy wouldn't be the last, either.

Ozzie was soon rewarded for his own patience. He could see Daisy as she stepped from the path that led from the many cabins scattered across the face of the mountain and merged with Main Street as the mountain dropped abruptly, leveling off and becoming Winding Ridge. He watched as she headed for the boardwalk that would bring her to his window.

Today Sheriff Moats crossed to the door and threw it wide, hoping to make an imposing figure framed in the opening. He addressed her, "Evenin', Daisy."

"Evenin', Sheriff," Daisy responded, continuing on toward her destination, looking less than interested in his lustful gaze.

"Saw that girl goin' up th' mountain," Ozzie called after her.

Daisy turned. "What girl?"

"You know, her mother died givin' birth—the one that ran away back when your so-called husband, Jacob, was holdin' her and another in the cellar house on your place."

"Forevermore! Sheriff, what're ya bringin' that garbage up for? Jeb's been livin' in th' city more an' more of th' time, an' not comin' around much at all. He's sendin' Joe with our supplies these days."

"Just don't want any trouble. I haven't had to put up with that big-feelin' detective from the city for the past coupla years, and I'd like it to stay that way."

"Ya make me laugh. I don't have no control of who comes to plague ya, Sheriff Moats, an' more especially th' detective from th' city. An' I don't care to neither."

"Your family, Patty in particular, keeps company with him," Ozzie spat. "I'm aware that he's been welcomed at your cabin on several occasions."

"Ya don't knowed what ya're talkin' 'bout. We can't stop the law from barging in on us when they're wantin' to." Angrily, Daisy bid the sheriff good day and continued walking toward the bar.

The sheriff watched, a wicked leer contorting his face.

After Daisy left the cabin, Patty sat and talked to Annabelle and Sara while the children ran, untamed, in and out of the cabin, busy at their play after having lost interest in Patty.

Drexel and Dakota were identical twins, and it was nearly impossible to tell them apart. The gregarious, rambunctious boys were miniatures of their darkly handsome father, Jacob McCallister, but the timid and tiny Kelly Sue favored Sara with her wild, stringy dishwater blond hair and freckled face.

"How long ya stayin'?" Annabelle asked.

"As long as it takes."

"Ya knowed we don't have much room, but ya're welcome to sleep with Sara an' th' youngins on th' sleepin' mats like ya did when ya was livin' here," Annabelle offered. "Ya knowed, I didn't like it, ya tellin' Daisy ya're goin' to stay at th' boardin'house 'stead of with us where ya belong."

"Ma, it'll be better for me to stay in town."

"Oh, I can see by your fancy dressin' an' talkin' that ya're too good to stay with your family, after livin' in th' city with Tuesday an' Cliff in their fancy house."

"Ma, you haven't even been in Tuesday and Cliff's house."

"I just knowed it's fancy." Annabelle was not to be deterred from her opinion. "I can tell by th' expensive way they dress."

"Whatever," Patty sighed, knowing she could never win an argument with Annabelle.

"What kinda backtalk is that?"

"I'm sorry, Ma, but I'm not taking a chance on being here asleep and Pa coming home and catching me unawares. You know very well that I'm not safe with him around."

"Ya betta watch ya don't get snotty like th' city women," Annabelle warned. "It ain't becomin'."

Letting out another huge sigh, again inviting Annabelle's displeasure, Patty determined to overlook her mother's small-mindedness where it came to people who did not live like she was accustomed to, and also of her ignorance of the deep hurt caused by the abuse her children's father had inflicted on them throughout their childhood.

"I told you, family is what I came back here for," Patty said. "I don't know what makes you think city people are snobbish. You've met Tuesday and Cliff, and you know how kind they are."

"If family is what ya came back here for, then why ain't ya stayin' with us? We're family," Annabelle insisted.

Patty chose to disregard Annabelle's repeated request for her to stay in the cabin. "When I say family, I'm talking about my birth mother. You never spoke of her and where she came from," Patty said, paying no attention to Annabelle's earlier warning to drop the subject.

Annabelle sighed, giving in a little. "I never saw a reason to bring up such a bad time."

"You mean her dying, giving birth to me?"

"Yeah."

"That's not what I'm wanting to hear about."

"Then what?" Annabelle asked.

"I want to know about before that. How did she come to be one of Pa's wives?"

"Ya'd have had to ask your pa that," Annabelle said. "I've never been made privy to Jeb's business."

"You know I can't ask him. And, Ma, you know why."

"I don't knowed no such thing," Annabelle pouted.

"Why do you tolerate a man who collects wives?"

"When he took me, he didn't have no other wives, but for the others it was a matter of survival, I suppose. Ya knowed it's th' mountain way."

"Who are my grandparents? Do I have cousins?"

"All I knowed is your ma's name was Betty."

"I already know that. Surely, you know something else."

"Nope. I don't," Annabelle said. "But maybe Aggie can tell ya somethin'."

"You're right. I bet she can. I'm going to drive up to her cabin right now. Ma, would you and Sara like to take a ride with me to Aunt Aggie's cabin?"

"I just can't get over the notion of ya drivin', but I reckon I would like to go," Annabelle said excitedly. "How 'bout ya, Sara?"

"I surely would, but we'd have to take th' kids, an' they'd be too much trouble getting' into everythin' at Aunt Aggie's pretty cabin an' messin' in th' car an' all. Hate to miss it, though. I love bein' in Aunt Aggie's cabin now that it's so nice."

"What do you mean, so nice?" Patty asked, a puzzled expression on her face.

"When th' Bookers were put out of it by Jeb—ya remember hearin' 'bout th' militiaman an' his family rentin' Aggie's cabin from Joe—Mr. Booker left it fixed fancy an' all," Annabelle said. "I'd sure like to see it for myself."

"Oh, yeah. Tuesday told me about it. I guess I just can't visualize Aunt Aggie's cabin as being something special to see."

"Oh, it is," Sara said. "Ya won't believe your eyes."

Annabelle had wanted to see Aggie's cabin ever since the day Daisy had moved Aunt Aggie back into her lifetime home—shortly after Benjamin Booker's arrest and Cecelia Booker's subsequent departure—talking about the wonders the Bookers had performed on the primitive cabin. Sara had had the pleasure on many occasions, but Annabelle was so overworked she didn't have the gumption, as she was so fond of saying, to make her way up the mountain on foot.

Patty and Annabelle climbed into Patty's car. Riding in a car, visiting, or merely leaving the cabin was a rare experience for Annabelle. They bounced up the rutted lane in silence, each of them lost in thoughts of the past. For Annabelle it had been many years since she had roamed the mountain. As a young girl, she'd spent much time walking just to have quiet time from parents and a family bursting at the seams with too many brothers and sisters, too little food, and all of them crowded into a very small cabin.

Those years ago, the inability to properly care for his large family was the primary reason that Annabelle's father had agreed to sell her to Jacob McCallister, a young and tremendously handsome man who happened to be Aggie's nephew.

As they approached Aggie's cabin, they could see her on the front porch, rocking to and fro in her favorite rocker. Her cats were her only companions; one kitten snuggled at her feet, another curled on her lap, and the tomcat was perched atop the back of the chair at Aggie's shoulder.

"My word, if it ain't Annabelle come callin' with a pretty, young girl at th' wheel, so it is," Aggie said. Her eyes were huge with wonder as she watched the silver-gray car approach. When it stopped near the steps to the porch, she clumsily rose from her chair, scattering the cats. She picked up her spittoon and moved to the steps to get a better view of the remarkable car—remarkable because all the cars she occasionally saw were, old, battered, and covered with dirt.

When the women climbed from the automobile, Aggie still hadn't recognized Patty. "Who ya got there, Annabelle?" Aggie asked, spitting into the spittoon and setting it on the banister as she leaned forward to squint at the girl.

"It's Patty. Don'cha recognize your own great-niece?"

"'Pon my soul. I didn't, so I didn't. How in tarnation did ya get rid of th' scar?"

"Plastic surgery," Patty answered.

"I've no idea what that is, so I don't."

"It's an operation performed by a doctor. Anyway, it was successful," Patty said.

"I'd never knowed ya, so I wouldn't. It's a miracle, so it is. I always knowed ya was destined to be a darn good-lookin' girl." At Patty's nervous laugh, Aggie added, "Well, ya was! Even with that purple birthmark, so ya was."

"Ya're right 'bout that," Annabelle said, puffing as she caught up with Patty. "I was so glad to see her. Ya knowed I thought I'd never see her again before I was dead an' gone."

"For land's sake, me too," Aggie said, hugging Patty, marveling that the girl had gotten so much taller. Patty made the tiny, spunky woman feel even shorter than she normally did.

"Let me sit down a spell. I can't believe my eyes, so I can't." Aggie reached for her spittoon and dropped back into her chair. "You've gotten so tall."

"After ya rest a minute let's take a look at your cabin. I've been wantin' to see it since Daisy told me ya got fancy fixin's."

"My lands, that's been a coupla years ago, so it has."

After some small talk, Aggie said, "Go inside an' help yourself." She hefted herself from the chair, and once again the cats scattered. "I don't have to take your hand an' lead ya, so I don't."

Annabelle opened the screen door and walked into Aggie's kitchen with Patty following closely behind.

When Aggie gained her feet once again, she followed them inside. "Don't just stand there with your mouth open, Annabelle. You're goin' to catch flies, so ya're."

Inspired by the lovely furnishings and the timesaving appliances, Aggie was keeping the place as nice as Cecelia Booker had. Liking things neat and nice, anyway, with the added incentive, she found the desire and energy to manage the necessary housekeeping chores.

Aggie had no vacuum sweeper, so she kept the rugs clean with her broom, and occasionally she hung them across her outdoors clothesline, giving them a good beating with a paddle and leaving them out a few hours for an airing.

Annabelle stared with obvious envy at the cherry wood furniture, the sofa, the bed with the soft downy spread, and most of all, the pretty, billowy, cotton curtains hanging at the sparkly, clean windows. The soft pastel colors in the rugs, curtains, bedspread, and sofa set off a cheerful atmosphere much brighter than Annabelle's colorless cabin and made a stark contrast to her drab existence.

"Aggie!" Patty exclaimed, remembering how gloomy the log cabin had been before. The last time she had been in it, it had been furnished with a homemade wood table with four chairs and a ratty cot that sat along the front wall. The loft had been partially dismantled for use as firewood. Everything in the entire place had been covered with a dingy film of soot contributed by the old woodburner and the potbelly stove, which had been removed by Booker to be replaced with more modern appliances.

"How lovely your place is. I can hardly believe my eyes," Annabelle said.

In an attractive arrangement, the bright furniture, wall hangings, and oriental rug that Benjamin Booker had purchased for his wife and sons and brought in from the city still adorned the loft, which was built below the steep pitched roof. The loft formed a partial second floor with wooden ladders, propped against the inner edge, serving as stairs.

The only thing Aggie had done to change the Bookers' decor was to retrieve her favorite rocking chairs from outdoors. Before Booker's restoration, they had always been placed within the radius of the potbelly stove's warmth. On her first day back, Aggie had dragged the two chairs back into the cabin, leaving the two more weather-beaten ones for her tranquil time outdoors. To anyone else the aged, colorless, unvarnished wooden chairs near the front door would undoubtedly look out of place in the newly decorated interior, but not to Aggie. In those very chairs, Aggie and her beloved nephew, Jacob, had spent a great part of his childhood talking companionably. In those same chairs she'd told him about the death of his parents. Through the years, she had sold her stepchildren one by one, and by her example she had unknowingly sent Jacob on the path to his downfall. Together, they had decided which of her late husband's ten children to sell first. He had kept her confidence, just as she had kept his in later years when he talked of his plan to kidnap Tuesday, bring her to his mountain cabin, and make her one of his wives.

The rocking chairs were also where one day in the future, against Tuesday and Cliff Moran's wishes, she would tell

Winter Ann who her birth father actually was and reveal the story of his life when she came searching as Patty now did, probing for her true family history.

"I can thank Joe for it, so I can," Aggie said. "He rented th' cabin to th' Bookers. I'm sure, though, ya didn't come all th' way up on th' mountain just to see my cabin, so ya didn't."

"No, Aunt Aggie, I didn't. I want to learn about my mother. There must be many family members that I don't even know about."

"Ya're probably betta off not knowin', so ya'ar."

"Oh, no! You're not going to get away with that," Patty said. "I want to know. I need to know if I'm one in a long line of people who have these dreams or if it's just me being plagued with them. I guess I need the comfort of knowing that there are others like me in the world. I feel like a freak!"

"Maybe ya're not goin' to like what ya find out, so ya're not. Specially with that fancy talkin' ya're doin' now that ya're livin' in th' city with those city folk."

"Aunt Aggie, let me be the judge of what I like and don't like, and there's certainly nothing wrong with improving oneself. Tell me what you know!"

"To tell ya th' truth, I don't knowed much, so I don't."

"Humph—" Annabelle grunted.

"What was th' gruntin' for?" Aggie asked. "Ya don't knowed what I knowed or don't knowed, so ya don't."

"I knowed that ya knowed too much for your own good," Annabelle said, "an' ya spend too much time talkin' 'bout it."

"Go on, Aunt Aggie! Tell me what you know!"

"Well . . ." Aggie relented, not in the slightest fazed by Annabelle's attempts to keep her quiet. "Betty was your ma's name, so it was. The old woman that—"

"Aggie, I think ya should leave well enough alone!" Annabelle tried yet again to silence the older woman.

"Quiet, Ma!" Patty insisted. "Aunt Aggie, were you about to say the old woman that lives at the edge of the forest is my grandmother?"

"Yeah. Her name's Myrtle. It was Myrtle's pa, old man

Moats, that sold her to Burl Landacre when she was a mere girl, so he did. Just like Burl sold Betty to Jeb, so he did."

"My grandmother. Her name is Myrtle Landacre?"

"Yeah. Myrtle was Betty's mother, an' that'd make Myrtle your grandmother, so it would."

"What?" Patty sat down hard on the chair next to Aggie. "How sad, living so close all my life, and only knowing of her as 'the old woman who lives by the edge of the forest.' And she's my grandmother!"

"Told ya to stop askin' questions," Annabelle said. "Told ya, you're goin' to dig up skeletons ya don't want to knowed nothin' 'bout."

Patty and Aggie ignored Annabelle.

"That's right, Patty, I was told that Myrtle was Betty's ma. It was one Sunday in church, so it was. It was Tommy Lee Hillberry's mother, when we was just young girls, as I re-member, that'd told me, so it was."

"That whole Hillberry family has been known to be trou-blemakers," Annabelle interrupted.

"Tommy Lee's mother wasn't a Hillberry then, so she was-n't, but she knowed 'bout th' mountain folk from way back. Now, pay attention to what I'm sayin', that don't mean it's true, so it don't, but Betty never did say nothin' 'bout her family. She was only with Jeb 'bout eight or nine months be-fore she died givin' birth to ya. I don't think she ever got used to livin' with Jeb an' all his women. Anyway, I don't knowed much 'bout Myrtle, but th' sheriff, Ozzie Moats, does, so he does."

Patty sat stunned. All of her life the children at school—hav-ing heard things from their parents in some cases, first-hand in others—talked about the old woman who lived by the edge of the forest, making fun and claiming that she was crazy.

"That explains why when I was a young girl and tried to tell anyone of my dreams they wouldn't listen, and, Ma, that's why you looked scared and made me stop talking about my dreams. You knew that Myrtle was my grand-mother, all along, didn't you?"

"Yeah, I had an idea, but not for sure, an' I didn't want to be th' one to tell ya," Annabelle said.

"Well, I told ya we're not sure, so we're not. But do ya really want to be known as th' granddaughter of a crazy woman? A woman that claims she can see th' future through her dreams?"

"Aggie, that's uncalled for," Annabelle said.

"It's okay, Ma. I just want the truth."

"Aggie don't knowed the truth when it's smacked her right in th' face."

Ignoring Annabelle's taunt intended to agitate Aggie, Patty asked her aunt, "What do you mean a woman who can see the future in her dreams? Is it like me?"

"Yep, that's what I heared, so it is."

"Patty, if Myrtle is found to be your grandmother, that don't mean that you're crazy too," Annabelle said ignoring Aggie, worried at the stunned look on Patty's pretty face. We're not sure—"

"Crazy too?" Patty was appalled. "Ma, you have no reason to call Myrtle crazy because of her dreams. Did people know about it?"

"That's why they think she's crazy. When she was younger, before she became a recluse, she was always warnin' people of things that was goin' to happen accordin' to her dreams."

"Everyone knows she's crazy, so they do," Aggie said.

"You'd think she was crazy even if not for the dreams. You're going by rumors, not fact, just like you thinking city people are snobs without even meeting them. As far as my grandmother is concerned, you don't know what you're talking about. I bet you've never met her or had a conversation with her, have you?"

"Maybe not, but ya can't ignore th' talk. Where there's smoke there's fire, I was always told."

"Oh, Ma, you're being prejudiced."

"I don't knowed what that means," Annabelle said.

"You just don't want to know what that means," Patty

said. "But I'm going to tell you. It means unfair, narrow-minded, and intolerant."

"I still say where there's smoke there's fire," Annabelle said stubbornly.

"There's talk that Myrtle could be th' sheriff's sister, so she could." Aggie added her two cents.

"Yeah, I've heard rumors to that effect," Annabelle said. "But ya just said ya don't want to hear 'bout rumors."

"Ma there's a difference between calling someone a witch and speculating on who's related to whom."

"I can only go by what ya're tellin' me," Annabelle said. "I only understand ya want rumors or ya don't want rumors."

"Bull! I still don't know why you didn't say so earlier. Aunt Aggie, you said the sheriff knew something—like it's of no consequence—when all along you both know that he's my grandmother's brother." Patty covered her mouth with her hands. "My great uncle! You're both holding back information!" Patty raged. "Good grief, I came all the way to the mountain to find out about my family and the two of you are playing games. Come on, I know you know everything."

"Alright, girl. Don't be actin' so uppity, but I'm goin' to overlook it an' tell ya what I knowed, so I am. Like I said, when Myrtle was a youngin', her pa sold her to Burl Landacre, so he did. Remember his son, John Bob? I knowed that man was thick as thieves with th' militia. Anyway, he was arrested for bein' involved in th' militia's activities two years ago when th' FBI came from th' big city an' broke up th' assembly at th' militia's compound. That's th' land that's runnin' from below my cabin, across th' mountain to Paul Frank Ruble's place, so it is. But John Bob's out now, an' mind ya stay away from him. I don't care if he is your uncle, he's a dangerous man."

Patty rose to her feet. "You're rambling, Aunt Aggie. Is that all you're going to tell me?"

"That's all I knowed, so it is."

"Where're ya goin'?" Annabelle asked, troubled by the look on Patty's face.

"I'm taking you home. Come on."

"But what's your hurry?" Annabelle asked. "I'm enjoyin' my visit. I haven't had time to look around at everythin'."

"I'm going to get to the bottom of this. That's the hurry." And at the crestfallen look on Annabelle's face, she relented. "Oh, go on, we'll visit a while. I'm sorry, Aunt Aggie. I haven't been very kind, but in all this talking neither of you have told me very much."

Patty took Aggie and Annabelle's hands, one in each of her own. "I'm not going to give up until I know everything."

Before Patty could change her mind about staying a while longer, Aggie patted Patty's hand and, with a little effort, rose to her feet to usher Annabelle through the cabin. Annabelle once again admired the expensive furnishings as she quarreled with Aggie about their usefulness. Followed by Aggie, she insisted on climbing the ladder to the loft and was particularly impressed. Having been familiar with lofts as a child, she had never imagined that one could be fixed up to be such a pleasant bedroom area. Together they moved around the space with Annabelle exclaiming over each new item. She particularly liked the colorful oriental rug that covered two-thirds of the floor.

After safely climbing back down the ladder, they ended up back at the table where Patty sat watching them, still smiling at their petty bickering. She realized that she couldn't remember a day in her life on the mountain that the two hadn't argued when they were around each other.

After a snack of Aggie's wonderful bread pudding, accompanied by talk of the old days, Annabelle watched morosely as Patty gathered her purse and car keys. Following her lead, Annabelle rose to her feet reluctantly, for although she and Aggie fought constantly when they were together, she was loath to leave her company so soon.

After dropping Annabelle at her cabin, Patty drove further down the mountain to visit Myrtle Landacre. Pulling off the rutted out road onto Myrtle's overgrown yard, Patty opened the car door cautiously, just wide enough to step out, to keep the heavy growth of brush from scratching up the paint. Looking as if she were marching to a beat that only she heard, she trampled the weeds, mashing them flat to the ground, and only then did she fully trust that the door would not be scratched as she closed it. Satisfied, she turned toward the front of the cabin and was startled to see an old woman standing in the doorway, intently watching her method of clearing a parking space.

"Hi, there," Patty called out, trying to sound cheerful, although she was actually terrified by childhood memories of the sinister stories told about the woman, stories that left the impression that people who went inside her cabin never came back out. "May I speak to you for a few minutes?"

"Don't knowed what ya'd want to talk to an old woman like me 'bout, but come on in, if'n ya want. I relish havin' company now an' again. Not that anybody comes a callin' on me. Nearest thin' I have to company is th' youngins that run past my cabin callin' me a witch an' such."

Surprised that the old woman freely referred to the children's pranks, Patty crossed the unkempt yard. By the time she'd reached the cabin, bits of dead leaves and weeds clung to her jeans. She entered behind the woman and was offered a chair at the table. The odor of decay and unwashed laundry hung heavily in the air, and the room was as messy as the cabin she had been raised in, before the women had been forced to take training in housekeeping and hygiene.

"Can I get ya somethin'?" the woman asked. "Do ya drink coffee?"

"Oh, no," Patty smiled. "I'm fine."

"What're ya wantin' to talk to me 'bout?"

"I'm looking for family. My mother's name was Betty Landacre, and I understand that you had a daughter with that name."

The old woman gasped, looking as if she'd seen a ghost. "Ya're my granddaughter!" Myrtle put her hand to her heart. "When I seen ya gettin' outta th' car, tramplin' th' weeds, I thought ya looked like my Betty."

"Please tell me about her," Patty said.

"My mind ain't as good as it used to be, but I'll try." The old woman wiped a tear from her cheek. "Betty was a good girl. She never gave me a minute's trouble. Like I said, ya look a lot like she did. She had wild dreams of leavin' th' mountain. I think she got 'em from lookin' at th' catalogs we used in th' outhouse."

"Oh," Patty said, covering her mouth with her hand. "I was the same way. Every day when I was a little girl, I dreamt of living in the city."

Myrtle smiled. "Ya had th' same notions, an' from th' looks of ya, ya got to realize your dreams."

"Yes, I did." Patty, no longer fearful, placed her hand on her newly found grandmother's arm for a second.

"Well," Myrtle continued, looking pleased at the rare human contact, "one day when my Betty was but a young girl, Burl, my husband, sold her. He never told me who he'd sold her to. An' afterward he'd not tell me where she was livin' or who she was livin' with. She was my only girl child, an' I've grieved for her all my life.

"Every day since Burl took my girl through that door cryin' for me to help her— she was merely fourteen at th' time—I've prayed she'd somehow come back home to me, an' here ya'ar, lookin' for all th' world like she did then."

"Then I really am your granddaughter," Patty said, teary-eyed. How ironic that she had escaped a fate similar to her mother's, at the hands of her own father, and was able to sit here now where her mother had been raised, chatting with her grandmother.

"I know who Burl Landacre is," Patty said, finally acknowledging to herself that he was her grandfather. "The little I knew about him only caused me to dislike him."

"He was a mean, uncarin' one," Myrtle said. "An' so was John Bob, my eldest, an' he's your uncle, ya knowed. I never got close to my son. I don't knowed if it was bein' so lost in my sorrow 'bout losing my Betty or just 'cause he was more drawn to his father an' his ways, seemin' not to need his mother."

"My pa, Jacob McCallister, was the man your husband sold my mother to. And, I'm sorry to say," Patty said, getting up and placing her hand on the old woman's shoulder, "she died giving birth to me."

Myrtle looked at Patty with tears in her eyes. "Don't worry yaself girl. I knowed she was gone. I seen it in my dreams over an' over. I've made my peace with it."

So there was someone else who had the dreams! A thrill of relief rushed over Patty in finding that she was not alone anymore. There was another just like her, and she stared at the one in wonder, so thankful that it was her very own grandmother.

"I have dreams too! Dreams of the past and future," Patty blurted. "Did my mother have them too?"

"Yeah, an' folks made fun at her too, just like they'd poked fun at me, an' I'm sure that ya suffered like that too, havin folks callin' ya crazy an' throwin' rocks at ya. That's why I've stayed to myself after I'd made th' mistake of tellin' people 'bout 'em, tryin' to help in my own small way by tryin' to warn 'em they was in trouble. Ya'll learn that ya can ward off trouble by knowin' ahead of time an' changin' your plans so's to keep outta trouble. Except ya can't control what ya dream 'bout. If I could've, I'd dreamt 'bout where my Betty was taken."

Myrtle leaned close to Patty, and a rare smile glowed on the old woman's face, making Patty realize that the old woman had obviously been pretty in her youth. "I'm so happy ya've come to see me. Gettin' to know ya will make up a little bit for losin' my Betty."

Patty smiled. "You can't know how happy I am to have found you. It seems too easy, and that scares me."

"I can tell ya that somethin's goin' to happen," Myrtle said. Patty shivered at the frank way Myrtle stated her prediction. "I just can't tell ya what. All I can say is for ya to be careful, be on guard all th' time. Ya shouldn't be doin' anythin' outta th' ordinary."

Patty winced; in light of the way she had been living for the past four years, coming to the mountain was something out of the ordinary in itself.

"Seems my dreams only come to helpin' those that're strangers to me, an' they sure enough don't want my help a'tall. My bein' right was what scared people, an' their fear was th' reason they'd accuse me of bein' crazy. It was just 'cause they couldn't understand, an' they'd have to put the blame somewheres."

"Now I know that Aunt Aggie and Annabelle knew exactly why you were made fun of, and that's why Annabelle always got so angry when I talked about my dreams. She knew I'd be a target for people's stupid fears, and they'd make fun of me as well. You know what? That would've been all it would have taken for everyone to connect me to you!"

"Yep, ya're right. I never thought of it, though. Like me an' your mother was th' object of their fear, so they called us 'th' crazy witches that live at th' edge of th' forest.' That was years ago, though. After Burl sold my precious daughter, th' taunts became just 'th' old woman who lives at th' edge of th' forest.' I knowed what was goin' on.

"It got worse after John Bob took a wife an' left home. That was soon after Burl was killed. People don't think I knowed it, but his own kind, th' ones in th' militia, what's got him. 'Spose he didn't follow their rules. He never was one to follow rules. Anyways, I haven't said a word to anyone 'bout my dreams for many years now, an' it ain't made no difference. In their eyes, I'm still crazy, an' it don't help me none when I have th' days when I can't keep things straight in my mind, not rememberin' what year or even what day it is. People don't forget, no they don't. An' they don't take time, like ya're, lettin' me sort out what I'm wantin' to say so I don't appear to be so crazy."

"You're fine, Myrtle," Patty said. "I've been told that the sheriff is my uncle. Is he?" she asked.

"Yeah, he is. But he don't like it, an' don't want no one to knowed it. I reckon he'd do anythin' to keep people from knowin' it. So if ya're plannin' to talk to 'im, ya're askin' for trouble."

"I need to find out. Does he have dreams like we do?"

Myrtle laughed, a rare sound in her cabin, causing her wrinkles to deepen. "I don't suppose he'd ever tell if he did. He'd die before tellin'. He don't want no one to think he's crazy like 'th' old woman at th' edge of th' forest.' He's 'shamed of bein' related to me."

Patty sighed. "I was one of the children who passed by here going to and from school, and I never realized that you were aware of the mean things that people were saying."

"Yeah, th' kids walkin' by always like to plague me with their taunts 'bout witches. It's gone on for years."

"I remember when I was in school here, they liked to torment you," Patty said. "I want you to know that I never did."

Myrtle smiled and patted Patty's hand. "I'm wonderin' why I never had dreams 'bout ya? I guess we'll never fully understand 'bout 'em or why we can't control what we dream 'bout. Anyway, ya don't talk like a mountain youngin.'"

"I'm living in the city and attending school there." Patty told her grandmother about her good fortune of meeting Tuesday and Cliff. And after spending a few hours talking, she rose to leave, saying she was going to talk to the sheriff.

"I wish ya wouldn't. He's not goin' to like hearin' that ya're stirrin' up th past. Like I said, he's 'shamed of bein' related to th' likes of me."

"I just want to talk to him. I've come this far."

After hugging her grandmother, Patty assured her that she'd be back. They would talk about moving Myrtle to the city and a better life, but first Patty knew she would have to finish school and get a job so she could do it. In the mean time, Patty would check around to learn if her grandmother was eligible to collect Social Security without ever having registered for a Social Security number. Patty was pretty sure it was a financial assistance that Myrtle had never known about. Hindering her further, her birth, like most people born on the mountain, may not have been recorded at the courthouse; therefore, she would not have been notified of such benefits.

Leaving the rutted-out mountain road, Patty drove along the cobblestone street that led to the boardinghouse. She pulled into a parking space that was parallel to the boardwalk. Taking Summer from the passenger seat, she tucked the doll under her arm and removed her bags from the trunk.

A feeling of doom welled up in her as she climbed the steps. She could not get the conversation with her grandmother out of her mind. "I can tell ya that somethin's goin' to happen," Myrtle had said.

Standing on the circular porch, she turned and surveyed the town. A few people were on Main Street, the only street running north and south, with half a dozen side streets intersecting it, running east and west. She knew that she stood out, dressed in trendy clothes with a designer traveling bag clutched in each hand and her doll tucked under her arm.

Turning back toward the entrance, Patty ignored the old men in the rocking chairs that were arranged the length of the boardinghouse porch. A few were smoking cigars or pipes; others were chewing tobacco and spitting ugly brown globs into the spittoons that were provided to control the potential mess of their nasty habit.

Patty crossed the porch, opened the screen door, and entered the common room to find that the registration counter was presently abandoned. She set her bags at her side and rang the bell for service. While she waited, she looked around the room. Although she'd been raised on the mountain and attended the town's church and school, she had never been in the boardinghouse. She was surprised to see that it was decorated in a tasteful manner, and it was more up to date than anything she had ever seen on the mountain or, for that matter, in Winding Ridge itself.

She had no way of knowing that a few years ago, during the time militia units from several states were banding together to build a secret tunnel and prepare for an assembly, the boardinghouse had had numerous travelers needing a place to stay. They were willing to pay good money to book rooms for months at a time, while doing their jobs during the week and traveling back to their homes on weekends. Melba, the proprietor, had used the windfall to modernize the entire place. Across the large reception area were several pastel sofas and armchairs attractively arranged under high-pitched ceilings. A stone fireplace was the focal point of the room.

Soon a maid came from an adjoining room and shoved a registration book toward Patty. "Sign the book. I'll give you your key, and you can pay Melba when she's back."

Patty signed the book, and relieved not to have to chat with the proprietor, lifted a bag in each hand. Having no bellboy to help and seeing no elevator, she mounted the stairway carrying her luggage herself.

The room was much nicer than Patty had hoped. There was a standard-sized bed, a tall, narrow, pine wardrobe, a desk, and a bathroom with a claw-foot tub. She was pleased to see that there was a shower, too.

She propped Summer on the bed, lifted her largest bag to the luggage rack, and removed her journal and pen. Soon she was sitting at the desk looking over the notes she had kept of her nightmares. Satisfied she had recorded them all, she began adding her latest information.

Before she was finished, she had filled two pages, recording the meeting with Annabelle, Aunt Aggie, and her newly found grandmother, Myrtle.

5

September 7, 2001
"Brandi, get in here."

The secretary released the call button. Picking up her steno pad and hastily entering her boss's office, she stood just inside the door admiring his coal black hair and handsome face. His strong, underlying masculine features did not take away from his striking good looks. "I'm here," she said.

"Close the door!" Jacob McCallister demanded impatiently.

Brandi Rose closed the door and crossed the plush carpeted floor, moving toward the expansive desk where her boss sat examining a six-inch stack of file folders.

Jacob McCallister had gone into accounting immediately after being released from prison, where he had made excellent use of his time by studying accounting, law, and carpentry. In preparing for his release, he had planned well and learned the skills he would need to build the kind of life he wanted for himself.

He had a scheme to get the payback he felt was due him. He would get even with Cliff Moran for interfering in his life by taking Tuesday for himself and getting him thrown into jail. Most important was for him to get Tuesday and his daughters back with him where they belonged.

To this end, he had no intention of being broke. To do what he wanted would take money. A great deal of money.

Prior to his imprisonment, he had earned an impressive amount of money in the trafficking and sale of children, babies that he himself had fathered. That business had led to his incarceration; he could not risk breaking the law anytime soon.

Lucky for McCallister, he still had the large sum collected from the couple who had wanted to buy Winter Ann, whom he had stolen from her crib while Tuesday slept. At the time of his arrest, the authorities had been unaware that he had already received and stashed the payoff. The couple buying the child were fearful of the consequences of admitting they had paid a handsome sum for a child they never got, and they never said anything to anyone, especially not the police, about the money. So Jacob was able to start his business in style and live in the fashion he had become accustomed to during his moonshine and black market years.

"This morning, I've made up my mind that before I go to New York for my meeting," Jacob said, watching Brandi approvingly as she gracefully crossed the room, "I'm going to take a side trip." He gave her his most charming smile.

"Again so soon? You visited the building site last week," Brandi Rose questioned.

"My plans are coming to a head. I'll be spending more time there, and you'll be on your own taking care of the office more often. This trip will be a few days longer than I'd planned." He absently motioned her to the chair next to his desk.

She took the seat, smoothing her short linen skirt over her nylon-clad legs, crossing them for effect and noting his reaction.

There was none.

He simply continued. "If I land the clients I'm after, there'll be tons of money coming into the business. And let me tell you," he slammed the files he was holding onto his desk, "I need all the money I can get for my future plans."

"You're talking about your appointment on September 11 to get hired on with the Wall Street client." There was excitement in her voice at the prospect of his having a connection in New York and the possibility of her being needed to travel with him on occasion.

"Yes, and don't doubt for a minute, it's a very important meeting," McCallister said, stacking the folders he had been updating atop the ones he had already piled on the desk for her to file later. "You can bet your sweet life, there isn't anything I'd miss this meeting for.

"Like I said, I'm taking a short trip before I leave for the New York meeting. I'll be back here in time to leave for the city as scheduled. I'll be in the office all day the day before I leave."

"You know I'll take care of everything." She blushed and said hesitantly, "I'll miss you." The young woman was usually careful not to show any affection toward him at all unless he prompted her to do so. When he wanted anything more from her than the performing of her secretarial duties, he was the one to make it known. Anytime they spent personal time together was always at his stipulation. He was unreasonably angered when she was forward with him without his permission.

His persona to friends and clients alike, in all things—and specifically in his relationships with women—was that of someone in total control.

Not skipping a beat in his account of events to come, Jacob gave Brandi a stern look, making it clear that he had not cared for her personal comments during their business conversation. "The entire trip, first to the new construction and then on to New York, won't be too long a time for you to manage things here. I've no doubt that you can handle whatever comes up."

"I'm sorry." Her face grew a deeper red. His look of annoyance stung, and she was offended that a simple statement letting him know that she would miss him had angered him so much. "Just tell me what you want me to do, and I'll see that it's done."

Paying no attention to her wounded look, Jacob continued his instructions. He shrugged off his displeasure with her, and his extraordinarily handsome face took on a good-humored expression as he anticipated his trip. His looks completely disarmed Brandi, as they did so many others, always putting him in the advantage.

"In addition to the accounting business, I want you to keep the builder supplied with materials for the project that I've undertaken. The usual supplier will contact you. During my absences, you may dispense with running the builder's requests for materials by me. Okay whatever he needs, and send a check covering the exact amount. As you know, I'm not one to leave others in total control of my business. As a result"—and surprising her significantly, he rose, moved to the front of the desk, and planted a kiss on her deep-red lips—"I feel the need to check the progress of the house, and I don't want anyone to know where I am. At the same time, I can't be bothered with incessant details."

"Yes," Brandi breathed. She smiled at the rare show of affection from her boss and occasional lover, totally forgiving him for hurting her feelings. "I'll see to it that whatever the builder needs is delivered to the site."

McCallister left the room.

September 8, 2001

As her best friend visited with her, Cora helped to calm Tuesday, who was worried that Patty hadn't called yet that day. The entire situation brought back unwelcome memories for Cora, but worrying about a potentially missing child was something she handled with optimism, because she was one of the lucky ones.

Thanks to Tuesday's husband and his unwavering detective work a few years earlier, Cora's daughter, Linda, had been found and brought home after being missing for two years.

Almost from the time Tuesday gave birth to Winter Ann, the baby cooed and laughed at the three-year-old Linda's antics, and they had become fast friends. Now Linda was six and Winter Ann was three. Today, while the women talked, the children played together happily in Winter Ann's upstairs bedroom.

"I don't think you have reason to be concerned," Cora said. "Patty's a very level-headed girl. In all the time she's lived with you, she hasn't given you a moment of worry."

"Until now, you mean," Tuesday said. "I still can't believe she went to the mountain against Cliff's and my wishes."

"Even so, she called yesterday when she arrived. She doesn't want you and Cliff to worry. Anyway, it's only been today you haven't heard from her. Yet, I might add."

"I know, and I hope I'm worrying needlessly," Tuesday said. "But I can't help it."

"She's caught up in being back at her old home after four years," Cora said. "A place I'm sure that she loved and hated. Plus, she went without your permission and probably doesn't want to listen to you hassle her."

"Oh, Cora, you know I'm not going to hassle her."

"Does she?"

"I guess not. I was adamant that she not go."

"So quit worrying."

"I know that she's very excited about the prospect of finding her family. Especially since her dreams lately have been revealing relatives from the eighteenth and nineteenth centuries."

"What do you think that means?" Cora asked.

"I'm sure I don't know," Tuesday sighed. "Sometimes it's so complicated."

"Don't worry," Cora said. Her smile revealed deep dimples, which were surrounded by clusters of delightful freckles spreading to the edge of her curly red hair. "It'll be okay."

"It's hard not to worry when I think of the dreams she's been having," Tuesday said. "She has one where Jacob is building a huge house in a remote area."

"Humph. That's a scary prospect. I mean if she's dreaming about it, sounds like she's going to be part of it."

"You mean both of us, because it sounds to me like he's getting a place ready for the two of us, just like he's always threatened he would. You know that he made it clear all along that he would get us back one way or the other."

Cora looked troubled, but said nothing as she waited for Tuesday to continue telling her what else was disturbing her.

"One strange thing is, Patty says that there is a second man in her dreams."

"Does she have any idea who it is?" Cora asked.

"No, not at all," Tuesday shrugged, "Not a clue."

"Are there other dreams?" Cora asked.

"Yes, she's told me about a few. In another one, she was alone on an abandoned road, and in yet another she was locked in a storage room of some kind."

"Was this on the mountain where she was raised?"

"She told me that she didn't know exactly where she was in the dreams."

"That's heavy," Cora said.

"What really scares me is that they both fit into her dreams of Jacob building a house in an isolated place.

I really don't like to think of that one," Tuesday said. "It's too much like before, and you know, putting words to them only makes them seem more real."

"Are you ever going to get him out of your life?"

"You know, Cora, it's as if Cliff, Patty, Winter Ann, and I are forever living in Jacob's shadow. Our every move is colored by his threat to get us back and by our knowing of his single-mindedness to get what he wants."

The girls came running down the stairs with Winter Ann in the lead. She spotted Tuesday at the table and ran to her, wanting to be picked up.

"What is it?" Tuesday slipped the girl onto her lap.

"Linda wants me to spend the night. Can I?"

"No, you may not," Tuesday said.

"Please," Linda begged.

Tuesday looked at Cora, "Is it okay with you?"

"Sure, we don't have any plans, and Linda loves to have her. And you know, I keep a few changes of clothes on hand for her." Cora nodded to the girls, "Go on upstairs now and play so Tuesday and I can talk."

"Okay, Winter Ann, you may stay the night." Tuesday kissed her on the forehead.

Winter Ann slipped from Tuesday's lap, and she and Linda joined hands and spun around the room in their excitement.

"Scat, get back upstairs, you two. You heard me. Tuesday and I want to talk."

"May we watch TV?" Linda asked.

"You'll watch one of the channels that you're allowed to. Okay?"

"Uh-huh," Linda promised vaguely, grabbing Winter Ann by the hand. They ran back up the stairs.

The women could hear Winter Ann ask Linda, "Know what?" as they ran up the stairs and bounded down the hallway to Linda's room. "No. What?' echoed down the stairs as Linda answered the question the younger girl constantly asked.

With the girls out of earshot once more, Tuesday continued telling Cora of her plans. "After all that's been happening, I'm going to start now, and I'm going to get to the bottom of this."

"What are you talking about, Tuesday?"

"Well, you know we keep tabs on Jacob—we have been since he was released from jail—but I want to do something more official."

"Like what?"

"Like hire a detective, keep up with his every move, that's what."

"Cliff is a detective!" Cora said.

"I know that, but he can't let Jacob consume all of his time. If we hire a private detective agency, they can keep someone on him around the clock. Anyway, we won't have to think about him all the time. I'm tired of living in Jacob's shadow. I'm tired of the darkness and doom its presence casts forever over my family and me. I'm going to find out what Jacob is up to. It's obvious from Patty's dreams that he's up to something."

"You know, Tuesday, had I not seen Patty's ability to see future events for myself, I'd say that you were crazy. But I agree with you. It's the only way you're going to be free from constant fear. I remember back when Patty was constantly dreaming that Jacob was coming for you, and even Cliff said not to ignore the dreams but to use them as a warning."

"And I didn't listen," Tuesday said. "I didn't take precautions, and he came in the night and took both of us from our beds."

"Don't make that mistake again, Tuesday!"

"I won't. I'll get Cliff to hire a detective right away," Tuesday said.

"Also, for comparison, make a list of everything Patty has told you of her dreams," Cora offered.

Finding the suggestion a good one, Tuesday rose from her chair and found a notebook. Sitting back at the table, she began the list, starting with the unknown man at the huge house Jacob seemed to be building. As she wrote, she was sure to note all the details from Patty's dreams that she could remember: the remoteness of the house under construction, a man and a boy who appeared to be working there, Patty standing along a lonely abandoned road, Patty locked in a storage room, and scenes of what she believed to be the lives of her eighteenth- and nineteenth-century family members. What were those all about?

Cora watched over Tuesday's shoulder as the list grew. "Keep this list with you and anytime you think of anything, write it down. Eventually the pieces will fit together."

"I know there's something I should be doing since I'm not hearing from Patty, but what?"

"I think you're overreacting a little. Even though Patty went to the mountain against your will, she considered your feelings and called yesterday to let you know where she was and that she got there safe. She'll call tonight or tomorrow. You'll see."

"I know. Now I wish that I'd paid more attention, went with her, something—oh, I don't know. I want to prevent anything from happening," Tuesday said. "You know, like Cliff's been saying, the dreams are warnings. If we heed them, we can put a stop to a new tragedy."

"What do you think the dreams of witch burning mean?"

"I don't know. I do think that it is an indication that she comes from a long line of people who have her ability to foresee the future in their dreams," Tuesday said. "Finding her family could solve that question."

"I agree," Cora said, " and if she finds a family member and gets them to talk about their own experience with unusual or foretelling dreams, she'll know she's not alone in her experience as far as her dream life is concerned."

"Wow!" Tuesday said. "I hadn't thought of Patty coming from a long line of ancestors who have been convicted of witchcraft. I bet Patty hasn't either." Tuesday wrote herself a note to talk to Patty about the possibility when she called.

Tuesday looked up from her pad. "Anyway, my first priority is finding out what Jacob is up to."

"Yes, that and keeping your list. We already know that we have the advantage in Patty's ability to see future and past events."

"You're right, and all this ties together somehow. I'm going to concentrate on everything Patty and I have discussed over the past few years. I'm going to write it down and compare it with Cliff's notes. I know he keeps notes on everything."

"I've got an idea," Cora said. "Have him get his notes on everything that happened here and at Winding Ridge as far back as the first day you met Jacob McCallister."

"I think you've got something there," Tuesday said.

7

Early morning on September 9, 2001

After a night of being asleep one minute and awake the next at the slightest sound—the sort associated with a large, old building that never quit settling on its foundation—Patty jumped from the bed, anxious to continue her search for other family members. She continued her hopeful position that they would turn out to be people like herself. Spurred on by the short time it had taken her to locate her grandmother, she was more than ready for the full day ahead of her, a day beginning with breakfast with Annabelle, Daisy, Sara, and the children, just as she had promised.

Afterward, she would drive to the county seat in Weston. It had the distinction of being the largest town for miles around. By arming herself with birth records from the courthouse there, she would be able to confront the sheriff with indisputable facts. At the courthouse, the information would be at her fingertips, provided her grandmother and great uncle were unlike many mountain folks whose births had not been recorded. The arrival of an infant in the remote mountains often was not recorded by a birth certificate because children were delivered at home; their families were unable to pay any kind of medical bills. Frequently, the child was sold or given to a mountain man who could take care of it or to a farmer looking for either another work hand or a mate for himself, his daughter, or his son.

It was possible that her uncle may not have been born on the mountain. She and her grandmother had not talked about it, but it did not matter. She wanted to search the records for all the Landacres, Moatses (her grandmother's maiden name), and McCallisters she could find. If Patty could find a record showing who her great uncle's parents were and could prove that they were the same as Myrtle's, he could not lie about being her grandmother's brother. The proof would leave little room for him to keep up the denial of his true family ties.

At the same time, she would check at the Social Security office and find out how to sign Myrtle up for a Social Security number at this late date in her life, hoping to speed up the process of getting her grandmother to the city and into a more comfortable life for her to live out her last years.

Suddenly she remembered she had not called home since the day she arrived, and to her surprise, now that she thought about it, she realized that that was two days ago! In her excitement about learning who her grandmother was, she hadn't thought about calling.

Flopping on the wonderfully soft multicolored quilt that covered the comfortable feather tick mattress, Patty picked up her doll from the floral, lacy pillow and sat her on her knee. "Oh, Summer, that's okay. I'll call Tuesday or Cliff from the pay phone at the gas station this evening with whatever new information I've gathered during our trip to the courthouse. They're going to be so excited that I've found my grandmother that they'll forgive me for coming here against their will. Who'd have ever dreamed that all along she was living only two miles below the cabin where I was raised?"

Ready to go, Patty slipped from the bed and tucked the doll under her arm as she surveyed the room. All she needed now was to grab her purse and scoop her car keys from the nightstand. Being part of a detective's family, she was excited about her very own investigation having such an early success and about how quickly everything seemed to be coming together.

Locking the door to her room, Patty ran down the stairs two at a time. She stopped by the desk to take care of her room charges. Taking her credit card from her purse, she handed it to the woman, waiting impatiently while she ran it through the machine. "Sign here," Melba said, pointing at the appropriate line. Under the watchful eye of the curious proprietress, whom Patty had missed when she had checked in the day before, Patty signed the receipt. She shifted her weight from one foot to the other, annoyed at the woman's slowness in taking care of the paperwork following the credit card transaction, and at questions about the make of her car and other information Patty did not believe the nosey woman needed. Determined not to get into a long, drawn-out conversation with the terribly overweight proprietress, who continued to study her with curiosity-filled eyes, Patty used one-syllable words and only nodded yes or no to the woman's questions.

The proprietor was as tightlipped as Patty proved herself to be now. When strangers she knew to be from the big cities, especially during the gathering of the militia, showed up asking questions, she was determined not to give out the least bit of information.

After she had booked the room for an indefinite time, Patty stuffed her wallet back into her purse, still holding Summer under her arm, and hurried out the front door. As she climbed gingerly into her car, she could still hear Melba's last question ringing in her ears, "Ain't ya a little too old to be playin' with dolls?"

Not noticing Tommy Lee Hillberry, who stood casually leaning against the side of the town bar with his right foot pressed against the brick exterior, watching the road as if he were waiting for someone, Patty reached over and settled Summer snugly into the passenger seat. Quickly starting the car, she steered toward the mountain trail, toward the cabin where she was expected to have breakfast with Annabelle, Daisy, Sara, and the children. Still highly motivated by her pursuit to find others like herself inside the circle of her birth family, she wanted to get the promised visit out of the way. She thought there would be time enough to spend at the cabin later on.

Not satisfied with Patty and her vagueness in answering her questions, the proprietress had followed her as far as the porch, curious about a girl too old to be carrying a doll with her and too young, in Melba's opinion, to be staying in the boardinghouse alone. She had watched as Patty skipped down the porch steps and hurried to her car, seemingly without a care in the world. "It just don't seem fittin' that th' young women travel alone these days," she said to the men who rocked on either side of the entrance, smoking their pipes or chewing tobacco and spitting their filthy juice into the spittoons she had provided so they wouldn't spit over the railing into her flower garden.

"Yep," old man Keefover offered from his squeaking rocking chair, "that girl puts me in th' mind of th' one we went lookin' for with my dogs goin' on four years back."

"It *was* that girl," John Bob Landacre remembered out loud and laughed, not having the slightest idea that he was talking about his niece. "Jacob McCallister's daughter. She's a city girl now. She was running away with a woman that McCallister brought from the city, a real looker, that one. I guess the woman realized she didn't want to stay after she got here and saw it wasn't up to her city standards."

"Yep, ya'd knowed about th' city as ya was one to spend time there," Keefover laughed, spraying brown spittle over his chin that he wiped away with his sleeve, enjoying ribbing John Bob about being afraid to spend his time in the city now. "That is 'till th' law got after ya an' your militia cohorts."

John Bob was safe from the law on Winding Ridge, and knew it. Sheriff Moats could care less about his involvement with the militia.

"Ah, leave him alone, will ya? John Bob's got enough troubles bein' a known militiaman. Anyway, we found them on Jacob McCallister's property," Melba remembered.

"Yep, he's another one in disfavor with th' law. He never had no truck with th' militia, but McCallister spent time in th' slammer for takin' that woman hostage," Keefover said.

John Bob sat with a scowl on his face while the others laughed. Most of them—and Tommy Lee's father, Andy Hillberry, in particular—had always envied Jacob McCallister's charm, his expensive extended-cab truck, and most of all the way women gravitated to him.

Before going back inside, Melba noticed that Tommy Lee Hillberry was climbing into an older model, glossy black Cadillac. She did not recognize the driver but had seen Tommy Lee being picked up by the same car before.

Tommy Lee had watched Patty as she danced down the steps from the boardinghouse, looking like a ray of sunshine. He did not miss the fact that the old men laughingly discussed her while ogling her every move until she drove out of sight. Tommy Lee frowned angrily at the way the men looked at her. He had for his entire life waited for the opportunity to take Patty for his wife. In his misguided mind, the only reason he had no chance to have her was because of Joe McCallister and his interference. He had no comprehension that Patty had her own plans for her future, plans that did not require grubbing for every bite of food, freezing in the winter, going without decent clothes, and living in an overcrowded cabin. She wanted an education and to live where she could use it.

In Tommy Lee's eyes, Patty looked out of place in the old, dilapidated town, dressed in her chic jeans and casual white, lace blouse with a light, sky-blue sweater draped fashionably over her shoulders.

His memories of her were of a girl dressed in feedsack clothes with stringy, unkempt hair surrounding a dirty face that was scarred with a purple birthmark that extended from her ear to her chin.

What had happened to that?

Arriving at the cabin, Patty entered from the backdoor leading into the kitchen. She stepped inside and was immediately enveloped by the heat radiating from the woodburner. "I'd forgotten how hot it got inside the cabin when you were cooking, Ma."

Annabelle turned down the battery-powered radio. Joe had bought it for them for Christmas the year before. "Ya never minded that it kept ya warm in th' winter," Annabelle said. "An' th' nights're gettin' nippy already."

"It's not cold now, Ma, and I don't remember the stove ever keeping me warm unless I stood so close to it that it burned my front while my backside stayed cold. You know as well as I do that when it really gets cold those stoves are useless in this drafty log cabin."

Annabelle took on a serious look. One hand on her left hip, she absently stirred the mush with a wooden spoon as she spoke. "It didn't hurt ya none. I knowed that ya're thinkin' ya was freezin' in th' winter an' goin' hungry all th' time. Look at 'cha. Ya're th' picture of health, an' I think ya have a good life now." She shook the spoon in Patty's direction, oblivious of the mush she dripped on the plank floor.

"I do," Patty relented. Sidestepping the spilled mush, she gave Annabelle a smile and a hug, grateful that the older woman had been, more than anything else, kind to her all through the years she had lived at the cabin. Annabelle had loved her, a little girl who was not her own. In her gratitude for Annabelle's motherly kindness in all matters not concerning her father, Patty suppressed an urge to tell Annabelle how the memories of her father's abuse tormented her still. *She never did anything to stop him. What about that?* Smothering her thoughts, Patty returned to the table.

"Daisy ain't goin' to get outa bed to have breakfast with ya. She worked till all hours last night." Annabelle said, opening the hot stove door and adding two large sticks of firewood that stirred the already crackling, burning wood into a little explosion of popping sparks eager to fly out the door. She slammed it shut before that could happen, fearful of mussing the fresh feedsack dress she had worn in anticipation of Patty's visit.

"Ma, I can see that you don't approve of Daisy and what she's doing, but I know from my own experience that it's something she has to do for herself. This is no way to live. Not for Daisy and me, anyway." Patty waved her arms around, encompassing the cabin's dingy interior that not only lacked modern conveniences but did not even have the barest necessities.

"Ma, th' kids're hungry," Sara said, coming into the room and interrupting the conversation.

"Sit at th' table, an' I'll dish up their food."

"They haven't been to th' outhouse yet. Ya can dish it up, though, 'cause soon as we're done we'll be ready to eat." Sara herded the children out the back.

"I don't knowed why ya an' Daisy's always been wantin' to live somewhere else. I've always been happy livin' here," Annabelle said in all sincerity. "Most of all, though, I like it when Jeb's here. But all this'll pass, an' he'll be 'round here more soon as th' law's off his back."

"Ma, the law is not on his back!" Patty said. "He's done his time. He's free. They let him out. He could come home if he wanted to, but he doesn't want to."

Annabelle set Patty's coffee in front of her and turned back to the stove.

At the hurt look on Annabelle's face, Patty left the table to take her hand. Feeling bad for being compelled once again to say what Annabelle did not want to hear, she blurted, "But it's all true, Ma. Maybe it's time you faced facts. He likes the conveniences and the good times that he can have in the city."

"Mark my word, he'll keep comin' home," Annabelle said with conviction, "just like he always does. That, I knowed."

Annabelle changed the subject. "Sit back down an' have your breakfast," she said as she set a plate of eggs and bacon on the table for Patty, who was relieved when she realized she was not expected to eat the mush. It was for the children.

"Ma, you know I don't drink coffee," Patty said, returning the cup to the sink. "I'll just have water if you don't have juice."

"We have juice. Daisy picked up some yesterday. Sit down. I'll get it."

"It's amazing to me the way you harp at Daisy for working, and at the same time accept the things she buys to make life better for you and Sara and the children."

"I don't harp," Annabelle huffed. "I knowed what's best. Now sit down and eat your breakfast 'fore it gets cold."

"Whatever." Patty gave up.

"Don't be impertinent," Annabelle admonished.

Patty rolled her eyes as she took a seat, and seemingly out of nowhere, the old tomcat jumped onto the table. Patty was startled, remembering the many times the cat had jumped on the table, tempted by food not meant for it, angering her father to violent behavior. Quickly, before the cat could get at Patty's plate, Annabelle grabbed it up by the scruff of its neck and, scolding it for disturbing her guest, flung the screen open and tossed him out.

Shortly, the screen door slammed again, and Sara appeared in the kitchen a second time with the three disheveled children following behind. "Ya're lookin' pretty, Patty," Sara said. "I knowed I said it before, but I hardly knowed ya now that ya don't have th' purple scar on ya face. Ya look really, really good."

"Thank you, Sara," Patty said.

"Ma and I've been talking about living in the city. I realize you've never expressed an interest in living there, and I know that we have never been close, but if you ever want to go, Tuesday and Cliff would help you. They've offered to help Daisy anytime she wants to go."

"I know, but Daisy is stubborn. She wants to do it herself."

"Most likely she's scared of the change and is stalling," Patty said. "Something will have to happen to get her to move. That's what happened to me. I wanted to go, but it took Tuesday's misfortune at Pa's hands to get me moving."

"Yeah, an' she helped ya."

"That's what it's going to take for Daisy, a push. It's a frightening move."

"I don't want to hear that nonsense," Annabelle demanded, slamming a tin plate on the table for one of the children.

It was no use. Patty would never get Sara to talk about living in the city while Annabelle was around, and Sara probably would never leave the mountain anyway. When they were children, Sara had never expressed a desire to leave and had not understood Patty's own longing to live in the city. Oh, but she was a carbon copy of her mother, Annabelle.

It was almost lunchtime by the time Patty left the cabin to collect whatever information she could from the courthouse. She was already eager to call Tuesday and share her news with her that evening, and at the same time let Tuesday and Cliff both know that she was fine so they wouldn't worry. She was hoping they would have a change of heart and stand behind her effort to learn all she could about her birth family. Surely they'd realize that she was an adult now and could take care of herself.

She left the cabin, promising to stop back that evening so Annabelle and the others would know that she had returned safely from her trip to Weston. She drove down Winding Ridge Hill to Route Seven, planning as she went to visit the sheriff on her way back to see Annabelle, before he went home for the day. At the intersection of Route Seven and Winding Ridge Hill Road, Patty turned right. Within an hour she was parking her car in front of the courthouse in Weston. She slipped from the car, locking Summer inside, and in minutes she found the record room. After learning from the clerk which books to seek out, she took out her note pad and began her search.

She found no birth records for any of the family members she sought. Shifting her focus to the house in her dreams, she asked a clerk how to find property transfers. On the advice of the clerk, she searched the grantee and grantor books and found a recording of a deed from Chase Martin to Jacob Mc-Callister for property that was in Braxton County. *I need to find this place. It's got to be the house in my dreams,* Patty told herself. *There are not many homes in the rural county, and the date of purchase is recent. Well, since it's the only property I can find, I'm going to check it out.*

One thing she knew for sure was that her father was not a land baron in anyone's estimation The only thing he ever owned, except for his secret house in Wheeling, was the run-down cabin on the mountain. At the thought of her father's ongoing hidden lifestyle, she felt a cold chill run down her spine. Taking a closer look at the deed, she found only the legal description, not a physical address. She asked the clerk how to find the address and was directed to the assessor's office, where she came to another dead end; the billing address was her father's house in Wheeling. She'd have to go around Winding Ridge making inquiries.

Patty tried to overcome the fear that came with learning that her father had purchased a property in a rural area; even just the fact that he bought a house fit into her dreams. Patty sprinted to her car and headed for Winding Ridge. Oh yes, it was time to talk to the sheriff. If her father spent any time at all in the area, the sheriff would know it. Something was going on with her father, and she was going to find out what it was. If she was going to be adult enough to take charge of her grandmother this was no time to run back to the city and hide behind Tuesday and Cliff.

In just a little over an hour Patty parked her car in front of the sheriff's office. Once inside she noticed the sheriff was alone; the deputy was nowhere in sight. "I need to talk to you, Sheriff. You'd know me as Patty McCallister."

"What do you want?"

"You know I'm your niece, don't you?"

"If you know what's good for you, you'll get out of here and go back to the city."

Patty could tell by the look on Ozzie's face that his anger was out of proportion to the question she'd asked. "You don't have to get so worked up. I'm not leaving until I'm ready. I'm going to learn all I can about my birth family in spite of your liking it or not."

"Little girl," the sheriff warned, "'if I like it' is the key. This is my town, and I'll not have you ruining my reputation."

"You've got to be kidding!" Patty said. "After what your brother did, and you keeping it quiet, especially with the fact that you're supposed to be a lawman, how can you believe you have a reputation to ruin?"

"I said get out," Ozzie fumed. "I'll not claim you or your grandmother as family. Never! Do you understand?" He heaved himself from his chair and pushed past her, on his way to the door. He opened it. "Get out!"

Frightened by his fury, she slipped through the open door and jumped as it slammed behind her.

"I'm leaving today, and I want the two of you to put more time in. I need the house finished as soon as possible," Jacob said.

Jacob McCallister, Tommy Lee Hillberry, and Ike Harris were gathered around the table in the kitchen, one of the rooms that had been restored and made ready for use. "I can hire help," Ike said. "There're plenty of men needing work."

"No. You know I don't want people knowing about this place," Jacob spat. "The two of you are two too many."

"Look, McCallister, I'm not one of your women to boss around and treat like a dog," Ike said. "Have you forgotten we're partners? Because if you have, I'm leaving, now! You know what? I don't even know what you're up to. And I don't like it."

"Don't get overly sensitive on me," Jacob laughed. It was no time for Ike to rebel. Jacob was too close to his goal. "I'm only being cautious."

"Cautious about what?"

"Tommy Lee, go out and unload the truck for me," Jacob said.

"Sure," Tommy Lee answered, not in the least interested in the men's conversation. "Where do ya want me put th' stuff?"

"Put it on the side porch," Ike said.

After Tommy Lee was out of earshot, Jacob said, "You know I'm getting the place ready for my family. I don't want anybody, and I mean anybody to know about my business. That means Tommy Lee too. His working here doesn't make him worthy of knowing my business."

An hour later, with the truck unloaded and Ike in town dropping Tommy Lee off, Jacob, satisfied everything was going well at the mansion, gathered his travel bag and briefcase from the room he used on his short visits to the site and left. When going to and from the building project, he used back roads to avoid traveling anywhere near Winding Ridge, although it added miles to go the opposite way on Route Seven to reach the next town that I-79 passed through. It would definitely not be to his benefit to be seen around Winding Ridge or the mountain.

In The General Store, Patty bought a few things, mostly because she never could during the time she was being raised in the small cabin above the small town. The few times she, Sara, and Joe dared to brave the store when they were kids, they were chased out. The proprietor knew the mountain children had no money to spend and feared they were planning to steal whatever they wanted, something that never occurred to them to do.

After paying for her purchases, she inquired about the property previously owned by Chase Martin. "I knowed th' man, but never knowed where he lived. I didn't even knowed he'd sold th' place."

"Do you have any idea who would know?"

"Nope. Sorry, but I can't help ya."

Patty went out to the street just as Tommy Lee was climbing from a black Cadillac. "Hey, Patty, I saw ya this mornin' goin' in your own car. I'm impressed ya can drive."

"It's not unusual. Don't you drive?"

"Wouldn't have nothin' to drive if I did," Tommy Lee said, envious of anyone who wasn't too poor to do something as cool as drive.

"Tommy Lee, do you know where the Chase Martin place is?"

"Nope." Tommy Lee knew of the Martins, but didn't know where they lived.

"Thanks, anyway," Patty said. "I'm going to try at the Post Office.

"Wait, Patty, can I take ya to th' movies? I have th' money to take ya. I can pay for ya an' me," Tommy Lee bragged.

She was embarrassed for Tommy Lee, having to turn him down, but not only did she have no desire to go to the movies—or anywhere, for that matter—with him, she had no time if she was going to find out all she could about her family.

"No, I can't. I've a lot to do before I go home. Thanks anyway." Patty turned away, missing the malicious look that replaced the smile on Tommy Lee's face.

Walking into the Post Office, Patty steeled herself for another bad scene like she had experienced in the sheriff's office and was pleasantly surprised when the Post Master said, "May I help you, young lady?"

She smiled. "Thank you. Yes. I'm trying to find out where a house is located. I found a deed granting ownership to Jacob McCallister from Chase Martin. Can you tell me how to find the address?"

"I can do better than that," the man said. "I know Chase Martin, but I never knowed he'd sold his place to that scoundrel McCallister." He picked up a pen and scrawled the address on a note pad, tore off the page, and handed it to Patty.

"Thank you," she smiled. "I appreciate your help."

"When you get to the bottom of Winding Ridge Hill, go left. It's about eighteen or twenty miles. You can't miss it. It's a run-down mansion, the largest house in these parts."

"Sounds easy enough."

"By the way, the house is in disrepair."

"Really?"

"Yep."

"Thanks." Patty turned to go.

"I never saw you before," the man said. "What in the world is a nice city girl like you doing in this nowhere town?"

"I used to live here," Patty said, and before the man could ask more questions, she waved and walked quickly out to the street.

She realized it was getting late and hurried to her car, heading for the cabin and dinner.

The next morning, after having breakfast at the cabin again and promising Annabelle she would return that evening, Patty had started out for Jacob's new property. Now, as she realized she had not seen a house or another human for the last twenty miles or more, her worry changed to panic, and she began looking for a place off the narrow road to turn around and head back the way she'd come. That was when she saw it, a spacious house with four white columns that spread grandly across the huge front porch. It was set back from the road, overlooking an enormous circular driveway that ran from Route Seven, swung gracefully past the elegant front steps, spanned the length of the wraparound porch, and curved back to meet Route Seven again.

She couldn't tell whether there were people living in the house or not. It was definitely the house she was looking for and obviously still under construction. The newness and grandeur of the house itself seemed odd, as it had been restored over an old stone foundation and built on grounds that had been neglected for years.

Ornate gothic gates, attached to a seven-foot, ancient wrought-iron fence surrounding the property, stood one at each end of a brick driveway with weeds that, sprouting along the entire expanse, made it evident that the fence and gates had been put up in the distant past and were rarely used now. The driveway met Route Seven at the beginning and at the end, forming a horseshoe. Each of the gates, wide enough to accommodate a car, was securely locked, but there was a third one, a narrow opening to an overgrown footpath near one end of the driveway, and it was invitingly ajar.

Patty pulled to the side of the road and climbed from the car. As she stood there wondering what to do next, she realized that the scene around her was hauntingly familiar. The hair stood up on the back of her neck as she surveyed the abandoned road, aware that the wind was whipping up, causing dead leaves to swirl around her feet in little funnel clouds. Her breath caught in her throat.

She was standing in her own nightmare.

8

*H*ER CHORES LONG FINISHED, ANNABELLE CONSTANTLY looked from the window, drawn by any sound at all coming from outside. Normally she would be rocking in her chair listening to her beloved radio at this time, but she had expected Patty to be back by now, and a female who knew the ways of the mountain men would never willingly travel alone at this late hour. Annabelle was despairing that she would see her again that day, figuring she must have gone straight to the boardinghouse.

"Ya look worried," Daisy said, entering the kitchen from the bedroom she and Annabelle shared alone, except when their husband was home.

"I'm wonderin' 'bout Patty. Thought she was comin' back this evenin'. She tol' me so herself when she'd come for breakfast this mornin'. She'd said she'd come back for supper."

Daisy had just left the comfort and warmth of the bed. She'd only been asleep for a few hours when she had climbed from the four-poster, and it was already time for her to get ready for her next shift at the bar. "She'll be here any time now. Ya was worryin' yesterday when she got back later than ya expected."

"Should've been here by now."

"How'd ya knowed what time she should be back?"

"I just knowed."

"So there's other places she could be. She's stayin' at th' boardin' house in town," Daisy said. "That's probably where she is now. I'm sure that she just don't want to be out too late 'cause she knows that th' militia could still be active 'round these parts. I'm sure she knows 'bout Jordan an' how they messed with her when she was travelin' by herself, an' that she only got away by th' skin of her nose with that Paul Frank Ruble's help."

"She should sleep here, an' take her meals with us, an' spend some time with 'er sister, Sara. She enjoyed her breakfast these last two mornin's, an' her supper last night, I could tell, an' she said so. I just don't knowed why she don't want to stay here," Annabelle complained.

Daisy looked around the room and laughed. "Well, I do! Ya remember how it was in th' city. Comfortable beds, food, heat in th' winter, cool air in th' summer, an' th' best of all there was an inside toilet. There was even a tub for bathin' that ya could stretch out in with hot an' cold runnin' water. Ya didn't have to fetch water in a bucket an' set it on a cook stove to get it warm enough for bathin'."

"I always fix th' bath water, an' she knows she wouldn't have to bother with it herself," Annabelle insisted.

"Forevermore, Annabelle, I just don't understand ya. Ya saw firsthand how nice it was livin' in th' city. After that, who'd want this?" Daisy swung her arm encompassing the room.

"I'm not convinced," Annabelle said. "Patty said she'd stop, an' I knowed she wouldn't go straight to th' boardin' house an' not stop here."

"Well, I'm sure she did. It just got too late an' she went to th' boardin' house where she has more conveniences than we do. I knowed it's probably not anythin' like we had in th' fancy hotels in th' city, but it's betta for her than here. Once ya get used to nice things it's hard to do without 'em."

"Just how would ya knowed that, Daisy?"

"I just knowed."

"We have nice things. We have th' potbelly stoves for heat in th' winter, an' ya can open th' doors to get air in th' summer," Annabelle said. "There's th' washtub we fill with water for our bath. An' th' best thing"—she stuck her nose in the air, indicating she felt that Daisy was acting high and mighty—"is we don't have folks livin' 'bove our heads, under our feet, an' on both sides of us."

"Oh, forevermore!" Daisy said in exasperation.

Early morning September 10, 2001

The boy left the town bar and he made his way along the cobblestone street. A passerby wouldn't have realized that he was heading anywhere in particular as he ambled past the boardinghouse and in the direction of The General Store.

Shortly, coming abreast of the store, he passed it and, turning quickly, stepped into an alley between the store and the movie theater. His activities were of no significance to anyone in the vicinity, busy with everyday errands, and so he went unnoticed.

Now passing far beyond the rear of the large buildings that faced Main Street, he continued his unhurried progress. Off the narrow alley was a dirt lane, running past a few houses and eventually disappearing into the thistles. Skirted by tall weeds that bent and swayed in the breeze, the virtually unused lane continued winding its way to the rear of a large two-story clapboard house that faced the main alley and sat one hundred and twenty-five feet back from it.

Moving off the dirt lane through a quarter mile of thick, wildly unkempt brambles and brush, he crossed the yard to the far side of the long abandoned house where, sheltered from view by densely overgrown weeds, a lean-to was attached to the side of the house.

Taking a key from his pocket, he unlocked the padlock and hurried inside the room that he thought of as "his place." The sun, no longer hindered by the door, filtered into the shadowy interior and sent streaks of light to the depths of the lean-to. Disturbed by the rush of air caused by the door's sudden opening and now illuminated by the bright light, dust particles performed an intricate ballet.

9

Late evening on September 10, 2001

After putting in calls to Cliff and Paul Frank, a panic-stricken Tuesday sat waiting for them at her kitchen table. She was more scared than she'd been for a long time, because she had not heard from Patty for three days now, counting this one. Patty had called the day she'd arrived at Winding Ridge. That call, in spite of the fact that Patty had gone against their wishes, had gone well; there was no reason for the silence now. It was becoming more and more obvious to Tuesday that something was wrong.

Following the ring of the doorbell, Paul Frank, hugely handsome in his State Police uniform, appeared in the kitchen. He was so much at home at her house that he felt no need to be escorted in, but he always rang the bell anyway, signaling his arrival.

Having heard his voice, Mary Lou came running down the stairs. "Are you going to the mountain to find Patty? I want to go with you," Mary Lou demanded, crossing the living room and heading for the kitchen, where the family spent most of its time. Paul Frank sat at the table, and Tuesday took a seat across from him.

"Sit down, Mary Lou," Tuesday said. "Paul Frank and I are talking about Patty going to Winding Ridge in search of her birth family and to see Annabelle and the others. I'm so worried about not hearing from her."

"She did go without your blessing." Paul Frank smiled.

"I know. I guess I can't expect her to keep in touch when she feels I'm being unfair."

"Let me understand this. You haven't heard from her the whole time?" Paul Frank asked.

"Yes. Of course, she called to tell me that she got there safely," Tuesday said calmly. "But that was three days ago. Since then, we haven't heard anything at all from her."

"Come on. I mean, that's not so long." Paul Frank smiled again. "What did you talk about?"

"Not much, just that she was on her way to the cabin."

"Did she say when she'd call back?"

"Only that she'd keep me posted."

"So what's the problem?"

"I know her. She wouldn't let me worry if she could help it." Tuesday put her face in her hands.

"I'd say she doesn't know you're worried. What's Cliff think?" Paul Frank asked.

"He doesn't even know that she hasn't called yet today. I don't think he's concerned yet.

I've been getting bad vibes, though. They're so real, like mental telepathy. I think she has the ability to send strong distress signals. That's why I called you today."

"Well, even though I believe she could just be so wrapped up in her search that she let time get away from her,"' Paul Frank said, "I'm not willing to take a chance on her safety. I'm going to go check on her."

"She may think we don't trust her on her own," Tuesday pointed out. "You know how she is about her independence. But I don't blame her after the life she endured for years. She's determined to get away from the total domination the mountain women suffer at the hands of men."

"I don't know about that, but she went without your permission. You and Cliff are responsible for her. I mean, it only follows that you would send someone to check on her. I'll offer my assistance in her search for her family," Paul Frank said. "Surely, she can't object to that. I've been trained in detective work."

"I'm going, too," Mary Lou announced.

"Mary Lou, no offense," Paul Frank said, "but I'm going alone."

Paul Frank had come to live in the city two years earlier. In that time both Patty and Mary Lou had became infatuated with him. After completing the required schooling, he'd been accepted in the State Police Academy. He'd also taken private speech classes, and as with the girls, not even a hint of the mountain remained in his manner or dress.

Cliff came in just then and joined the others at the table. "I'd say from the looks of it the two of you have a plan."

"We're trying to figure out why we haven't heard from Patty if she's not in trouble."

"On the chance the solar phone doesn't work, she could have found a pay phone," Cliff offered.

"I know she knows where at least one is because we used it on our way off the mountain running from McCallister. Or," Paul Frank added, "she's upset that the two of you wouldn't back her in her search."

"It could be she's totally immersed in her search and isn't thinking," replied Cliff.

"The two of you are only saying that she may or may not be in trouble. I realize that," Tuesday said. "That's what we've been weighing all day. She would not worry us. And it all comes back to when we last talked. She promised to keep in touch."

"There's no doubt about it," Cliff said. "We have to check it out, keeping in mind Patty is a teenager and keeping in touch may not mean the same thing to her as to us."

"Sure," Paul Frank said, "I mean, she's probably so excited about seeing Annabelle and the others and being on the mountain again. Can you imagine? She's seeing it through different eyes after living a totally different lifestyle here. Gosh, she's probably not paying attention to time."

"Maybe, but let's not take a chance. We'll assume that she needs us," Tuesday said. "I can't ignore this feeling I have that she's in trouble."

Hearing the men in the kitchen, Winter Ann darted down the stairs, her dark curls bouncing around her shoulders. She crossed the room toward Cliff and Paul Frank, who were, except for her mother, her very favorite people.

"I want to go, too," Winter Ann demanded. "I want to find Patty." She jumped on Cliff's lap, throwing her arms around his neck. In all this activity, her hair ribbon had slid to one side and hung lopsided over her ear. Tuesday reached around her head and removed it.

"Whoa," Cliff laughed. "You're going to knock me off my chair one day."

"And I'll pick you up," Winter Ann laughed.

"Know what?" Winter Ann looked toward her mother.

"No! What?" Tuesday answered.

"I'm going with Paul Frank and Daddy to find Patty."

"I don't think so, young lady. You're going to stay put where I can keep an eye on you. Mary Lou, would you please take Winter Ann upstairs and see if she has any homework?"

"Oh, Mother, I'm only in preschool. I don't have homework." Winter Ann was mature for her tender age; Tuesday herself had always been the same way, but she had no way of knowing that since her only family, her parents, had been killed in an auto accident eight years earlier, and her grandparents had died when Tuesday was a girl, never getting to meet their only child's daughter, and leaving no one to reminisce with her now about the old days.

After the girls disappeared upstairs, Paul Frank announced, "If you don't hear from her tonight, I'll leave at six in the morning. It's just getting daylight at that time."

"I agree," Tuesday said, "just in case there's something wrong."

"But what?" Cliff asked. "Do you think the militia would be interested in her?"

"There's no telling," Paul Frank said. "On the mountain, it could be anything."

"What about McCallister? Has the detective found anything?" Tuesday asked.

"Not yet," Cliff said. "I should be getting a report from him later this evening."

"I hate to even think it, but maybe he's the reason we haven't heard from her," Paul Frank said. "If he's after Patty, you can be sure that he's going to come after Tuesday and Winter Ann, too."

"Be careful, Paul Frank," Tuesday pleaded. "You know I don't ever want Winter Ann to know that Jacob is her biological father. Not ever."

"I'm sorry," Paul Frank apologized. "I know I shouldn't even allude to any connection between the two of them."

Cliff said. "I'll let you know what the detective has found out as soon as I hear."

The detective was to know where McCallister was at all times. If he wasn't in town, and Patty had not returned, Cliff would assume he was in some way responsible for Patty's disappearance and would join Paul Frank in his search on the mountain.

Disregarding the earlier pleas from Mary Lou to join him, Paul Frank called in for a short emergency leave of absence and prepared to leave at dawn for the mountain where he'd spent the first eighteen years of his life.

Winter Ann, forgetting about her mother's request for her to remain upstairs and unnoticed by Mary Lou who was to keep an eye on her, had wondered back to the kitchen. She came up behind Paul Frank, and tugging at his shirtsleeve, asked him her perpetual question. Actually, she'd adopted it from her favorite character in a story that her mother had read to her many times at her repeated request. "Know what?"

"No. What?" Paul Frank asked.

"Patty and Mary Lou are your girlfriends. Why can't Mary Lou go with you to find Patty?"

"Where'd you get that idea, Winter Ann?"

"I just know. So why aren't you taking Mary Lou with you?"

Paul Frank squatted to be nearer the small girl's height. "You be a good girl, and I'll bring you something from the mountain."

"Nuh-uh! I want you to tell me why you're not taking Mary Lou!" The little girl stomped her foot.

"Winter Ann, you're being rude," Tuesday admonished the girl. "You mustn't ask personal questions, and how many times have I told you not to stomp your foot to get your way?"

"I'm sorry," Winter Ann looked very apologetic. "But why can't Mary Lou go?"

Tuesday sighed; her daughter was the most inquisitive child she had ever encountered. She was also the most intuitive, always asking questions far beyond her age. "Just because, and for your information neither one of them is his girlfriend. When Paul Frank does get a girlfriend, he'll have only one. People don't have two."

"Why not? Both of them want him for a boyfriend."

Paul Frank and Tuesday looked at each other, smiling. "I'm sorry, but she's incorrigible," Tuesday said.

No one except Cliff had noticed when Mary Lou had appeared briefly in the kitchen doorway only to turn quickly and run up the stairs. "I think we have some hurt feelings here," he said nodding toward the stairs. "Tell me if I'm stepping out of line, but it's obvious that both the girls have feelings for you. Why are you keeping yours to yourself?"

Paul Frank was silent for a few minutes, a frown on his face. "I guess I'm not ready. I've been working on my career, and I've been saving to buy a house of my own. You've seen my tiny room at Monica's rooming house." Paul Frank made a sweeping gesture with his hand. "I do like one of them very much, but when I make a commitment, I want to have something to offer. I mean, I want a life like you and Tuesday share."

"There's something to be said about working to get ahead and being prepared for a relationship. But I'd say the most important issue here is that the other girl needs to be moving on rather than waiting for you."

"I don't know. I mean, I'm hoping that I don't have to hurt anyone. Since it's not meant for me to be with one of the girls, the man for her will eventually come into her life."

"Paul Frank," Tuesday interjected, "I think you should speak up. Drawing it out will only hurt the other one more."

"When I get back from searching for Patty, maybe I'll do just that."

Mary Lou was listening from the top of the stairs. "Please let it be me," she whispered.

After Paul Frank left, Cliff fished the phonebook from the drawer in the phone stand. Thumbing through the pages, he found the listing for accountants. McCallister and Associates was listed among the numerous firms. Cliff and Tuesday had already known that Jacob McCallister had an accounting firm and that it was located in Wheeling.

Under the circumstances, Cliff had reconsidered and decided not to wait for the report from the detective. He wanted to speak to McCallister himself. He dialed the number and a soft, feminine voice answered, "How may I help you?"

"I'd like to speak to Mr. McCallister," Cliff said.

"Sorry, he's not in today."

"When do you expect him?"

"If you'll leave your phone number, I'll have him return your call."

"Will he be in tomorrow?" Cliff asked.

"No, I'm not sure when to expect his return, exactly. Anyway, you just missed him." Cliff let out his breath as if he had been holding it for a long time. The voice continued, "He just got back from a building project he's involved in, and he left right away to meet with some new clients. He'll be out of the office for the next couple of days at least."

"Thanks, I'll try back later." Cliff hung up, frustrated. If McCallister had really been out of town and had come back, it didn't necessarily mean he was not on Winding Ridge at the same time as Patty. And McCallister's secretary had said he was leaving town again; maybe he was going back to the mountain.

Taking a page from Tuesday, and at the private detective's request, Cliff gathered his notes going clear back to the day he had first met Tuesday and Jacob McCallister at Cora's home. After setting down the name of every detective who was closely involved in the case when Tuesday went missing, Cliff began calling them one by one. After getting nowhere he called Hal Brooks; Cliff had left the best for last.

"Hal," Cliff said when his old partner answered, "I need to see you. There's a situation going on, and I've decided to get Jacob McCallister out of my life once and for all."

"Something happen?"

"I'm not sure," Cliff said, "but Patty went to Winding Ridge to locate her birth relatives and we haven't heard from her for several days. Naturally we always think of McCallister when anyone in this family is in trouble. I've decided to find out what he's up to these days and to keep track of him in the future."

"Do you have a specific reason to think that McCallister is up to something? Or is it just caution on your part?"

"Yes. It's her dreams," Cliff said. "I guarantee he's up to something, and to tell the truth I'm afraid that he has Patty now."

"If not for being involved in the case before, I'd be hanging up on you right now, thinking you were a nut case. Since I know that you're not—how can I help?"

"I believe I'll find some answers in my notes from the time that I met him and Tuesday at Cora's house. Also, there may be answers in Patty's dreams."

"Tell you what, I'll get my notes together and be available anytime you say."

"I mostly want to brainstorm with you. We always come up with something when we do that."

"I'll be mulling it over."

Cliff asked about the twins that Hal and his wife had adopted when they were only toddlers. Daisy's first set of twins, the little girl and boy were Hal and his wife's pride and joy. Due to the newest emergency, Cliff and Hal talked over their fear that McCallister might see the children somewhere and recognize them as his own; the boy bore a strong resemblance to his natural father.

After the phone conversation, Cliff took out his notes on Patty's most recent dreams and nightmares. When McCallister's secretary mentioned that he was checking on a building project, it brought to Cliff's mind the huge house McCallister was building in one of Patty's nightmares. Also, Patty had commented that the house was in a remote area. Patty had mentioned a dream in which she was stranded on an isolated road with nothing in either direction as far as she could see. In another she was locked in a dark place with no food or water. In the margin next to this one Cliff wrote, "This sounds like McCallister's m. o. It's just like the time he locked the two women in the cellar house."

"I don't want to frighten Tuesday, but everything is starting to point to McCallister. But why is it just Patty? Is he stalking around somewhere, waiting for the right circumstances to pick up Tuesday and Winter Ann?" Cliff said to himself as he wrote in his notepad. He added, "No way! This is not going to happen again."

Patty was huddled in a dark corner. The event at the mansion's gate, where everything had started going bad, came back to her. As she stood along the isolated road, the stranger had suddenly appeared behind her and asked: "Are you deaf and dumb, girl? I asked you, what're you doing here?"

Patty had frozen, terrified at the harsh sound of the man's

voice. "I'm looking for the owner of this house," she explained.

"I could help you if I wanted to," the man said. And that was when she'd noticed that her old schoolmate Tommy Lee Hillberry was standing behind him.

"Why ya lookin' for th' one that owns this place?" Tommy Lee asked.

At first she was relived to see a familiar face. That was before she noticed the look of glee and lust in his bloodshot eyes.

"I have my reasons," she had croaked.

I'm in that huge house! Why are Tommy Lee and the man working on that huge house? I know it's Pa's house. Did he hire them to kidnap me? How could that be? I'm here just by happenstance.

It was not that she had not taken heed of her dreams, warnings that Cliff believed could help her avoid wandering into harm's way, but once again, Patty had, without design, walked right into her nightmare.

I feel like I've been drugged or something, she thought. The last thing that I remember is Tommy Lee bringing me rusty water and a stale sandwich. The man with him must have provided the food. Tommy Lee would have no way to get a sandwich made from prepared food even if it was stale. How could I have been so dumb to just stand there when I first saw them? I don't even know which one pulled a feedsack over my head and threw me over his shoulder.

There was a thump at the door. She froze.

Deep in the tunnels a county away, the six boys, bored and as usual unsupervised by parents who left them with too much time on their hands, were hanging out surrounded by their ill-gotten stash.

"We've got to be more careful, bein' seen 'round th' places we rob," Robbie Rudd said.

"We don't want to be caught. No way," Kevin Clarke said and pushed Timmy Sturdivant back against the tunnel wall in annoyance. To stop the ruckus Timmy's brother Erik grabbed Kevin and twisted his arm.

"Ya mean when we ran into old man Keefover this mornin'?" Coop crowed. "He ain't never sober enough to knowed what's goin' on around him, anyway."

"Yeah," Kip Willis said throwing a punch to Kevin's stomach, "him an' anyone else that'd be snoopin' around our business. One thing for sure, we don't want my dad to catch us."

"What a grasp of th' obvious ya have," Timmy snickered as he pushed Kip outside the ring of light. "Don't knowed why I'm dumb enough to hang out with th' deputy's son. Anyway, we have to be careful of Toughman's gang, too. They'd steal our stash quicker'n we got our hands on it in th' first place."

"Lucky for us they don't come around much," Kip said.

"They're too lazy to travel the distance," Coop said. "Anyway, I'm more worried about Joe McCallister. He's like his pa. He can break the law, but just let somebody else do it an' he's down on ya like he thinks he's the law."

The gangs were rivals and often engaged in fights. Toughman's gang claimed a portion of the tunnel ten miles deeper in the mountain miles away from where Rudd's gang met. They used the tunnel that ran beneath Broad Run and Centerpoint, and with Paul Frank living in the city, they freely used the entrances at his home place at Broad Run. But Rudd's gang preferred the newer entrance and caverns built by the militia below McCallister's cabin on Winding Ridge, and that's where they normally spent a large part of their day.

The boys brought their loot to one of the huge chambers the militia built for storage rooms for Armageddon. They had furnished it with stolen chairs, cots, quilts, and cooking utensils. They stole most of their food—and many other items to make their clubhouse a place they could hide out in comfort. They enjoyed never having to go home to eat or sleep for that matter, except for the fact that if they did not show up at home once in a while, their parents would send the sheriff after them.

They kept such a low profile that mostly Tommy Lee Hillberry was blamed for the gang's crimes, stealing and terrorizing young girls being their favorites. Although Tommy Lee was continually after the girls, not caring if they wanted his attentions or not, he seldom stole from others.

The boys were planning to rob a place where they had found more booze than they had seen outside a bar. The last time they'd gone there, they were able to get in and out unobserved. The place was being restored and held many items of interest to them.

10

Dawn of September 11, 2001

He parked in front of the boardinghouse and looked up the street. Checking into an inn was new to Paul Frank. He'd never had the money, the need, or the desire to travel. His only wish, since he had gotten away from his family's underprivileged mountain life, had been to improve his lot, and he had.

Inside, the huge woman at the counter peered suspiciously at Paul Frank. "How long ya stayin'?" she asked. "I need paid in advance."

"I don't know. I mean, I'll have to pay you day to day."

"No problem, long as ya're paid ahead a day," Melba said, looking him over. "If I'd knowed ya, it wouldn't've made any difference. Ya're from th' city, I reckon."

"I live in Wheeling now, but I'm from Broad Run above Centerpoint," Paul Frank said.

"Folks don't usually come back to these parts after leavin'."

"I'm looking for someone. Before I rent a room, I'd like to ask you a few questions, particularly about Patty McCallister."

Paul Frank noticed that the woman raised her eyebrows sharply at the mention of Patty's name.

"Ain't none of my business, an' I suppose it ain't none of your'n neither. I mind my own business, an' it ain't my place to knowed some other'ns," the proprietor told him, echoing almost exactly the words she'd spoken to Cliff Moran four years earlier when he'd rented a room from her.

"Please, her life may be in danger," he urged.

As though she hadn't heard him, Melba pushed the ledger forward for Paul Frank to record his name and address. When he reached to sign, he saw "Patty Moran" written in the next-to-last line. "I'd forgotten," he said as he turned the book back toward the proprietor. "Her name is Patty Moran now. I see that she did check in on September 7th. It's right here." He pointed to the name and date.

"Boy, I ain't here all th' time, an' I don't see everyone that checks in. Anyway, ya had th' name wrong. Furthermore, I don't like people comin' in askin' questions 'bout folks what ain't none of their business. Seems to me every time that happens trouble starts. What part of that didn't'cha understand th' first time I said it?"

"Look, I'm with the State Police, and it's important that I locate her as soon as possible."

"I don't care if'n ya're with th' king of England, I'm not in th' business of findin' th' lost. I'm in th' business of rentin' rooms an' mindin' my own business. If ya're lookin' for somethin' lost, I think Th' General Store has a lost an' found department."

"Miss," Paul Frank pleaded, "you know how dangerous the mountain can be, especially for a young girl on her own. Don't make me call in backup."

"All right, all right, I knowed who ya mean," Melba said. "To tell ya th' truth, I'm worried too, or I'd not tell ya nothin' 'bout her, law or not. Mark my word! She's stayin' here day to day like ya're, but I ain't seen her since day before yesterday. She's payin' by credit card an' she'll check out when she's ready."

Around six-thirty that same day, and not mindful of Daisy's need for sleep, Annabelle hefted her generous bulk from the warmth of the tattered quilts covering the feather tick that served as a mattress for the four-poster bed, to attend her morning chores. She was fully awake, worry about Patty up-permost in her mind; meanwhile, Daisy, following a late shift at the bar, had been asleep for a scant two hours and re-mained huddled under the quilt.

Annabelle was content to live in the remote cabin, ab-sorbed in her household tasks as always, just as she knew Jacob McCallister expected her to be. Annabelle's loyalty, as well as Aunt Aggie's, lay with Jeb. He was the center of their lives, and they both lived for his more and more infrequent visits. Much to their regret, now that Joe could drive, he was in charge of the household in his father's prolonged ab-sences. Joe demanded the same day-to-day routine from them that Jeb did.

Annabelle shuffled into the kitchen, her wiry hair escaping in frizzy strands from the knot she always wore, and turned on the radio. It was set on her usual station; chatter from her favorite morning talk show filled the air, chasing the early morning quiet from the cabin. Happy to be hearing voices from a larger world, Annabelle pulled a farmer's match from her pocket and struck it across the top of the woodburning stove. She held it to the scraps of paper and twigs that she had arranged the night before.

The fire caught quickly, and Annabelle waited, watching as it burned strong and bright. Lifting a few pieces of kin-dling from the wood-box stored at the side of the stove, she placed them carefully so as not to smother the flame. Just be-fore she closed the oven door, the kindling caught and flames shot out, throwing bright flashes across the kitchen. The homemade furniture near the stove, caught by the fire-light, sent tall shadows dancing over the log walls, creating a false sense of cozy comfort. Soon the warmth radiating from the stove overcame the chilly morning air.

At seven, the sun rose above the mountaintop that tow-ered regally above the small cabin. Made even more in-significant by a huge outcropping of rocks just above the clearing, the cabin nestled snugly among pine trees. Sunlight filtered through the small window above the woodburner, erasing the shadows and bringing its own brightness and warmth to the bleak rooms. Soon it would be too hot inside, and the kitchen area would be particularly unbearable.

Drexel appeared in the doorway, pulling aside the ragged curtains that separated the children's bedroom from the kitchen. Trailing behind him were the other children and Daisy. It was clear from the looks of Daisy's red puffy eyes that she had not gotten her required sleep. Along with Annabelle's early activities, the children crawling onto the bed upon their waking had rousted her much too early.

"Sara, can't ya tend to th' youngins so I can get some sleep," Daisy wailed to the girl when she came in from her morning trip to the outhouse. "They're all over me in th' bed."

"Sorry, Daisy. I thought they'd gone outdoors when I did," Sara apologized, taking charge of the children.

Sara settled the children on the benches attached to the table, Drexel and Dakota on one side, with herself and tiny Kelly Sue on the other, to even out the weight and keep the whole thing from tilting. She reached for the radio, twirling the knob until she found a station that was playing music.

The battery-powered radio was a wonder for Annabelle, Daisy, and Sara. Annabelle adored listening to the news and talk shows. Sara and Daisy always chose music first and talk shows and the news second. The three of them even loved the commercials. Hearing interesting conversation and being informed about what was going on in the outside world gave them food for thought and fresh, different life experiences— outside their sphere of influence—to think about, talk about, and look forward to. Each and every day they were learning about something they had not even known existed. The radio provided for them a new eye on the world, which added color to their dreary existence. Without the radio, their short trip to Wheeling four years earlier would have faded quickly and become just a distant memory. With its stories of people from many walks of life, including women who were living lives of their own choosing, the radio was a constant reminder of just how isolated their lives were.

Sara loved the music more than the others did. Before Joe brought them the radio, she had had no idea about music or how entertaining it was to listen to or sing along with. Routinely, she fought with Annabelle to turn the radio from news to music.

"Okay if I listen to music awhile, Ma?" Sara asked.

"Ya knowed I like to hear th' people talk."

"Ya didn't used to care 'bout th' world outside th' mountain," Sara teased.

"Didn't really knowed there was a different world out there 'till I was forced into it. It's makes it interestin' to hear 'bout it now that we've seen it first hand."

"Ma, let me turn-n-n it! After th' youngins eat, an' before I take 'em out to play, I'll find ya a news station."

"That's what ya was goin' to do anyway, so why'd ya even ask?"

"Just wantin' to be nice," Sara said, smiling her triumph.

"Humph," Annabelle grunted.

"What ya fixin' for breakfast, Ma?" Sara asked as she switched stations.

"Flapjacks, but we're goin' to run out of 'em an' everythin' else we have to eat, if Joe don't tend to gettin' supplies in pretty soon."

"He'll bring 'em in time," Sara said, tossing her head. "He ain't forgot us yet. I knowed he don't want his child to go hungry."

"I don't guess he's wantin' Daisy's twins or th' rest of us to starve, either," Annabelle huffed, "but that don't mean he's goin' to take th' time from 'is new city life to take care of 'is obligations."

"Ma," Sara said, "ya worry too much."

"Somebody has to worry," Annabelle fumed. "It sure ain't goin' to be ya an' Daisy."

Sara rolled her eyes and turned up the volume on the radio. Humming along with the music, she tuned her mother out.

Half an hour later, they had finished their breakfast to the tune of rap music, which Annabelle detested. Sara changed the radio dial to Annabelle's favorite morning talk show, and leaving the cleanup to her mother, she led the children outdoors to play in the morning sunshine.

Alone in the kitchen, just before nine o'clock, Annabelle was busy with her chores, intently listening to an irate caller tell about a drunk driver killing her friend one evening a week before. Her friend had crossed the street, relying on the approaching vehicle to observe the stop sign. Instead, he ignored the stop sign as if it had not been standing there for years and ran down the woman, dragging her for twenty feet, too drunk even to realize that he'd hit someone.

The caller's voice choked as she asked, "How is it that the man was released on bail the same day, so he's able to continue driving around the neighborhood?"

Annabelle had found the story distressing, and was fully absorbed in the program when suddenly it was interrupted.

"Of all th—," Annabelle started to complain, but when what the intruding newscaster's excited voice announced, "This just in, a passenger airliner has crashed into a tower at the World Trade Center in New York," she forgot all about the first story and became intrigued by the breaking news. She continued her work, but kept her ears tuned to what the man was saying. Although she had no idea of the true magnitude of the tragedy, her attention was total.

After about fifteen minutes of speculation about the incident, the newscaster's tone became more agitated and his voice picked up volume. "It seems that another passenger jetliner has hit the second tower at the World Trade Center! This is not only too coincidental to be an accident, it's virtually impossible for a huge jet to suddenly—out of the blue—hit such a building on a bright sunny day. A pilot could see those structures for miles.

"And folks," the newscaster's voice broke, "there are thousands of people in those buildings this time of morning."

Annabelle finally sat down, forgetting her chores. The announcer's husky voice was filled with a deep emotion that she'd never heard coming from her radio before. His unthinkable words held her captive.

A short time later, when he revealed that yet a third passenger jetliner had crashed into the Pentagon in Washington D.C., his personal reaction hindered his ability to speak professionally.

"Daisy, get in here. Somethin' is happenin'." Annabelle hefted herself from the bench at the table and called for Sara to come in. The three women gathered around the radio. The chores, Daisy's primping, and the children's playtime with Sara were totally abandoned. And then the familiar voice of the newscaster told of the fourth airliner crashing in a field in Pennsylvania.

The women spent the entire day huddled around the table, listening to the horrific news, having no idea how the tragedy was going to affect their lives.

11

11:00 am September 11, 2001

After settling into his room at the boardinghouse, Paul Frank headed for McCallister's cabin on the theory that Patty would have gone there as soon as she arrived on the mountain. As the cabin came into view, memories of two years earlier rushed into his mind: the time he and Jordan had spent in the tunnel, the militiamen and their families gathered for the rally, and most of all, his deepening relationship with Cliff Moran and the realization that being a lawman was what he wanted for himself.

He parked near the back door in the circle of dirt defined by many years of McCallister's use of the area as a parking pad for his truck.

Inside the cabin Annabelle, hearing the whine of the truck engine, stopped what she was doing and opened the back-door to see who it was. "'Pon my soul, if it ain't th' boy from Centerpoint," she said to the others still huddled around the table. Along with Annabelle, they were mesmerized by the haunting news of the terrorists' blows.

"I bet my bottom dollar he's here for Patty." Annabelle rightly guessed.

"Tell 'im to come on in," Sara said. "My, it'll be good to see 'im again."

"Is anyone with 'im?" Daisy asked.

"It's just me," Paul Frank said as he followed Annabelle into the kitchen, lighting up the somber room with his broad, white-toothed smile.

"Don't ya look th' handsome city boy!" Daisy gave a low whistle imitating the men in the bar who whistled at her from time to time, showing their appreciation for her extraordinarily pretty face and trim, shapely figure.

Paul Frank grinned, mostly for the charming way Daisy had whistled.

"Ya sure dress up good," Sara commented.

"How can ya'all joke around when people're suffering such misery and loss, an' when we're so worried 'bout Patty an' her whereabouts?" Annabelle complained.

"That's why I'm here. Tuesday and Cliff and I are also very worried about Patty. We've not heard from her since the day she arrived on the mountain." Suddenly realizing all of what Annabelle had said, he asked, "What do you mean people are suffering misery and loss?"

"Haven't ya heard?" Daisy asked. "Ya're a city boy now. I'd think ya'd knowed what's goin' on in th' world before we did."

Paul Frank looked around at the worried faces and shrugged.

"Come an' sit down. It's all that's on th' radio," Sara explained, moving toward the center of the bench to make room for him.

"We're at war," Daisy offered.

"What on earth are you talking about?" Paul Frank looked as if he thought the women had lost their minds. "I mean, what would you know about war?"

"Listen!" Daisy exclaimed.

The newscaster was talking to an expert from a nearby state, asking questions about how a firefighting team could possibly deal with a disaster of such magnitude. After exhausting the subject with the expert, the newscaster began his story from the beginning.

"For those just tuning in," the newscaster said, as he did every fifteen minutes now, "at approximately eight forty-six this morning, a jetliner crashed into the south tower of the World Trade Center. Fifteen minutes later a second jet hit the north tower."

Paul Frank listened with the others. His face showed his unguarded fear and disbelief as the full story was repeated, as it would be for days and months to come. All this had happened as he was on the road from Wheeling to Winding Ridge. Paul Frank had been listening to a CD while in his truck and had heard nothing of the tragedy.

The voices from the radio forgotten for a time, they began talking among themselves, going over what the newscaster had said. The women shot questions at Paul Frank, looking to him as though only someone who lived in the city could make sense of this madness.

"We can't do anything about the terrorist attack," Paul Frank said after a while, bringing the women back to the world that they lived in and could relate to, "but we can do something about finding Patty. Tell me everything that happened while she was here. I mean, I want to know everything she said."

Back in his room, having gotten nothing helpful from Mc-Callister's women, Paul Frank called Cliff using his solar phone. "I'm really worried now, Cliff. No one has seen Patty since the third morning she was here."

"I'm looking into the possibility that McCallister has made good on his threats and has taken her again. I hate to even say it, but absolutely everything I uncover points to his involvement in her disappearance," Cliff replied.

"What about Tuesday and Winter Ann? I mean, we've always believed that if he acted on his threat he'd take all three of them."

"I'm sure that's his long-range plan," Cliff said, "but now I believe that somehow he found out that Patty was going to Winding Ridge alone and took the opportunity to get to her."

"Besides that," Paul Frank said, "I heard about the attack on the World Trade Center. Will that hinder our search for Patty?"

"So far I can't see anything that will interfere with our search as long as we don't have to fly. Maybe you don't know, but the airports are shut down indefinitely."

"No, I didn't know," Paul Frank said. "I don't know much except what I've been hearing on the radio."

"It's awful. As I said before, Tuesday is thinking along those lines, but I didn't want to talk about it when you were at the house. Anyway, right now we'd better get back to finding Patty. Do you remember the nightmares she's been having about her father?"

"Yes, I do," Paul Frank said. "About seeing a big house, about being locked in a dark room, and about standing along an isolated road. I know there are others, but they're not coming to mind right now."

"I think the dreams are revealing things about her situation right now and may, if we can figure them out, lead us to her whereabouts. They fit in with McCallister's vow to—as he would put it—reclaim Patty, Tuesday, and Winter Ann and reunite his family. See if you can put together any of the dreams with anything you come across in your search."

"Sure. I mean, it makes sense to me."

"Not being able to locate McCallister is what has me the most worried," Cliff said.

"We should've kept closer tabs on McCallister." Paul Frank blinked away his tears of frustration, "I have this sick feeling that he has everything to do with Patty's disappearance."

"So do I. I thought keeping closer tabs on McCallister wasn't possible while trying to live a normal life, but under these circumstances, I'd say you're right. We did everything but follow him around twenty-four hours a day, and apparently that wasn't good enough. Anyway, we'll get to the bottom of this. Just keep in touch. By the way, don't go and do a disappearing act on me like Patty did. If I don't hear from you first thing in the morning and every four hours after that up until you go to bed, I'll assume that you're in trouble, too. I'd have no choice but to immediately get a team together and head for the mountain. It's imperative that we keep each other posted."

Late night of September 11, 2001
It had been a long day, the day that would to be forever known as 9/11. Annabelle waited for Daisy's return from the bar. As she rocked in her favorite chair, its to-and-fro movement created a hypnotic "squeak-squeak, squeak-squeak" rhythm. She sat cloaked in darkness, watching the stars as they blinked on and off. She was thinking about Patty's out-of-the-ordinary behavior. She had always been such a thoughtful and obedient child, and how peculiar it was that she had not come to say good-by, especially since she had assured Annabelle that even though she would be staying at the boardinghouse, she'd have breakfast with her and the others each morning.

Interrupting her thoughts, a car stopped in the distance, and the echoing sound of a door slamming reached Annabelle's ears. Shortly, Daisy appeared in the moonlight. Her feet hidden by the high weeds, she appeared to be gliding above the ground, a lovely apparition silently floating across the yard.

The rocking chair's comforting creaking sound guided Daisy to the steps leading to the front porch, where Annabelle waited. Daisy had used a well-worn path leading from the dirt driveway. The driveway itself branched off from the rutted-out dirt road that ran from the town at the foot of the mountain and dead-ended at Aunt Aggie's cabin four miles above.

"Who's bringin' ya home? Ya're askin' for trouble from Jeb. Ya thinkin' he ain't goin' to tolerate ya workin' in th' bar? Well, ya can bet he ain't goin' to abide ya runnin' with men in their cars."

"Annabelle," Daisy began, as she sat in the rocking chair next to her, "I'm tired of ya worryin' 'bout what Jeb's goin' to do. He ain't never here no more. He don't ever bring our supplies 'cause he has Joe do it for 'im."

"Ya knowed that ain't true. He comes 'round lots of times an' ya knowed it," Annabelle warned. "An' ya'd betta think on this, it'd be th' same thing if Joe'd catch ya. Ya knowed that he'd tell Jeb in a flash."

"Let 'im. It won't be too long 'til I have enough money to go to th' city," Daisy said defiantly.

"It's your funeral," Annabelle said. "Anyway, that's not what I've been waitin' up this long night to talk to ya 'bout."

"So, what is?"

"It's Patty," Annabelle said. "I'm worried. She still hasn't come back."

"Guess she went back to the city an' her fancy new home."

"Ya knowed she wouldn't go without sayin' bye."

"I don't knowed no such thing," Daisy said, annoyed by Annabelle's constant worrying. "Stuff happens. She has a fine, new life, an' she ain't worryin' 'bout what's goin' on in this cabin. She knows by now from livin' in th' city that it's a worthless excuse of a place to live."

"Just 'cause ya don't care 'bout nothin' but yourself, don't mean th' rest of us feel th' same way."

"Just 'cause I can't abide this cabin no more," Daisy moaned in frustration, "it don't mean that I don't care 'bout others—ya knowed I do. Ya're angry 'bout me wantin' to move to th' city an' not wantin' to admit I'm right."

A roaring engine distracted the quarreling women, and not knowing who to expect this time of night—Joe or Jeb— they quickly arose from their chairs and raced across the front porch, moving through the living room and quickly crossing the kitchen to reach the back door.

The lane that unraveled from the mountain trail ended at the foot of the back steps. It forked off the gravel road, winding its way to the porch. The wide dirt area there had been made over the years by McCallister's parking his truck at the rear of the cabin. It was completely out of sight to anyone using the gravel road to reach the top of the mountain.

To Annabelle's regret, in spite of the fact that she missed
having her son with her on the mountain, it was he and not
Jeb who stepped from the truck. She could see Joe in the circle of light spilling from the cab, looking as if he'd walked
straight from the pages of one of the Sears Roebuck catalogs
they kept in the outhouse in lieu of toilet paper. Before they
got the radio, those catalogs had also served as the family's
only window on the world. Their colorful pictures, of beautiful people in striking clothes, had sparked Patty's and
Daisy's fantasies of exciting city lives, which Annabelle considered nothing but foolish dreams.

Especially now in his store-bought clothing, Joe was a mirror image of his father. Both had memorable, brooding, brown
eyes, dark hair, and incredible muscular builds. But the father's good looks were enhanced by his charm, and he was
blessed with a rare charisma. His captivating smile won the
attention and quick friendship of those he came in contact
with—more specifically women. Joe McCallister's good
looks, on the other hand, did not hide a threatening expression that bordered on a mean scowl. As a result, women were
not immediately attracted to him, nor did he make friends
easily, if at all.

That difference in the men was instantly apparent, but
after getting to know each of them, acquaintances and col-
leagues discovered that they bore the same self-centered,
chauvinistic, mean-natured personalities, and ultimately
found them to be the shallowest of men.

"It's late. What're ya doin' up at this hour?" Joe asked,
slamming the truck door and dousing the pool of light.

That was a close call, Annabelle thought. She was shaken
but mightily relieved that at least Daisy was in and she did-
n't have to account for her absence.

"Patty's missin', an' we just couldn't sleep, that's all. That
Paul Frank Ruble was here, too, askin' questions 'bout Patty.
Now, he's out lookin' for her," Annabelle explained.

"Next thing, we heard ya comin' an' stepped outdoors to
see who it was comin' at this hour of th' night. It ain't prop-

er for visitors to come callin' at all hours," Annabelle contin-ued, babbling in her nervousness at being caught being up so late. "Should've knowed it was family."

"What'd you mean, Patty's missin' an' he's here looking for her?"

"Yeah, that's what I just said," Annabelle answered. "She'd come here to visit an' wouldn't spend th' night. Be-fore she'd gone missin', she was stayin' in th' boardin' house yonder in town, puttin' on airs."

"Oh, Ma, she's not doin' no such thing. She just got used to nice things, that's all," Joe shrugged.

"Since ya're up, ya can fix me somethin' to eat." He hand-ed Annabelle one of the two grocery bags he carried. She took it, and they crossed the porch and entered the kitchen, where Annabelle emptied her bag on the table. Daisy put the contents of both bags away, leaving the fixings for sand-wiches out.

Soon Annabelle had prepared a sandwich for Joe, and one each for Daisy and herself. Both women relished the taste of the store-bought bread and lunchmeat. The prepared food was a rare treat for them

"Ya sick, Ma?"

"No. Why'd ya ask such a question?"

"Said you couldn't sleep, and Daisy here's still dressed," Joe looked at Daisy with a scowl on his face. "Kinda on the sleazy side, if you ask me."

"I haven't gone to bed yet," Daisy said, leaving out the fact that she had not gone to bed because she'd been work-ing in a bar filled with men. "It ain't none of your business how I dress," she snapped.

"Ah, but it is, and I find the both of you stayin' up this late hard to understand," Joe said suspiciously. "I can't ever re-member either of you stayin' up past dark, an' it was dark hours ago."

"Can't sleep when ya're worryin'," Annabelle said, deter-mined to steer the conversation in another direction before Joe noticed that Daisy smelled of cigarette smoke and beer.

He'd add that to what he called her sleazy appearance and figure out she'd been at the bar for sure. "We was only worried 'bout Patty, she—"

"Yeah, you said she was visitin'. But I'm surprised about her comin' back here for any reason, though, since she's livin' in style with Tuesday and Cliff in Wheelin' these days."

"It was a coupla days ago, she'd come to see us," Annabelle said. "I thought ya'd knowed. Ya live in th' same city."

"Ma, Wheelin's a big place. I never see her. You know I live in Pa's house. Tuesday and Cliff don't want anythin' to do with the two of us.

Anyway, why'd she come to see you?"

"She's wantin' to learn 'bout her family," Annabelle said.

"We're her family," Joe replied, "even if she's thinkin' she's too good for us now that she's livin' with Tuesday and Cliff."

"It's not us she's lookin' for. She's wantin' to learn 'bout her birth mother's folks."

Having been roused from a sound sleep, Sara appeared in the doorway that separated her and the children's room from the kitchen. She leaned unnoticed on the doorjamb, the limp curtain absently draped across her shoulder, listening for a short time before resentment and jealousy compelled her to speak.

"Joe, maybe ya have Patty hid somewhere for ya self. I knowed ya always wanted to keep her an' me on th' mountain to keep house an' have your babies for ya."

"Shut up, Sara," Joe said, giving Sara a dark look. "I'm tired of your troublesome ways. Get back to bed. You don't know what you're talkin' about. I've no such notions about what you're sayin'. That was a boy's dreams. Now I'm a man too smart to end up in jail like our pa did. He's just plain lucky to be out of jail from what I've learned about the law. I like the city and the city women. Anyway, livin' on the mountain's too hard. Why'd you think I only come 'round when I have to?"

"Joe, Sara, quit your bickerin'. Patty's surely in trouble. Ya've got to see if ya can find her," Annabelle pleaded.

"Are you crazy? It's the middle of the night. I'll see about her in the mornin'. Now I'm bone tired." Joe pushed his plate back and stood.

"By the way," Joe said as an afterthought, "I don't knowed if you heard on the radio I bought for ya all, but this mornin', the World Trade Center buildings in New York City and the Pentagon in Washington, D.C. was destroyed by terrorists. And because of that the country's at war."

"Yeah, we heard 'bout it on th' radio, but I don't exactly knowed what th' Pentagon's all 'bout. I can't even imagine th' New York City's buildin's that're over one hundred stories tall," Annabelle said.

"But we seen big buildings when Cliff Moran used th' law to take us to Wheelin' for questioning," Daisy said. "I'm goin' to live there one day, an' talk like you're learnin' to. Ya just watch and see."

Joe ignored her wish to live in the city, but he was happy that she had noticed his improved speech. "The buildings you saw ain't nothing' compared to the ones in New York."

"How's that?" Daisy asked.

"They're like miniatures of them," Joe said. "The buildings that was bombed in New York City make the ones in Wheeling look like toy buildings. Those buildings in Wheeling was around twenty stories tall. Even after seein' them, you can't imagine a building bein' over a hundred stories tall?"

"No, I just can't imagine that!" Annabelle exclaimed. "I was overcome with plain old admiration at th' ones that was twenty stories tall. They looked like they was goin' to touch th' sky. Well, I still don't believe I wasn't dreamin' 'stead of really seein' 'em."

"I'll have to admit it," Joe said. " I couldn't imagine them either, if I hadn't seen them on the TV, an' I've been livin' in Wheeling next to the ones that're twenty stories or so for a coupla years now. But if you had seen the attack on a TV screen, you'd have been terrified out of your minds."

"What scared me most just hearin' 'bout it," Daisy said, looking frightened, "was th' thousands of people that died in th' buildin's an' those in th' air planes too."

"I just can't think on it," Annabelle said, shaking her head. At the same time, her fingers were busy attempting to tuck a few flyaway strands of hair back into the knot she always wore atop her head. "Why'd someone want to kill that many people?"

"They're terrorists," Joe said. "They don't like the way we live in the United States of America." At the puzzled look from Daisy, he added. "Mostly it's the city people they don't like. Most people in our country don't live like we've lived here all our lives. They have more than enough food, and homes you wouldn't believe, and from what I see they don't appreciate it. You wouldn't believe the waste. They don't know or care that there's people that don't have nothin'."

"From what I heard," Annabelle added, "th' killers killed their selves too. They knowed they was goin' to die with all th' others."

"They hate us that much!" Joe added.

"Yeah, there was only a hand full of 'em dyin' for their cause. Look at how many they killed, although we can thank God that thousands got out." Daisy choked up, hardly able to think about the grief the families and friends of all those wounded and dead were going through.

"It's scary," Sara said. "If Cliff hadn't made us go to th' city when Pa was in trouble, I don't think I'd've been able to come close to imaginin' buildin's that're standin' that tall. The biggest buildin' here is the theater, with two stories. We wouldn't've been able to understand 'bout th' TV's ya're talkin' 'bout either."

"Yeah," Daisy said, "but they have one—" she stopped abruptly, turning red. She was going to say that there was one at the bar—a big mistake since none of McCallister's women had ever been permitted to go inside it, let alone work there.

"Ya was talkin 'bout war. "Annabelle said, changing the subject, knowing Daisy had almost gotten all of them in trouble. "Are we in danger?"

"Sure," Joe said, basking in the role of someone in the know. "That's what war is, a killing time, a very dangerous time! Accordin' to the news reports, there'll be other attacks. Don't'cha listen to th' radio that I brought ya?"

"We tol' ya we did," Daisy said. "That's how we knowed.

"Annabelle spends all her time listenin' to th' news. That's when she can get th' radio away from Sara, listenin' to her loud music."

"So what?" Sara jumped in. "I like th' music. We need somethin' fun to do 'round here."

"Shut up, Sara," Joe said. Noting her hurt look at his thoughtless remark, he softened a bit.

"Hey, Sara, I'll take ya shoppin' at Centerpoint before I leave this time."

"No kiddin'?"

"Believe me, I heard th' news," Annabelle said, ignoring Sara. "I heard all of it, an' th' fright an' sorrow of it all almost caused me to have heart failure."

"I'm turnin' in now," Joe said, "and Daisy, we'll talk in the mornin' about your dress, and you can explain why you smell of beer and cigarette smoke."

"Don't ya want to knowed who Patty found out her grandmother is?" Daisy said, trying to divert Joe's attention to a different topic.

Annabelle was relieved that Daisy had thought of something to sidetrack Joe. She knew full well that had it been Jeb coming home this night, he would not have let Daisy's appearance go uninvestigated. Not for a minute.

And if he ever discovered that Daisy had been working in the bar, with Annabelle and Sara's knowledge, there was no doubt that each of them would feel the full force of his wrath.

"Who?" Joe was intrigued.

"Myrtle Landacre. Ya knowed, th' ol' witch that lives at th' edge of th' forest."

"No way! You're kidding me," Joe said, forgetting about Daisy.

"Nope," Sara said gleefully. "Aunt Aggie said it was true, too."

"I just don't believe it," Joe said.

"Well, ya ain't goin' to like who her great uncles is then," Sara continued.

"Tell me!"

"It's Ozzie Moats an' Aubrey Moats," Annabelle said.

Joe started laughing. "The old sheriff's goin' to be fit to be tied."

"Well, if Patty ain't told him—an' she ain't that I knowed of," Annabelle interrupted, "he don't knowed she knows, an' I want it to stay that way."

"Why's that, Ma?"

"Just don't want no trouble started," Annabelle said. "I think we've had enough trouble to last a lifetime."

12

Morning of September 12, 2001

Cliff was in his office, swamped with the many problems connected with the terrorist act that had blindsided the nation and the world, when he got the first report from the private detective he'd hired to tail McCallister.

"What'd you learn?" Cliff held the phone to his ear with his shoulder, making a final note on his pad.

"Sorry, but it sure looks like Jacob McCallister was in the 9/11 disaster yesterday morning," Jeremy Clarke responded.

"What!" Cliff lost all interest in what he had been doing.

"That's right. I'm sorry, but he was there."

"Sorry! That'd be the best news I've heard in a long time. But why are you so sure?" Cliff stood and turned toward the window behind his desk, nearly dragging his phone to the floor. He turned back and caught it just in time. "Convince me."

"Well, there are no remains," Jeremy said, "if that's what you're wanting. But according to his secretary, he had a meeting scheduled in New York the morning of the eleventh and boarded the plane as planned. His desk calendar showed he had an appointment at the World Trade Center with a potential client at nine that morning. All of the facts place him at the building during the attack."

"Man, this changes everything," Cliff said.

"What?"

"It's a long story.

"When was the last time the secretary saw or spoke to him?" Cliff asked.

"The ninth, the day before he left for New York," Jeremy said. "I followed him to the airport on the tenth. So I know that he went from home to the airport without taking time to stop by the office. And he hadn't planned to, anyway, according to his secretary."

"So you're sure he boarded the plane?" Cliff asked.

"I followed him to the airport, to the ramp leading into the plane."

"Are you certain he stayed on it as it left the ground?"

"Absolutely," Jeremy answered. "And I can't think of a reason for anyone to buy a ticket and get on a plane, only to get off again. What'd be the point? Anyway, I stayed until the plane taxied to the runway and took off."

"Too bad I didn't have you follow him." Cliff leaned forward, ready to make notes. "You'd have known that he'd actually entered the World Trade Center building and could verify that he was still in it when it came down. Man, if I had foresight, you'd have been right there and we'd know for sure if he was inside or not."

"Whoa, back up," Clarke said. "I'd be dead now, and you'd have nothing."

"Sorry," Cliff laughed. "You're right, you'd have been in the World Trade Center along with everyone else. I guess you can thank me for having a cheap budget and not realizing how imperative it was to know McCallister's whereabouts at all times."

"You can say that again," Jeremy said. "Thanks!"

"What else have you got?"

"Because of the airlines being shut down, if he, by some miracle, wasn't killed in the attack, he'd have to return by another means," Jeremy said. "We know that he hasn't returned to Wheeling by air. Anyway, I've no doubt he was in that building."

"Good riddance," Cliff said.

"I beg your pardon? That's the second time you've shown you're happy about the prospect of McCallister's death. A bit unusual, I'd say."

"I know it sounds callous, but the man has been a threat to my family for several years. And I can't help but be relieved that he's gone."

"Humph, it's like that then."

"You've got that right."

"Well, it's official, so you can believe it. Everything he did for days leads directly to his being in that building during the attack."

"Set my mind at rest. I want you to turn every stone. Keep checking. Talk to everyone who knew him or did business with him. Double check with those you've already talked to. Call me as soon as you've done everything that can be done."

At a knock at the door, Cliff said a quick good-bye and put the handset in the cradle.

Jim Jones, otherwise referred to as J. J., walked into the room and crossed to Cliff's desk. "You wanted to see me?"

"Sure do," Cliff said. "I've got a situation, and I need you to take over my cases. Here are the files. Ed Tallman will fill you in. You can meet with him in the morning."

J. J. took the files and scanned each one carefully. He had worked with Cliff and was familiar with his reputation, and he was honored that he was chosen to take over Cliff's case-load.

After J. J. left, Cliff decided to visit McCallister's office in person and question his secretary himself.

Arriving at the reception area where McCallister's secretary was stationed, Cliff found her busy at her desk, looking far more like a fashion model than a receptionist. He was not the least bit surprised at McCallister's choice of a secretary.

Cliff crossed to her desk.

She had looked up as Cliff first strode into the room. "May I help you?" she asked.

"I certainly hope so." Cliff gave her his most charming smile. He had a way with women and used his magnetism when he needed to.

"I'm here to verify Jacob McCallister's death."

"I don't know what you're getting at. Everyone knows that he died in the World Trade Center attack, and we here have suffered a great loss. I can't imagine your rude intrusion into our grief."

"I'm sorry, Miss—" Cliff waited for her to introduce herself.

"Brandi, Brandi Rose," the unusually attractive woman disclosed.

"I'm sorry to upset you, believe me, but I have a job to do.

"Without a body—or any tangible evidence for that matter—how can you be sure that he perished in the building?"

"Well!" she said, turning to face Cliff fully. "If he were alive, he'd be here, wouldn't he?"

"Maybe. Maybe not."

"Sir, he had an important appointment scheduled that very morning in the World Trade Center, with very influential clients. It was crucial to our firm, as getting these particular clients would mean a great deal of additional income flowing into the company. I can assure you that nothing could have stopped him from keeping that engagement— that is, short of getting killed." She sobbed as the reality of the state of affairs settled in on her.

"That's a good point," Cliff said.

"I'm sorry, but I do realize that you need to be sure."

"I do."

She shrugged soundlessly.

"He has family, you know," he said.

She looked surprised that the detective standing in front of her seemed to know anything at all about Jacob's family. She did not comment, though. Her boss always made a point in keeping his personal life close to his vest, and she was not about to divulge any information, man of law or not. "I told you, if he was not in that building, he'd be here taking care of business, which there is plenty of."

"You're right. I didn't mean to come down so hard on you," he said, regarding her with an apologetic grin.

At last, she returned his irresistible smile, her eyes brightly shining through her tears. "It's so sad to think of him losing his life like that. He's so young, and he has everything: looks, charm, money, a good life."

"Do you know anything about his past?" Cliff asked.

"Not really, but I don't see what his past has to do with the 9/11 tragedy. Jacob is one of the nicest men that I've ever met. He was a great boss and friend."

"McCallister has family, and his children and an aunt are his closest relatives,' Cliff said.

"I thought the wife was a man's closest relative," Brandi Rose said sharply.

Cliff raised his eyebrows. "I know of no wife. His aunt raised him. And the reason I was so hard on you was that I wanted to be sure McCallister actually was killed before we inform her. No need to upset her unnecessarily if, for some unknown reason, he didn't show up for the appointment or got out of the building somehow. He may be lying in a hospital unidentified and injured, unable to return to Wheeling at this time."

"I never thought of that," Brandi Rose gasped, "and I've been so upset that I forgot to mention to the FBI when they were here that he had a rental car, but knowing where it is now may help."

Cliff removed his note pad from his breast pocket and made an entry in it, looking up to ask, "Did you make the reservations for the airline ticket and the car for him?" He took a softer tone.

"Yes, I did."

"Do you have a copy of his itinerary?"

"Yes. It should be in his desk. Shall I look for it for you?"

"Yes, please."

She stood and crossed the room to McCallister's door.

Cliff followed, stepping in front of Brandi to open the door. "Why didn't you give the papers to the FBI?"

"They didn't ask for them," she shrugged.

"May I look around his office?"

Holding the office door open, the girl looked up at him with great tears threatening to spill from her huge brown eyes. "Please do. You could stay here all day if you think it would help, but I know in my heart he's gone."

"I don't want to hurt anyone. I just want to verify his death so his family can collect on his death benefits. Believe me, they need it."

Brandi Rose released her tense grip on the doorknob and glided into McCallister's office. She opened a desk drawer and quickly found McCallister's schedule. "I think this is what you're looking for."

Cliff accepted the papers, noting that the office was overly plush for an accounting firm started by an ex-con and in existence for only two years. He turned to the woman and dismissed her with a thank you.

With the itinerary tucked safely in his pocket, Cliff sat at McCallister's desk and surveyed the expansive top before he touched anything. Quickly noticing a photo of Tuesday displayed on the left corner of the huge desk, he felt a sick knot form in the pit of his stomach. McCallister had indeed not abandoned his goal of getting Tuesday and the girls back. Also, Cliff realized that anyone who didn't know better would, in all probability, automatically assume that a picture of a woman placed on a man's desk was that of his wife or girlfriend.

Next to the photo was McCallister's phone, and next to that was his appointment pad. It was open to September 11th. The entry for the 9:00 a.m. space read: World Trade Center/ South Tower/103rd floor/new client interview.

Next, he leafed through the previous days, weeks, and months. Cliff removed the pages from the pad and put them in his pocket. He snooped through the papers sprawled across the huge oak desk but found nothing incriminating.

Back in the reception area, Cliff thanked the secretary. "I'm very sorry for your loss. It's a hard time for the entire world."

Brandi Rose looked at Cliff with tear-filled eyes. "I feel sorry for the aunt you mentioned. Jacob spoke of her on several occasions. I got the impression that he thought a great deal of her." Brandi blinked, causing a tear to fall down her cheek, leaving a path in her carefully applied makeup. "His wife, I feel most sorry for her."

"His wife?" Cliff asked. "You mean the woman in the picture on his desk?"

"Yes, isn't she lovely?" Brandi Rose looked a bit jealous. "Jacob has, I mean had," she corrected herself, "a wife and two daughters. He never talked about them much, but he had definitely planned to reunite with them."

The sick feeling in the pit of Cliff's stomach worsened at hearing firsthand McCallister's determination to get to Tuesday and the girls once again.

"Is something wrong?" Brandi Rose asked.

"No." An accomplished professional at all times, Cliff regained his composure. "I'm fine, just surprised. I didn't know that he had a wife," he said, having decided against telling Brandi that the woman in the photo was not her boss's wife but Cliff's own.

"Oh, yes. Had it not been for her, we would have been married." She put a hand over her mouth as if she'd said too much.

"Really, you're involved with a married man then?" Cliff asked, realizing that he was being rewarded with further information because he had not set Brandi straight about Tuesday.

"Was involved." Brandi 's face had reddened from her temple to her neck. "I shouldn't have said anything. It's just the shock of losing him. But I guess now that he's dead it doesn't matter that I've revealed it to you."

"Then you must know if he had any friends."

"I know of only one," Brandi said, shrugging. "His name is Ike Harris."

Cliff wrote the information on the pad he always carried in his pocket. He had already filled a page with notes while searching McCallister's desk drawers. "I swear I've heard that name before. Where does this Ike Harris live? And how did McCallister know him?"

"I really don't know," Brandi said. "All I know is Ike has a wife who lives in his hometown of Grant Town, and that Ike, as well as being a friend, is employed by Jacob in the building project."

"You mentioned a building project before. Tell me about it."

Brandi Rose had never disclosed her boss's business, and she wasn't about to start now. "I don't know anything."

"Okay, what about his wife?" Cliff asked.

"The only conversations we had of a private nature were the few times when he talked about his aunt or his wife and daughters."

"Tell me about them."

"He said that his wife was beautiful, kind, and intelligent. He said he was building a dream house for his wife and his daughters, and he'd vowed that he'd never let them go again."

"That must be the building project, you spoke of. Did he tell you of any sons?" Cliff asked.

"No." Brandi raised her perfectly shaped eyebrows. "And I believe if he had other children he'd have told me."

"Did he tell you where he was building the house?"

"No. I told you he was a very private person," Brandi said. "He never told me much at all."

"So that would account for him not telling you about his grown son who lives with him here in Wheeling."

Brandi did not respond. She simply gazed at him with glistening, pain-filled eyes.

"Sorry if I seem cruel," Cliff said, "but I can assure you that I know Jacob McCallister much better than you do. Believe me it's imperative that you tell me everything that you know about him."

"He did tell me that Ike Harris was in charge of restoring his family's new house and that it was part of a grand old estate that he was able to get at a bargain price. That's all I know." Brandi looked pointedly at Cliff, who looked skeptical and said, "Really?"

Cliff added this startling information to his notes. The facts fit into Patty's dreams so perfectly that it was uncanny. He was anxious to discuss everything with Hal Brooks and Jeremy Clarke.

"One more thing," Cliff said, turning back toward Brandi's desk, "I need you to gather the invoices, orders, and anything connected to the building project. Anything that will help determine where that house is."

"Why on earth would that be any of your business?"

"Look, I can get a search warrant," Cliff bluffed. He held his breath. That information was crucial. There was no time to waste and maybe not enough evidence to persuade a judge to grant a warrant, but Brandi did not know that.

Cliff waited, going as he usually did on the theory that he who speaks first loses.

13

Evening of September 12, 2001

Instead of heading back to the city to enjoy his days off, Joe stayed on in his quest to find Patty. He had decided to put aside his confrontation with Daisy for later, for a time when he might want some leverage to bend her to his will. Besides, he didn't really have a taste for punishing someone who had been a second mother to him during his early years.

He was so intrigued by Annabelle's story of Patty's new-found family that he drove down the mountain to visit Myrtle Landacre. When he arrived, he pulled his truck into the weeds, getting it as far off the gravel road as he could.

With no smoke rising from the chimney and no activity around the cabin, it appeared that no one lived in the old, unpainted structure. The warm weather partly accounted for the lack of smoke, although most of the mountain cabins had chimneys that discharged smoke from woodburning stoves used for cooking no matter what the temperature.

Like Patty before him, he made his way to the front door through a tangle of brush and rubbish. He had barely knocked when the woman opened the door just wide enough to stick her head out. Up close she made a frightening picture, with her steel gray hair topping her wrinkled, weather-worn face. A few loose tendrils of her hair moved in the breeze.

"Good to see ya. I've been expectin' ya," the woman croaked, her greeting prompted by a series of unrelated dreams involving various visitors, most of whom she did not recognize as anyone she had met before.

Four years earlier, while searching the mountain for Tuesday Summers and Jacob McCallister, Cliff Moran had stopped at this very house, too. Just as Cliff had, Joe got the impression that the old woman did not know what she was talking about. He was unable to understand the old woman as Patty had, and the fact that she rambled on about her dreams only confirmed to Joe that he had been right all his life—she actually did live in her own world of fantasy and deserved to be called "the old witch who lives at the edge of the forest." She certainly wouldn't be able to give him any reliable information, he decided. But seeing as Patty had been there to talk to her, he entered the cabin as the old woman opened the door wider.

"I'm looking for my sister, Patty," Joe said, continuing to be put off guard by her strange welcoming remark. The mention of her revealing dreams didn't set very well with him, either, just as Patty's talk of dreams had unsettled him in their youth.

"Don't knowed ya, but I knowed ya're here lookin' for your sister."

"Is there anyone else living here?" Joe asked.

"I live all by myself. Don't hardly ever see no others," the old woman said, exposing the few badly snuff-stained teeth that she had left in her mouth.

"Just tell me if you've seen my sister," Joe demanded.

"What's your name?" the old woman asked, squinting at him through watery, old eyes. "How d'ya 'spect me to knowed who your sister is if'n I don't even knowed your name?"

"I'm Joe McCallister. My family lives on th' mountain above you. My sister, Patty, told our ma she was comin' to see you," Joe said. "I know she's been here by now. She's missin'."

The old woman offered him a chair at the table that held a few tin plates, an old, dog-eared Sears Roebuck catalogue, tin cups, and various unprepared foods in sacks and boxes. Having taken care of her social duties, she sat in a rocking chair that was near the old potbelly stove.

"Missin'?" Myrtle asked.

"That's what I said, and I think that you know somethin' about where she is."

"I didn't even knowed she's missin'," Myrtle said, a worried frown covering her face, deepening her wrinkles.

"There's trouble afoot," Myrtle predicted, raising her eyebrows. "Ya've been livin' in th' city," she said, changing the subject.

"How'd you know that?"

"It's your speech. Ya're startin' to lose th' mountain brogue. I knowed ya used to, when ya was a youngin, practice talkin' like your pa. Now, after ya've been livin' in th' city, ya're doin' pretty good."

"It's nice of you to notice." Joe relaxed a bit. How did she know about him? Did she know what she was talking about, or was she just rambling on as others over the years consistently believed? "How'd you know anything about how I talk, or about me livin' in the city?"

"I dreamt 'bout ya from time to time, but I never could figure out why 'cept I reckon it's 'cause I was destined to meet ya. After all ya're my granddaughter's half-brother. What's goin' on now is all tied in with th' goin'-ons over th' last six years. When that detective stopped by to talk to me an' thought that I was tiched in th' head an' ran off without payin' attention to what I was sayin', I knowed I'd be brought back into th' mix some time or another."

Joe stood up. "I think I'd better go. I have to look for Patty."

"Why, boy? Ya're afraid of me! I'm just a lonely old woman, an' ya don't have nothin' to fear from me. Please sit back down."

Joe pulled the chair he had been sitting on from the table and turned it around, sitting astride it and resting his chin on his crossed arms at the top rung of the ladderback. "Like I said, I'm lookin' for my sister. You said all this is tied in with what happened over the past years. Are you sayin' Pa has somethin' to do with us not findin' her?"

"I can't say."

"Well, was a pretty, dark-haired girl here to visit you? She would've been askin' you about her mother, Betty."

"So ya knowed ya're lookin' for my granddaughter. Yeah, she was here," the old woman said, her face brightening. "She's a pretty one, don't'cha think? She wanted to knowed 'bout my Betty. She's th' girl's mother." Myrtle looked doubtful as a new thought crossed her mind." Ar'ye my grandson?"

"My pa was the man who took Betty to wife," Joe said. "Me and Patty have the same pa, but not the same ma, although my ma raised her as if she was her own daughter."

'I knowed who her ma is," Myrtle said shortly. "My husband sold my Betty for two hundred dollars to some mountain man. He never told me where she was. It nearly broke my heart, an' for some reason I don't knowed 'bout, I never dreamed where she was. It's a bother that I don't seem to dream 'bout th' matters that I most want to knowed." She wiped a tear from her cheek and continued, sniffling, "For some reason, I don't knowed why I have 'em, and I can't control 'em"

"So, it's finally out. You're Patty's grandmother?" Joe said, squirming at the old woman's obvious distress.

"I guess I am, but ya don't need to look so shocked. I knowed what folks're thinkin'." She held her head up, gaining control of her emotions. "They're thinkin' that I'm a crazy witch."

Joe cringed with the knowledge that she was aware of what people thought of her. He had spent a great deal of his youth yelling taunts at the old woman when he passed by, traveling to and from school. He'd also given Patty a rough time when she talked about her dreams, accusing her of acting crazy, like this old woman.

"Don't worry. I knowed what th' people 'round here think of me. If th' truth be known, I knowed a lot more than most." She leaned closer to Joe and smiled. "I even knowed that ya was goin' to come an' visit me."

"How's that?" Joe looked very uncomfortable.

"Don't act dumb. Ya knowed 'bout my dreams. I just told ya I dreamt it. Ya knowed 'bout Patty's dreams too, but ya wouldn't listen to her no matter how much she was pleadin' for ya to."

"Why should I? The women folk don't talk about anythin' that's worth listenin' to. And you sound just like Patty. She's always talkin' about her dreams to anyone who'd listen. More often than not, no one would," Joe said, looking even more uncomfortable.

"Everybody thinks I'm a witch." Myrtle smiled, exposing her snuff-stained teeth. "An' so do ya."

"Not me. I don't think nothin' of the kind," Joe lied.

Myrtle raised her eyebrows. "My granddaughter don't think I'm a witch. No. She understands. She's just like me an' her mother 'fore her. After I told th' girl that her mother was my daughter, she hugged me, sayin' she was goin' to take care of me, happy to have found her family." Myrtle paused for a response. Getting none, she continued, "She come here knowin' that th' sheriff was my brother. She said that she had to talk to 'im." Myrtle looked directly into Joe's eyes and asked pointedly, "Did you knowed Ozzie was my brother?"

"No. I don't expect he'd want anyone to know," Joe answered. "I just found out when everyone got all worried when Patty went off without tellin' anyone. Anyway, Patty knows now too. Aunt Aggie told her. It seems like she knows everythin'."

"Ya think'n my granddaughter just went off without tellin' anyone?"

"Why not?"

"I knowed she wouldn't do that. That one has a pure heart. Wouldn't want to cause no worry. Anyway, young man, my granddaughter ran outta here happily lookin' to talk to her uncle," the old woman said with pride. When she smiled, her wrinkles, etched by sad memories and harsh weather, carved even deeper across her face. "Didn't get a chance to make her understand that Ozzie was not goin' to be happy to be connected to me. She was too happy to have found her family. Said she'd be back. Goin' to take me to th' city to live."

"You? In the city?" Joe smirked.

"Didn't I just tell ya? She's goin' to take me to live with her when she can get her own place an' take care of me proper," Myrtle said wistfully.

"Did she say anythin' else?"

"Nope. Just that she was happy she found me. Ah, let me tell ya, young man, I'm th' one's happy to have a part of my Betty back in such a lovely granddaughter. Since she left here, though, I sense a great dark cloud hoverin' over her, an' I'm worried. Somethin' is coming to fruition. My dreams ain't tellin' me what it's 'bout, but somethin' evil's afoot. I kin feel it in my bones."

A cold chill ran down Joe's back, and the hair stood up at the back of his neck. There was a force of energy in the room he could not begin to comprehend.

"Oh, boy, I see ya'ar frightened, an' it's as ya should be," Myrtle said, leaning forward so close to Joe's face that he drew back, unnerved, as her hot breath caressed his face. "I knowed ya gave my granddaughter a bad time 'bout her dreams when she was a mere child an' needed support from her family. I knowed what ya was interested in from both your sisters—what I didn't knowed then was that she was my granddaughter."

Joe jumped from his seat. "If you knew so much, how come you didn't go to my cabin and get your daughter in the first place and bring her back home?"

"Ain't ya listenin', boy? Just like I said before. Now! I told ya that I hadn't knowed then who my man took my daughter to or that she had a baby, a child that was my flesh an' blood. Oh, how I wish I did, an' how I wish I could've saved her from ya an' her pa."

"Dreams ain't worth much then, are they?" Joe snickered. "Anyway, that's the way I always seen it. If they were, you'd have known she was your granddaughter."

Myrtle agonized. "Don't ya go makin' light of me an' my granddaughter's dreams. They don't tell us everythin's goin' to happen, just enough to protect ourselves an' others if they listen an' heed 'em proper. It all started with my family generations ago, when my great, great, great grandmother was burned at th' stake for bein' a witch."

"This is getting weird," Joe whispered under his breath.

"Oh, ya think so, do ya?" Myrtle had heard Joe's low murmur and angrily turned to face him. "Th' ability to see th' future through my dreams came down to me from my mother an' grandmothers, an' on to my daughter an' then to my granddaughter Patty! She has a job to do. She has to make somethin' right, I suppose. If'n she don't, our trouble will pass on down th' centuries. I knowed one thing for sure, if ya want to see her again, ya'd betta find her, and find her fast."

"I have to go." Joe rose from the chair and backed toward the door. "Thanks for taking the time to see me."

In a shot he was out the door, with her last remark still ringing in his ears. Just as he settled himself inside his truck, another truck he did not recognize pulled in beside it.

Sorrowfully, Myrtle wiped a tear from her eye as Joe sped away.

14

Evening of September 14, 2001

Cliff had spent the time before dinner on a phone conversation with Jeremy Clarke, discussing the investigation into McCallister's death and his link to Ike Harris, the man that Brandi Rose said was working with McCallister on the building project. Cliff had learned that Harris had shared a cell with McCallister during his stint in prison.

"Before 9/11," Jeremy said, "I hired two men alternating with me to keep McCallister under constant surveillance, like you wanted. I've sent you some background information on them. They're brothers, Logan and Remington Michael, and they're the best in the business. Now I have them digging in to positively confirm McCallister's death. We're trying to locate Ike Harris and the building project as well."

Ike Harris's working with McCallister worried Cliff, especially since the project matched Patty's dreams so well. He would not tell Tuesday about it until it was unavoidable.

Later, Cliff and Tuesday sat with dinner plates in front of them, his empty and hers untouched. Mary Lou and Winter Ann sat in their places at the table, looking at their worried parents. The conversation was somber, and just to escape their worry about Patty for a bit, they talked about the terrorist attack and how it might affect them personally.

The family was dismayed and saddened by the overwhelming news reports on every TV station. It had been that way since the morning of the attack three days before, and the President's pronouncement that the United States was declaring war on the terrorists weighed heavy on their hearts.

"Know what?" Winter Ann asked.

"No. What?" Tuesday gave her a weak smile, attempting to hide her fear from her daughter.

"We can go find Patty. I'll go too!"

"That's very sweet of you, but Paul Frank is looking for her."

"I can help." Winter Ann laid her hand on Tuesday's cheek.

"He'll find her."

Poor child, Tuesday thought. *I've been so worried about Patty and the war that I haven't seen how worried Winter Ann is about her big sister.*

"If I thought you and the girls would be safe here," Cliff said, "I'd go to help Paul Frank. I just don't know what's best at this point. There could be more attacks, and we could all get separated."

"How can we know what's the right thing to do?" Tuesday worried. "This is all so foreign to us."

"One thing for sure, if another attack happened, and we were separated, it would create an even worse situation."

"I can't even bear to think of that," Tuesday said.

"Now that McCallister's rental car has been identified under the bombed out buildings and he's counted among the dead in the World Trade Center attack, we don't have to worry about him bothering our family," Cliff said. "But on the other hand, there's no telling what could happen to Patty on that mountain."

"I thought you were still investigating Jacob's death, you know, making sure!" Mary Lou exclaimed.

"Oh, we're sure. I just don't want to take any chances, that's all."

"I can hardly believe that we're finally free of living in Jacob's shadow. It hung like a dark cloud over our lives every single day. But you're right about Patty not being safe on the mountain, regardless. We know how women are treated there. And, although the militia's been disbanded, we have no idea whether those militiamen who avoided arrest or simply slipped through the cracks are continuing their misguided, illogical cause."

"What do you suggest we do?" Cliff asked.

"Winter Ann, go upstairs and watch TV for a while. Mary Lou, go with her and find a program for her to watch, okay?"

"I want to go with Daddy and help him find Patty. I want her to come home!" Winter Ann cried, her eyes huge with alarm.

"No one's going anywhere. Now go," Tuesday said more sharply than she intended.

She'd always put the child's needs first, but in her own overwhelming fear, she lost sight that Winter Ann needed to be shielded from the threat of more violence.

Winter Ann slid off her chair, looking first to Tuesday and then to Cliff for solace. Finding no compassion in her parents' faces and holding back her tears, she ran for the stairs. With each step, her dark curls bounced around her cherub face.

With nothing left to say, Mary Lou followed behind.

As soon as Mary Lou and Winter Ann were out of earshot, Tuesday pleaded, "Cliff, please wait until we hear from Paul Frank before you go to the mountain."

"You're right," Cliff said. "Paul Frank's more than capable, and he knows the mountain better than I do."

"If it weren't for Jacob's death, I'd be sure that he was responsible for Patty's not contacting us. But if it's not him, then who is it?"

"I have this persistent, nagging thought in the back of my mind," Cliff said. "It's bugging the hell outta me."

"To do with Jacob?"

"Yes. It's something his secretary said, and I can't put my finger on it."

"Think! It may be important!" Tuesday pleaded.

"I'm going to call Jeremy Clarke and see if he's found anything. I'll look through my notes after we clean up from dinner. And I'd like to see the notes you have on Patty's dreams."

"Sure. It's Mary Lou's turn to clean up, so we can get started after I check on the girls. Winter Ann looked pretty scared when we sent her upstairs." Tuesday took a quick, nervous sip of her iced tea as she remembered Winter Ann's fear. "You can go ahead and get your notes together, and mine are in that drawer under the microwave. I'll be upstairs with Winter Ann. She's hearing too much of what is happening and needs to be reassured. I'm afraid that I've been so wrapped up in my own worry that I've neglected her." Tuesday broke down and began shaking and sobbing; the combination of grave family problems and a world crisis was simply too much.

Cliff rose from his chair, and pulling her to her feet, took Tuesday in his arms. "I'll find Patty if it's the last thing I do," he swore.

To her absolute horror, Tuesday felt another surge of fear from Patty, and her legs gave way. Cliff was caught off guard as together they crumpled to their knees. Still holding each other, they sat on the floor, arms entwined.

Or was it Patty? Tuesday thought, and fainted.

15

As Joe was leaving Myrtle's cabin, Paul Frank drove up. He was heading toward Aggie's cabin this time, cautiously driving on the high ridges that had been created over time by tires spinning in mud and snow, digging out deep ruts.

Spotting Joe as he crossed Myrtle's littered front yard to reach his truck, Paul Frank pulled in and called out to him. "You're looking for Patty?" he asked.

"I am."

"Me too, but I'm not having any luck. I've already been to see your mother and the others. I'm on my way to Aggie's now."

"Well, Patty's been here." Uncharacteristically, Joe cooperated by answering Paul Frank's questions for the sake of finding Patty. "But Myrtle said she was goin' to see the sheriff after she left her cabin. You may not know it since you were reared at Centerpoint, but the local folks believe that Myrtle's a witch."

"Why would Patty be interested in a woman everyone thinks is a witch?" Paul Frank asked.

"Accordin' to Myrtle," Joe explained, pointing his thumb back toward the neglected cabin, "Patty just learned she's the old woman's granddaughter. And you'd think that she'd be bummed out about bein' related to a witch, but Myrtle says Patty's plannin' to take her to the city and take care of her."

"I'm not surprised. Patty desperately wants to know who her family is."

"Yeah, but regardless of what Myrtle says, Patty wouldn't want to be related to a crazy old woman," Joe said.

"Just how do you know the woman's crazy?" Paul Frank asked. "I mean, my guess is that you've never spent any real time talking to her."

"I know it because everyone else does," Joe said. "You could walk through town askin' anyone you'd pass, and they'd tell you the old woman is nuttier than a fruitcake."

"I bet no one has really bothered to get to know her. I mean, to me it sounds like just so much small town gossip," Paul Frank said.

"She's a witch," Joe said, jabbing his finger at Paul Frank, "and Patty should've never come here lookin' for her."

"Get out of my face," Paul Frank said and involuntarily stepped back, livid at Joe's offensive behavior.

"Did Myrtle say anything else?"

"Said Patty was goin' to visit Sheriff Moats."

Paul Frank turned to leave.

"You look here," Joe called out. "I'm warnin' you, stay away from Patty. I don't want you around her."

Paul Frank continued walking toward his truck. Finally, he turned and said, "Joe, get with the times. Women haven't been treated as property for years, and you'd better watch your step along that line. You're flirting with the shady side of the law if you obstruct Patty's movements to suit yourself. She doesn't want or need you to run her life. You've been away from the mountain long enough to see that it doesn't work that way in the real world. I mean, I really wouldn't want to see you end up behind bars like your father."

Joe picked up a rock and threw it as hard as he could. And it would have been a surprise to anyone who knew Joe had they been watching, since his aim was normally excellent, that the rock whizzed past Paul Frank's ear and landed well beyond him. It also would have been a surprise that Joe gave up after one rock.

Paul Frank had stood his ground, refusing to duck, and looked Joe in the eye. It was obvious that Joe had missed on purpose; his intent was to provoke Paul Frank. Joe was smart enough not to attack a lawman, even if he wasn't in uniform.

Joe dropped his gaze first, and turning his back, lurched toward his truck.

Soon after watching Joe scramble into his truck, Paul Frank, putting off his visit to Aggie, climbed in his own and headed off the mountain toward the sheriff's office.

"Can I help you?" Jess Willis asked, hiking up his pants and setting the broom behind the file cabinet.

"I'm looking for Sheriff Moats," Paul Frank said.

"I'm deputy Jess Willis," the tall, lanky deputy replied self-importantly. He reached out and shook Paul Frank's hand. Then squaring his shoulders and keeping one hand on his holster, he tipped his regulation deputy's hat. "The sheriff's out on business at the moment. Maybe I could help you?"

Paul Frank replied, "I'm here unofficially, at the moment, but I'm a State Police Officer from Wheeling."

"I remember you." Jess grinned, relaxing his pose of importance. "You're from Centerpoint. The detective from Wheelin' took you in and saved you from livin' a miserable mountain life."

"Funny, I didn't realize you were a comedian. I remember you, too. We met back then. This time, I'm here looking for Patty Moran. You know, I mean Patty McCallister." Paul Frank explained, as it was unlikely that Willis knew that Cliff and Tuesday had officially adopted her. "I was told that she came here to talk to the sheriff."

"Thought you might be here about the terrorist act."

"What would this time-forgotten-mountain town have to do with the World Trade Center attack?"

Jess shrugged his shoulders. "Can't think of any other reason for you being here. And I have to say, I don't care much about your puttin' down my town."

"Man, I'm sorry. I mean, didn't have any intention of belittling your town."

"No offense taken," Jess said graciously, hiking up his pants with his thumbs again.

"I'm here because I'm anxious to find Patty and get back to the city," Paul Frank said. "I mean, you can't be sure what's going to happen now that the whole world's on alert. I don't like being separated from my friends or my job at a time like this. Anyway, do you know anything about Patty's whereabouts? Was she here?"

"Not that I know of, but she could've come by when I was out," Jess said. "Do you know when she came to see the sheriff?"

"It could've been the seventh or maybe the eighth," Paul Frank said.

Jess moved to the sheriff's desk and scanned the daily logbook. "The sheriff was here all day both days, and I was in and out. We do log all complaints and calls. She's not listed. I'd remember if she'd been here. I know who she is and I recall that she'd ran away to the city around the time her father, Jacob McCallister, was on the run for kidnappin' and child endangerment charges.

"I wouldn't be surprised if she had been here," Jess continued, "and because she's a mere mountain girl to the sheriff, he didn't bother to log the visit."

"Sounds like Moats. He sure is a piece of work," Paul Frank said.

"You probably don't know the half of it," Jess offered.

"Can I count on you to keep an eye out for Patty?" Paul Frank asked. "I mean, it's not like her to stay out of touch with her family."

"No problem, that's what we're here for," Jess said, sincerely. He was dedicated to helping all the people in the county, including those on the mountain. Not so with the sheriff, who catered exclusively to the townspeople, seeking their support. They were inclined to forget the mountain folk existed, and Ozzie Moats followed suit. After all, most of the mountain people could not read or write and generally did not vote.

Paul Frank shook the deputy's hand once again and, leaving his card with him, strode back out onto the street to question the pedestrians.

Later, still having learned nothing about Patty or her whereabouts, Paul Frank headed toward McCallister's cabin. As he was passing Myrtle's cabin, he impulsively decided to stop there. He swung into the brushy area that made up Myrtle's yard.

Before Paul Frank could reach the door and knock, the old woman opened the door and invited him inside. "I've never had so much company," she said with a rare grin on her face.

"I understand that one of your visitors was Patty McCallister. Is that right?"

"It sure is!" The old woman grinned again. "She's my granddaughter, ya knowed."

"Joe told me," Paul Frank said. "He was here earlier."

"Ya, he was. He's a bad one, an' don't have no good intentions when it comes to his sister Sara an' my Patty."

"I know," Paul Frank said.

"I had a dream last night," Myrtle said with tears shining in her eyes. "I don't knowed what it means, but Patty was confined in a small room. She was lyin' in a corner terrified in th' dark. I knowed she's not had enough food or water for some time now. I'm pretty sure she's alive, but I do knowed there's death in th' room."

"Have you seen anyone else in your dreams?"

"There's a man hoverin' 'bout'."

"Can you describe him?"

"No. There's only an impression of 'im. I've often wished I could control what I dreamed 'bout when I'm needin' to knowed somethin', but that's not th' way of th' mind."

In his eagerness to get on with his search, Paul Frank stood. "Thank you for talking to me. I'll keep in touch. I know you're worried, and you'll want to know when I find her."

"Thank ya, son. Ya're a good, kind man. Mind ya be careful, though. I can feel you're in grave danger now."

Paul Frank sat in his truck and dialed Cliff's number from his solar phone. "I've just spoken to Myrtle Landacre. As it turns out, she's Patty's maternal grandmother."

"Is that good? I've no idea who she is."

"Probably not," Paul Frank said. "She's a sad old woman with no one to care for her, and you know Patty, she'll do it herself or else."

"She'll manage her grandmother *and* college," Cliff said. "You know how hard she works and how much family means to her."

"You're right, I mean, I'm sure she's thrilled she found her so soon. She talked to her the second day she was here. But that's all there is to report," Paul Frank said. "Patty's still missing."

"Was her grandmother any help about what happened to her?"

"No."

"Where does she live?"

"Just below McCallister's cabin. The mountain folks and the townspeople all think she's a witch."

"You know," Cliff said, "I remember now. I met her when I first traveled the mountain. I must say, I can see how a rumor like that could get started. I couldn't make any sense out of her chatter. I guess, unlike you, I wasn't asking the right questions."

"Myrtle did tell me she and Patty had their dreams in common."

"Has she had dreams concerning Patty?"

"Yes. She said Patty's in a small dark room with no food or water." So as not to alarm Cliff, Paul Frank left out the part where Myrtle said she sensed death in the room. "Also, she said there's a man hovering about keeping her there."

"Paul Frank, that describes two of her dreams. Let me read mine and Tuesday's notes for you and maybe you can come up with a clue as to where she is and who has her. Hold on."

When Cliff and Paul Frank were finished with their review, Paul Frank started his truck and began driving slowly up the mountain only more convinced that time was growing short.

Hearing the sound of an engine and thinking Joe had returned, Annabelle ran out the backdoor to wait on the porch, with Sara following close behind. It was not Joe's truck driving up the lane, though. It was Paul Frank Ruble.

"Hi, Sara, Annabelle," Paul Frank greeted them.

"What ya doin' back here so soon?" Sara asked.

"I'm still looking for Patty. Tell me that you've heard from her."

"There's nothing," Sara said. "Only thing I can say is, she was here one day and gone the next."

"She's been missing for six days now," Paul Frank said, more worried than ever after his last conversation with Myrtle. "Is anyone other than me out looking for her?"

"Joe is," she said, "but he thinks she's on her way back to Wheelin'. Ma thinks she'd come an' say good-bye first, though. An' so do I!"

They led Paul Frank into the kitchen where the children were playing underfoot, ignored by their mother, Daisy, who went about her daily chores. He was pretty much a stranger to the women and children, although he and Sara had met now and then as she and Joe often shopped in The General Store in Centerpoint.

"Can hardly believe ya're a lawman now," Sara said.

"You know I'm not here on official business."

"I don't knowed what official business is," Sara said and looked at her mother for explanation.

Annabelle shrugged and said, "Sounds like trouble to me. When lawmen come on th' mountain it always means trouble."

"I talked to Jess Willis about Patty's disappearance," Paul Frank said. "He had no idea."

"Have ya checked th' boardin' house?" Sara asked.

"Yes, I did. I mean, I'm staying there so I checked first thing. She rented a room and hasn't checked out."

"Th' sheriff ain't goin' to do anythin'. Women ain't important to him, and he'd be glad if he never saw any of th' mountain folk walkin' 'round his town."

"I was hoping she'd be back here by now. At first I believed she was just too busy visiting and looking for her family to call home, but now I know that something is terribly wrong. It's time for Cliff to get some men up here."

"Oh, dear," Annabelle wailed. "I've been hopin' ya wouldn't call Cliff. I don't think I can deal with th' law crawlin' around th' mountain an' makin' our lives turn upside down all over again."

"Surely, you want Patty found," Paul Frank exclaimed. "She could be in trouble!"

"Oh, yeah, I'm worried 'bout her an' want her found," Annabelle said. "I just feel uneasy when th' law comes nosin' 'round. Seems to me they cause more trouble than they fix."

"You just don't like it that they found out about Jacob McCallister's black marketing scheme and put a stop to what he was doing. I'm sorry that you lost a husband and caretaker, but he had to be stopped," Paul Frank said.

It was obvious that Annabelle had no idea how many lives Jacob McCallister had destroyed. 'I just don't want no more trouble."

"We must find Patty. Her life may be in danger. So tell me what you can. Is there anyone on the mountain who would do her harm?"

"No, not that I knowed of," Annabelle cried.

"Any old boyfriends?"

"She never had a boyfriend. Her an' Sara were thick as thieves with Joe."

"Patty's a real pretty girl. Were there any boys after her attention? Maybe one she turned away?"

"There was one," Sara said, joining the conversation. "Tommy Lee Hillberry. Joe was always chasin' him off."

"So I'd be correct in saying that Tommy Lee didn't care for Joe."

"Ya would," Sara said.

Annabelle looked from Sara to Paul Frank with a sinking heart. She knew that Tommy Lee was rumored to have terrorized young girls and even raped a few.

Daisy had been in the bedroom getting dressed for work. Now she appeared in the kitchen. "I heard ya all talkin', an' I'm goin' to tell ya somethin'. There's been talk at th' bar that Tommy Lee has been accused of raping two girls from town." She revealed what Annabelle was keeping to herself. "I seen how mean he can be. I seen him hangin' 'round town pesterin' th' girls that're walkin' up or down th' streets."

"Where does he live?" Paul Frank asked in alarm. "There was a man and boy at the mansion in Patty's dream."

"Humph," Annabelle snorted. "Those dreams're th' cause of her troubles if ya ask me."

"We didn't ask ya," Daisy snapped.

"There's no call for ya to talk to me thataway," Annabelle fumed.

"I'm sorry, Annabelle." Daisy gave Annabelle a quick hug and turned to Paul Frank. "If ya drive me to town, I'll show ya."

"Ya don't have to be at work for a coupl'a hours," Annabelle said.

"I need to do some shoppin' at Th' General Store," Daisy said.

"Let's go," Paul Frank said.

Daisy pointed out the ramshackle cabin to Paul Frank. Sitting a hundred yards beyond the rutted-out, dirt road and secluded deep in a wide valley that dropped off sharply below the road, it was centered on an impressive acre of rare bottomland, and it was the very next cabin below McCallister's. Litter marked the warn paths—walkways trampled through the tall weeds to and from the cabin and road. Untouched, taller weeds surrounded the cabin while hundreds of wildflowers, many topped with butterflies and all swaying in the breeze, encircled the entire valley.

After depositing Daisy at the entrance of the bar and warning her that she was tempting Jacob McCallister's wrath, Paul Frank headed back to the Hillberrys' cabin.

At the entrance to the property, he turned in and drove across the overgrown track that merged with the main footpath, which eventually led to the front of the cabin. It was obvious that motor vehicles rarely traveled the distance; the Hillberrys owned none. They were too poor even to keep horses for transportation. Jumping from the truck, Paul Frank scanned the surrounding area. He saw no one. Patty's car was not in sight, nor were there any signs that she had been there.

Off to the side of the cabin was a hog pen filled with four, fat, rutting pigs. Chickens pecked at the barren, dry ground surrounding the waterlogged hog pen, where the animals were mired in squishy mud, and around the cabin, hunting the feed that had been scattered for them that morning.

Before Paul Frank could knock on the door, a skinny woman, ageless and toothless, opened it. "What ya doin' on my property?" she asked.

"I'm looking for Tommy Lee Hillberry."

"We don't cotton to strangers here'bouts. Now, go away!"

"Please, I need to find him. It's very important!"

"What ya wantin' him for? No one ever comes lookin' for him. He don't have no truck with th' likes of ya."

"Look, how can I convince you how important it is? I must talk to him. Where is he?"

"For one thin', I don't knowed where he is, an' I sure don't knowed ya. Do like I told ya, an get off'a my property." With that she slammed the door in his face.

Having no other choice, Paul Frank gave up and made his way across the footpath, through the old discarded beer cans and what appeared to be the entire collection of the Hillberrys' unwanted possessions. Obviously, the Hillberry men had a taste for beer. Paul Frank decided to check out the town bar, where he'd just left Daisy.

After pausing a moment just inside the door to let his eyes adjust to the dark, and involuntarily wrinkling his nose at the smell of stale beer and cigarettes, Paul Frank crossed the wood plank floor and sat at the bar. Daisy appeared at his side.

"Did ya find out anythin'?" she asked.

"No, and after seeing the many beer cans strewn over the yard, I thought I might have better luck looking for him here."

"Should've thought to tell ya, Tommy Lee an' old man Hillberry hang out here 'bout every day. Usually, though, they get drunk an're thrown out every time, too."

"Can you find out if they were here yet today?" Paul Frank asked.

"Sure. Be right back." Daisy crossed the room and spoke to some men who were playing poker in the far corner. She learned that Tommy Lee had left about two hours before and had been very drunk.

Returning to the bar where Paul Frank waited, Daisy said, "We just missed him. The men told me that Tommy Lee left shortly before I got here for my shift, tellin' the men that he had a date. A date! I never knowed of Tommy Lee havin' a woman."

Daisy went on, "Don't knowed of any female that even liked him. He's a mean one, an' he's always causin' trouble, just like his pa."

Paul Frank left immediately to call Cliff on his solar phone. As he sat inside his truck in front of the bar, he opened the conversation without preamble: "I'm almost positive that Tommy Lee Hillberry has Patty."

"I remember him," Cliff said. "I spoke to him when I was searching for McCallister back when all this first began. I wasn't having any success, and then I spotted Tommy Lee. For twenty bucks he told me that McCallister lived above Winding Ridge on the mountain. I also met Tommy Lee's father in Sheriff Moats' office. He constantly hounded the sheriff for allowing McCallister to continue selling his own children, insisting that Ozzie's department was failing to do its job of protecting the people in the county. I suspect his real motivation was jealousy that McCallister had huge amounts of money to flash around town and an expensive truck to take him anywhere he wanted to go."

"Did you know that Tommy Lee has always had a thing for Patty?

"No, I didn't."

"Sara told me that from the first time Tommy Lee saw Patty when they were kids, he stalked her constantly, trying to get her alone. Apparently Joe kept him away from her for the most part. Joe and his father are said to be the only two people that Tommy Lee fears."

"Joe's on the mountain?" Cliff asked.

"Sure enough."

"What's he doing there?"

"He brings the supplies for his family," Paul Frank answered. "I mean, it's obvious that's the reason McCallister allows his son to live with him in Wheeling. That way, McCallister can keep an eye out that Joe takes responsibility for the women, leaving McCallister to his own interests."

"What about Patty's car?"

"Not a sign of it," Paul Frank answered. "Of course if I spot her car, I'm hoping to find her too."

"Finding it may mean finding her, but on the other hand she may not still be in possession of it," Cliff said.

"From what I know about Tommy Lee, he may be dumb enough to leave her car out in plain sight of where he's keeping her," Paul Frank said.

"Have you been to his house?"

"Yes, and no car. His mother wouldn't cooperate either. I'm going to have to use my badge to persuade her to allow me to search the house since she refused to talk to me or let me in. If I make it official that I'm a lawman going after Patty's abductor, she'll see the light. From the looks of the Hillberrys' cabin, it could be the small dark place in Patty's dream. And, Cliff, I think it's time to call in help. The more time passes, the more sure I am that Jacob McCallister's involved in this."

"Can't be, and I've meant to tell you—he was killed in the World Trade Center tragedy. Maybe you'd better tell the women, and especially Aggie. The way I remember it, he was her life."

"Wow! You don't say? I mean, I hate to say it, but the world will be better off," Paul Frank predicted.

"I'd be happier if there was a body to spit on, but all the facts prove he was there. One break was a rental car, booked by him at the airport just after his scheduled arrival. It was found near Ground Zero, where it had been buried under tons of debris."

"I'm sure his signature on the rental forms was verified," Paul Frank said.

"Oh, yes. There's no doubt about it. They were signed by McCallister himself. He picked up that car."

"It's a relief to know that he's not responsible for her disappearance," Paul Frank said.

"I know, and now I can rest easier knowing Tuesday and Winter Ann are safe from him. Except for the threat of another terrorist act, I'd be on that mountain with you by now."

"I can see that. The entire family could be separated if something else happens. Well, as soon as I can, I'll talk to Aggie and the others and let them know. While I'm at it, Aggie may be the one to give me some idea of where Tommy Lee is holding Patty."

"Assuming that he has her," Cliff said. "Remember, don't assume too much, or you might miss something. Just because we can be sure it's not McCallister, we don't want to let our guard down."

"You're right, but it sure is a relief to know he's out of the picture.

Now, I'm going to check Tommy Lee's cabin," Paul Frank replied. "You never can tell—his mother just might go along with him holding a girl there."

"Yes, she might," Cliff said. "Aggie went along with Mc-Callister. Annabelle, Daisy, and Sara all witnessed McCallister's mistreatment to each other's children, as well as Tuesday, and never did anything to help them. Be careful that you don't tip Tommy Lee off that we're on to him," Cliff said. "If he gets suspicious, he'll move her."

"I doubt that'll happen. I mean, he's pretty drunk right now from what I hear."

"Do what you can. In a case like this, time means everything."

At the thump Patty came out of her daze, shaking her head as if to clear it. Startling her even more, the door creaked open, and a light shone in her eyes, effectively blinding her. Tommy Lee, weaving side to side, barely able to manage the door and handle the tray he carried, stepped in leaving the door ajar.

"Hi, Patty. Ya're my girl now, an' I've brought ya somethin' to eat, an' then I'll show ya some real lovin'. Wouldn't ya like that?"

Over the other foul odor that was ever-present, Patty could smell the liquor on his breath even from where she crouched against the wall like a trapped animal. Shaking with fear, she waited for her eyes to adjust to the sudden light and for her chance at freedom.

Tommy Lee, counting on her drugged state to keep her in line, squatted at her side with the tray wobbling in his hands. Suddenly, like a bolt of lightning, she sprinted for the door. Tommy Lee dropped the food and water he had brought for her, and with his own lightning speed, leapt forward, skidding on his stomach, and grabbed her ankle. She fell hard on her hip, hitting her head on the doorjam. Stunned, she crumpled to the floor.

With pain throbbing in his knees and bile filling his throat, Tommy Lee crawled out the door and kicked it shut; then he rolled against it and threw up.

When Patty's head cleared, she stood and tried to open the door. She had not heard the lock being engaged as she had when Tommy Lee had left her there the first day or on his frequent visits since. When she turned the knob, the door opened a crack proving Tommy Lee had not locked it. She pushed harder and the door would not open any further as it was stopped by something solid. She could see through the crack that it was Tommy Lee, out cold, sleeping it off.

It was obvious to Patty what had happened. With Tommy Lee's blue jeans visible through the crack in the door, she knew she had very little time left to think of a way out of her situation. The boy's intentions had been unmistakable. He had made it clear that he believed she wanted to be his girlfriend.

16

OZZIE MOATS STOOD OUTSIDE THE STREET ENTRANCE TO his office. He frowned as Paul Frank left the bar, jumping into his truck and quickly making a U-turn. The sheriff eyed Paul Frank's progress, noting that the boy stood out in his creased slacks and sports jacket, so unlike the mountain men. Put him in mind of Jacob McCallister's fancy dress and top-of-the-line truck.

"Good day, Sheriff Moats," Paul Frank called from his truck. He opened the door, stepped out onto the boardwalk, and approached the sheriff. "I'm looking for Patty McCallister. Have you seen her?"

"Nope."

"I've reason to believe that Tommy Lee Hillberry is behind her disappearance. Have you seen him?"

"Nope. And I don't appreciate a young whippersnapper pokin' his nose in my business."

"You sure don't sound like a professional man whose been elected to the job of upholding the law." Paul Frank flashed his badge. "I mean, am I talking to the sheriff of this town or not?"

Ignoring the insult, the sheriff spit between the cracks of the boardwalk. Poking his own badge with his thumb, he said, "I'd say that by this here sheriff's badge I'm wearin', you'd know full well who I am. Am I goin' to be plagued all my life with the likes of you big-feelin' city lawmen?"

"Actually, Sheriff Moats," Paul Frank gloated, "I'm an unassuming mountain boy who, by sheer luck, moved to the city."

"Yeah! So you are. Almost didn't recognize you." Ozzie looked quizzically at Paul Frank. "Seen you and heard of your dealin's with the ones from the city."

"I'm sorry. I should've introduced myself. I mean, I'm Paul Frank Ruble from Centerpoint." He held out his hand in a friendly gesture.

"Yeah, I've heard of you," the sheriff acknowledged, but he ignored the extended hand. "You was mixed up in the breakin' up of the militia some time back. You got thick as thieves with that big-feelin' Cliff Moran."

"You're right. He's a great man," Paul Frank said with a grin, making like Ozzie was complimenting Moran.

"It's not my view of 'im." Ozzie spat in irritation.

Paul Frank couldn't keep the annoyance out of his voice at Ozzie's irrational view of upholding the law. "After Moran and others broke up the militia, I left the mountain with him and have been making something of myself."

"Yeah, I can see that," Ozzie allowed. "With them fancy clothes an' your fancy way of talkin' you could fit in anywhere. Anywhere but here that is. We don't like folks puttin' on airs around here."

Having said his piece, the sheriff held his hand below his mouth next to his chin and a large blob of soggy tobacco landed wetly in the center of his palm. He lifted a copper spittoon from a wooden crate next to a rocking chair near the office entrance and, with a twist of his wrist, he guided the tobacco wad into a day's worth of brown spittle. "So what's a fancy gentleman like you doin' in a town like this?" The sheriff replaced the spittoon, enjoying the sarcasm that dripped from his voice.

"Have you seen Patty McCallister or an unfamiliar car around town?"

"Don't tell me it's another kidnappin'," Ozzie snickered, plucking his poke of tobacco from the inside pocket of his jacket. He pinched a new wad, shaped it to his satisfaction, and inserted the roll into his jaw between his teeth and cheek, forcing the right side to swell to three times its normal size.

"I sure hope not, and I wouldn't think a lawman would think it funny learning someone was in trouble in his jurisdiction. Something's not right," Paul Frank said. "I mean, she came here to learn what she could about her family, and we haven't seen her for a while."

"What're you talkin' about?"

"You know, her mother was brought to McCallister's cabin to be one of his women, and Patty's only wanting to find out who her mother's family is. All she has ever known is that her mother's name was Betty."

The annoyed look on Ozzie's face turned to one of anger. "Why would she want to go stirrin' up trouble?"

"What do you mean? She's only looking for her family."

The sheriff turned away, and Paul Frank could no longer see his expression. "Sometimes it's prudent to leave well enough alone."

"Would you mind explaining that to me, Sheriff?"

"Yeah, as a matter of fact I would." Ozzie stepped forward, expecting that his huge bulk and authority as county sheriff would intimidate the young man.

Paul Frank didn't move, forcing the sheriff to step back.

"I don't get you, Sheriff. I mean, a girl may be in trouble and all you can think of is not stirring up town gossip."

"It's not gossip, I'm worried 'bout," the sheriff spat. "It's trouble I'm interested in wardin' off."

"And what trouble might that be?" Paul Frank asked.

"Just never you mind. This conversation is closed," Ozzie said and disappeared into his office.

Just like Cliff Moran had years before, Paul Frank learned that there would be no cooperation from the local law enforcement. He got back into his truck, and as he started to pull out into the street, he saw Andy Hillberry, Tommy Lee's father, staggering up the road. Waiting for the man to come abreast of the truck, Paul Frank considered the questions he would ask

"Hello there, Mr. Hillberry. How's it going?" Paul Frank leaned from the open window on the driver's side.

"Fine. Jus', jus' fine. An' jus who'ar ya?" Hillberry slurred his speech. He had been intent upon heading home, ignoring the sheriff's office as he staggered by. Andy made it a point never to annoy the sheriff when he was drinking; he'd been locked up in the jail for twenty-four hours too many times in the past. But when he was sober, he freely ranted at the sheriff about any lawbreaker he could think of. In the past it was Jacob McCallister who had been the focus of his loud accusations.

"I'm Paul Frank Ruble, from Centerpoint."

"That 'posed ta mean somethin' ta me?" His rear end wobbling from side to side, Andy clutched the truck bed for support, looking like a man ready to be frisked.

"I guess not," Paul Frank said, opening the door and leaning out so he could see Andy's face.

"Where's your son, Tommy Lee?"

"What' ya wantin' him for?"

"I mean, I just want to talk to him."

"I don't keep track of 'im. He's a big boy. He don't need his pa to keep tabs on 'im."

"When's the last time you saw him?"

"Wait a darn minute, young man." Andy released the side of Paul Frank's truck, meaning to step closer to Paul Frank, and had to grab the truck door to steady himself. "I don't have to answer your questions. Ain't none of your business where Tommy Lee is." Andy made a small, involuntary lurch toward Paul Frank. Righting himself, he settled back into his unstable stance.

"Maybe not, but I need to talk to him."

"What 'bout?

"A girl," Paul Frank said.

Andy leered, thinking of Tommy Lee with a girl. "I knowed he found one, must've been yesterday. Least I think it was yesterday. No, 'twas th' day before."

In his excitement of telling of his son's good luck, Andy lost his grip on the truck, tottering a bit and then righting himself once again. "He was th' happiest I ever seen him, gettin' dressed in his best shirt an' jeans. Said he was keepin' her at his own place."

"His own place?" Paul Frank said carefully, knowing Andy could tire of the conversation at any time or become suspicious of the questions and stagger away.

"A boy needs his own place." Andy said, a loud wet belch coming from deep in his throat, and tottered again, catching the bed of the truck with his right hand just after he lost his grip on the door with his left.

"I can agree with that." Paul Frank played his game. "I mean, where is it, anyway?"

"Ah—if ya don't knowed, I ain't goin' to tell." Andy leaned his full weight against the truck bed for support. With a solid brace behind him, he felt steady on his feet. He pushed himself away, weaved from side to side, turned uncertainly, and lurched up the street toward the mountain and his home. Reeling from left to right, in an exaggerated penguin walk, he staggered up the street and disappeared.

In keeping to his plan of talking to Tommy Lee's mother, Paul Frank headed up the mountain toward Andy Hillberry's cabin, passing the old man making his unsteady journey home.

Tommy Lee's mother saw the truck coming from her window above the woodburning stove in the kitchen. She moved to the porch and waited for the truck to come to a stop near the back of the cabin. In the distant past, the occupants had had the money to purchase vehicles, and they had parked them there, making a hard-packed, rutted-out area.

"Hello again," Paul Frank said as he jumped from the truck and faced the old woman.

"I told ya to get off'n my property. I'd appreciate it if ya'd stay away."

"I promise that I will." Paul Frank held up his badge. "I mean, as soon as you tell me where Tommy Lee's place is."

The old woman looked surprised at Paul Frank's request, but the badge meant nothing to her. She had never been in a position where an officer had the need to flash one; she'd never even been in the presence of a law officer. "What'd ya knowed 'bout Tommy Lee's place?"

Paul Frank had thought fast, using the little knowledge he had gained from his conversation with Tommy Lee's father. "Ah, Andy just told me I might find him there."

"Then, ya're goin' to have to get Andy to tell ya th' rest of it!" Undaunted by the sight of Paul Frank's badge, the old woman disappeared inside the cabin and slammed the door, ending the conversation.

"Okay. So much for that. I mean, she sure wasn't impressed by my badge," Paul Frank said in frustration, knocking on the door once again. The woman opened it a few inches, looking angry at his continued intrusion. "Am I never goin' to get shed of ya?"

"I don't want to be rude or scare you, but I am going to take a look through your cabin." Paul Frank pushed the door open easily as the frail woman did not have the strength to oppose him.

Walking through the cabin, Paul Frank was surprised at how clean and neat it was. Otherwise, it was obvious how poor the family was. For all his trouble, he simply discovered that the woman was in the small cabin alone.

Ending his search back at the front door where he had started, Paul Frank turned and thanked the woman. "If you don't tell me where Tommy Lee's place is, I'll go knocking on every door on the mountain and in town, if that's what it takes to find someone who knows where it is! It'd go easier on him if you cooperated," Paul Frank implored.

The woman stood unmoved by his plea and made no comment.

Paul Frank gave up and left.

Priming himself for his visit to Annabelle and Aggie, Paul Frank retraced his steps across the unused driveway. He climbed into his truck and headed back to the mountain road. About halfway there, he passed Andy Hillberry sprawled in the bushes alongside the lane leading to his cabin. Apparently, when Andy was on a binge, he made his way home in stages. Walking, sleeping, walking, sleeping, walking.

September 15, 2001

Rounding the turn just before Aggie's cabin, Paul Frank saw Joe's truck parked near the front porch. "What'd you know? Joe's still on the mountain. I mean, he must've been serious about looking for Patty," Paul Frank said under his breath.

The two inside had heard the truck pulling up to the porch, and Aggie rushed to open the door to see who was coming this time. "Who's that?" Aggie said.

"It's only Paul Frank Ruble," Joe said. "I just had a run-in with him a while ago."

"What about?"

"He's out lookin' for Patty, too," Joe said.

"What in th' world would he be doin' lookin' for Patty?" Aggie asked. "From here he looks like the ones comin' from th' city, so he does."

"Yeah, it's Cliff and Tuesday that's rubbin' off on him. Anyway, the last I seen of him, he was lookin' for Patty," Joe answered.

"Sara was here tellin' me, so she was," Aggie said. "She walked up here so's I'd knowed in case Patty'd come 'round here, an' I could tell her to get on home to Annabelle so she'd not be worryin' herself sick."

Paul Frank jumped from the truck and approached the two who had moved onto the porch.

"I remember ya, so I do," Aggie recognized Paul Frank as he approached the porch. "Ya're th' one that ran off with Tuesday an' Patty, knowin' Jeb had threatened to kill me if I let them outta my sight. I don't knowed what business ya think ya have with me after th' dirty ya did me, so I don't."

"I knew he wasn't going to kill you, Aggie," Paul Frank said. "I'm the one he's planning on killing. If you remember, he said he'd get me if it took him a lifetime."

"Well, what ya wantin' nosin' 'round here?" Aggie asked.

"Aggie, Joe. I'm afraid I've got some bad news," Paul Frank said.

"I'm sure glad you're here, Joe. Your aunt's going to need your support."

Aggie grabbed her chest, going pale all of a sudden. "Please don't tell me that my Jeb's hurt," Aggie pleaded, using the pet name she had always used for Jacob, the one important person in her lonely, isolated life. "I've had all th' bad news I can take today, so I have."

"I'm sorry," Paul Frank said, "but he was in a meeting at the World Trade Center when the planes hit." Joe stood there with his mouth open, so Paul Frank put his arm around Aggie and led her inside the cabin to her favorite rocking chair. He couldn't help noticing how modern the cabin's interior was and thinking how there must not be another cabin like it anywhere on the mountain. Then he remembered that Booker had lived there with his wife and sons during the militia's unlawful assembly two years earlier. The man was rich, a former senator; it wasn't surprising.

"Can I get you something?"

"Where's his body?" Aggie asked, tears streaming down her face. She refused to sit in the chair.

"It looks like most of the bodies are never going to be recovered," Paul Frank said.

"Ya mean to tell me there's no body, an' ya're standin' there tellin' me that my Jeb's dead."

"It has been verified," Paul Frank said. "He was definitely in the building."

"Well, he wasn't there, so he wasn't. Jeb wouldn't get hisself in a pickle like that, so he wouldn't." Although Aggie stubbornly held to her conviction that her nephew was still alive, she had turned deathly white. But everyone knew he was a master at disappearing, never to be found until he was ready to surface. Why, he had proved it time and again.

Aggie's knees gave away and she began sinking to the floor. Paul Frank put his arm around her waist, pulled her arm across the back of his neck, and led her toward her bed. "You need to rest a while," he said, gently pushing her onto the bed. He lifted her legs up to rest on the comforter and fluffed the pillow for her head. Giving up her protests, she closed her eyes to be alone in her misery.

"Joe, I've done my job. I've told you," Paul Frank said. "I mean, believe me, the facts put him in that building at the time of the bombing.

"Anyway, the other reason I'm here," Paul Frank said, changing the subject, "have you any word on Patty yet?"

"No. Nothing," Joe shrugged.

"Aggie, have you seen or heard from her?"

Looking over at his great aunt curled in a fetal position on the bed, Joe jerked his head toward her and said spitefully, "Sara told her about Patty bein' missin', and she don't know anythin'."

"Will you let me know if you find her, Joe?" Paul Frank asked.

"Why should I?"

"Because there are people who are worried about her."

"Sure, I'll let you know," Joe lied. "That is, if you agree to do the same."

"I'd be happy to."

"Is there anything else?" Joe asked.

"I have one more question. Do either of you know of Tommy Lee having a place of his own?"

"No," Joe answered.

"I talked to his father. I mean, he was stoned out of his mind, but he told me Tommy Lee had a place of his own."

"What! Ya thinkin' that he has Patty?"

"It looks more and more like it. Tommy Lee's father told me that he had a new girlfriend. I'm afraid he was talking about Patty."

"Have you talked to the sheriff?" Joe asked.

"Won't do 'im no good, so it won't." Aggie advised from the bed still in curled in a ball.

"Why's that, Aggie?" Paul Frank asked.

"He's related to Patty's family, so he is," Aggie kept her back to Paul Frank. "He's ashamed of bein' related to th' old woman that lives down by th' forest 'cause everyone thinks she' s crazy."

"You're talking about Myrtle, aren't you?"

"Yeah, I am."

"Yes, I have talked to him. And you're right, he's not willing to help or even admit there's a problem," Paul Frank said.

"She's his family, so she is," Aggie said, her voice muffled in the pillow.

"I don't know why he wants everyone to think his family is the perfect all-American family," Paul Frank said. "I mean, he has a brother in jail for kidnapping and a sister that is rumored to be crazy. Makes me wonder what he thinks of himself."

"He thinks he's the all-time great sheriff," Joe said. "He struts around town with his badge flashin' on his sheriff's uniform, or sits at his desk reading girly magazines, while Jess Willis does all the work. He's thinkin' the people believe the town is quiet and peaceful because he's the sheriff. He has no idea they laugh behind his back."

"How does he get elected then?"

"'Cause no one else'll run," Joe said. "I think Jess Willis's plannin' to run next election, if Ozzie don't scare him outta it again. He's afraid he'll lose and the sheriff'll make it even harder for him to continue to act as deputy."

"All I can say is Jess Willis was one hundred percent more helpful with the arrest of the militia and their leaders than Moats was. But enough of the sheriff. I mean, are you sure that you have no idea where Tommy Lee keeps his own place?"

"He really has his own place? Do you know that that family is dirt poor? How's he goin' to pay for a place of his own?"

"I don't know, but it looks like he has," Paul Frank said. "Maybe his place is an abandoned building. His father told me that yesterday Tommy Lee was bragging about having a girlfriend that he had taken there. According to Daisy, he's never had a girlfriend."

"You can say that again," Joe said. "He's a creep, and people say he's raped a few girls."

"If that's true, I mean, why hasn't he been charged and thrown in jail?"

"The sheriff says he's investigatin' it," Joe said. "And the fathers of the girls don't want anyone to knowed because they know a girl'll never get a decent husband if everyone knows she's been with another man."

"What kind of thinking is that?

"That's just the mountain way. Anyway, there're only rumors. Nobody knows anything for sure. But as for his own place, I'm thinkin' on it, and I'm gettin' a few ideas."

"Let's hear them," Paul Frank said.

"Now's not the time for talkin', it's the time for doin'." Joe grabbed his jacket, "I'm goin' to scout around. If one of us finds her, he'll take her to my cabin where she belongs, and Annabelle can tend to her if she needs it. You don't need to worry, she's my responsibility, not yours. I've been takin' care of her and Sara most of their lives, and I'll take care of them now."

"That's bull, and you know it. Patty and Sara spent most of their lives starving and suffering abuse from you and your father. I'm taking her home to Tuesday and Cliff. That's where she wants to be, and that's where she belongs."

"We'll see 'bout that," Joe said and was gone in a flash.

Paul Frank moved closer to the bed and placed a comforting hand on the grieving woman's shoulder. "Aggie, do you have any ideas about where Patty could be?"

"No. I don't, so I don't."

Before Paul Frank left, he spent a few minutes consoling Aggie about her nephew. He told her he'd let her know of any new information gathered on McCallister, and if any of his personal possessions were found in the rubble, he promised to see that she and Annabelle got them.

Aggie stubbornly clung to the belief that her nephew was not dead.

"That does it. Patty needs to be protected from Joe and the likes of him. When I find her, I'm going to tell her how I've felt about her for a long time now," Paul Frank promised himself as he returned to his truck.

"First I better tell Annabelle, Sara, and Daisy that McCallister is dead. Somehow, I don't think Joe is planning on doing it anytime soon." With that thought in mind, Paul Frank drove toward McCallister's cabin, dreading the ordeal of telling his other dependents that he was gone for good.

As always, the occupants heard the truck outdoors and spilled out onto the back porch, looking to see who was coming to visit. Hating the job, Paul Frank sat in the truck for a minute gathering his thoughts. Finally, with no more reason to delay, he slipped from the truck and met the women on the porch.

"Can we go inside? I have something to tell you."

"Don't tell me Patty's hurt or worse," Annabelle said, seeing the serious look on Paul Frank's face. "Don't tell me that."

"No, not her," Paul Frank assured Annabelle.

"It's Jacob."

"What? What 'bout him?" Annabelle asked.

Daisy and Sara moved to each side of Annabelle, sensing something was very wrong.

"Yes, what is it?" Daisy asked.

"He was in the World Trade Center building on the eleventh, and he's dead."

"No-o-o-o-o—" Annabelle screamed. "I won't have ya comin' in my house tellin' me hogwash like that." She collapsed to the floor with Daisy and Sara hanging on to each of her arms.

"Let's get her to the bed," Paul Frank advised. It was the only thing he could think to suggest.

After getting Annabelle settled, Sara and Daisy joined Paul Frank in the kitchen. "Are you sure? Daisy asked. "Because I can't believe he'd have any reason to be in New York of all places."

"It's official."

Every once in a while Annabelle could be heard wailing in the background, sending icy chills down the spines of the others.

Tears spilled from Sara's eyes, but for Annabelle's grief only. Understandably, she had none of her own. Daisy, ever dedicated to McCallister, having always been his favorite, was stunned by the news, but she had long since made peace with the idea of spending the remainder of her life without him.

Dry-eyed, Daisy put a comforting arm around Sara, who flinched each time her mother wailed her grief.

18

September 16, 2001

The next day as Annabelle stood looking out the window above the woodburner, she got a huge surprise. "Looky there, Sara," Annabelle said. "Aunt Aggie's comin' off th' mountain! Ya'd betta get out there an' help her climb down th' trail yonder. She's goin' to go an' break her foolish neck if she falls down that rocky path."

A few minutes later, Annabelle watched as Sara helped Aggie down the path to the back door. "What'cha doin' here?" Annabelle asked, as she led the two inside the kitchen.

"I come to talk about Jeb, so I did." Aggie said and gratefully sat at the table.

"Yeah, I enjoy talkin' 'bout 'im," Annabelle said, having decided to ignore Paul Frank's report on Jacob's death. "I miss 'im, an' I can see 'im appearin' at th' door at all hours, bringin' supplies an' tellin' stories, when he has a mind to tell 'em that is. He even brings us special presents sometimes."

"That ain't what I have on my mind, so it ain't," Aggie said.

"What's on your mind then?" Annabelle asked. "Can't do much more'n talk 'bout 'im when he's in th' city."

"Oh, I want to talk 'bout him all right, so I do," Aggie said. "I want to tell ya I don't believe my Jeb's dead, so I don't."

"I don't neither, but what 'bout Paul Frank comin' here tellin' us that it's true?"

"I don't care what anyone else's sayin', so I don't. I want to knowed what ya think 'bout Jeb."

"I believe Jeb's hidin' somewhers, laughin' 'cause th' law's thinkin' he's dead. Anyway, what would he be doin' in some big, hundred-story buildin' in—"Annabelle's brow wrinkled as she took a minute to remember the name—"New York City?"

"That's the dumbest thing I ever heard," Sara said. "Pa'd have no reason to hide from th' law, pretending he's dead. He was let out of jail after doin' his time."

"Ya don't knowed what ya're talkin' 'bout, Sara," Annabelle said. "I'd knowed in my heart if my man was dead."

"Well, I don't believe it neither, so I don't, but it sure would do my old heart good to see 'im for myself, so it would."

"That's what I'm wantin', too," Annabelle said.

"Have ya heard from Patty?" Aggie asked. "Maybe she could get word to 'im to let us knowed he's all right, so she could. She knows th' city now."

"Aunt Aggie, I done made a special trip to your cabin an' told ya we ain't heard as much as a peep out of Patty," Sara said.

"Aggie," Annabelle said, "ya knowed Patty don't have nothin' to do with Jeb no more. She's afraid of 'im. Anyway, I've been powerful worried 'bout her. We've not heard a word."

"I'm stayin' here for a few days, so I am," Aggie said.

"There's no need for that. Sara'll come tell ya if we hear somethin'," Annabelle said. "After getting' used to your fancy bed an' your fancy cabin, how're ya goin' to sleep on a mat on th' floor in this place?"

"I can sleep in th' bed, so I can."

"Oh, no, Aggie. You're not puttin' me or Daisy out of our bed an' on th' floor."

"What's this 'bout puttin' Daisy on th' floor?" Daisy appeared in the kitchen; the curtains swayed in the doorway she had just passed through.

"Me an' Aggie think that Jeb is alive, an' she's talkin' 'bout stayin' here until he comes home or, knowin' her, till his body is carried in."

"Oh, forevermore," Daisy said. "Jeb's dead, an' ya both knowed it. His rental car was found at th' buildin', an' he had an appointment at th' same time th' buildin' was hit. He was there!"

"That ain't enough for me, so it ain't."

"Oh, Aunt Aggie, ya'd not believe Jeb was dead if his body was laid out in his coffin an' sittin' right in front of ya. Why, ya'd say, 'He's just sleepin', so he is,'" Daisy mocked Aggie.

"Well, I don't believe it neither," Annabelle said, siding with Aggie, possibly for the first time in their lives.

"Forevermore," Daisy said again in exasperation. "Th' two of ya can sleep together an' pine away waitin' for Jeb. As for me, I'm goin' to th' city soon. I almost have enough money saved, an' th' woman at th' shelter's lookin' for me an apartment."

"How's she talkin' to th' woman in th' city?" Aggie asked, looking to Annabelle, a frown of skepticism on her face

"I'm standin' right here, Aggie. Ya can ask me," Daisy grumbled. "There's a phone at the town bar, an' I call her from there when I need to."

"It's fine with me if ya move to th' city," Annabelle said. "I'll have Jeb all to myself if ya're not here."

"Annabelle, no one's goin' to have Jeb," Daisy said. "Not anymore. An' if I had someone else to watch th' twins, an' if it wasn't so much farther to walk to work when I don't have a ride, I'd go an' stay at Aggie's cabin until I move. It'd be worth it to get away from th' two of ya bickerin'."

"Just who's goin' to watch your youngins when ya're at work when ya're livin' in th' city?" Annabelle asked.

"Ya're thinkin' I haven't thought of that, aren't ya?" Daisy said. "Well, ya're wrong! Th' shelter is helping' with that, an' th' welfare will help me till I'm on my own."

"Jeb won't like it one bit if he finds out ya're acceptin' welfare, so he won't."

"Aunt Aggie! Annabelle! Face it. Jeb's dead."

19

*T*HE AIR WAS GETTING A CHILL IN IT, AND PATTY COULD tell that it would not be long before nightfall. Nevertheless, it was still plenty light enough for her to see the blue-jeaned behind of Tommy Lee, who continued to lay in drunken unconsciousness.

After repeatedly kicking at the door, attempting unsuccessfully to force Tommy Lee to move, she sat just inside the doorway. Clutched in her fist was her only weapon. She sat where she could keep an eye on Tommy Lee, not wanting to be blindsided when he came to. Earlier, right after he'd passed out, she'd taken the time to search for something she could defend herself with, knowing she was no match for him. In her search, she'd found a small stack of used lumber under a pile of rubbish, mixed with old rotting leaves. Rusty, spike nails protruded from many of the pieces, and she chose one that was four feet long and one inch thick with three inches of a nail's point exposed.

While Patty sat fearing for her safety, tears streamed down her face unchecked as she remembered a small part of the chat she had had with her new-found grandmother. A few words in a conversation had ended her dreams of the life she and Paul Frank might have together, had made her realize that she wasn't good enough for him. Her grandmother had revealed that, although all she had wanted in her life was to get her daughter back, she had feared that if her daughter had somehow returned home, she would not have had a chance for a normal life after having been used by a man and then tossed away. Myrtle told Patty that she knew that no man would want her daughter after she had been with someone who was not her husband, so in reality, since the deed was done, she was better off staying with the man her father had sold her to. Patty had suffered the same fate at her brother's and her father's hands, and so she put herself in the same category. After listening to her grandmother, Patty had come to the conclusion that the relationship with Paul Frank she'd long hoped for was simply impossible. Patty deduced that surely Paul Frank knew; that was why he continued to treat her like a sister.

Oh, I'm so glad that I put off asking Paul Frank to my school party. It would've been so embarrassing if he said no, that I'm only like a sister to him. Her uncontrolled sobbing broke the eerie silence. *Besides, if I never start a relationship with him, I'll never have to know for sure that he thinks I'm damaged goods, soiled like my grandmother says my mother was.*

Involuntarily, Patty sobbed more loudly.

Tommy Lee moved.

Catching the movement from the corner of her eye and controlling her emotions with great effort, Patty stood. She raised the weapon above her head, waiting for him to gain his feet, reach for the door, and open it. As she waited quietly, afraid even to breathe, Tommy Lee grunted like the pig he was and with clumsy difficulty got to his hands and knees. He appeared to be confused as to where he was. Then a look of determination changed the expression on his face from bewilderment to one of purpose. He made it to a wobbly, upright position, and as he turned to grasp the door handle, Patty firmly held the homemade weapon over her head. The door opened a crack and his stench preceded him as he moved inside the room.

His rank body odor, combined with the smell of vomit on his breath, made her gag.

20

MARY LOU AND TUESDAY SAT AT THE TABLE, EACH HOLD-
ing a cup of tea. They contemplated what was happening. "Do you think that Paul Frank'll ever find Patty?"

"Of course I do," Tuesday said carefully, and then her control cracked. "Why did I not realize that she'd go regardless
of what I said to try and stop her? It was obvious she felt
compelled to find her birth family. I'm so worried!"

"I know this is not the time, but do you think Paul Frank
knows which of us he wants?"

"No. I have no—"

"Know what?" Winter Ann had heard Mary Lou's question. She had entered the kitchen still wearing her pajamas.

"No, what?" Tuesday gave the expected answer.

"I think Paul Frank likes you and Patty." Winter Ann
climbed into a chair next to Mary Lou with a serious look all
over her doll baby face. "But I think he wants Patty for a girlfriend."

"Winter Ann, you know no such a thing!" Tuesday scold-
ed the little girl, who was going only by her own childish
perception. "I don't even know."

"Why do you think that?" Mary Lou asked the little girl.

"'Cause of the way he looks at Patty."

"What do you know of romantic looks, or romance for that matter, young lady?" Tuesday scooped the cuddly, flannel-wrapped Winter Ann onto her lap and hugged her.

"I don't know. I just think he looks like he likes her." Winter Ann looked serious as she tried to explain herself. "Like you and daddy."

"Winter Ann, go get dressed, and I'll come up and comb your wild hair."

Winter Ann scampered up the stairs; it seemed she never walked as running got her around much faster. Tuesday turned to Mary Lou, who looked crestfallen.

"Mary Lou, eat your breakfast. Winter Ann is only four years old, and she couldn't know what's in Paul Frank's mind. Anyway, there's a chance she's right and, if she is, you'll have to understand and do your best to get over him. On the other hand, he could be interested in you, and Patty will have to deal with that."

Tuesday left the kitchen and climbed the stairs to help Winter Ann with her hair. Tuesday tickled her in the places that made her giggle the most. "Now, you can have breakfast."

When they returned to the kitchen, Winter Ann ran to Mary Lou and asked, "Know what?"

Afraid it was going to be more of the same, Mary Lou rolled her eyes and looked at Tuesday asking, "No, what?" Any other reply would only cause Winter Ann to ask her question until she got the response that she wanted.

"Mommy and me are going to make cookies, and when Paul Frank brings Patty home they'll have cookies and milk."

"That's nice," Mary Lou said and hugged the little girl while she looked at Tuesday over Winter Ann's thick, bouncy, dark curls. "Am I invited?"

"Oh, yes," Winter Ann said. "I wouldn't have a party without you."

"Winter Ann, would you go upstairs and get my sweater. I feel a little chilled."

"Okay, Mommy. Where is it?"

"It's on the chest at the foot of my bed."

As soon as Winter Ann had charged up the steps, her chubby little legs just long enough to manage them, Tuesday immediately turned to Mary Lou. "Why do you look so pale? Is something wrong?"

"I'm worried about Patty." Mary Lou looked as if she were going to cry. "I know I sound selfish worrying who Paul Frank is going to choose when Patty's very life may be in danger. But I am worried about Patty. Bad things happen on that mountain. Bad things—especially to women."

"I know," Tuesday said. "I'd never have believed myself what horrible things can happen there, though, if I'd not been held against my will by McCallister and used however he pleased."

*T*HE BOARD CAME DOWN HARD ON TOMMY LEE'S HEAD and he crumpled to the floor, blood running down the side of his face. Luckily for him, the nail hadn't made direct contact with his skull, hadn't pierced deep into his brain like it might have. It did tear a large gash in his scalp leaving a flap of bloody skin and hair hanging over his left ear.

He was halfway sober now, after his two-hour sleep on the cool, damp ground just outside the door. Getting away from Patty, who continued to hold the board over her head for another swing, was Tommy Lee's only thought. Crablike, with his rear end only a few inches above the floor, he scrambled backward toward the corner, not taking his eyes away from Patty's weapon. "Please don't hurt me. I love you," Tommy Lee pleaded.

"You make me sick, Tommy Lee. You leave me in this damp, dark, excuse for a room for days with no food and precious little water, and you whine for me not to hurt you. You're lucky that I don't drive this spike nail right through your worthless head."

Tommy Lee reached the corner and sat soundly on his rump as he held his arms in front of his face, peeking between them. He begged Patty not to hit him again.

"Where's my car?" she demanded.

"I'll tell ya if ya promise not to hit me again."

"I don't have to promise you anything." Patty gave the board a small swing in the direction of his injured head. "Tell me where my car is."

"It's in th' old garage behind th' house."

"You mean behind this shack," Patty hissed.

"No, behind th' mansion," Tommy Lee whined.

"Is that where we are?"

'Yeah, in a shed behind th' grandest house ya'll ever see, when it's finished," Tommy Lee said proudly. "Your pa's mansion."

"What! What did you say?"

"Ike Harris, th' man ya saw with me th' other day, was hired by your pa to build a mansion for ya an' Tuesday an' Winter Ann. 'Course your pa don't knowed that I knowed any of it."

"Does my pa know you brought me here?"

"That's for me to knowed an' ya to find out." Tommy Lee smirked as though he had just said the coolest thing.

"I knew it was Pa behind all this," Patty said. "How could I not? All my life my father has treated me as if I was born for his enjoyment and profit," she sobbed. "You are a no good—" Patty was at a loss for words. "You keep me here, making like I'm your girlfriend. I—"

"Now ya're hurtin' my feelin's," Tommy Lee whimpered. "I always thought if it wasn't for Joe, ya'd be my girlfriend. He's th' one keepin' us apart."

"Ah-h-h-h! You have the nerve, talking about hurt feelings," Patty hissed. "You're just like Joe and my pa, oblivious to anyone's feelings but your own."

With the door open, the structure was revealed as a simple shack. The interior was finally clearly visible to Patty. An old, small, worktable covered with discarded building materials, with a single chair next to it, occupied the corner across from where Tommy Lee cowered. The floor was wood plank, and there were no windows. At the corner nearest the door were several boxes filled with magazines and other clutter that was important only to Tommy Lee. Next to that was a body-shaped lump wrapped in an army blanket.

"What is that smell, anyway?" Patty asked, knowing from the overwhelming smell that whatever it was it was dead.

It was obvious that Tommy Lee knew what she was talking about because he turned and looked in the direction of the object of her fear.

"That's my other girlfriend," Tommy Lee leered.

"Give me my keys!" Patty demanded in a quivering voice, making a threatening gesture with the weapon she still clutched in her hand.

She was now shaking with fear. She was sure there was a dead person under the blanket. It was not an animal. Since Patty had been confined there, there had been no movement from under the blanket. She realized she was dealing not only with a lovesick maniac, but with a murderer as well, and she wondered how she could cope. She was positively weak with hunger and thirst.

"Th' keys're in th' car," Tommy Lee bleated.

In a desperate attempt to get away from Tommy Lee once and for all, she demanded, "Stand up and pull all your pockets inside out, Tommy Lee, or I'll use this again." She moved forward a few steps in a threatening manner and, for emphasis, swung the board in small arcs above her head.

Tommy Lee stood and pulled out his jacket pockets. The keys fell to the floor, sliding through a crack at his feet.

"Hi, Daisy," Paul Frank said. "You ready to go home? I mean, I'll give you a ride. I want to check what's going on at the cabin. Maybe Patty's come back."

"We wish," Daisy said. "Thanks for thinking to give me a ride. Can ya give me a minute?"

"Sure."

A little while later, they stepped into McCallister's cabin.

"I'd hoped Patty was with ya," Aggie said.

"I wish I'd found her, too," Paul Frank said. "That's why I'm here."

He nodded toward Aggie. "I'm surprised to see you here, Aggie."

"I come to see Annabelle, so I did. I don't believe that my Jeb is dead, an' I knowed Annabelle wouldn't've either."

Annabelle was still as pale as she was when Paul Frank had told her about Jacob. "Yeah, we don't believe Jeb was in that building."

"You need to accept it—Jacob McCallister is dead," Paul Frank said with obvious concern in his voice.

"Just because we knowed about the attack don't mean nothin'. There's no body, so he's not dead," Annabelle said.

"We talked about that. It wasn't found," Paul Frank said patiently. "They don't expect to find many bodies. The heat was so intense that there was not much left of anything, especially bodies that were crushed and burned under the ruins. Actually, all that was left of those two buildings were twisted pieces of steel and dust."

Annabelle's tear-stained face crumpled at the talk of Jacob being crushed to death. She rose to her feet and began moving about the kitchen, preparing dinner.

"With no body, ya can't be so sure," Annabelle shrilled with her back toward the others. "I can still see 'im walkin' in th' door carryin' supplies from town. For one, I'm not goin' to accept it. He's goin' to come back."

"I don't knowed why you're carin' so much. He's mean, an' he doesn't care 'bout us. I'm sad an' glad he' gone," Sara said with tears filling her eyes.

"Sara, he's your father, an' I don't want to hear such disrespect outta your mouth," Annabelle said.

"He's mean an' ya knowed it," Sara sobbed. "He made mine an' Patty's lives miserable."

"Okay," Daisy intervened, "let's not speak ill of th' dead."

"Ill of th' dead!" Sara screeched. "All ya ever cared 'bout when he was here was primpin' for 'im. Well, he ain't here no more an' I'm glad!" Sara stomped from the room and flung herself down on her mat.

"He ain't dead! So he ain't!" Aggie slammed a pot down on the woodburning stove, making her point.

"What is it? I mean, why are you all denying the truth?"

"You'll see," Annabelle said. "You'll see, he ain't dead."

"We can't do anything about that now, and the important thing is finding Patty! I mean, as time goes by, the chances of finding her get slimmer.

Sara, come back in here." Paul Frank pulled back the curtain that separated her room from the kitchen. She stood, letting the quilt she had been hugging to her knees fall to the floor, and followed by the trio of children, returned to the kitchen, where she slumped to the bench at the table.

Kelly Sue climbed onto her mother's lap. The twins returned to their homemade toys at the foot of the potbelly stove.

"Now I want all of you to listen to me," Paul Frank said sternly. "Andy Hillberry told me that Tommy Lee had his own place. Also, he told me that yesterday Tommy Lee told him that he had a girlfriend. I mean, we all know that he never had a willing girlfriend, so it sounds like he very well could have Patty at his place. Do any of you have any idea at all where that is? It's imperative that we find out and soon."

"I sure don't knowed anythin' 'bout Tommy Lee," Annabelle offered.

'I don't neither," Sara said, "'cept that he used to hang 'round Patty when he could get away with it, when Joe wasn't 'round."

"I don't knowed anythin', but I sure can ask around. Maybe someone at th' bar knows somethin'," Daisy offered.

"I just knowed he's a scoundrel, so I do."

"Do that, Daisy," Paul Frank said, ignoring Aggie, "and I'll keep in touch with you in case you find out something. I mean, I'm getting very anxious about Patty's safety."

Night was falling fast as Paul Frank left. He got in his truck and drove around, moving up and down every trail, knocking on doors and getting nowhere. With no other ideas, Paul Frank took his phone from his pocket and called Cliff. "Man, I'm at a dead end. No one seems to know anything. After talking to Andy Hillberry, I'm sure Tommy Lee has Patty secured somehow at his place, but I don't even know if his place is a house, a cabin, a shack, or what."

"Think, Paul Frank. They're dirt poor. If Tommy Lee has a place, it's a shack or tree cabin or something of that nature. What about Centerpoint? Have you looked there?"

"I don't know of Tommy Lee ever hanging around Centerpoint or that side of the mountain, for that matter. I mean, neither Tommy Lee nor his father have jobs. How would he come and go so easily? There's no way his family could buy or keep up a car or even a horse."

"All I can say is to keep doing what you're doing," Cliff said. "If you can, talk to Andy Hillberry again. You never know, he might reveal something that'll help you."

"Thanks, I'll keep in touch."

"Paul Frank, I'm coming to help. I'm getting worried."

"I think you can hold off for a while. What if there's another attack? Anyway, Joe's out searching too, and I'm hoping that I cross paths with him soon. Maybe he's come up with something. Why don't you wait until morning, and if we haven't found her by then, I'd say get in your truck and head this way. You know, you can be here in about four hours."

"All right, I'll wait, but only till morning. With McCallister out of the picture, I'm only concerned about leaving Tuesday and Winter Ann because of the possibility of another attack on our country," Cliff said. "You know, I have faith in you; otherwise, I'd have been there by now."

"Thanks," Paul Frank said, "I'm doing my best at this end. Cliff, just so you'll know, I mean, you were right about my coming forth about my feelings for the girls. Patty is the one, and I'm going to tell her the minute I find her. The longer she's missing, the more I regret that I haven't said something."

"I'm glad to hear it, but don't worry. The two of you are young and have the rest of your lives to share."

Cliff's encouraging sentiment, meant to boost Paul Frank's morale, served instead to give him an eerie feeling of dread.

A little later, Paul Frank found himself on the final stretch of road that leveled off a half mile before reaching the main artery connecting the businesses of Winding Ridge. "I never thought of it! I haven't covered every possibility," Paul Frank shouted in his excitement of thinking of a likely place to search for Patty. "There're side streets running off Main Street."

Bouncing over the cobblestone street, which consisted of three city blocks before it ended at the sheer mountain face where the town could no longer spread out, he looked carefully to his right and left. When he came to the first cross street, he swung around to the right. After stopping at each of the eight houses and knocking on the doors, he continued driving closer to the outcropping of rocks for another half a city block. Getting as close to the drop off as was safe, he jumped from the truck, and peering over the edge, he saw Route Seven at least a mile below, winding its way around the foot of the mountain, following the profile created by the drop off.

He wheeled the truck around and crossed Main Street, finding there were only three houses on that side, and the road dead-ended where the rocky face of the mountain rose starkly skyward. After checking the houses that were grouped together on one side of the road, he backtracked and turned on Main Street, continuing toward the end.

There was an alley halfway up the block, wedged between The General Store and the movie theater. Paul Frank turned onto the narrow street between the three-story buildings. Directly behind the store and theater were two smaller buildings. The one on the left was a smaller replica of The General Store, except it faced the alley rather than Main Street. The other building sat on the right side, facing the alley and was a twin to the movie theater.

Much farther back from the group of four buildings, at a distance about the length of a ball field, stood a two-story house. At least a hundred yards back from the road, it was mostly hidden by huge pine trees. A second two-story house was situated merely a dozen feet from the alley. Choosing the nearest one, Paul Frank knocked first at one door and then another before realizing the house was vacant.

He quickly strode back to his truck, got in, and drove along the lane to the second house. He left the truck once again and began walking around, knocking on doors and looking into windows. The house looked as if it had been abandoned for some time. Rounding the corner at the rear of the house, he spotted a shack with large patches of trampled weeds all around it. He hurried to the building.

He pried the padlock open and walked inside. Certain that this was Tommy Lee's place, Paul Frank searched for any item that might point him to Patty. He found a pile of discarded beer cans in one corner, piles of blankets in another. Girly magazines rested on an old butcher's block that had been made into a table, which was flanked by two rickety wooden chairs.

Paul Frank sorted through the magazines and found a blueprint neatly folded at the bottom of the stack. Quickly he unfolded it, knowing it could be something important; it was definitely out of place in the cluttered shed.

"Wow!" Paul Frank shouted in his excitement at finding a clue to Patty's whereabouts.

It was late evening when the call came. Tuesday answered the phone. "Let it be Patty," she prayed. "Hello."

"Hi, honey. Have you heard from Paul Frank?"

"No. I haven't, and I'm getting more and more worried."

"I have. We talked earlier. If he doesn't find Patty by morning, I'm going up there."

"What can you do that he can't?"

"I can take some help," Cliff said. "I'm sorry we didn't take more drastic steps earlier on. I know full well that time is of the essence in missing person cases."

"We sent Paul Frank, and you said he's good."

"Yes. He has excellent instincts, he knows the mountain, and he won't stop until he finds her. Anyway, if we don't hear something soon, I'm leaving first thing in the morning."

As Tuesday hung up the phone, Mary Lou came up behind her. "Was that Paul Frank?"

"No, it was Cliff. If we don't hear anything by morning he's taking a few men and going to the mountain."

"Please let me go too," Mary Lou exclaimed. "I'll never see the mountain again otherwise."

"Cliff would never allow it, and you know it. This is official business."

"You could come along, too. I know that you want to. Cora would be more than happy to watch Winter Ann," Mary Lou prodded.

"What would be the point? You said yourself that you don't know the mountain," Tuesday laughed. "When Paul Frank, Patty, and I stumbled across you for the first time, you were hopelessly lost in a snowstorm on the mountain and had no idea where you were."

"I know, I know. I'm just so worried about Patty and Paul Frank now. It's so hard to sit around and do nothing."

"I understand. I feel the same way," Tuesday said, embracing the girl. "All we can do is wait."

22

*W*ITH A SWIPE OF HIS ARM, PAUL FRANK CLEARED the table of the clutter and spread out the blueprint. There was no electricity in the shed; he had gone to his truck and retrieved a flashlight so he could read the diagram.

The blueprint was for the construction of a very large house. At the bottom right corner was a note: *Ike, I want this house finished as soon as possible. If you need help there's a boy on Winding Ridge, Tommy Lee Hillberry, who'll be happy to earn a few bucks. You can find him in the town bar most days. I'll meet with you in a few days to go over the plans with you. I'll notify you in the usual manner. Have a good day. Jacob.*

Paul Frank excitedly scanned the entire paper and found an address scrawled in the same handwriting: *Route 3, Box 119, Short Run. Pass the road running up to Winding Ridge, go about twenty miles, and you'll see an old foundation set inside a tall, wrought-iron gate. That's the site of the house.*

"I've got to call Cliff," Paul Frank said aloud to no one as he ran back to his truck to get his solar phone.

"Cliff, I found Tommy Lee's place."

"Good work!"

"There's a blueprint for a huge house. It fits in with Patty's dreams. Also, there's a note written by McCallister to a man named Ike."

"I got it from Jeremy Clarke that Ike Harris is the name of the man McCallister was in prison with.

What's the note say?"

"McCallister suggests that Ike hire Tommy Lee to help with the house. And the best thing is, there's an address and directions to the house. I'm going there right now."

"Okay. I'll round up Randy McCoy, and we'll be on the mountain today."

23

*P*AUL FRANK WASTED NO TIME IN HEADING FOR THE CON-
struction site. He traveled down Winding Ridge road
and turned left. Speeding along, he frequently checked the
odometer dial as the miles rolled around it. When he saw he
had gone fifteen miles, he started watching for the wrought-
iron fence that marked the property.

Just as the gauge turned over to nineteen miles, Paul
Frank saw the mansion up ahead.

"Yes! That's it!" Paul Frank slowed to a stop and then
backed up the truck and pulled it off the road out of sight. As
he walked along, he stayed close to the overgrown brush,
keeping out of the view of anyone who might be around.

When he came to the gate, he opened it and stepped onto
the footpath. A grand, new manor rose from an old foundation. Although obviously not finished, it was still impressive.

His eyes followed a wide path of worn-down weeds, and
about two hundred yards back, the corner of a one-story
building caught his eye. As he drew nearer, he could see that
hidden behind a tall row of pine trees was an ancient wooden
garage with doors that opened outward. The building leaned
slightly to the left, and the padlock was hanging open. Paul

Frank freed the lock from the latch. As he pulled at the door on the left, he heard an angry, hissing growl. He continued pulling, but very slowly because the door dragged in the dirt making it difficult to open, and because he did not know what size animal was making the noises. He did not relish the thought of a wild animal that outweighted him by hundreds of pounds jumping out and attacking him.

Suddenly, a roly-poly raccoon squeezed through the small opening, its teeth bared, still hissing and growling. As Paul Frank backed away, the raccoon suddenly jumped at him, knocking him back a few steps by the force of its fifteen-pound body. "Holy cow!" Paul Frank exclaimed. "That hurts!" The frightened animal had attached its claws to Paul Frank's blue jeans, digging in painfully. As soon as it had a solid grip, it bit deeply, drawing blood, before jumping away.

Paul Frank hopped around on one foot before trying to pull up his pant leg to check for damage. His calf was too large for the opening of his pants to pass over, so he took his knife from his pocket and cut a slash in the jeans so he could assess the damage. "Man, I mean, that's nasty," he said out loud, "and that damn animal could be rabid. Well, too bad, but I just can't do anything about it until I find Patty."

Getting over the initial shock of the painful bite, Paul Frank angrily jerked the door the rest of the way open and gasped at what he saw. "Dear Lord in heaven, I hope this is a good sign," he prayed.

There, inside the ancient garage, stood Patty's silver Avalon.

Paul Frank limped around the car, trying all the doors and finding them all locked. He peered inside and couldn't see anything unusual. *Patty was here somewhere.* The car was the only thing in the garage, so Paul Frank closed the doors and surveyed the area more closely.

To the north of the garage and a short distance from the mansion sat a small building separated from the house by a breezeway overgrown by many years of untended vines. What caught his attention were the trampled weeds that marked the area in the same way as the packed-down brush around the garage.

Favoring his injured leg, Paul Frank approached the small structure. He saw that the building had no windows but found an entrance on the far side. There was a padlock on the door identical to the one on the garage, but it was not engaged.

Cautiously, he opened the door. The fading light filled the room, and to Paul Frank's horror, in the far corner he saw Tommy Lee holding Patty as a shield. Having heard the activity out by the garage, Patty had let down her guard and Tommy Lee had taken advantage of the situation. He grabbed the board, reacting in his usual cowardly manner, and was prepared to sacrifice her for his own safety.

To keep her from bolting, Tommy Lee had his left arm wrapped around her neck. He brandished a board threateningly above his head. "Don't come any closer, ya big-feelin' city turd!" Tommy Lee demanded. "I won't be responsible for what I do if ya don't listen to me."

Paul Frank stopped in his tracks.

This time Patty took advantage of the situation, knowing that Tommy Lee was expecting the assault to come from Paul Frank, believing that he had Patty under control. So suddenly she bit Tommy Lee's arm, making him loosen his grip. As he favored his injured arm, she forced her elbow sharply into his ribcage. Then with all her strength, she rose to a crouch and, turning in a quick pivot, pushed Tommy Lee's arm backward so hard that the nail was forced into the wood above his head, lodging the board fast to the wall.

Patty stumbled as she ran to Paul Frank, and he gratefully took her in his arms without taking his eyes off Tommy Lee. "Boy, you have some answering to do!"

"Ah, I didn't mean no harm," Tommy Lee whined. "I love Patty, an' I knowed she loves me too because when we was kids she was th' only one that treated me like I was worth talkin' to. That's except when she couldn't 'cause her brother Joe'd run me off, tellin' her she couldn't talk to me."

"Patty, where are your keys?" Paul Frank asked, ignoring Tommy Lee.

"They fell through the floor boards when Tommy Lee took them from his pocket." She moved to the area where she remembered the keys falling.

"We'll get them later," Paul Frank said.

"What happened to your leg, Paul Frank?"

"Ah, it's okay," Paul Frank didn't want to worry Patty after what she'd been through.

"No, it's not," she said. "What happened?"

"A raccoon bit me. I mean, he got me as I was forcing my way into the garage where Tommy Lee hid your car."

"You need immediate care, Paul Frank. The raccoon could have rabies. I don't remember how soon after being bitten you need the shots, but we aren't taking any chances."

"Okay, okay. Let's call Tuesday and Cliff first. They're worried out of their minds."

Paul Frank took the phone from his pocket and dialed Cliff and Tuesday's number.

"Hello," Tuesday answered.

"Tuesday, it's me Paul Frank. I've found Patty. She's okay. You want to say hi to her?" Grinning, he handed the phone to Patty.

"Hi, Tuesday, I'm fine. I'm sorry you were worried."

"What happened?"

"It's a long story. I'll tell you when I'm home, that is if you'll take me back after worrying you so bad."

"Don't be silly. You're my daughter. And I want you home just as soon as you can get here. But, Patty, I'm very disappointed in you for disobeying Cliff and me. We know how much going to the mountain meant to you, though, so Cliff and I are going to overlook it this time—if you promise never to pull a trick like that again."

"I promise," Patty whimpered. "I found my grandmother."

"I'm anxious to hear about that, as well as everything else that has happened. I'll have dinner ready for you. You should be home by dinner time if you leave now."

"If you don't mind, Tuesday, I'm going to take the time to tell Ma and the others that I'm okay."

"Of course, but hurry home. I'm dying to know absolutely everything that happened."

"I also want to see my grandmother again. The sheriff's my uncle and I want to talk to him. You don't mind if I stay a few more days, do you?"

"Patty, you don't know what is going on in the world now. There's going to be a lot of catching up to do. I'm sure Paul Frank will fill you in. I want you to come home now!"

"Tuesday, I really need to do a little more digging into my family history. I'm going to stay. Please understand, and forgive me."

"I'm going to talk to Cliff about it, so for now I'm not going to make an issue of it, but keep in touch," Tuesday said. "I want you back here as soon as possible. And now tell me everything," she demanded.

Realizing that Tuesday deserved to be informed, Patty quickly gave her the short version. "I was taken hostage by Tommy Lee Hillberry," Patty said, "and another man. From some of the things Tommy Lee told me, he's a friend of my father, and he, along with Tommy Lee, was involved in my disappearance."

"Jacob?" Tuesday said. "Patty, I want you home!" The dread she felt at the thought of him stepping into their lives again made her forget about his death at the hands of the terrorists. Out of pure raw fear, she nearly fainted and landed solidly in the easy chair next to the phone stand.

"Yes, the man's a friend of Pa's, but Paul Frank has already told me that he's dead. The place I was held hostage in was his mansion. Tommy Lee said so. It's the one I have nightmares about. Tuesday," Patty sniffled, "can you believe it, I was held in the house of my dreams. The one Pa is building for us, or should I say, 'was'? And there's something else too. There's a body wrapped in an army blanket in the lean-to where he was holding me. Paul Frank and I are going to check it out. We wanted to let you know that I'm okay before we get into that."

"You don't know whose body it is?" Tuesday asked.

"No," Patty sobbed into the phone. The gravity of what she had gone through was catching up with her now that she was safe.

"You're coming home!" Tuesday said.

Taking advantage of the emotional conversation, Tommy Lee began creeping toward the door in an attempt to get out of the room unnoticed. As he crossed the threshold, Paul Frank caught the movement out of the corner of his eye. He grabbed Tommy Lee by his belt and jerked him to his feet, twisting him around to face him. Tommy Lee kicked him in his injured leg, causing Paul Frank to nearly black out with the pain of it. Tommy Lee scampered away like a rat before Paul Frank could catch his breath.

"Dammit," Paul Frank shouted, and sat on the floor favoring his injured leg.

"I have to go now, Tuesday. I'll call you later!" Patty said and cut the connection.

"Are you okay?" Patty sat on the floor next to Paul Frank.

"Yeah, it just hurts like thunder."

"I want to get my car, Paul Frank. Do you think you can move around with that leg injury?"

"Yes, it stopped bleeding, but you're too weak, Patty. Let's wait until later."

"Please, Paul Frank. I don't want to leave it here. We don't know where Tommy Lee ran off to, but he's certain to come back, and he knows where the keys are, and if we don't get them and take the car, he will. It makes me sick to think of him driving my car."

Paul Frank could not argue with that. They walked around the building where there was an opening to the crawl space.

Paul Frank squatted, getting in position to crawl under the building. With a groan of pain, he moved forward on one knee.

"No, Paul Frank, your wound is open, and it's hard to tell what kind of infection you'll get under that old building. I'll look for the keys. I'm smaller than you anyway."

His leg pained him too much to argue. Although he hated to, he moved away from the opening.

Early morning September 18th

Annabelle spent a major portion of her time either gazing from the window above the woodburning stove or standing at the back door, holding the screen open, as she watched the road and willed Patty to return.

"Ma," Sara admonished, "ya're goin' to let th' flies in to eat us up if ya don't quit holdin' that screen door open."

"I can't take it no more. Patty can't've disappeared into thin air."

"Ma, she's got to be somewhere," Sara said. "People don't just vanish. Joe an' Paul Frank'll find her. You'll see. It'll be th' last place ya expected."

Annabelle turned and walked toward the bedroom she shared with Daisy. "Where're ya goin', Ma?"

"I'm goin' to wake up Daisy, that's where."

"Ma, ya knowed she worked 'til th' wee hours in th' mornin'. Let her sleep, for heaven's sake."

"It's for her own good, Sara. Jeb's goin' to come walkin' in that door one day, an' there'll be more trouble than ya can shake a stick at. Not only for Daisy, but me too. Ya knowed he counts on me to keep things goin' th' way he wants."

"Ma!" Sara exclaimed. "Pa's dead, an' ya knowed it."

"Don't ya talk like that," Annabelle shot at Sara. "There's no body, an' 'til I see a body, he's not dead. One day soon he's goin' to walk in that door with a smile on 'is face an' a story to tell." Annabelle sat soundly in a rocking chair, her face twisted as she tried her best not to give in to tears.

"Ma, it'll be okay." Sara put an arm across Annabelle's back. "Joe'll take care of us. He's just like Pa. He's been doin' it ever since he's been drivin'."

"Does Joe ever mention Frank Dillon? Ya knowed, I been thinkin' of 'im," Annabelle said. "Remember when your pa was on th' run, keepin' outa jail, an' Frank talked Joe into movin' us to his cabin?"

"Oh, yeah, I do. I never saw anythin' like Big Bessie an' th' way she wanted to boss us around. Ya didn't like her much, Ma, did ya?"

"No, I didn't," Annabelle said. "Remember how she an' Aggie argued from daylight 'til dark?"

"Why ya bringin' Frank Dillon up?" Sara asked. 'Ya knowed he's in jail."

"With th' situation we're in it just made me think of Frank's women, an' who's takin' care of 'em now that he's in jail. I'm pretty sure he didn't get out on probation like your pa did."

'I don't knowed," Sara said. "Ma, ya're thinkin' that Joe's takin' care of Frank's women!"

"Somebody has to be takin' care of 'em," Annabelle said. "They're just like us. We'd starve without Jeb or Joe to bring us our supplies an' stuff."

"Daisy wouldn't let us starve. Even with Joe bringin' supplies, Daisy is always bringin' us extras, from time to time," Sara disagreed. "She'd bring us anythin' we needed from Th' General Store, an' I could get a job in th' bar too."

"Oh, no," Annabelle raged. "I'm not goin' to stand by on pins and needles 'bout th' both of ya getting' caught workin' in that bar filled with drunks. Ya're my daughter, an' I'm not goin' to stand for it."

"Oh, Ma, if it comes to that, that's what I'll have to do."

"Just who'd ya thinkin's goin' to take care of ya an' Daisy's youngins?"

"Ma, ya would if'n ya had to."

"Don't be so sure," Annabelle said.

Eager to get her mother's mind off the bar and her father, Sara changed the subject back to Dillon's women. "But I just bet Joe takes Frank's women supplies when he brings 'em to us."

"I'd wager that you're right," Annabelle said, "and I'd wager it's on orders from Jeb. Frank took care of us when Jeb was on th' run, an' I'm sure Jeb'd feel obliged to return th' favor."

"I'm goin' to walk to their cabin an' see 'em," Sara said. "No one's looked for Patty there that I knowed of. Maybe she's there hurt an' they're takin' care of her till she's better. An' anyway, when we find her, I'll tell her 'bout visit'n them, an' she can let Mary Lou knowed how her mountain family's doin'. Patty can tell her all 'bout it when she gets back to th' city."

"Ya goin' to take th' youngins?" Annabelle asked. "I'm not up to chasin' after 'em today."

"Ya knowed they'll all be wantin' me to carry them," Sara complained. "I can't carry three youngins."

Daisy entered the room with her twins hanging on her legs. "Go on, Sara, I'll watch th' youngins. I'm off work tonight, an' I can't sleep anyway with Annabelle naggin' me to get up every ten minutes. Anyway, I didn't want to sleep all day when I can sleep tonight."

With a purpose of her own and freed from the constant demands of the children, Sara happily started down the path to Frank Dillon's cabin.

24

*P*ATTY WAS JUST ABOUT TO ENTER THE CRAWLSPACE WHEN she saw the pain etched on Paul Frank's face. "Are you okay?" she asked.

"Just mad that Tommy Lee got away."

"No matter," Patty said. "Where's he going to go anyway? He has no car, no friends, no money, and for certain, he has no brains."

"We can deal with Tommy Lee later. I have information you should know about."

"What's that?" Patty looked concerned.

"I found a blueprint for the mansion that's being built beyond this shed. There's a note at the bottom of it. The note was written by your father to a man called Ike Harris."

"Oh, no." Patty's face lost all its color. "I just can't take it anymore."

"Don't worry," Paul Frank reassured her. "McCallister will never hurt you or Tuesday again. He's dead."

"You said that earlier, and I was so glad to see you and to get away from Tommy Lee, it just didn't sink in. What happened to him?" Patty didn't know whether to laugh or cry.

Paul Frank told her everything, starting with the attack on the World Trade Center and ending with the death of her father.

"Wow! How can I possibly take all that in? I guess that was what Tuesday meant about my coming home, that there're things going on that I don't know about. I'm scared to think that we may be at war and lives are being lost, but I'm so relieved I don't have my father shadowing me any more. The man my father wrote the note to must be the one that Tommy Lee's helping. The man that is—was— working with my father."

"How does Tommy Lee get here and back? Do you know?"

"The man working with Tommy Lee drives an old, black Cadillac. I saw it parked outside the few times that Tommy Lee came in to bring me water and food, if you could call it food. Once he brought dried-out biscuits, something I'd thought I'd never have to eat again since escaping the mountain with you, Tuesday, and Mary Lou four years ago. Another time, he brought a chunk of meat he'd torn from a roast. It was so poorly prepared and preserved that I almost gagged just on the smell of it, but when you get *that* hungry you'll eat anything." She sobbed again.

Paul Frank took her in his arms. "The proprietor at the boardinghouse told me that she saw a man in a black Cadillac pick Tommy Lee up just across the street from the boardinghouse a few times," he said, his chin resting on her dark head.

"That's him," Patty said, "the man working with him at the mansion. He was rude and brutal looking, and Tommy Lee called him Ike. Paul Frank, where is he now?" Patty cried suddenly. "We don't know where Ike or Tommy Lee is."

"I know, and I won't feel that you're safe until we know where the both of them are, preferably behind bars."

After retrieving the car keys, Patty and Paul Frank drove their respective vehicles into town and headed for The General Store for a soda and some fast food for Patty.

Patty had been secretly worried about her doll and what Tommy Lee might have done to her out of meanness, and she had been relieved to see Summer propped up in the front seat of the car, just where she had left her. She was glad to have the doll with her now.

After The General Store, the next stop was Sheriff Ozzie Moats' office.

Patty was apprehensive that the sheriff would fail to bring Harris and Hillberry to justice for taking her hostage, leaving them to come after her again. Tommy Lee, a genuine chauvinist just like her father, was too poor and uneducated to come after her in Wheeling, so she wasn't so concerned about him. But Ike Harris had the means to go anywhere he wanted; he could come after her wherever she was.

Paul Frank opened the door to the sheriff's office and waited as Patty, brushing potato chip crumbs from her blouse, stepped inside and confronted the sheriff. "With no thanks to you, I've just survived being held against my will with little food or water."

The sheriff sat at his desk looking annoyed at Patty's outburst, frowning as the two young people entered the room. "What're you doin' here again, boy? Haven't I told you I'm tired of puttin' up with your unfounded claims?"

"What do you mean, unfounded claims?" Paul Frank bellowed.

"Your tellin' me that that girl there was missin'," red-faced with anger, his finger pointed at Patty, Moats continued, "when she's runnin' the mountain with the likes of you." The sheriff threw out his arms in as if encompassing the entire mountain "That's what I mean."

"Sheriff, you're constantly jumping to conclusions. Only an hour ago Patty here was locked in Tommy Lee Hillberry's shed. There's a dead body in there, too, wrapped in an old army blanket. I want you to arrest him immediately."

"I came here before cleaning up so you could see what I've gone through," Patty exclaimed. "And all you can say is that you're tired of unfounded claims."

"Wait a doggone minute," the sheriff barked and brown spittle sprayed from his mouth. "I make the decisions around here. I'll not have a wet-behind-the-ears city boy tellin' me how to run my town!"

"Sheriff, there's a dead girl in Tommy Lee's shed, and he is responsible."

"Just who *is* this girl?" the sheriff asked.

"We're not sure," Paul Frank answered, "but Patty thinks it might be one of Frank Dillon's women. One thing for sure, we know that Tommy Lee killed her."

"Did he confess to it?" Ozzie spat.

"Yes, as a matter of fact he did," Patty said.

"You don't even have a name for this girl."

"Just because we don't know who it is doesn't mean there's no body. We were never around Frank Dillon's family much because they never attended school or church. Anyway, it's been a couple of years since I've seen any of them, and that was briefly, at the courthouse in Wheeling, when my pa and Frank Dillon were on trial, so I can't be sure," Patty said sheepishly. "I was too frightened being locked up with a dead body to look at it. I didn't, until Paul Frank came for me, and even then I didn't take a good look."

"What evidence do you have against Tommy Lee, Mr. Big-feelin' City Boy?" The sheriff asked Paul Frank, ignoring Patty. In his irrational anger, he arose from his chair with too much intensity, jarring the desk forward.

"For starters, the girl's body is in the same shed Tommy Lee locked Patty in. I mean, it doesn't take a brain surgeon to figure it out," Paul Frank said. "Plus, weren't you listening? He admitted to it to Patty."

"That's right. Tommy Lee told me that he didn't mean to kill her, that he only wanted a girlfriend," Patty offered. "It's almost like he has no idea that he did something wrong."

"I'm supposed to take the word of an ignorant mountain girl in such a serious matter?" Ozzie's nostrils flared, and he pounded on the desk with a closed fist. .

"In other words, a female doesn't have the brains to testify against a man?" Paul Frank spat.

"I'm taking Patty to Annabelle, and just so you know, I've called Cliff Moran. He'll bring in the proper authorities to take care of the situation. It's glaringly obvious now, and from past experience, that you have no intention of doing your job."

Leaving Ozzie muttering unintelligibly in his frenzy at the mention of outside lawmen sticking their noses in what he considered his business, Paul Frank guided Patty out the door and helped her into her car. He hurried to his truck, prepared to follow her up the mountain.

Ozzie had no intention of arresting Tommy Lee, and he was furious about Paul Frank's interference. Compared to Cliff Moran and his back-up detectives, though, Paul Frank was a mere fly in the ointment. Ozzie Moats could handle him.

Up until the time that his brother Aubry was arrested, along with McCallister and others, for being involved in selling children, Ozzie had constantly lived with a deep fear that Aubry would get caught and drag their good name through the mud, making a laughingstock of Ozzie as an honored sheriff. Now that his greatest dread had happened, Ozzie continued to be protective of his family name and also of his town. Having outside lawmen crawling around his territory, intent on keeping the men from running their families as they saw fit, was out of the question. If they had to discipline their women, so be it.

The women and children gathered around Patty, genuinely delighted that she was safe. While the others talked, Annabelle dragged a washtub into the bedroom. She and Daisy began filling it, a bucket at a time, with water straight from the wood-burner, where it had been heated to a comfortable temperature, for Patty to have a much-needed bath in privacy.

Patty saw what they were doing and insisted, "I'm not

going to bathe here when I have clean clothes and all the conveniences in my room at the boardinghouse. I'm not!"

"Ya ain't safe by yourself. Ya knowed you're scared to be alone with Tommy Lee an' that man on th' loose. An' it's no trouble for us a'tall. Look, we've filled th' tub with hot water. All ya have to do is step in it."

Patty knew that Annabelle was right, and she was too tired and too weak from hunger to fight. She gave in. Besides, she wanted to be there when Paul Frank returned from looking for Tommy Lee. She was more than a little worried about his leg.

Forgetting their intentions of privacy, the women stayed in the room to fret over her and talk. They were trying to be helpful. Between them Daisy and Sara found an outfit from their meager belongings for Patty to wear.

While the others fussed, Aggie sat on the four-poster bed, looking thoughtfully at Patty, who sat scrunched in the round washtub with her back pressed against the galvanized ridges, her heels pressed uncomfortably against her buttocks, her feet set on the bottom with her toes flattened against the lower ridges of the tub, and her knees tucked under her chin.

"Tell me 'bout life in th' big city," Aunt Aggie asked, preparing to open the subject of her nephew.

"I'm surprised that you want to hear about that," Patty said, lathering the soap briskly on the ragged washcloth. Bubbles dripped onto her knees, which shined wetly where they jutted above the water line. As she bent to reach her feet, her chin touched her knees and became covered with the same soapy bubbles. "I've tried to talk to you about it and you never listened before."

"What I'm wantin' to knowed, so I do, is 'bout what kind of things your pa was doin' in th' city. Did he have a woman?"

"Aunt Aggie, I haven't seen Pa since I've been living in Wheeling."

"Ya tellin' me that ya didn't see your pa even once?" Aggie said. "I can't believe that, so I can't. Why ya'd be passin' 'im on th' street sometimes, so ya would."

"What would you know about life in the city?"

"I knowed more than ya think. I've been to th' city. I'll tell ya about it one day, so I will."

Patty was not convinced. "Oh, Aunt Aggie, the city's so big you could go a lifetime and not pass the same person twice."

"Okay then, I knowed ya knowed things from ya dreams, an I want to hear 'bout them, so I do."

"Oh, you do, do you? How come you never wanted to listen when I was little and needed someone to help me understand what they were all about?"

"There was no point then in encouraging' ya to act like an old woman that people thinks is crazy, especially when she just happens to be your grandmother, an' we didn't want no one to knowed it."

"I would have wanted to know it, Aunt Aggie," Patty said. She was becoming increasingly uncomfortable with the ridges in the bottom of the tub cutting into her buttocks. She leaned over the side of the washtub, feeling for a towel. Gracefully, under the circumstances, she stood and wrapped the towel around her body and stepped from the tub.

"I would have never been ashamed of my own kin," Patty admonished.

"That ain't what I'm here to talk 'bout, so it ain't. I'm wantin' to talk 'bout your pa. I just ain't goin' to believe he's dead, so I ain't."

"Aunt Aggie, there's nothing to tell. Paul Frank believes that Pa's dead, and so do I."

"Ya mean ya just hope he's dead. I knowed how ya feel 'bout your own pa, so I do. Ya knowed somethin', so ya do. I can see it in your eyes. I think ya knowed your pa's not dead, an' ya just don't want to admit it. Ya knowed it by your dreams, so ya do."

"Aunt Aggie, don't make me sorry that I didn't just go back to the boardinghouse to clean up and wait for Paul Frank."

Paul Frank spotted Joe's truck first, then spied him leaning against the theater, one leg bent with his foot on the building behind him, chewing on the stem of a dried leaf, and looking as if he didn't have a care in the world. He was watching the light traffic, motor and foot, going up and down Main Street.

"Hi, Joe." Paul Frank pulled alongside where Joe was. "I found Patty. She's with Annabelle and the others."

"Got to say, I'm glad," Joe said, taking the leaf momentarily from his mouth. "I've run outta places to look. Did that snake Tommy Lee have her?"

"He did. Did you know your father was building a huge house at Short Run, about twenty miles from here?"

"My father never tells me anything," Joe said, his demeanor making it crystal clear that the subject was closed.

"I mean, you must know something, living in the same house and all."

"Hate to disappoint you, but I don't know anythin' about my pa's business."

"Ever hear him talking about Ike Harris or Tommy Lee?"

"No! Did you take Tommy Lee to the sheriff?" Joe switched to the subject at hand.

"Didn't. He got away, and we haven't found him again. I need your help. I mean, the sheriff's not interested in justice, and I'm not looking for any help from him."

"The law up here ain't goin' to do nothin' to Tommy Lee. On the mountain it's fittin' for a man to do whatever he wants to his women. But me, now, I have no problem with givin' Tommy Lee his due for botherin' Patty," Joe said and pushed off from the building he was leaning on.

"He killed a girl, too. The body was left in a corner wrapped in an army blanket, like a discarded piece of rubbish, in the same place he had Patty," Paul Frank said.

"Do you know who it was?" Joe looked alarmed. Big Bessie had told Joe that Sally Ann had gone off and not come back.

"No, but Patty thinks it's one of Frank Dillon's women."

"Mr. Big-Feelin' Law Man, I'm afraid you might be right. Sally Ann's been missin' for over a week now," Joe said through gritted teeth. "I'm responsible for them till Frank gets outta jail.

I have two reasons now to get that little weasel!"

"Just hold on there," Paul Frank said, stopping Joe as he made a move for his truck. "Don't take the law into your own hands, or you may be the one whose standing inside a jail cell, staring back out from between iron bars."

"Not to worry," Joe said. "I'm not goin' to kill him."

"I think that Tommy Lee's not only stupid, he's a brick short of a load. I mean, more than that, he's dangerous," Paul Frank said. "So watch yourself."

"Are you kidding? I can handle it. I may not be a fancy lawman like you, but I can handle myself," Joe said, "and you'd be smart not to forget it. By the way, how'd he kill her?"

"We don't know. We didn't examine the body. It was obvious that the girl had been dead for a while."

"Crap!" Joe threw the leaf with the in the street and headed for his truck. "Sally Ann was one of my favorites since, thanks to you, Mary Lou ran away." He jerked the truck door open, turned back toward Paul Frank, and called, "I haven't forgotten either. I'll get you for it too. Just you wait and see. Boy, you'd betta take care of that leg. Looks nasty."

Paul Frank watched as Joe swung into the driver's seat, revved his engine, peeled out, roared out the cobblestone street, and disappeared among the outcropping rocks and pines as he headed up the mountain.

Just then Deputy Jess Willis came from the alley next to the sheriff's office. He stepped from the shade into the sunlight on the boardwalk. Seeing the deputy appear from out of the shadows, Paul Frank crossed the street. "What's up, Jess?"

"The usual. Nothing." Jess smiled and shrugged. "Did you find Patty Moran yet?" he asked.

Just in time to mock Jess's question, Sheriff Moats came out to see what was going on. "You mean did you find Patty McCallister?" He spat, obviously not liking that his deputy used Patty's adoptive name, since he hated Cliff Moran even more than he hated the mountain people living above his beloved town. "I'll answer that question. No, he didn't find her 'cause she wasn't missin'. She's an ignorant mountain girl, and everyone knows that you can't make a silk purse outta a sow's ear."

Not favoring the sheriff with a response, Paul Frank updated Jess Willis about Patty's ordeal. "The sheriff knows that we found her," Paul Frank said. "I mean, we came here first to make a report. Tommy Lee Hillberry had her locked up at a building site on Short Run."

"And you're telling Jess this because—?" Ozzie asked, stepping forward, not liking to be upstaged by his deputy.

"Sheriff, you're the most uncooperative lawman I've ever met. I mean, it does the rest of us a disservice when anyone uses the title of sheriff on you. Anyway, we need to find Tommy Lee fast. He's a danger to the young girls around here. Jess, when you find him put him in a cell until Cliff Moran gets here with the marshal."

"I don't need you tellin' me what to do. You don't have no evidence that Tommy Lee killed the girl," Ozzie spat. "I'd say you'd do better to take care of that leg than stick your nose in my business."

"As an officer of the law, I'm telling you to see that he's locked up," Paul Frank demanded. "You'd be wise to have him in your custody by the time Cliff Moran gets here. By the way, Joe McCallister said that Sally Ann, Frank Dillon's woman, has been missing for a few days. She could be the girl in Tommy Lee's shanty!"

Paul Frank turned and without another word climbed inside his truck. Enough time had passed for Patty to have her bath, and Paul Frank made his way back up the mountain trail.

Reaching the path leading to the back of the cabin where Frank Dillon's wives lived, Sara broke into a run. She waved at Big Bessie, who had appeared on the back porch to see who was running toward the cabin. "Hi, Bessie, it's me, Sara McCallister."

"I was hopin' it was Sally Ann," Big Bessie said, wringing a dishtowel nervously in her hands.

"Why ya lookin' for Sally Ann? Where could she be, anyway? She don't have no where to go."

"Well, she's been gone for days. I don't keep track of time very good, but I knowed she's been gone a week or more."

"Oh! How strange! Patty's back on th' mountain, an' she's been missin' since after th' second day she'd came, an' ya all have a girl gone, too."

"What do ya think happened?" Big Bessie asked.

"I sure don't knowed," Sara said, stepping onto the porch. "It's strange, both of them missin'."

"Maybe Patty took Sally Ann an' ran away to th' city like she done before, when she'd run from ya all's pa an' taken our Mary Lou with her."

"No, she don't have anything to run away from. She came home drivin' a fancy car an' all. She wouldn't have gone back to th' city without sayin' goodbye, an' she sure wouldn't have taken Sally Ann without tellin' ya, unless Sally Ann was in trouble somehow. She told me she wanted to visit with ya all while she was on th' mountain so she could let Mary Lou know, when she got back to th' city, how ya'll're gettin' on. Anyway, that's why I thought she might be here."

"I told Joe that Sally Ann had gone off somewhere an' not come back when he brought our supplies th' other day. He was real mad that I didn't knowed where she'd gone to. He didn't believe th' ruffians a'round here had enough nerve to bother a woman he was in charge of, an' thought maybe she'd gone off with a man she fancied, an' ya knowed how that'd set with 'im. I told 'im that was a laugh. I don't knowed where she'd meet a man bein' stuck in this cabin with only women an' children to talk to."

"I've been wonderin' 'bout it, ya knowed, if Joe was bringin' ya all what ya need," Sara said. "I knowed Pa would have expected 'im to. Like your Frank did for us when Pa was on th' run."

"Yeah, he does."

"That's what I suspected."

"Well, Sara, come in an' sit for a spell," Big Bessie invited and turned to open the screen door to let Sara pass through.

Melverta and Emma Jean were at the table peeling apples for Big Bessie to make applesauce to fill the many canning jars that covered one end of the huge table. "Sara, what a nice surprise. I never thought I'd set eyes on ya again!"

"I didn't either, but Patty's gone off an' not come back. I thought I'd check to see if for some reason she'd come here an' didn't come back 'cause she got sick or somethin'. An' like I told Big Bessie, I was curious if Joe was takin' care of ya like Frank Dillon did us when Pa was runnin' from th' law."

"It's a shame isn't it?" Melverta said. "'Cause Frank an' your pa never allowed us to visit no one, I guess we just got in th' mind of keepin' to ourselves even with them gone, but visitin' one another's nice, an' I'm glad to see ya.

I suppose Big Bessie told ya that Sally Ann went off an' didn't come back either."

"Yeah." Sara said.

"Ya have any ideas 'bout where Sally Ann could be?" Emma Jean asked.

"No. No more than I have an idea where Patty is, but we need to keep in touch so's when we find one of 'em we let th' others knowed."

A half dozen rocking chairs were arranged around the potbelly stove below the loft, where bed mats were strewn over most of the floor. Rocking companionably, Sara and the women enjoyed their visit. Sara had feared Big Bessie when she lived in Dillon's cabin; now, to her surprise, she found that talking with her was a treat. The younger girls had started attending school, knowing that Frank Dillon would not approve of their getting an education. They were well aware that Joe would have forbidden it, on Frank's behalf, but did not have the fear of Joe they had of Dillon, who was in prison and out of their lives for a very long time.

Except for Big Bessie, who waited patiently for Frank Dillon's release, the girls were intent upon getting away from their life of poverty. Big Bessie kept their plans from Joe but threatened to divulge them to him if the young women disobeyed her. They knew the threat to be backed up by the power of her ham-like arm, which was quick to swing at an offending girl's head at the slightest provocation.

The girls were not the oldest students in the school. Others were attending who were older than the average student, having been held back for poor attendance or illness, many having being kept home too often to help parents with the never-ending chores.

"Do ya all ever see Tommy Lee?"

"Yeah, we do," Melverta said, "but only after school. Ya knowed he don't go anymore, an' he's usually drunk by th' time it lets out. I bet he don't get outta bed till noon."

"Has he ever bothered ya?"

"Are ya kiddin'? He's always askin' for one of us to go on a date with 'im," Melverta said. "We all're a little scart of 'im, especially Emma Jean. When he's around, she goes to stutterin' so bad ya can't understand her a'tall."

"Y-y-ya're a-a-a-ways b-b-b-ein' mean, t-t-to me, M-m-melverta," Emma Jean stuttered, throwing a wet dishcloth at her.

"He even likes Melverta," Eva Belle said laughing, grabbing the dishtowel from Melverta's shoulder where it had landed. "He ain't even carin' that she looks more like a boy than a girl."

Sara smiled and changed the tone of the conversation. "My sister Patty came home for a visit, an' we're thinkin' Tommy Lee took her to his place," Sara said. "Do ya knowed where that could be?"

"No." Melverta looked around for confirmation and, looking back at Sara, shrugged. "I do knowed that there's a gang of boys, led by Robby Rudd, meetin' in th' tunnel. Remember th' one th' militia was tryin' to tunnel into with th 'one they was buildin'?"

"What 'bout them?" Sara asked.

"For one thing Robby struts 'round with a rifle, an' he's crazy enough to use it if he feels threatened. They terrorize the young girls around here, an' go stealin' 'round th' county. Stealin's how they stock food an' household stuff for their clubhouse, as they call it."

"Them b-boys an' T-t-t-tommy L-l-lee's d-d-dangerous," Emma Jean said. "T-t-they've hurt some o-o-of t-th' y-y-younger g-g-girls in s-s-school. E-e-everyone knows it t-t-too."

"Yeah," Melverta said. "But Tommy Lee's always botherin' us th' most, sayin' he's goin' to get hisself a girlfriend, an' mark my word, he'll do whatever he has to do to get her. Th' others just want to rape an' torment th' girls, then they let 'em go, but Tommy Lee wants to keep 'em locked in his place."

"I didn't knowed they was hangin' 'round in th' tunnel," Sara said. "I bet Joe knows, though. He don't tell me nothin', an' I don't knowed nothin'. All I do is take care of Kelly Sue an' Daisy's twins."

"Tommy Lee's pa's always hittin' an' beatin' 'im, tellin' 'im he ain't no good," Eva Belle said. Her huge blue eyes looked too large in the small face that hovered above her petite frame. "Ain't no wonder he's bein' so mean."

"Yeah, I knowed he's mean all right," Sara said. "He was always after Patty when we was goin' to school in town. He always watched for his chance when Joe wasn't around, an' he'd try to make her talk to 'im. Her mistake was she felt sorry for 'im an' talked to 'im."

"He's too crazy to talk to," Melverta said. "He's no good a'tall. Drinkin' all th' time, an' watchin' th' girls with his tongue hangin' out."

"Maybe one of th' boys has Patty confined in th' tunnel," Sara guessed.

"It could be," Melverta said. There's no way we could knowed."

"I've enjoyed talkin' to ya, an' we'll keep in touch 'bout this," Sara said, "but I'd better get back home to th' kids. Th' others don't have no patience with them. And I need to tell Paul Frank an' Joe 'bout th' tunnel right away."

"If those boys have 'em, I sure feel sorry for 'em," Emma Jean said.

Melverta and Emma Jean offered to walk halfway with Sara, knowing they'd enjoy their time away from the cabin. They were loath to end the chance to talk to someone other than their sister wives.

Sara got to her feet and, bidding Big Bessie goodbye, followed Melverta and Emma Jean out to the path going up the mountain. Single file, they climbed up the first part of the steep trail leading to the cabin Sara shared with Annabelle, the children, and Daisy.

Feeling clean once again after her primitive bath in the washtub, Patty dressed as she continued to answer the women's questions. At the same time, the children, allowed back in the room now that she was dressed, vied for her attention, going undisciplined by the adults.

The huge question on the women's minds was if Tommy Lee had raped Patty. "I thank God that the only hardships that I suffered were fear, hunger, thirst, and loneliness," Patty declared, putting the others' minds at ease. "Tommy Lee was very drunk, and from all his drinking and poor nutrition he was pretty unstable."

With a slam of the screen door, Sara came into the kitchen in time to hear the tail end of the conversation. "Oh, Patty, I'm so glad your safe. Where've ya been?"

"Tommy Lee had me locked in a shed at Pa's mansion." Patty resigned herself to another round of questions.

"I was thinkin' one of th' mountain boys had ya in th' tunnel. I just found out that the ones led by Robby Rudd have a club in th' tunnels, an' they take girls there. Melverta said they go around stealin' from folks' houses to fix it up."

"I heard Daisy mention 'bout that a time or two," Annabelle said. "I never thought much 'bout it though. It didn't surprise me that th' boys would use th' abandoned tunnel for a hideout."

"Hideout?" Sara said. "Sounds like they're hidin' from th' law, th' way ya put it."

"Maybe they are." Annabelle arched her eyebrows.

"I don't think Joe's tied up with them," Sara said, "but I've heard that he gets them to do his dirty work for 'im some times."

"I don't believe that a'tall," Annabelle declared. "Now Tommy Lee hangs with 'em sometimes, but Joe's like 'is father, not mixin' with the no-good mountain men."

"Did he rape ya, Patty?" Sara disregarded her mother's disclaimer.

"No. He just starved me," Patty said, her eyes huge in her pale face. "But, let me tell you, I was afraid the whole time that he was going to rape and kill me. And if I'd known about the Rudd boy and his gang hanging out in the tunnel, I'd have been scared out of my mind that Tommy Lee was planning to take me there."

"I'm happy ya didn't get hurt that a'way," Annabelle said. "I guess ya don't need a youngin in your life, now that ya're gettin' an education an' all."

"Ma, what about me?" Sara said. "She don't need a youngin' without a husband like I have it! Look at me, I'm tied down with my daughter, an' I can't finish my education or be out where I'd meet a man to marry, an' anyway we all know no man would marry a woman that was ill used by another man, especially one that has a child outta wedlock."

Patty flinched. In her eyes, she was in the same situation, except she did not have a child. And she didn't believe that not having a child made her any more marriageable.

"I didn't knowed ya felt that way," Annabelle said, watching Sara as she darted after Kelly Sue, who was getting clobbered by Drexel on one side and Dakota on the other.

Sara scooped her daughter from the floor just in time for the child to miss a hit to her nose from Drexel. "Ma, I'm a woman, not someone's baby maker. I want a life just like anyone else. I want a husband an' my own home filled with children with the two of us takin' responsibility for 'em."

Annabelle stood and went over to Sara and took her in her arms. "I guess I don't think of life out of these walls 'cause I don't have dealin's with others. Why, it takes all my energy just makin' sure we survive, an' ya was always hangin' onto Joe. Ya was even jealous when he looked at one of Frank's women."

"That was then, Ma, but I know better now. Believe it or not, I learned a lot in th' city too. It wasn't just Daisy learnin'. Th' difference with Daisy an' me is, she wants to take what she learned an' live in th' city, where I want to take what I learned an' stay on th' mountain just like ya, Ma. Except I'd like to go to th' movie theater an' to th' barn dances they have in town. I'd like to go to church an' get to know other people to do those things with. Anyway, I was just feelin' sorry for myself. Go on an' sit down. Right now we need to see 'bout Patty."

"Yeah," Annabelle agreed, "but I'll not forget that ya have needs too. Ya're too young to be stuck only carin' for th' youngins an' havin' nothin' for yourself."

Sara patted her mother on the back. "With bein' excited 'bout Patty gettin' back safe, I didn't tell ya everythin' about my visit with Frank Dillon's women. They're worried 'cause Sally Ann's missin'. She's been gone for over a week now."

"Oh, no!" Patty sobbed.

25

*A*FTER WALKING SARA PART WAY HOME, MELVERTA AND Emma Jean took advantage of the occasion to go into town, leaving Big Bessie to believe they were still with Sara. Every time they got the chance to hang out at The General Store, where they liked to look at the clothes and other merchandise, they took it. As they neared town reaching the foot of the mountain, they came upon Tommy Lee, who was headed to town as well. Having no interest in shopping, he was on his way to get drunk at the bar.

Out of boredom rather than spitefulness, and heedless of the danger she put Sara in, Melverta made a point of telling him that Sara was at their cabin, asking a lot of questions about him, intentionally giving the impression that Sara was interested in him.

Melverta walked on for a few feet and tauntingly called to Tommy Lee, "Heard that you had a date with Patty McCallister."

Stupidly believing that Patty had enjoyed his company, Tommy Lee grinned widely. Puffing up his chest, he said, "I guess that really important information gets 'round town pretty fast.

Who told ya'?"

"Sara. Guess she's jealous," Melverta lied.

"M-m-melverta, ya're bein' mean, t-tryin' to s-start t-t-t-trouble," Emma Jean said. "H-h-he's goin' t-t-o p-plague t-t-them t-to death now."

The women had not let up on their endless questions to Patty when Paul Frank returned from town.

"Patty, can I talk to you?"

"Sure. What is it?"

"Let's go for a walk."

"What about your leg?"

"It's okay for now," Paul Frank said, "I'll take care of it."

They left the cabin and walked toward the barn with Paul Frank limping slightly. Patty grabbed his arm and pulled him the other way. "I don't want to go in the barn. It has too many bad memories."

"Okay," Paul Frank said. "I mean, I don't want to upset you."

"Let's go down this path a little ways," Patty said. "When I was in school, this is where Joe and Sara left me to wait for them when they went off to be alone. I was supposed to wait for them before I went home because Pa would know we were back from school and weren't doing our chores. Come on, I'll show you."

Patty led Paul Frank to the site where she used to sit and think, throwing pebbles over the side of the cliff and waiting after she threw each one to hear it hit the rock ledges below.

"We can talk here."

They sat at the edge of the cliff where an outcropping boulder made a comfortable bench from which to view the magnificent valley below.

Paul Frank took Patty's hand and looked into her eyes. Patty turned her face away and withdrew her hand.

"What's wrong, Patty?" Paul Frank asked, looking surprised at her rejection.

"Nothing." Patty said a little too sharply. "You said you wanted to talk."

"Yes. I had planned to wait until I was more established and had more to offer, but when I thought I had lost you forever, I decided to tell you how I feel now."

"Please, don't!" Tears filled Patty's eyes.

"What's wrong? I've been sure that you felt the same as I."

"You'd be better off with someone else."

"Patty," Paul Frank said, taking her chin in his palm, "everyone thought you were crazy about me. What happened?"

"I don't want to talk about it now," Patty said as she turned her head away from him again. *I'm not good enough for any man after what Pa did to me,* she thought.

"Okay, I understand," Paul Frank said, although he did not. "Let's go back to the cabin. I need to connect with Cliff, and I haven't been able to find that snake Tommy Lee yet. We'll talk later. Okay?"

"Okay," Patty said, "but right now I want to tell you what Sara found out." She told him about the gang that used the tunnel.

"Did she tell you who any of them were?"

"She said Robby Rudd is their leader, and he carries a gun. He's the son of the bar owner where Daisy works."

On the way back Paul Frank called Cliff's cell phone. "How soon are you going to get here?"

"We're about an hour and half out," Cliff said. "We stopped to eat after I spoke to you last. I'll meet you at the boardinghouse."

"Fine, see you there. I've got a lot to tell you."

They walked up to the truck they had left parked at the cabin, and Paul Frank put his phone inside. "Since I'm scheduled to meet Cliff in an hour and half, I'm going to scout around to see if I can find Tommy Lee," he said to Patty.

"Sure, Paul Frank," Patty said, relieved not to have to explain her feelings until she sorted them in her own mind. She really needed to speak to Tuesday about them. "I'm going to visit with Sara a while. She needs to talk. I'll meet you and Cliff at the boardinghouse."

"Okay, I'll see you then."

"You know, Paul Frank, I'm surprised that Cliff is still coming to the mountain, since you've rescued me and we know that it was Tommy Lee."

"Well, we're interested in this Ike Harris," Paul Frank said. "And you said yourself that the house your father was building is identical to the one in your dreams. Cliff wants to check it out."

"We both know you can't arrest a man for building a house," Patty said, sorry for the sadness and hurt she now saw in Paul Frank's eyes because of her refusal to discuss their relationship. But she did not know what to do; she could not tell him of the sexual abuse she suffered as a child. After the conversations she'd had with her grandmother and with Sara, she very much needed to talk to Tuesday about what she should do. Was she not good enough for a decent man because of her past? Even Sara believed that she herself was no longer considered fit to marry.

Paul Frank laughed. "No, I can't arrest a man for building a house, but I think he can be charged as an accessory to a crime. And, Patty, I'm not through with our conversation. Somehow I know you feel the same for me as I do for you. I'm not taking no for an answer."

"Paul Frank, I—"

"We'll talk when I get back,' he interrupted her.

"Okay, that's fair enough," Patty said.

"I wish you'd tell me now what's bothering you, though."

AFTER LEAVING PATTY AT THE CABIN, PAUL FRANK ventured back to the mansion where she had been held. He intended to question Ike Harris, and he had a suspicion that Tommy Lee was hiding out there. When he arrived at the huge mansion, Paul Frank pulled his truck to the side of the road and parked in the same spot he had earlier. Leaving the truck and walking along the gated property's boundary line, Paul Frank could visualize Patty standing at the side of the road, as she had described in her dreams, looking left and right with the dead leaves swirling around her ankles.

As Paul Frank drew closer to the mansion, he heard a series of swift movements to his right and swinging around him.

Suddenly, a twig snapped behind him, and he turned. He was eye to eye with the barrel of a gun.

The blast of the gunshot echoed long after Paul Frank fell to the ground.

*P*ATTY, HEAVY-HEARTED, REMAINED AT THE CABIN UNTIL she felt it was time to meet Paul Frank at the boarding-house. It was a much-needed quiet time, and spending it with her half sister Sara was proving to be good for her. Maybe she could forget her own problems by trying to help Sara with hers.

"What have you been doing besides taking care of the children and helping Annabelle with the chores?" Patty asked, starting the conversation.

"That's it, Patty. Th' youngins keep me busy nearly all my wakin' hours. Anyway, I think it'd be more interestin' to hear 'bout your life."

"I love living in the city, Sara. There's always something to do. I've made a few friends in school, and Winter Ann, Mary Lou, and I have become like sisters." Patty noticed Sara looked a little hurt and suspected that she was jealous that Mary Lou, someone she had only met a couple of years ago, had become more of a sister to Patty than Sara had ever been.

"You know, Sara, given the circumstances, we did pretty well as sisters. I love you a lot."

"I feel th' same way, but I guess I was always afraid of your talk of dreams an' such," Sara admitted, looking sheepish. "I was jealous of ya an' Joe, too, an' I knowed betta than that now. It did me a world of good just visitin' th' city an' livin' with Frank Dillon's women. They was th' first real friends I ever had. Ya knowed th' way it was, th' kids at school had no use for us."

"What did you think of the city when you were taken there for questioning?"

"At th' time I was afraid of it," Sara said. "There's so much I didn't understand, an' I knowed that I couldn't take care of myself there. It was too foreign. Ya was doin' okay there, but ya had Tuesday and Cliff."

"They would have helped you," Patty said. "They still would. So would I."

"Maybe someday, but for now, I really want to stay here. Since pa's dead, I'm not worried 'bout Joe, an' I'm goin' to do th' things I never have. Daisy has offered to pay me for watchin' her twins, an' I can go to th' movies, get back to goin' to church, meetin' people my age."

"Sara, that won't last long, because without a doubt, Daisy is moving to the city, and you absolutely must get a job. You cannot continue to be dependant on Joe the rest of your life."

Preoccupied with her work, Annabelle made her way from the children's bedroom to the kitchen with her arms loaded down with dirty clothes. "I got th' water boilin'. Sara get th' washtub for me. It's still sittin' at th' foot of th' four poster with Patty's bath water in it."

"Come on, Sara. I'll help you." Patty said.

The two girls half dragged, half carried the tub, swinging it from side to side, slopping water, from the bedroom, across the kitchen, and out the back door. They emptied the tub well away from the cabin, keeping the area around the place dry. Then they carried it back into the kitchen, where Annabelle filled it with hot water from the large pot heating on the stove.

Taking a washboard from its place on a spike nail behind the potbelly stove, she stood it inside the tub. Next, she dropped the children's clothes in the tub and added a little soap. "Sara, ya knowed I can't get on my knees no more. Get busy an' start scrubbin' th' clothes."

"I'll wash some, too," Patty offered. She knelt at the side of the tub, picked out a small shirt, and firmly scrubbed it up and down the rough ridges of the washboard. She held the shirt up and, dubbing it clean, tossed it in a bucket of cold water Annabelle had sat alongside the tub for rinsing.

"Sara, there's no need to work so hard. You remember in the city there's water inside for washing, bathing, and cooking. There are machines for washing clothes and drying them."

Looking grateful for Patty's help, Sara smiled and said, "Maybe someday."

As they worked quietly, Patty tried to swallow the miserable lump in her throat. She had not wanted to put Paul Frank off, but she didn't know how to tell him about the childhood rape at the hands of her father or the relationship she had had for a short time with her half brother. *I don't know what I was thinking, planning to invite him to my senior party,* she thought. *I don't know why I just didn't admit all along that I'm damaged goods.* She stifled a sob. In the back of her mind, especially when she was with her young, carefree classmates, she'd always felt defiled.

"What's wrong, Patty? Ya look like ya're goin' to cry."

Patty forced a smile. "Nothing really. I just had a bad feeling." She shrugged her shoulders. "You know, a sick feeling in the pit of my stomach. It's happened before, when something bad happened. I'm glad to be here visiting with you. I'd like to help you make your life better, if you'll let me." Patty reached out and took Sara's soapy hand in her own.

"Since Pa's gone, I really feel like I can do it," Sara smiled, "but ya knowed I'm goin' to have to battle Ma. She thinks we have to live just like Pa and Joe want, like we don't have minds of our own. I'll have to fight her, but I promise, I'm goin' to start doin' what I want to do for a change. Just like ya an' Daisy are. I don't want to die like Rose did, not even once havin' any pleasures in my life."

Patty smiled encouragingly and then suddenly looked at her watch. "I should be going now. I'm supposed to meet Cliff and Paul Frank at the boardinghouse."

"Wel-l-l-l-l, 'pon my soul!" Annabelle exclaimed, overriding the girls' conversation. "It's that detective, Cliff Moran. That nice, redheaded young man is with him."

"It's not like you didn't know he was coming!" Patty said, pushing past Annabelle in her haste to get to Cliff.

"Cliff!" Patty ran to him as Annabelle held the screen door, getting out of Patty's way. "I'm sure glad to see you. Hi, Randy."

"Patty, it's good to see you're okay," Randy said. "We were sure worried about you."

"Cliff, Randy, I think something's gone wrong."

"That's what I was afraid of when the two of you weren't waiting at the boardinghouse," Cliff said. "We left word with Melba that we'd been there, in case we'd gotten our wires crossed."

28

*H*AVE A SEAT," SARA SAID. "WOULD YA LIKE A COLD drink?"

"Thank you, Sara. I would," Cliff said, and Randy nodded his assent.

While Sara got drinks for the two men, Patty sat across from them. "Have you seen Paul Frank yet?"

"No. We came straight here. Guessed you'd be the one to know where he was," Cliff grinned.

Blushing, Patty wondered if Cliff knew about Paul Frank's feelings for her and that he had been planning to tell her how he felt about her. "I don't, except that he's been out looking for Tommy Lee. I don't know if you've been told, but Tommy Lee killed a local girl. We think she was one of Frank Dillon's women."

"Paul Frank mentioned something about it."

"It was awful. She was being held in the same shack I was." Patty shuddered. "We told the sheriff, but you know how he is. Tommy Lee is on the loose, and Paul Frank is trying to find him. I have a very bad feeling, Cliff."

Sara set a lemonade in front of Randy and one in front of Cliff.

Randy took a long drink, savoring the sweet, cool liquid.

Annabelle, ever watchful, noticed Randy wore an expression of longing each time he looked at Patty. *He's got romantic notions 'bout her. I can plainly see it in his eyes.*

"I want you to stay here, and we're going to look for Paul Frank."

"Please, Cliff, let me go with you. I know the mountain, and I want to go back to the mansion. I think that's where Paul Frank was heading."

"Your going with us sure would save a lot of time, since we've no idea how to get there."

"That settles it, then," Patty said. "Give me a minute."

"Now, Cliff, do ya think Patty should be puttin' herself in harm's way again?" Annabelle asked, stopping Patty in mid-stride as she headed for the living room to grab her light jacket.

"Dunno what ya're thinkin'," Sara said, "but I don't think Tommy Lee'd be able to hurt Patty with Cliff an' Randy 'round to protect her."

"What 'bout this Ike they're talkin' 'bout?" Aunt Aggie said. "He sounds pretty dangerous to me, so he does."

"Oh, for crying out loud, will the two of you quit worrying?" Patty said, turning on them.

"The lot of ya're acting like a dog with a bone," Sara said. "She's goin' to be safe with Cliff an' Randy, an' Paul Frank's out there somewhere too. They'll catch up with 'im."

Every time Paul Frank's name was mentioned, the sick feeling in Patty's stomach got stronger.

Too troubled about Paul Frank's failure to be at the boardinghouse as planned, Patty did not take the time to evaluate the sick feeling, and ignoring Annabelle's doom and gloom, she hurried from the room and got her light jacket. Returning to the kitchen with the sleeves tied loosely around her neck, she said, "Okay, guys. I'm ready."

Amid warnings to be careful, the three of them left the cabin.

*T*HE LIGHT WAS FADING FAST AS CLIFF, RANDY, AND PATTY made their way to the house of Patty's nightmares. It was an easy trip; Patty remembered the way very well.

As they neared the rare straight strip of road that fronted the adjacent property, Patty suggested that Cliff pull off to the side so as not to announce their arrival. They approached the mansion on foot, and she strongly sensed something out of the ordinary.

"Cliff, the place looks abandoned, and I can feel it. There's no one here."

"Good," Cliff said. "We can nose around without anyone bothering us."

They moved on, with Patty now in the lead and Randy bringing up the rear. They walked through the open gate to the walkway that led to the huge front door.

Suddenly, Patty screamed and fell to her knees.

"Victor, why do you want to change your looks? You are the handsomest man I've ever seen!" Donna Saracco asked.

"Look, Donna, I'm willing to pay you handsomely. Don't ask questions. I only want to look like someone else for a year or so. After that I can change back if I want."

"It's 'Doctor Saracco,'" Donna said.

"Oh, is that right?" he said, "It wasn't 'Doctor' last night."

"I wasn't angry with you last night. We'll have to do it here," Donna said. "The staff would be suspicious if they saw me working on a man without the slightest disfigurement, one who couldn't be more handsome."

"Who cares about them? But you, you needn't be suspicious. I have my reasons."

"I have to know more about why you want it done or I won't do it!"

"Okay, but it's embarrassing for me to tell you. I want you to have a high regard for me. How can we have a relationship if you don't?"

"Just tell me."

"I faked dying in the World Trade Center attack."

"Why, Victor? Was it insurance?"

"No, I was in a very unhappy marriage."

"Victor Newman! You led me to believe that you were not married," she spat. "I would never have gotten into a relationship with a married man knowingly. Never!"

"Okay. Okay, I'm sorry," he lied. "I wanted you that bad. Doesn't that count for something?"

"I'm not going to do it."

"Look, do you really want me to go to jail for faking my death?"

"No, of course not, but if you're not wanted for a crime, or haven't fraudulently collected insurance, I guess there's no crime in faking your own death."

"Humor me." He kissed the corner of her mouth and stroked her dark brown hair.

"All right," she relented. She had never been able to refuse the handsome man anything. "But I love the face you have."

"If you really love me, my face shouldn't matter."

"Okay, okay. When do you want it done?"

"Now. Afterward, I'll get a buzz cut. You've always said that my hair is the first thing you noticed and the biggest turn-on for women."

"Oh, yes." Donna said. "Just looking at you makes a woman want to run her fingers through that thick, black, beautiful wavy hair while gazing into your deep brown eyes."

"Blue contacts!" he said. "I would never have thought of it."

"Yes," she said, getting caught up in his enthusiasm, "and I think filling in the cleft in your chin and making your lips fuller would be sufficient to do the trick. I can change the shape of your eyes, too. We can't change your voice or your personality, though. You'll have to watch for that."

"Sounds great. I can be confident that I'll be okay, especially if I don't have any close contact with anyone who knows me well."

"Oh, yes. Passing you on the street, sitting in the same restaurant, or even in a short encounter, no one will be able to recognize you."

"Absolutely?"

"Oh, yes. I'm sure of it."

30

*T*HE WOMEN SAT AROUND THE TABLE, THEIR CHORES AND radio forgotten. The children, apparently sensing something was not right, played uncommonly quiet games just outside the back door, keeping within view of the adults at the table.

Aunt Aggie lifted her head, listening. "Sounds like Joe's truck comin', so it does."

"Wel-l-l-l, now ya knowed who's comin' by th' sound of a motor," Annabelle said.

"Dunno what your talkin' bout, so I don't. Ya're actin' like ya never noticed that I always knowed whose comin'."

Following the slam of a door, Joe leapt up on the porch, ignoring the steps and scattering the kids. He threw open the screen door, allowing it to crash against the outside wall of the log cabin. At the unusual sight of the women sitting at the table doing nothing, he stopped in mid-stride.

"What the—"

"You're goin' to unhinge that door if'n ya don't stop slammin' it thataway," Annabelle grumbled before Joe could finish.

"You all look as if something happened. Is it Patty? She's okay, isn't she?"

216

"Far as I knowed, she is," Annabelle said. "She went off with that city detective, Cliff Moran, and Randy McCoy."

"What?"

"Ya mean ya didn't knowed they was on th' mountain?" Daisy asked.

"No," Joe answered. "I had no idea."

"Where've ya been?" Annabelle asked. "Thought ya'd be long gone back to th' city by now."

"I have to get back to my job soon, but I've been helpin' to find Patty. You know that, Ma."

"Well, she's been found, so she has," Aggie said. "I'd've said you'd been back to your big money job in th' city by now."

Joe laughed. "You women don't know what big money is."

"Humph," Aggie snorted.

"I'm figurin' on settlin' up with Tommy Lee. He killed one of my women."

"One of your women?" Sara stood, knocking her cup to the floor. "Ya mean one of Frank's women, don't ya? Who do ya think ya're, a big shot? Everyone knows that those women're Frank's women."

"Frank's in prison," Joe spat.

He crossed the room and, for the first time in his life, slapped Sara, unknowingly solidifying her new resolve to make something of her life.

Annabelle gasped; he looked so much like Jeb at that moment. More than ever she realized that Joe was a carbon copy of his father and always had been.

Sara drew her hands to her face and dropped back to the bench she had been sitting on. The children clambered inside and surrounded Sara, crying in fear for her.

"Joe, sit down," Annabelle ordered. "There will be none of that in this house ever again."

Joe turned on his mother. "I'm in charge here now. Pa isn't here. He's dead, and I'd say you'd be well off to remember that, especially if you want to continue gettin' your monthly supplies. Do you understand that?"

Annabelle bristled, knowing she had to let him have the upper hand. Daisy didn't make enough money to support all of them. Besides, she was saving all she could, toward moving to the city. "I'm just sayin', I don't want ya to go mistreatin' anyone here. It ain't fittin'."

Ignoring his mother, Joe left, slamming the door behind him.

Annabelle and Aggie settled back to their radio and their chores, resigned to the men in their lives forcing their will on the women.

Sara quietly seethed.

31

*O*H, CLIFF, IT'S PAUL FRANK!" PATTY SOBBED, HOLDING his head tenderly in her lap.

Cliff knelt beside Patty and touched Paul Frank's temple, checking for a pulse. There was no mistaking—the boy was dead. There was no pulse and the warmth had already left his skin.

"I'm sorry, Patty, there's nothing we can do for him now." Cliff tried to pry Patty's right arm from around Paul Frank's torso. But ignoring Cliff, with her left hand cradling Paul Frank's head, she leaned forward and kissed his blue lips. She was not to be moved so easily, and unable to pry her free, Cliff stroked her cheek, feeling the wetness of her tears.

After a very long time, Patty sat up and wailed, "Why? Why? How did this happen?"

"I know it feels so unfair to you." Cliff held his own grief at bay, striving to be strong for his adopted daughter and to say the right thing. "But in my job people die every day. No one can predict who or why. We have to accept it when it happens."

"But, Cliff," Patty pleaded, tears streaming down her face, "why was I not warned in my dreams? Oh, my heart is breaking in two . . ."

"Patty, I don't know, and your heart will mend in time, I promise you."

"My grandmother!" Patty's eyes grew wide. "She may have had a warning dream. Please, let's go see her."

"We will, Patty. First we have to take care of Paul Frank."

"Oh, I know," she sobbed, leaning close to him again and resting her cheek against his. "I don't want to leave him here like this."

"Also, we have to find out who did this. If we don't, all our lives could be in danger."

"I'll stay with Paul Frank and you go to the nearest phone and get an ambulance up here," Patty said.

"It's too dangerous, Patty," Cliff said. "Whoever did this could come back, I'll stay with him. I can call an ambulance on my solar phone, now. You and Randy can go to the sheriff's and tell him what's going on. I think it's better to deal with him in person. We're out of Ozzie Moats' jurisdiction. Anyway it'll give him something to do. Have him call the sheriff's office in charge of this county."

"Okay." Randy had been standing quietly in the background, choking back unshed tears, so moved was he by Patty's sorrow.

Patty stumbled unsteadily to her feet.

"Are you going to be alright?" Cliff asked softly.

"I have to be," Patty answered. "Oh, Cliff, it hurts so much, I can't bear it."

Cliff had stood too, and gently put his arms around her trying to give her a measure of comfort. Patty sobbed and sobbed as if her heart actually would break just as she had said. When she had calmed down, Randy stepped in and took her arm and led her to the truck.

One by one, Joe had searched each of Tommy Lee's hangouts, including his home, and ended up at the bar. Tommy Lee was in the corner sleeping one off. Joe strode across the room, grabbed Tommy Lee by the scruff of his neck, and jerked him to his feet.

Awake, Tommy Lee swallowed his profane objection at seeing it was Joe McCallister's formidable bulk standing in front of him and holding him to his feet by only one of his powerful arms.

"What'd ya want, jerking me outta sleepin' thataway?"

"You're lucky that's all I'm doin'," Joe said. "I'm takin' you to jail where you belong. Come on!"

Crossing the room, heading for the entrance, Joe made a fine figure dragging the smaller Tommy Lee, stumbling and whining, behind.

In no time Joe was ushering Tommy Lee into the sheriff's office across the street.

"What the—" Sheriff Moats began and was struck mute by a no-nonsense look from Joe, who lifted the key ring from its peg at the entrance to the cell block.

"Sheriff, Tommy Lee confessed that he murdered Sally Ann, and in my book that's enough to hold a man."

"What you or anyone else thinks, boy, is of no consequence to me." The sheriff's face was blood red with anger; the next step would be steam whistling from his ears.

Before Ozzie could say anything more, the door flew open again, and Patty, followed by a stranger, stepped in. At closer inspection, Ozzie recognized the man as a city detective who had been involved with Cliff Moran in the investigation of the militia two years ago. Ozzie kicked his chair. It spun around twice before it banged into his desk and came to a stop.

By that time, Joe had Tommy Lee locked in a cell and was replacing the key ring back on its peg.

"Sheriff, I'm Randy McCoy. Maybe you remember me from the last time I was here. Patty and I have come to report another murder."

Angrily, Ozzie swung his chair back to face his desk, still showing his displeasure at the intrusion into his domain. He sank heavily into the comfortable cushion.

Patty's face was still wet from the deluge of tears.

Joe noticed her distress. "Patty, what is it?"

"Paul Frank has been killed," she sobbed.

'I'll handle this!" Ozzie left his chair. He swung around his desk, shouldering his oversized form between the other men and Patty. "Where did it happen?"

"There's a mansion at Short Run. It's being restored. I believe my father is—was—the one having the work done."

In the background, Tommy Lee was hollering to be let out. "I ain't done nothin'. Let me outta here. If ya let me outta here, I'll tell ya who done it."

"Keep your mouth shut," Joe said. "Or I'd be more than happy to shut it for you. Just remember you're the one bein' held for murder."

"Ya just got th' word of a girl, an' ya knowed nobody's goin' to listen to her. She's just cleaned-up mountain trash—"

'Hold it!" Randy demanded. "This quarreling is going to get us no where."

"I knowed who killed Paul Frank," Tommy Lee said. "I heard 'im sayin' he was goin' to kill Paul Frank. I heard it with my own ears."

Ozzie fumed intensely; he had not bothered to check out the murder, and as a result had effectively invited the city lawman to take over. He himself would never arrest a man for killing a woman, but he should have foreseen what would happen, what with Paul Frank Ruble nosing around. He would have been better off doing things by the book. Now they knew he had not even taken the time to look up Tommy Lee for questioning, and thus had unwittingly left Tommy Lee's arrest to Joe, a mountain boy. Now he had to face the consequences; he had put the sheriff's office in a bad light.

Randy moved over to the cell. "Okay, boy, who killed Paul Frank?"

"Joe." Tommy Lee pointed an accusing finger at Joe. "I heard 'im threatenin' Paul Frank right to his face."

"Who's goin' to believe that drunk?" Joe sneered. "What if I did threaten' him? Don't mean I did it. I wouldn't've shot him anyway. I'd beat him to death and called it a fair fight."

Patty flinched as the unbidden vision of Paul Frank being beaten flashed into her head.

"Don't leave town," Randy ordered.

"I have to report back to work," Joe sniveled.

Not ready to accept that Joe was responsible for Paul Frank's death (although he had no doubt Joe had threatened it), Randy said, "Leave your work and home addresses with the sheriff. If you don't, I'll automatically assume you're the one who shot Paul Frank. Killing a lawman goes down mighty hard. And if you're the one who did it, you'll never again see the light of day."

Randy turned to Patty. "We're done here. Let's get back to Cliff."

"Fine," she answered. Her face was as pale as plaster-board.

"Ozzie," Randy turned back and said, "do you think, if I took her there, the town doctor would see Patty as soon as possible?"

"Go on. She knows where his office is." Ozzie was mortified enough to be willing to cooperate for a change. "I'll call and let him know you're coming." Continuing the rare moment of cooperation, he added, "I'll see to it that Joe here leaves those addresses with me."

"Thanks," Randy led Patty to the car, calling Cliff on his solar phone as they went.

Careful not to disturb anything, and staying close to Paul Frank's lifeless body, Cliff searched the immediate area for possible clues. There were footprints between the body and the mansion. He broke a few branches from a small pine tree and laid them over the clearest ones so they would not be disturbed.

A vehicle drew close, and Cliff moved toward the gate. He saw it was Randy and Patty. On their heels an ambulance, siren screaming, skidded to a stop in the soft dirt on the shoulder of the road. Cliff shook his head; you could count on a call for transporting a body to turn into one of emergency.

Randy stepped from the car and went around to help Patty. She was a little calmer, as the doctor had immediately given her a sedative, having learned of the situation from the sheriff. The stop had taken only five minutes out of their time.

"Randy, how about taking Patty to the cabin for Annabelle and Aunt Aggie to take care of her. She really doesn't look very good."

"No. I won't go," Patty wailed.

"I already tried that," Randy said, "but I did take her by the doctor's office, and he gave her something." Changing topics, he said, "We have a suspect."

"Who?"

"Joe McCallister. Tommy Lee heard him threaten to kill Paul Frank."

"That's interesting."

Patty swayed. Cliff took her in his arms. "Patty, you can't do anything here. We need to tell the others anyway."

Suddenly, her knees buckled and if not for Cliff's strong arms, she would have crumpled to the ground in a heap.

The paramedics ran to her side. "What happened here?"

When the call came, Tuesday was preparing for bed. Winter Ann was asleep in her room, and Mary Lou was studying in hers.

Crushed by the news, Tuesday felt a renewed fear for Patty and Cliff.

"Who did it?" Tuesday asked, dry-eyed, her tears choking in her throat.

"We don't know," Cliff said. "I hate to give you this kind of information over the phone, but Cora is on her way over to stay with you, so you'll not be alone."

As if conjured by Cliff's telling, Cora rang the doorbell.

The women were cleaning up from their evening meal when Joe appeared at the backdoor.

"Come on in, Joe," Annabelle coaxed. "I saved ya a plate. It's nice an' warm in th' oven."

"Thanks, Ma." Joe let the screen door slam behind him.

"What's wrong?" Daisy asked.

"It's that boy from Centerpoint, Paul Frank. Someone killed him."

"Oh, no!" Sara gasped. Over the time she'd gotten to know him, she'd also gotten to like the handsome, thoughtful boy. "Who'd do such a thing?"

"Don't know," Joe said. "It don't make sense to me."

"Ain't no reason for it," Aunt Aggie said, "except for Jeb to do it, so it's not."

"Oh, Aunt Aggie," Daisy said, "you knowed Jeb's dead."

"Do I?" Aunt Aggie asked, raising an eyebrow. "Now ya just think on it. Who wanted Paul Frank dead? I heared it myself, so I did, Jeb tellin' Paul Frank he'd kill 'im for lettin' Patty an' Tuesday go, an takin' them to th' city. He meant it too, so he did!"

Everyone was quiet. Although each of them had heard Joe make the same threat time and again, they knew what Aggie said was true.

"I for one don't believe Jeb's dead," Annabelle said stubbornly, against all the facts.

"Would ya rather he be a murderer?" Daisy said.

"I don't believe that neither," Annabelle said with little conviction.

At the sound of a car approaching, Joe quickly moved to the door. He recognized the driver as Randy McCoy. As he watched, Patty opened the passenger door and climbed from the front seat, and before her knees gave away McCoy had come around to help her and caught her around her waist.

With Randy's support, she walked toward the backdoor, shoulders hunched, head hanging in despair, clutching his arm; she made her way to the door.

"Is she hurt?" Annabelle asked the detective, opening the door for them and alarmed at Patty's state.

"Not physically," Randy said. "She was with Cliff and me when we came across Paul Frank's body. She'll be all right, but it'll take time. Don't let her out of your sight! Don't leave her alone with Joe! That's an order." The only alternative was leaving her alone in her room at the boardinghouse, but she was too out of it to be on her own. Plus, he didn't think for a minute that Joe would harm Patty. More to the point, he wanted to control the girl, keeping her with him.

The detective left, and the women put Patty to bed in the four-poster.

32

*H*E PUSHED HIS PLATE ASIDE AND SMILED AT THE BEAUTI-
ful woman seated across from him.

"Victor, if we're going to continue being so close, I want to move in together."

Tossing his napkin in his plate, his expression instantly changed from a charming smile to a mean, spiteful look. "So you think you're permitted to make demands on me?"

"I'm sorry," she apologized fearfully. "It's just that—"

"It's just what?"

"In a relationship, couples share their lives more closely."

He laughed. Apparently his anger had dissolved.

"It's okay then," she relaxed noticeably.

"I have no intention of getting into a so-called sharing re-lationship," he continued in unusual good humor. "We've only been seeing one another a few days."

"Still, I want to know more about you."

"If I told you, I'd have to kill you." Had it not been for the faint smile on his lips, Carla would have believed he meant what he had just said; still, she stiffened. Even after a charis-matic smile had spread fully across his face and she returned it with one of her own, she had the feeling that his remark had not been an idle one.

What she did not know was that they had met before. One of many one-night stands, she had no idea that she had been with him before or that she was being used to test his new look.

CHAPTER

33

*I*N THE LATE AFTERNOON, A PALE AND LISTLESS PATTY SAT AT the table talking to Annabelle, Sara, and Aunt Aggie. All the while, snug in the four-poster bed, Daisy lay snoring. The night before, in a hurry to get back to his job, Joe had set out for Wheeling. Shortly after Joe left, Daisy had returned to her job at the bar. Now she was taking a long nap because she was scheduled to work again that evening. As usual, without Jacob or Joe there to discover she was defying them, she was taking advantage and putting as many hours in as she could.

Patty was in shock at Paul Frank's death, but she knew she wanted to see her grandmother and talk to her about everything that had happened since their last visit. In her wobbly state, though, her stomach turned at the smell of the evening meal being prepared.

"Ya're lookin' peeked," Aggie said. "Ya need a proper supper, so ya do."

"No! Please, I don't want anything to eat. But if there's lemonade made, I'll take some."

"Stay where ya're an' Sara'll get it for ya," Annabelle said. "Sara, step an' fetch Patty a drink."

Sara was bent over the washboard scrubbing the children's clothing. She rose to her feet with a groan. "Can't ya see I'm up to my elbows in soap suds?"

"Go back to your chores, Sara. I'll get my own." Ignoring Annabelle's bidding to let Sara wait on her, Patty moved to the stove where the cups were lined up inside a wood crate. The rectangular box—bottom to wall—had been nailed next to the stove and worked very well as a cupboard with the lower end serving as a shelf for dinnerware and cups. Patty chose a cup and poured her own lemonade.

Sara went back to her work. "I would not've minded, Patty. I was only aggravated at Ma for expectin' me to 'step and fetch it,' as she's always sayin'."

"It's okay, Sara. I'm not helpless."

"At least someone cares if I'm treated like a workhorse," Sara complained.

"No one's treatin' ya like no workhorse," Annabelle said. "We just want Patty to get better. That's all."

"Get better? What're you talking about? I'm not sick! I'm mourning the loss of a dear friend, and I'm going to find out who killed him too. Just see if I don't. That's what he'd do if it were me. I have to be strong. That's the way we were together. If not for him, I'd still be living on this time-forgotten-mountain being abused by my father and brother."

"Now, Patty, there's no call for ya to speak ill of your father an' brother."

"Ma, quit hiding your head in the sand," Patty said in frustration. "You knew what was happening to me when I lived here. And, furthermore, Pa's dead!"

"I won't hear it, so I won't," Aggie said, snuff-stained spittle spraying from her mouth in her annoyance. "I've been thinkin' I need to go back to my place, so I do. Jeb'll come to my place first when he's ready to come home."

"Patty'll take ya after her bath," Annabelle said, glad to get Aggie and her constant complaining out of the cabin, knowing Aggie's true reason for wanting to leave was that she was missing the comforts she enjoyed in her renovated home. Besides, she had found out all she could from Patty.

"Patty, ya drink your lemonade, and after Sara's done with the wash tub, I'll fix ya a bath." Annabelle sat beside the grieving girl. "There's water a'heatin' now."

"Ma, I've had my last bath in this cabin. I will bathe at the boardinghouse in a tub with hot and cold running water. After I go visit my grandmother, I'm going back to my room, get my bath, and go to bed. My clean clothes are there, too."

"Patty, it ain't safe to go runnin' 'round th' mountain alone, so it ain't."

"It sure ain't, if Pa's not dead like ya and Ma insist on be-lievin'," Sara said.

"Oh, stop it all of you. You all know very well that Pa's dead," Patty said.

"Can't think of anyone but your pa that'd want to kill Paul Frank, so I can't. Heard him with my own ears, swearin' he was goin' to kill him for helpin' ya an' Tuesday run away. He's plannin' on killin' that detective Cliff Moran, too, so he is. I heard 'im sayin' it myself, so I did. Said he'd kill them if it was th' last thin' he ever did."

"Patty, there's some truth to what Aggie's sayin'. Who would want to kill such a nice young man as Paul Frank, ex-cept your father?" Annabelle asked as she placed a plate with a biscuit and strawberry jam in front of Patty. Patty took a few bites just to please Annabelle, but the food was taste-less to her. The danger implied by Aunt Aggie's comments failed to penetrate Patty's grief over Paul Frank.

"You would rather believe Pa's a murderer than admit that he's dead!" Patty exclaimed.

"Of course not," Annabelle retorted, "but th' facts are th' facts."

Patty rolled her eyes, looking at Sara, who shrugged her shoulders.

"Ya don't need to be lookin' like we don't knowed what we're talkin' 'bout, so ya don't."

"Just finish your drink," Annabelle admonished.

As Patty finished her lemonade, Cliff and Randy pulled in behind her car in the parking area at the rear of the cabin. Annabelle invited them in and offered them coffee and jelly biscuits. Tempted by the aroma, they accepted right away.

From the neatness and the much more pleasant smell inside the cabin generally, as well as from the mouth-watering aroma of food preparations, the men could tell that since the women's stay in Wheeling at the center for abused women two years before, they had made improvements in their sanitary habits. Another change for the better was the area beside the back porch. It had been cleaned up, and gone was the putrid odor generated by bathwater and dishwater full of food particles left to rot on the ground. The women apparently had found a more sanitary way to dispose of the dirty water.

Randy watched Patty as he enjoyed his jelly-and-butter-covered biscuit. He had met her on the mountain during the previous investigations and again in Wheeling, and had learned from Cliff that she had a long-time and deep-seated crush on the highly respected, handsome Paul Frank Ruble. Randy had feelings for Patty, but in light of her very visible grief over the loss of Paul Frank, he kept them to himself.

"Cliff, I'm hopin' ya can talk some sense into this girl, so I am," Aggie said. "She's bound an' determined to go to her grandmother's cabin an' then th' boardin' house, so she is."

Watching Patty, Cliff took note that she had the glazed look of someone in shock. This was no time for her to go driving around the mountain alone. "Patty," Cliff said, as he took her hand in his. She did not look at him, fearing he was about to forbid her to finish the work she had come on the mountain to do. Finally, as she knew he was waiting for her to meet his eyes, she looked at him. "I must continue," she pleaded.

"I know. We're going with you. You're in shock. I promise I'll just drive, and you can go where you feel the need. Randy and I can be helpful to you. And you never know, we may learn something about Paul Frank's murder."

"Okay," Patty said. She knew from experience that she could trust her adoptive father. "First the boardinghouse. I want to shower and change. I can't bear another primitive bath here in this cabin." Patty produced a feeble shadow of a smile.

Cliff and Randy thanked Annabelle for the coffee and biscuits as they took their leave. At Randy's reminder that someone needed to meet the forensic team, they decided that Randy would use Patty's car to get to town and would wait at the sheriff's office for the forensic team. Cliff would escort Patty as she continued her search for her family, now with the added job of looking for Paul Frank's killer. Her hope was that her grandmother might somehow be helpful through her dreams.

As they traveled toward town, Patty talked about her grandmother and the revealing dreams that they had in common. "Why do you suppose I dreamt about the mansion and not of the danger it held for Paul Frank?"

"I can't answer that, but maybe your grandmother can. You said she knew the family history, and the ability to know the future was not given just to her and you, but many others for hundreds of years."

"Yeah," Patty said. "According to my grandmother, they were very open about it."

"It must have been very frightening not being allowed to talk to anyone about it when you were a child."

"Being made fun of was the hardest part," Patty said in a flat voice.

"That's never any fun," Cliff smiled and reached over and laid a hand on her shoulder. "It'll get easier, I promise."

She tried to return his smile, knowing that he meant well. "Paul Frank is gone, and it hurts so much," she said simply.

Cliff swallowed a lump in his throat.

As they neared the boardinghouse they were quiet, comfortable in each other's company.

"Here we are," Cliff said. "While you're in your room, I'm going to check Paul Frank's room."

"How're you going to get in?"

Cliff held out a key. "I thought to get it from Paul Frank's pocket. I didn't want to wait for a court order. He's the same as family, and I want to check his room. Maybe I'll find something. At least I can repack his things and—"

"And what?" Patty asked after Cliff failed to continue.

He put a comforting hand on her shoulder and guided her inside the boardinghouse. "Go to your room. I'll book one for McCoy and myself. We can meet here in an hour."

Walking toward the counter, Cliff nodded to the proprietor.

"I'd like a room for two," he said, laying his credit card on the registration desk.

"I remember ya," the woman said, grinning. "Ya're a detective, an ya been here before. Never saw th' likes of a man askin' so many questions 'bout such that weren't none of his business, a'tall."

Cliff laughed; he remembered that it had taken him a few days, on his previous stay four years earlier, to figure out that all her complaints were just her style of talking.

Later, feeling some better, Patty returned to the lobby to meet Cliff and Randy as they had planned. The men were waiting, deep in a conversation, obviously concerning the murder of Paul Frank.

"I'm ready to go," Patty said when the men turned and noticed her standing at the foot of the stairs. "If you don't mind, I'd like to see my grandmother first."

"Sure," Cliff said. "Let's go."

They climbed into the front seat, Patty in the middle, still unusually quiet, and set off for Myrtle Landacre's cabin.

It only took ten minutes to get to Myrtle's cabin. They had planned that Patty would go first and knock on the door, but that turned out to be unnecessary. Myrtle was at the wide-open door, waiting. "I knowed ya was comin'," she called to them. "I dreamed it." She squinted her eyes, peering at the men as they followed Patty to the door.

Patty ran to her, and Myrtle took her in her arms. When Myrtle looked at Patty, her face softened from the harsh look of an old crone to one of a loving grandmother, and Cliff and Randy could see her as Patty did.

"Come in," Myrtle invited.

Her place was in much better order than when Cliff had paid her a visit four years before. He had no way of knowing that having Patty in her life had given her the motivation to care more about her own existence and her immediate surroundings. She had kept her home in flawless order before her husband had sold her daughter, Betty, but after that Myrtle had had no enthusiasm to continue making things nice—until Patty had entered her life.

The group sat around the table. Patty was the first to speak. "Grandmother, did you know that I was being held against my will by Tommy Lee Hillberry?"

"It wasn't clear, Patty," Myrtle said. "I knowed ya were bein' starved for food an' water. I knowed there was death around ya, but I knowed it wasn't ya."

"Paul Frank was shot. Did you know that?"

"Nope, I didn't. Don't knowed what or why my dreams're what they're, an' what they're not. I just have them."

"Then you didn't know enough about what's been going on to help?"

"Oh, no, or I would've." Myrtle patted Patty's shoulder. "Ya knowed that."

"Yes," Patty smiled. "I do know."

"Can you tell us anything?" Cliff asked in desperation.

"Nope, but it'll come together," Myrtle said.

"Frankly," Cliff said, " I think it was either Joe McCallister, who has been known to have threatened Paul Frank's life, or Ike Harris. Harris was the one Brandi Rose, McCallister's sectary, was in contact with for supplies for the mansion."

"Harris is my bet," Randy said.

"What about Tommy Lee Hillberry? We know he's a murderer—he killed that girl," Patty said.

"You've got something there," Cliff said.

"You're right," Randy said, "and Tommy Lee hadn't been arrested yet. The sheriff left him free to do as he pleased, knowing full well he had already committed murder."

It was late, and Tuesday and Cora sat at the table drinking coffee and crying. Mary Lou was sleeping, thanks to Doctor Hess and a tranquilizer.

"Does anyone know how to contact Paul Frank's sisters?" Cora asked.

"I don't know, and I don't know anyone who would. I suppose someone in Centerpoint might. The proprietor of The General Store in Centerpoint knew everyone, but he's in jail now."

"Oh, Cora, I can't believe Paul Frank will never come walking through the front door ever again, with that beautiful smile on his face." Tuesday wept. At the sound of small feet swiftly padding across the dining room, she quickly wiped at her tear-stained face.

Winter Ann ran to her mother and Tuesday took her in her arms, settling the child in her lap.

"I can't sleep," Winter Ann whined.

"But you must. You need your rest."

"I'm scared about Paul Frank."

"I know, but you needn't be." Tuesday pushed Winter Ann's disheveled hair away from her face. "He's with God now. You know that's where Christians go when they die."

"Yeah, I know. Christians are the people that do what God wants them to."

"My," Cora said, "you sure are learning your Bible lessons."

After quieting Winter Ann's sobs and convincing her to get into bed with Mary Lou, Tuesday sat by her daughter's side until she was asleep. When they retired for the night, Cora would be sleeping in Winter Ann's bed with Linda.

Quietly, Tuesday returned to the kitchen, where she joined Cora. "You don't know how grateful I am for your staying with me right now," Tuesday said.

"As if you hadn't done the same for me the two long years my Linda was missing from our lives."

"That's what friends are for." Tuesday said, giving Cora a quick hug. They put their cups in the dishwasher and were about to go upstairs when there was a knock at the door. Tuesday opened the door, keeping the security chain latched, and peered out.

"Tuesday Moran?" the man asked, flashing a badge.

"Yes."

"May we come in?"

"What's it about?"

"We're investigating Ike Harris and Jacob McCallister in the murder of Paul Frank Ruble."

"What are you talking about?" Tuesday said. "Jacob McCallister is dead, and what would I know about Ike Harris?"

"May we come in?"

"Let us see your identification." Cora had walked up behind Tuesday.

"That's okay, Cora. I remember him from the militia's unlawful assembly on Winding Ridge. You're J. J., aren't you?"

"That's right. This is Bart Howard. You've met him as well. He was part of the rescue team when you where being held by McCallister four years ago"

"Come in and have a seat," Tuesday offered.

"We know that Ike Harris was working with Jacob McCallister on a building project. That's where Patty has been this past week; she was being held by Tommy Lee Hillberry and Ike Harris. We know that McCallister owned the place at the time of his death."

"Where are Ike Harris and Tommy Lee?" Tuesday asked. "I'd say they're a dangerous combination."

"Tommy Lee's locked up in jail on Winding Ridge at this time," J. J. said. "As for Ike Harris, we don't know where he is."

"It sure looks like Harris is behind the murder," Bart said. "At the least we can pick him up for breaking parole, seeing as he has been keeping company with McCallister, a known felon."

"Why's that?" Tuesday asked.

"Ike's on parole. It's the rules. You get two felons together, you're asking for trouble."

"I can tell you where he lives. I remember it was in Jeremy Clarke's report. I'll find it." Tuesday went to a desk across the room and pulled out a folder. She turned to the right page. "Here it is," she said, pointing at the paper. "Grant Town. It says Ike lives there with his wife."

"Assuming he committed the murder, he's probably too smart to go back there while the heat's on," Howard said, "but maybe not. We'll check it out."

The men left, and Tuesday hurried to call Cliff on his solar phone. "Cliff, J. J. and Bart Howard were here. They're on their way to Grant Town where Ike lives. Where are you?"

"We're talking to Myrtle Landacre. Thanks for calling me about J.J. and Bart. I need to touch base with them before they pick up Harris. I have a few unanswered questions, and I can use their help."

"Like what?"

"Like why did the building project continue after McCallister's death?"

"Maybe Ike didn't know," Tuesday said.

"No, I don't think so. I talked to Brandi Rose, McCallister's secretary, and according to the information I gathered while in his office, she was authorized to fill any orders from Harris and would've been in touch with him. I'm sure that I convinced her that he was dead, and I've no doubt she would've told Harris."

"But, Cliff, without McCallister there was no reason for Ike and Tommy Lee to continue the job. You can't get paid by a dead man."

"Something smells like a rat."

"Don't tell me that you think Jacob's alive after all!" Tuesday said.

"That's too bizarre. If he was alive, he would have turned up at his office."

"He doesn't have to hide," Tuesday said. "It's not as if he's wanted by the law. As far as the law's concerned, he's done his time."

"That's true. There's no reason that I can think for McCallister to fake his death," Cliff said.

"He had no way of knowing that the World Trade Center was going to be attacked, anyway."

"No, but he was there and could have taken advantage of it," Cliff said.

"But why?"

"That, I don't know," Cliff said. "But what bothers me is, it seems that the work at Short Run should've ground to a halt when Jacob died in the disaster," he went on. "But it didn't, and if Harris was involved in Patty's disappearance it could've only been on McCallister's orders. Harris had no motive for detaining her. I have to ask myself, how could McCallister be dead and all that continue?"

"You're right," Tuesday said. "If not for the work continuing we could believe that Tommy Lee acted alone, that he alone was behind Patty's disappearance. The one thing I can take comfort from is that Tommy Lee would never come off the mountain to get her.

"Ike Harris, though, surely was only acting on McCallister's orders," Cliff said, "and I can't see any reason he'd be interested now that McCallister's gone."

"*If* he's gone."

"That's the key." Cliff shifted the bulky solar phone to the other ear.

"What are we going to do now?"

"Tomorrow I have to make arrangements for Paul Frank to be transported home. I hate leaving Patty here on her own, but she is determined to finish what she started, and Myrtle can look after her."

"She's got to be in shock," Tuesday worried.

"Yes, she is. But she feels if she drops it, Paul Frank will have died in vain."

"I can see that, but if there's any chance at all that Jacob is not dead, she's in danger! And, Cliff, so am I!"

"You know what? Joe's been living with his father for a couple of years now. He has the same agenda as Jacob," Cliff said. "That's got to be it. I can't get around it any other way. McCallister has no reason to fake his own death."

"Oh, yes! I never thought of Joe carrying on with Jacob's plans. He always wanted to follow in his father's footsteps. I feel better now, Cliff. You always make me feel better."

"Well, don't worry about Patty, I plan to keep her safe until she comes home."

After the call from Tuesday, Cliff, Randy, and Patty got up to leave.

"Myrtle, please, if you learn anything, let me know," Cliff said. "Can you make it to town, and leave a message at the boardinghouse, if you need to?"

"Who'd ya think gets what I need at th' store? My son, John Bob sees that I have money every month, an' I take it to Th' Genera Store an' get what I need. Th' walk does a world of good for this old body of mine."

"I knew we could count on you," Cliff said.

"No problem! I can do it," Myrtle testified. "Ya just watch ya back, Mr. Cliff Moran, 'cause in my dreams ya have a dark cloud over ya head. Someone wants ya dead. That's for sure. Don't knowed who it is, though."

FTER HIS MAKEOVER WAS COMPLETE AND HAVING TAKEN the time to test it by visiting Carla, a short-time acquaintance, Jacob McCallister traveled to Short Run and the mansion only to find that Ike Harris was not there. He had disappeared as if he'd never been there at all. His personal things were gone, which was unusual. Previously, he'd gone home to visit his wife occasionally but never took all his things with him.

McCallister had come to the mountain prepared to find out what was on Harris's mind and silence him if necessary. Harris would eventually figure out, as supplies kept coming in to complete the house, that Jacob had not really been killed in the attack on the World Trade Center Towers. Ike would hold it over McCallister's head. He wasn't having any of that.

"Damn!" Jacob yelled out loud in frustration, kicking a can of paint across the room. "Maybe he's already wise to me. I've got to find him. I can't have anyone walking around thinking that I wasn't killed that day. And what about Tommy Lee? He knew I was behind the scene, keeping the supplies coming. He's not too dumb to figure it out." Jacob threw things aside as if trying to find an answer.

"No one would believe him, anyway. But, man, I can't take a chance on it." McCallister picked up the paint can he had kicked, thankful that it had not opened, spilling its contents. "I don't want to have to keep up the pretense of being Victor Newman any longer than I have to. I've got to get rid of Tommy Lee and Harris, the only two people that could possibly have an inkling that I'm still alive, before I'm ready to make a comeback.

"As for Tommy Lee, I wouldn't be connected to him in a million years. Anyway, dead men don't kill. Ike Harris is another matter, but the fact that I did time with him shouldn't raise eyebrows when he turns up dead. With them gone, there's no one else to worry about. My family wouldn't open their mouths about anything I do, period."

McCallister waited until dark and went into town. He parked his truck on a side road and walked past the jail, keeping close to the buildings where the light from the street lamps could not reach him. The sheriff's Jeep was gone; the jail was dark. The only ones inside would be those locked in cells. He crossed the alley and walked to The General Store. He knew Tommy Lee was more likely to be found in the bar, but he chose to stop by the store first. There he could pick up any gossip that might be going around. If nothing else, it would be an opportunity to check out his new look before attempting the bar.

He eased through the door and allowed it to close behind him. He walked to the right and away from the men gathered around the potbelly stove, rocking in their chairs, trading stories, and smoking their pipes. As McCallister moved around the store, he learned there were only a few patrons shopping, but the subject of the conversation, among the men around the potbelly, was Joe McCallister. Joe, they were saying, had thrown Tommy Lee in jail, after the sheriff had tried to sweep the matter under the carpet, for murdering a girl from Frank Dillon's household.

After purchasing a package of batteries so as not to cause comment about why a man would come into the store and walk right back out without spending as much as a penny, McCallister returned to his truck. He got a flashlight from the glove box, shoved it into his pocket, and turned back to the jail. Investigating each alley behind the various business-es, he found a wooden crate behind The General Store. It was the right height to raise him to window level.

He checked that the gun silencer was firmly attached and shined the light into the cell. He could not see the cot or Tommy Lee, who was sleeping on it just below the window, out of McCallister's line of vision. He could not get a good shot.

All of a sudden, with a crash, McCallister broke the win-dow with the butt of his gun, quickly turning the gun back around as Tommy Lee scurried to the bars and rattled them, yelling for help. There was none. McCallister simultaneously pointed his gun and his light toward the sound of Tommy Lee's screams. Without removing his gloves, he took aim and shot the boy in the temple, silencing him forever.

After ending Tommy Lee's life, McCallister crossed to the town bar. On the way, he muttered to himself. "Harris, after Cliff Moran, you're next. I promised I'd get him, and I do keep my promises. I can only be hanged for murder once."

During the days he had spent with Carla it was obvious that she had no idea that they had met on another occasion. Based on her reaction, or rather, lack of one, McCallister was confident that no one would recognize him.

Jacob never got to know the regulars at the bar in all the years he had patronized it. Tonight he strode through the door boldly convinced he would not be included in their conversations. Midway down the long bar, he froze in his tracks at the sight of Daisy running around among the ta-bles, serving drinks, wearing jeans that were too tight and a sweater that was very low-cut.

Unable to control his temper, he walked up to her and grabbed her arm, causing her to drop her tray of drinks. Booze and broken glass splashed up their legs.

"What the—" Daisy began.

35

WITH DAISY WORKING AT THE BAR AND AUNT AGGIE back in her cabin, Annabelle had the bed to herself. She was awakened from a sound sleep by the noise of a car veering off the road to the dirt lane leading to the cabin. Thinking it was Daisy coming home from work, she turned over and drifted back to sleep.

The next thing she knew, the door crashed open.

"Oh, my word. Oh, my word!" She sat up and searched the floor for her oversized slippers, finally sticking her feet into them, and hurried into the kitchen. "What's goin' on now?"

To Annabelle's surprise and horror, Daisy was sprawled on the bench at the table, where she had been pushed. She was looking defiantly at an extremely handsome man who was glaring at her, ready to strike her.

"What's goin' on in here?" Annabelle gasped.

"Annabelle, that's precisely what I want to know. Let me hear it. What do you have to say for yourself?"

"Jeb!" Annabelle turned pale at the sound of her man's voice coming from the mouth of a stranger. "Ya look different, but I knowed it's ya. I'd knowed that voice anywhere."

"So you know who I am," he said.

"I'd knowed ya anywhere," Annabelle said. "Especially your voice. Everyone thinks ya're dead. I knowed ya wasn't."

"That doesn't explain why Daisy here was working in the town bar," Jacob said. "Or most importantly, why you're allowing it."

"I can't tell her what to do," Annabelle said, trying to hide her anger. It always made her furious when he was so unreasonable about expecting her to keep everything going just as he wanted it. When he was absent, he counted on her to keep control of the others, period. "Daisy's not a child. She's got a mind of her own, that one."

"You would think that after you spent weeks thinking that I was dead, I'd get a warmer welcome."

"Ya'd think that after ya'd neglected us for so long, ya'd be a little happier to see us, 'stead of comin' in here an ' yellin' that everythin' ain't th' way ya want it."

"Both of you get to bed, and don't think you've gotten away with your disregard for my wishes, Daisy. I'll deal with you in the morning. I want to talk to both of you, and I don't want to do it in your new home, the cellar house."

As the women went to the bedroom, Jacob searched the kitchen for something to drink. In the corner of the kitchen, at the bottom of a stack of wood crates used for a cupboard, he found a bottle of whiskey. He took it to the living room, sat on the sagging horsehair sofa, and took a long drink.

He had missed his dinner, and soon he was half drunk, having second thoughts about locking Daisy in the cellar house, knowing he wouldn't get away with it any more than he had the time he locked Tuesday and Patty there. He decided he would take Daisy to the mansion. It was perfect. He could not allow her her freedom any longer. He could keep Annabelle quiet; she would die to avoid getting him into trouble, but not Daisy, not any more. Sara was another matter.

McCallister was snoring within the hour.

Daisy had waited to hear him snore, planning to get away before he awoke. She knew that if she were still there the next morning, he would lock her in the cellar house for disobeying him. She was not about to take his abuse one more day of her life. She had money enough to leave. She'd been saving every bit she could for the two years she'd been working at the bar and had it stashed in a small metal box. She would have left sooner, but without him around to make their lives more miserable, it had been easier to procrastinate, having Sara and Annabelle to take care of her children.

The one important thing Daisy did not realize was that Jacob McCallister had truly become a dangerous man now that he was guilty of murder. He simply could not allow her to her live outside his sphere of authority knowing that he was still alive. Unwittingly, she was taking advantage of her one chance to ever leave the mountain safely.

She tucked the moneybox under her arm, shook the twins and Sara awake, and hissed in Sara's ear, "You're not safe here, Sara. Please, I can't explain, he'll hear us. Get out tonight! Come with me or go to Dillon's cabin."

"I can't leave Ma, Daisy," Sara whispered. "I have to stay here—for now—and protect her. I really don't believe Pa'd hurt her badly."

Daisy shrugged.

"Come on, boys. We mustn't wake your father, so be quiet an' follow me."

The boys were too frightened of their father to make noise and risk waking him, and they obediently and silently followed their mother into the kitchen, where she hurriedly dressed them for their trip to town.

Without so much as a sound they were out the backdoor.

Well out of hearing of the others back at the cabin, Daisy dared to speak. "Drexel, hold tight to mommy's pant leg so ya won't get lost. I need to carry our moneybox, an' I can only hold one little hand at a time."

"What's a moneybox?" Drexel asked.

"It's a box that holds money, you dork," Dakota said.

"Dakota, where did ya hear that word?"

"Which one, Ma?"

"Dork."

"Ya knowed that's what Joe calls us."

"Yeah, I remember hearin' 'im callin' ya that," Daisy sighed.

"Where're we goin'?" Drexel asked.

"Remember I told ya that we was goin' to th' city one day?"

"Now?"

"I didn't think it was goin' to be in th' nighttime," Dakota said. "I'm sleepy in th' nighttime." The little boy rubbed his bleary eyes.

"Ma, can I hold your hand now, an' Dakota hold your pant leg?"

The walk was long and difficult in the pitch black of night, but Daisy was determined to make the trip as fast as possible. It would be a disaster if McCallister woke up and followed her. They would not have a chance if he followed in his truck, catching up with them before they reached the boardinghouse and safety.

"He must not know that Cliff Moran's in town," Daisy said in frustration, "or he wouldn't've come here, or maybe he thought his changed appearance would fool everyone."

"What'd ya say, Ma?" Dakota asked.

"Nothin', I'm just keepin' us company. Ya have to keep walkin'."

"Well, ya sound like ya're scared," Drexel whined. His mother's fear was contagious. "Ya're not scared, ar'ya', Ma?"

"No, honey. Don't be scared. We're goin' to be just fine from now on. I promise."

"Okay," the boys whimpered in unison.

In a particularly rocky stretch, Dakota and Drexel sagged to the ground. They were too tired to continue. "What am I goin' to do?" Daisy moaned. "We must get to th' boardin' house before your pa catches us. Okay, I'll take turns carrying ya." She picked Dakota up and kept walking. Drexel, spurred on by the threat of his father catching up, stumbled as he followed, gripping his mother's pant leg.

When they came to the foot of the mountain where it leveled off, forming the flat where the town of Winding Ridge stood, Drexel whined, "Is it my turn yet?"

Daisy set Dakota on his feet and picked up Drexel. "Come on, now! We're just goin' to that buildin' yonder."

After what seemed a lifetime to Daisy, they came to the boardinghouse. She opened the door and, with the children following, walked into the lobby. By that time it was dawn, and Monica was just shuffling behind the registration desk. "Can I help ya?"

"Please, there's a man stayin' here. His name is Cliff Moran, an' I need to see 'im," Daisy sobbed in fright and fatigue.

"Okay, calm down. I'll call his room. We have intercoms in them now, 'cause when th' militia gathered here'bouts a coupla years back, they wanted 'em. An' with all th' money they was payin', I couldn't see my way to refuse," she babbled proudly as she punched in his room number. After pushing the appropriate numbers she said, "There's a women with two kids lookin' for ya in th' lobby." After Cliff had responded, Monica looked at Daisy and said, "Ya heard 'im, said he'd be right down."

Shaking in fear of the door bursting open and Jacob stalking through, Daisy led the twins to a sofa along the wall of the lobby and laid Drexel on one end and Dakota on the other. She sat between them.

Cliff could not believe his eyes. "Daisy, what in the world are you doing here?"

"I need help," she sobbed. "Jeb's back an' he caught me workin' in th' bar. He's passed out, but he plans to lock me in th' cellar when he wakes up. I'm not stayin' an' takin th' abuse any more. I have money." She held out the box. "Take it."

"Hold on for a minute," Cliff said and sat next to her, taking her hands. "Jacob McCallister's not dead? Are you sure?"

"I'm sure. He's alive, but he changed his hair an' his face some way. His eyes're blue now. How can that be?"

"You're *sure* it's him?"

"Oh, yeah, it's him. I'd knowed his voice anywhere. Anyway, after ya really look at him, ya can tell who he is."

"It all makes sense. He's got to be th' one that killed Paul Frank," Cliff said.

"He's bent on killin' ya too," Daisy warned.

"Let me get you and the boys a room, and we'll put your money in a safe." Cliff went over to the counter and booked a room with two beds for Daisy and the boys. Also, he got a key to a hotel guest safe and put Daisy's moneybox inside. "Here's the key, Daisy. Don't lose it. The door automatically locks when you go out. You'll need it to get back inside."

After escorting Daisy to her room, Cliff hurried to his room and rushed in as soon as Randy opened the door.

"Jacob McCallister's not dead after all. He showed up at the town bar and forced Daisy to go back to their cabin with him, threatening to lock her in the cellar house. I have to let Tuesday know."

"While you're doing that, I'll call Hal Brooks and have him get someone to keep an eye on your house in Wheeling."

Safely inside the room, Daisy tucked the boys in one of the beds. After thanking Cliff for his protection, she had locked the door behind him. By the time he was speaking with Randy, she was already flopped on the bed, exhausted. A couple of hours later, she awakened to the boys' splashing water in the bathroom. She hurried to the adjoining room and saw the mess they had already managed to make.

"What do ya think ya're doin'?

"We're playin'," Drexel said.

Daisy noticed their dark pants. "Did ya boys wet ya'selves?"

"Ya was sleepin' an' wouldn't wake up," Drexel said. "We couldn't wait no more, an' couldn't get out th' door to go to th' outhouse."

Daisy laughed. "I guess the two of ya had no way of knowin'." She pointed to the commode. "That's th' outhouse, but it's in th' house."

With huge eyes the boys stared inside the commode. "It don't look like no outhouse," Drexel said.

Daisy put the stopper in the sink and filled it with water. Next, she filled the tub. "Okay, boys, undress an' get into th' tub. You need a bath."

With yelps of glee, the boys did as she said, delighted with the huge tub. They were too big now to get into the washtub at the cabin at the same time, so they had been bathing alone. They missed playing together as they had when they were toddlers. As they splashed happily in the boardinghouse tub, she rinsed their wet clothes in the sink. Then, letting the clothes soak, she dried the youngsters and wrapped them in towels. She set them on the bed to play while she rung out their clothes and laid them over a towel rack to dry.

Pushing her fear to the back of her mind, she admonished the boys to stay out of trouble while she bathed. After drawing a fresh tub of water, she closed the door part way and took a quick bath, then soaked her tense muscles briefly. She rinsed herself then and dressed in the same clothes she had worn the day before, thinking that if she'd had a pair of extra arms when she'd left the cabin, she could have carried the nice clothing Tuesday had given her a few years ago.

There was no turning back. She'd made her bed and now she had to sleep in it—as Aunt Aggie was fond of saying.

Patty knocked on the door. Daisy jumped, startled at the unexpected sound. She wrapped the towel that she had been drying her hair with firmly around her head and opened the door.

"Daisy, you shouldn't open the door to anyone. You know Pa will be looking for you."

"I think he'll run. He knows I'm goin' to tell that he's not dead."

"You don't know that! Anyway, we're not safe till he's gone."

Patty noticed the twins playing, their towels forgotten. "Where are their clothes?"

"They wet in them. I was asleep an' they didn't know what th' commode was for."

"They'll take all day to dry. I'll go to The General Store and get them each another outfit. You need one too, don't you?"

"All I have now, except for my boys an' my box of money, is on my back. I couldn't pack anythin' an' take th' chance of wakin' Jeb. He'd've stopped me for sure. I couldn't've carried anymore, anyway."

There was another knock on the door, followed by Cliff's voice calling, "Open up! We have supplies."

Patty opened the door and found Cliff and Randy both toting boxes of carryout food.

"Oh, that smells good," Daisy said.

The boys jumped from the bed they'd been using as a trampoline. "I'm hungry," they squealed in unison.

The men laughed at the naked boys. "What happened?" Cliff said.

"Wet clothes. I'm going after outfits for them," Patty said. "Randy, will you accompany her?"

"Sure. I think they look even more adorable when they're dressed."

Patty smiled.

"Get up to the table," Cliff instructed the boys.

They ran to a small table that functioned as an eating place or a desk, and each of them managed to climb on a chair. Cliff set hotdogs, hamburgers, and fries down in front of them.

"Here's the drinks," Cliff said. "Eat up."

"Thanks," Daisy said.

"Thank you!" Cliff said. "By coming here, you've saved us maybe months of work."

"Not to mention people's lives," Randy said, looking pointedly at Cliff. "More particularly, Moran's."

"How'd you manage to get off the mountain with that large moneybox and two small boys?" Patty asked.

"Fear that he was goin' to lock me up. I'd made up my mind years ago I wasn't goin' to put up with him an' his selfish demands all my life. I've seen first hand now how it is livin' around people that don't expect ya to just exist for their wants."

"I'm glad to hear that," Patty said.

"While the boys are occupied, you can tell me what you know," Cliff said, pulling up a chair.

"I only knowed he'd cut his hair, an' his eyes're really blue an' shaped different. Ya knowed his eyes was always dark brown. His face's different too, some how. Like, his chin, it don't have that dent in it no more. Th' one like ya got."

"Cleft." Randy grinned.

Cliff looked up from taking notes and smiled. "How was he dressed?"

"He was dressed like he always did when he was goin' to th' city. Ya knowed, he had on nice pants with a crease in 'em. A button-up shirt an' a jacket. Not like when he spent time on th' mountain, always wearin' jeans an' a flannel shirt."

"Okay, after Randy and I make a sweep of the mountain for McCallister, we're taking you, the twins, and Patty to Wheeling," Cliff said.

"I thought Patty'd want to stay here."

"She did," Cliff answered for her. "But it's not safe for the family to be scattered with McCallister on the loose. She can return when this is over."

Patty nodded her agreement.

"After Patty and Randy come back from shopping, I want the two of you to stay put in your rooms unless Randy or I am with you. Understand?" Cliff asked.

"Yes, Cliff, we'll stay," each of them answered.

"We're going to go after McCallister while we know where he is."

"He's probably out lookin' for me by now," Daisy said.

The boys were getting catsup all over themselves.

"You'd better get the outfits and get back here," Cliff said. "Looks like the boys need another bath."

As Patty and Randy left the room, the boys ran into the bathroom. They were intrigued with the running water. They loved climbing onto the commode seat, leaning over the edge of the sink, and with one turn of a handle, making the water splash into the sink.

That same morning, Annabelle was quietly working in the kitchen. She knew when Jeb woke up he would be furious to find out that Daisy was gone and had taken the twins with her. The food she had been preparing was almost ready when she heard him moving about the living room.

"Turn off that damn noise," he said as he appeared in the kitchen. "I'm hungry."

Regretfully, Annabelle complied and turned off the radio.

"What time is it?" he asked.

"How'd I knowed what time it is?" Annabelle asked.

She could not get used to his changed looks. "Sit ya self down. It's 'most ready."

"I missed your cooking, Annabelle," Jacob said, a rare compliment coming from him.

"Why, thank ya!" Annabelle beamed.

Halfway through his meal, Jacob noticed that they were the only ones in the kitchen. "Where's everyone?"

"I don't knowed. Sara and Kelly Sue might've gone vis- itin', 'cept it's unusual for them to get outta bed before me an' be out an' about on top of that. Daisy, though, she never goes outdoors 'cept to th' outhouse an' cellar house. Or to work." Annabelle looked sheepish mentioning Daisy's job. "Since I've not seen her all mornin', my guess is that her an' her twins must've run away."

Jacob stood up, and if it had not been for the fact that the bench he had been sitting on was attached to the table, he would have knocked it over. For the first time in his life, Jacob McCallister showed real fear. Annabelle could see it in his eyes.

He sat back down.

"What ya goin' to do?"

"I don't know," Jacob answered. "This isn't supposed to be the way it goes. I've always kept you women on the mountain away from influences in town. Now that Daisy's been working in the bar, she knows too many people, and locking her in the cellar house would only bring the law down on me."

Jacob threw his tin plate at the washtub on the woodburning stove, where Annabelle had her dishwater waiting for the dirty dishes. It landed in the water with a splash.

"I have no idea what to do or where to look. I'm going to visit Aunt Aggie." He slammed out the back door, leaving Annabelle with her mouth agape. Her Jeb, not knowing what to do? No, he would get Daisy and punish her. Annabelle turned the radio back on and set about her work.

As the truck moved swiftly up the mountain, Jacob racked his brain, trying to come up with a solution to his dilemma. As long as no one knew he was alive and on the mountain while the murders happened, he would be safe to switch back to his original looks eventually, with all this forgotten. He had to get rid of Cliff Moran.

His aunt had heard the truck's engine humming in the distance and was on the porch hoping to see who it was. When Jacob stepped from the truck and smiled, she knew. "Jeb, what happened to your face?"

As he moved closer, she could see his blue eyes. "Jeb, ya have blue eyes, so ya do. How could that be?" All color had drained from Aggie's face.

Seeing his aunt in such a state, he removed the contact lens from his right eye. "Oh, my word," Aggie cried.

Jacob spit on the contact and put it back in his eye. "It's okay, Aunt Aggie. It's just a contact lens. You know, like glasses without stems that go over your ears."

He took the tiny woman in his arms. His mother's sister, the one who raised him from a child after he'd lost his parents, was probably the only person that he really loved. To him, his children were only for profit. He had sold them one by one, with the exceptions of Joe, Patty, and Sara, and he'd kept them only to increase his supply.

"Jeb, why're ya disguising yourself again? Could only mean trouble, so it could."

"You know that everyone thinks I'm dead. I needed to come to the mountain, so I disguised my self."

"An' why's that?"

"You know why! I want Tuesday and Patty back. Now, Daisy has run away."

"I tol' ya when ya brought Tuesday here 'em years ago that ya'd pay for it, so I did. No one'd bothered ya for sellin' your children to th' mountain men, but ya go makin' trouble with th' city folks, ya're goin' to get locked up, so ya will. See if I ain't right."

"Aunt Aggie, I don't need a lecture. I need help."

"First off, Daisy has money and has been talkin' to some folks in th' city 'bout goin' there to live. It ain't goin' to be easy to stop her, so it ain't. My guess is she's already told people that ya're still alive. Looks to me like ya're goin' to have to stay in disguise for a very long time if ya don't want no one to find ya, so ya're. An' ya're goin' to have to do some more changin'. I knowed who ya was right off, so I did."

"I sort of expected that. You raised me, after all. Who knows me better than you do?"

"Don't take no chances goin' out an' about lettin' people see ya."

"I'll be okay," Jacob said.

"Now, ya ain't told me what ya're hidin' from. Just what did ya do?"

"Aunt Aggie, don't be like my women, always ready to think the worst where I'm concerned."

"I ain't, so I ain't," Aggie said. "Ya knowed I always stand up for ya no matter what."

"I'm sorry. I know you do."

"Ya can't stay on th' mountain either if ya don't want spotted. Daisy knows ya're here, so she does."

"I think Daisy's only interested in getting away from me."

"Maybe ya're right," Aggie said. "All I want is for ya to come back to th' mountain where ya belong, so I do. I miss havin' ya comin' up th' mountain from your cabin to visit with me, bringin' my snuff to me an' talkin' 'bout everythin' we've been through all these years."

"I guess we don't have time for that now," Jacob said. "We need a plan."

"I just don't understand why ya have to hide behind a disguise, so I don't."

"Aunt Aggie, you don't have to understand. Just help me. I'm afraid I don't have much time."

"Ya need help doin' what? Gettin' off this mountain? If that's what ya're talkin' 'bout just get in your truck an'go. Nobody's goin' to knowed ya now just because I knowed ya."

"You're sure of that?"

"I'm sure of that, so I am."

Jacob rose from the rocker, kissed his aunt on the cheek, and all too soon Aggie watched as her beloved nephew drove off the mountain. As she rocked, a tear ran down her cheek.

36

WINTER ANN QUICKLY DARTED TO THE BAY WINDOW. She had heard the slamming of car doors, followed by voices. It was what she had been waiting for all day. Ever since her mother had told her that her father and Patty were coming home that evening, she had waited in the living room, where she would be the first one they saw when they came through the door.

Just as Patty entered the house with Cliff following close behind, Tuesday ran to him, not wanting to wait one more moment to be in his arms. Patty picked up Winter Ann and, lifting her high in the air, swung her in a circle until she giggled with delight.

Mary Lou skipped down the stairs two at a time and joined in the joyful reunion.

"Are you hungry, Daddy?" Winter Ann asked. "Mommy has been cooking dinner for you all day."

"I could eat a horse." Cliff grinned at the child. Then suddenly it hit them all that Paul Frank was gone for good. He would never come into their house, bringing with him his lighthearted air and good humor, would never be at their table to share a dinner that Tuesday and the girls had spent the day preparing, and the initially joyful gathering turned somber.

After the meal, the girls went to their rooms, and Tuesday and Cliff sat in the living room with their coffee, where they discussed Paul Frank's funeral services. Only then did Cliff tell Tuesday about McCallister's faking his death and disguising himself before coming back to the mountain. He told her it was likely McCallister, and not Ike Harris, who had killed Paul Frank.

Tuesday became hysterical with fear upon learning that Jacob was alive after all. Cliff held her tight in his arms and pressed his cheek to hers, muffling her cries so as not to alarm the girls. It took him most of the night to calm her enough to tell her of his plans.

The next morning Cliff left the house after arranging to meet Randy McCoy, Jim Jones, and Bart Howard at his office.

After a discussion that lasted three hours, the four men split up. Randy McCoy and Cliff Moran were going to stay in the city—Cliff had no intentions of being away from his family, knowing that McCallister was on the loose—while Bart Howard and Jim Jones went back to Winding Ridge. The men were taking no chances that would allow McCallister to get away. At her own request, Daisy had been taken along with her children to the women's shelter, but before she went she had given a good description of Jacob's new disguise.

"Cliff, there's a chance that Ike Harris is the one who murdered Tommy Lee Hillberry and Paul Frank Ruble," Randy said.

"Okay, why do you believe that?"

"Ike was working at the mansion. Maybe Paul Frank had a confrontation with him."

"Why would restoring a house give cause for murder?" Cliff asked.

"I don't know, but there could be more to this than we realize. All I'm saying is, we can't pick McCallister up without a good reason."

"I think we have a good enough reason to hold him for questioning," Cliff said. "He faked his death, he's in disguise, he was on the mountain when the murders were committed, and in Daisy we have a willing witness. Let's start in his office. I called Hal last night, and he was able to get a search warrant for McCallister's office and his house."

J. J. and Bart reached the mountain just after lunch. They made their first stop the sheriff's office. Both Ozzie Moats and Jess Willis were there, the sheriff at his desk and the deputy cleaning the cells.

"What do you have on the murders so far?" J. J. asked the sheriff.

Ozzie stood and remained silent.

"Are you doing anything at all?" Bart asked.

"As a matter of fact, we are," Ozzie said.

"Let's hear it," J. J. demanded.

"What the—" Ozzie uttered, his anger rising. "You might think you can come to my town and run my investigations, but I'm not goin' to have it."

"What investigation?" Bart asked. "That's all we want to know. What are you doing? Look, there are two women who are in danger until we find and lock up the man who murdered Tommy Lee and Paul Frank. You seem not to have any concerns at all about that."

"Just what do you want me to do?" Ozzie asked indignantly. "There were no witnesses. No one knows anything."

"How do you know that? You haven't even gone door to door and asked. Someone shot Tommy Lee from the alley that turned off Main Street. The killer had to have walked or driven down Main Street and stood on the crate that was found under the window. Someone could have seen the killer carrying the crate to the window from wherever he got it. They would have no way of knowing it was important to report it if no one asked them!"

"I wanted to get out and investigate," Jess said as he stepped from the cell he was mopping, "but the sheriff felt the cells needed cleaned."

"Jess, get back to work. This is none of your business."

"I'm deputy, and it is my business," Jess said, dropping the mop into the scrub bucket at the entrance to the cell. "It's not a deputy's job to do the cleanin' while you sit at your desk readin' magazines or standin' at the door gawkin' at the women walkin' by."

Ozzie's face got blood red as he listened to Jess, who had never been so disloyal to the sheriff. He had always done as Ozzie asked with very little backtalk, and certainly never in front of others. "You want to keep your job, you'd better mind your business and keep to your place. This is none of your concern. Go back to work."

"Wait just a minute, Jess," Bart said. "I want you to get out there and knock on doors. Find out if anyone saw someone suspicious that night."

"Now, *you* wait just a minute," Ozzie sputtered. "You can't come in here orderin' my deputy around."

"Sheriff, you're not doing your job," J. J. said. "We need help, and it's obvious that you aren't willing. Jess is, and we're taking advantage of it. Let's go, Jess."

The deputy hesitated, hiked his pants up by his belt buckle, grabbed his cap, and not even looking back at Ozzie, he swaggered out the door, following the two men onto the street.

"Jess, you know the town better than we do. How would you divide it?"

Feeling important, Jess stood as straight and tall as he could. He hooked his right thumb in his holster and with his left hand straightened his tie. "I'd say for one of you to take the upper side of Main Street, while the other takes the lower side, going off the side streets. I'll take Main Street and the alleys runnin' off of it. I think it's more likely that the people will talk to me. You know how they are with strangers, but tell the ones you talk to that you're workin' with me, and they should be more cooperative."

"Okay, let's meet back here when we're finished," Bart suggested.

As the men set off, Ozzie stood in the doorway, a scowl covering his face.

Brandi Rose looked up startled when Cliff and Randy strode into the office, where she was packing things away. "What are you doing here?"

"I have something to tell you, and it's going to be a shocker," Cliff said, "so brace yourself."

Brandi Rose stared back at Cliff. Her huge eyes, round and worried under thick lashes, revealed that she was expecting bad news. "All right, what is it?"

"Jacob McCallister is not dead. He faked it. We're investigating the possibility that he murdered two men."

"Oh, I'm so happy!" Brandi Rose beamed, her expression magically changing from fear to joy. "When is he going to come back to work?"

"Didn't you hear me?" Cliff asked. "He's wanted for murder. It's not likely he'll hang around here."

"You can't mean it," Brandi Rose pleaded. "Jacob is the nicest man I know."

"He can be when he wants to be," Cliff said, "but don't let that fool you."

"We have a search warrant," Randy said. "We're going to search the place, and we need your cooperation."

"There's nothing to hide here. You're wasting your time, but go ahead." Brandi Rose went back to what she had been doing.

"Stop packing," Cliff ordered. "We'll just have to unpack it anyway."

Brandi Rose sat back in her chair. Her face was pale, and her hands shook. "If he's not dead, he'll come back here."

"Nothing could make me happier," Cliff said as he dumped a neatly packed box on the floor.

"Oh, no! Do you have to make such a mess?"

While Randy went to check out McCallister's office, Cliff stayed busy opening the boxes that Brandi Rose had packed, keeping an eye on her. He sorted through carefully so as not to miss anything that might point to McCallister and the motivation for his crimes. Still, Cliff noticed Brandi Rose's dazed, unbelieving look.

"It's a certainty that McCallister is alive. He went back to his mountain home. It's been verified. The women he keeps in his cabin saw him."

"Women? What about his wife?"

"He has no wife," Cliff answered. "The picture of the woman on his desk happens to be my wife."

Brandi Rose was speechless.

"I realize that this is a lot to take in all at one time, but Jacob McCallister is not the man you thought he was. He's been in prison for kidnapping and child endangerment, among other things. He has women and children living in poverty in his cabin on the mountain above the town of Winding Ridge. And now he's guilty of murder!"

"I just can't believe it," Brandi Rose sobbed.

"That's the effect he has on women," Cliff said. "It's why he can get away with it."

"But your wife, how—"

Randy returned suddenly to Cliff's side and said, "I need to talk to you in private."

"Hold on a minute, Randy. Brandi Rose, I want you to leave everything as it is and go home." Cliff handed her his card. "Call me if you hear from him."

Brandi Rose looked at Cliff defiantly but did not speak.

"If you don't cooperate, you can be charged as an accessory to the crime. You won't be the first. By the way, I'm assigning a man to watch you. I'd advise you not to warn McCallister. You won't get away with it."

Keeping her silence, Brandi Rose left.

"Okay, what have you got?" Cliff asked.

"His home address. I found his safe hidden in a closet."

"I don't believe it! How did you get the safe open?"

"One of my informers taught me. You remember, I told you about it."

"Oh, yeah!" Cliff said grinning. "I told you you'd be tempted to enter a life of crime every time you came across a safe."

"Yeah, right, very funny. Anyway, it's filled with money—I can't even guess how much. I found some papers, too, including the deed to his house here in the city."

"Wow, that's great! Call for more men and we'll go search the house."

"Remember his son Joe lives there, too."

"We'll watch out for him," Cliff said. "McCallister could be hiding out there, thinking we haven't had time to ascertain where he lives."

37

*A*FTER LEAVING A MESSAGE ON BRANDI ROSE'S ANSWER-ing machine at home, Jacob waited impatiently for her call. He paced throughout his house, rifling through drawers, closets, and desks, searching for money he might have tucked away and forgotten. Although he didn't want to add another person to the few who already knew he was alive, he could think of no other way but to involve her. It was best for him to keep out of sight; he could not be the one to go back to his office for the money he had stashed there.

The phone rang, making him recoil.

Jacob picked up the receiver. "Yes."

"Jacob, is that you?"

He did not speak.

"It's me, Brandi Rose!"

"Good, I was waiting for your call," Jacob said.

"Yes. I just got the message. I just got here from the office."

"You've been at the office? I'm surprised you've kept it open this long."

"At first Ike and I didn't know what to do, so we just kept going."

"What stopped you?"

"The law."

"What?"

"There are two detectives in your office right now."

"Is one of them Cliff Moran?"

"Yes, he came here snooping around right after 9/11 and again today."

"Damn. Listen, I need your help. It involves you running away with me. You'll have to give up your friends and family."

"I'd go anywhere with you," Brandi Rose breathed.

"Good, we've got to make plans. I need the money from my safe. The combination is left three, pass it twice, right nine, and left two."

"Got it!"

"Now, do you know where Ike is?"

"I thought he was still at the building site."

"No, I've been there."

"I don't know then," Brandi said.

"I was hoping he was in communication with you. It makes me nervous that he left without saying anything. Was he acting strange or anything?"

"No, not at all. What are you getting at?"

"I have a bad feeling, not knowing where he is or what he's thinking."

"I thought everything was fine with him," Brandi Rose offered.

"We'll figure that out later. Meanwhile, here's what I want you to do."

Jess Willis had diligently knocked on every door on every house and business on Main Street, taking him every bit of two hours. When he was done, he tucked his notebook into his breast pocket and headed back to the office. He had hardly stepped inside the door when Ozzie jumped him with a barrage of verbal abuse. Jess had no intention of cowing down to the sheriff this time.

Refusing to get into a war of words, Jess took the handle of the mop and resumed cleaning the cells. Ozzie sat at his desk with a self-satisfied smirk on his face. His small, beady eyes followed Jess as he finished his job.

An hour later J. J. and Bart returned from their door knocking just in time to catch Jess as he finished up his housekeeping duties. Quickly, he ushered the detectives into a small room with a wooden table and six chairs. There was a window high on the wall, a twin to the one that was broken when Tommy Lee was shot. The bars cast long shadows across the scarred table where the sun shone brightly through the glass.

"Hope one of you two got something," J. J. said. "No one I talked to saw anything unusual or otherwise that night."

"Nothing," Bart said.

Smiling, Jess leaned back in his chair, lifting the front legs off the floor. At the same time he removed his notepad from his breast pocket. Settled, letting the wall support the chair, he hooked his foot behind the chair rung. "I thought it was hopeless," Jess said, "'til I knocked on Hump Rudd's door. He's the bar owner. His wife, Fran, was home. She don't hang around the bar 'cause her husband don't want her out there. She didn't want to talk to me at first, but finally I persuaded her."

Having gotten the full attention of the detectives, Jess squared his shoulders and allowed the front legs of his chair to fall back to the floor. Leaning his forearms on the table for emphasis, he continued in a voice full of pride. "She told me that she was taking fresh air on her front porch, sittin' in her swing and mindin' her own business, when she saw a man comin' down the street. He couldn't see her 'cause of the vines that Hump has growin' around and through the latticework 'round his porch. What made her pay attention was the man comin' down the street kept goin' into each alley he came to. 'You know, like he was lookin' for somethin', she said. 'Finally, he come outta one with a crate and disappeared into the alley next to the jail.' A few minutes later, according to Fran, he came out onto the street, without the crate he'd been huntin' for so diligently just minutes earlier."

"I hope she was able to give you a description of the man," Bart said.

"She said he was tall and muscular lookin', he had dark hair closely cropped, and he was dressed much nicer than the men she was used to seein' in Windin' Ridge."

"Does that sound like McCallister?" J. J. asked Bart.

"When I asked, she said it wasn't McCallister," Jess said quickly.

"Matches my notes," Bart said. "Look at your notes, J. J. Cliff told us that Daisy said McCallister had cut his hair in a buzz cut. We know he has very dark hair, dresses nice, is tall, and lifts weights to keep his arms, chest, and legs muscled out."

"The best thing is," Jess continued in his high-pitched, excited voice, "the man went from the alley beside the jail straight to the bar. We need to find who was in the bar that night and get their version of his description."

"We know that McCallister was in the bar that night," Bart said. "That's the night he practically dragged Daisy out of there."

"If he's the only man fitting Fran's description, it's got to be McCallister that shot Tommy Lee."

"Remember, Fran said it wasn't McCallister. But first," Bart said, "we need to find out what Ike Harris looks like. A description of dark, short-cropped hair, tall, and muscular could fit a lot of men. There's an excellent possibility that he could be the one who murdered Paul Frank and Tommy Lee."

"Sure," Jess said, "and if Ike doesn't fit Fran's description and there wasn't a man other than McCallister fitting it in the bar that night, I'd say we have McCallister dead to rights."

"Okay, Jess, since you're a town man and the people will cooperate with you, find out each and every customer who was in the bar between five and ten o'clock in the evening. Question them closely about whoever was there then. Let us know if you need help."

"As long as Fran says it wasn't McCallister, we don't have much to go on."

"Get to it, Jess," Bart smiled and then stood. "You're doing a good job."

"Wait just a minute!" Ozzie's huge bulk filled the doorway. "I'll give my deputy orders. You big-feelin' detectives ain't goin' to run my investigation."

"Like I said before, looks to me," J. J. sneered, "like you don't have an investigation."

"Just what have you been doing on the case?" Bart asked.

"I don't have to report to you, or anyone else for that matter," Ozzie spat, turning his back on Bart and J. J.

"Jess, you can go on and question the folks that were in the bar durin' the shootin'. But mind, I'm the one givin' the orders around here."

Jess left with Bart and J. J. following at his heels, the detectives looking too disgusted for further conversation with the sheriff.

On the way to McCallister's house, Cliff, who was riding shotgun, took the call from Bart Howard wanting a description of Ike Harris. Leafing through his notes, Cliff found the pages on Ike Harris, McCallister's former cellmate. Harris was tall and thin and had sandy blond hair and a receding hairline. He was twenty years older than McCallister.

Bart updated Cliff on what they had come up with to date—a description that could fit McCallister, and the woman who gave it denying it was McCallister.

Randy concluded, "As far as we know, McCallister has never murdered before."

They pulled up in front of the house, and the other men piled from the cars and surrounded it in mere seconds, leaving Cliff and Randy free to approach the front door.

Cliff tried the door, but it was locked, so he rang the doorbell, knocking at the same time. "Police! Let us in, or we'll break down the door. We have a search warrant." There was no answer. Before Cliff could give the order to break in, though, the door opened from inside.

"We were able to force the French doors around back," an officer explained. Cliff and Randy hurried inside, and the men quickly swept the house.

Following Jacob's orders, very quickly while Cliff and Randy were still conducting a search of Jacob's office, Brandi Rose had cleaned out her savings, rented a car, and went to meet him at the bus terminal, where he had picked up a second stockpile of money he had stashed in a locker months before, in the event he had to make a quick getaway one day or couldn't get to his office safe.

Brandi Rose entered the bus terminal and glanced around, but she did not see Jacob. He was supposed to be at the terminal by now; she began to panic. A man who had been sitting on a bench with a large suitcase at his side approached her then, with a great smile on his face. "Brandi Rose, it's me, Jacob." He took her arm.

She gasped.

"I told you on the phone I'd changed my appearance. I didn't think it was that good, since Annabelle, Aunt Aggie, and Daisy all knew me right off."

"Oh, my goodness, it's you! You look so different," Brandi Rose said.

"Is everything ready?"

"It's done," she said, still sounding stunned.

"What did you do with your car?"

"I put it in my garage and locked the house, just like you said. I called my sister and told her that my job ended and I was going to California and look for work. She knows that I have enough money to live on for some time. There won't be any questions. I've lived in California before. I guess I have a reputation as a gadabout."

"Great!" Jacob took his bag and her arm. "Let's go. I'm sure that big-feeling Moran is just steps behind you."

"I know, and believe me, I've felt the small hair on the back of my neck tingle every time I see movement from the corner of my eye."

"He's a jerk," Jacob spat.

"Let's go," he said again as he pulled her arm, moving her along.

"To California?"

"No. Believe me Moran will check it out. It doesn't matter if your family thinks it's not unusual for you to drop everything and move. He'll leave nothing to chance."

"Where then?" She tripped as she hastily short-stepped trying to keep up with him in her tight skirt.

"You'll see," Jacob said, impatient at the need to drag her along.

Cliff was angry at himself that Brandi Rose and McCallister were gone. He had known that Brandi Rose would pick up the phone and call McCallister, warning him they were coming, but had not anticipated they could touch base with one another so quickly because he had expected that McCallister would have taken more time leaving the mountain in the first place. Having barely minutes to prepare to leave town, they must have only been scant minutes ahead of them. Cliff sent the extra men away, and he and Randy conducted a complete search of the house.

"What's this?" Randy asked, holding up an old, worn blueprint.

"Let me see." Cliff took the map. "It's a drawing of the tunnels running beneath the mountain above Winding Ridge. Wonder what McCallister's doing with it?"

"I've no idea," Randy said. "As far as I know, McCallister was against the militia."

"Yes, he was. He was furious that his son Joe was so deeply involved in it."

"You know," Randy observed, "this map seems out of place. It was wedged between the sofa and the end table."

"Like maybe McCallister was studying it and hadn't remembered to put it away because he had to leave sooner than he expected. From the looks of the rest of the house, he keeps things in their place."

"Joe lives here, too," Randy reminded Cliff. "More than likely, he would be the one interested in the map, as he was the one involved in the militia."

"Let's not make any assumptions," Cliff said. Folding the blueprint, he put it in his pocket and forgot it.

Later that day, Cliff and Randy had learned that according to her family, Brandi Rose had closed up her house and, out of the blue, left for California that very day.

NNABELLE WAS HAVING HER USUAL EARLY-MORNING breakfast. She had the radio tuned to her favorite station and was stunned when the newscaster began a story about the murders of two men on the mountain above the small town of Winding Ridge. At the same time, she was excited that anyone in the outside world even knew about the remote town.

He mentioned Jacob McCallister by name then, and Annabelle gasped, clutching her chest, horrified to learn that he was suspected of the murders and was thought to be on the run with a woman named Brandi Rose, who had been his secretary.

The secretary too had recently disappeared after cleaning out her bank accounts and informing her family she was returning to California. In his most melodramatic voice, the newscaster added: "Brandi Rose has not been seen or heard from since she made that final call to her sister. No travel ticket bought in her name, no credit card charges, nothing."

"My word," Annabelle breathed, "who'd ever thought people out there knowin' 'bout our state of affairs up here on this time-forgotten-mountain."

The door slammed and startled Annabelle. "Sara, I thought you'd gone an' run off with Daisy."

"No, I've been at Dillon's cabin. They have a radio too. Joe got it for them."

"So ya heard. Your pa's gone to California with that woman."

"Yes, I heard it last night. Ya must've been sleepin'. I'd say Pa's in trouble now," Sara said.

"Ya knowed, I'd bet that when Jeb was in trouble a coupla years ago there was talk 'bout it on th' radio an' we just didn't knowed it."

"Ya're probably right, an' we didn't knowed it 'cause we didn't have a radio then."

"I hope th' law don't come around lookin' for 'im here," Annabelle worried. "I can't abide it when th' law's comin' 'round askin' questions I can't answer."

"I don't believe th' law's goin' to be back here, an' I don't think Pa's comin' back here anytime soon, or I sure wouldn't be here. When there's trouble, Pa disappears for a coupla years. Ma, what're we goin' to do now that Daisy's gone?"

"Well, we're goin' to do th' same as we always done."

"Ya knowed Joe don't come 'round enough to keep us supplied. Daisy was bringin' in most of our food an' all."

At the hum of an engine outdoors, the two women stopped talking. Someone had driven into the back yard. The engine cut out, and then a door slammed.

Sara rose to her feet and hurried to the back door. It was Deputy Willis. "Hi, Jess, it's been a long time."

Jess strutted across the packed-dirt yard and crossed the porch. "I'm looking for McCallister, again," he said meaningfully. "I don't want no hard time from the two of you. Just tell me where he is, and it will save us all a lot of time."

"Are ya kiddin'?" Annabelle sputtered. "Ya knowed he don't tell us anythin'."

Jess pulled the screen door from Annabelle's hand and, pushing her gently aside, walked into the kitchen. He moved swiftly through the cabin, already sure that McCallister was not there, but needing to check it out for the report he would be sending to Cliff.

Back in the kitchen, Jess, basking in his self-importance, stood facing the women, firing questions at them.

"Why don't'cha just wait a minute?" Annabelle demanded. "We tol' ya we didn't knowed where he is. He don't tell us nothin'."

Empty handed but confident that he had done his job, the deputy left. His final report would include a review of his search and interrogation at the cabin and would also state that the forensic report he had received indicated that the bullet used to kill Tommy Lee Hillberry was not the same caliber as the one found in Paul Frank Ruble. His report would conclude: "After searching the houses in town and on the mountain, I believe that Jacob McCallister has left the immediate area. I will continue to make spot checks until you inform me that it is no longer necessary to do so."

Cliff and Randy could not find a trail to follow. The only thing they knew at this point was that after closing her house Brandi Rose had rented a vehicle. The car was found in Morgantown, where it had been left at a car rental company, apparently sometime in the night. It had been rented under Brandi Rose's name.

"You know what?" Cliff asked.

"Tell me."

"I just remembered the blueprint we found in McCallister's house, the one of the tunnel. Do you think he would hole up there?"

"I can't visualize him staying in that tunnel very long," Randy answered. "But he could move around in it, exiting into any one of the many towns the tunnel connects. It would be impossible to trace him. The entire tunnel spans three states."

"I hadn't thought of it," Cliff said.

"All he'd have to do is get to the mountain without being spotted."

"What if he didn't go to the mountain to enter the tunnel?" Cliff said. "What if he went in from a town he picked at random?"

"Or maybe he didn't leave the mountain in the traditional manner. He used the tunnel instead."

"If he hadn't been careless with the map, we'd never have thought of it."

"I think you've got something there," Randy said. "But I still think the map was of more interest to Joe. Under the circumstances, McCallister wouldn't be so careless."

"We can't take that chance. The best thing is, we don't even have to find out where they went in. We'll go in from Winding Ridge and check it out. We have the advantage. We have the map to guide us around the tunnel."

"I think just the two of us should go," Randy said. "With too many men, we may give ourselves away."

"I'll get us a couple of bicycles," Cliff said. "They'll be quiet, and we can get around much faster than walking."

Just then the fax machine line rang and a page covered with a large scrawl slowly fed out. Cliff picked it up; it was the report Jess Willis had written following his search for McCallister.

"It looks as if we have two murderers," Cliff said.

"Maybe, maybe not," Randy said reading the report over Cliff's shoulder. "A killer could use a different gun."

"You could be right, but I think you're reaching."

The men planned to leave first thing the next morning. They made a list of what needed to be done and divided the jobs between themselves, agreeing to meet at Cliff's house at 8:00 a.m.

"Oh, no, Cliff," Tuesday pleaded. "Please don't go."

"I have to. You know we can't let him run loose. He'll never leave us alone."

"It's not that, Cliff. You have no way of knowing that Jacob's traveling by way of the tunnel, or even if he's running. You told me the woman at Winding Ridge said the man she saw on the street going into the alley didn't even look like Jacob. Somehow I don't think he's a killer. He just wants to manipulate women."

"Why is he running then?"

"Because he knows Daisy went straight to you when she ran away and that you're after him. I would bet my life on it."

39

*O*N BIKES, CLIFF AND RANDY ENTERED THE TUNNEL from Paul Frank Ruble's property at Broad Run. They were careful to keep their flashlights pointed at the ground just five or ten feet ahead. They rode deeper into the tunnel, scattering the rodents as they passed. After riding just a couple of miles in the eerie darkness they heard voices up ahead. Under cover of the boys' conversation, they propped their bikes against the wall of the tunnel. Careful to keep out of the glow of light made by a few flashlights and a lantern, they crept close enough to hear clearly.

They recognized one of the voices as Joe McCallister's. He was telling the others that the murder of Paul Frank Ruble was being blamed on his father, and he was going to find out which of them was responsible. "I know you mongrels were robbing the place 'cause you knew Ike Harris wasn't there. What happened? Ruble came on you, and you got scared and shot him?"

"No," Robby Rudd blubbered, confident to speak freely in the presence of his friends. "We wasn't stealin' that day. We had one of th' Keefover girls there. We had her blindfolded and gagged so she wouldn't make any noise or knowed where she was. Anyway, Ruble came on us. It was like he came outta nowhere. He musta parked a distance from th' property and walked in, ya knowed, usin' th' element of surprise. It scared us 'cause we'd heard Ruble was th' law. I seen him before he seen me, an' knowed I had to do somethin'.

"I picked up my rifle an' crouched. I circled 'round 'im usin' th' weeds as cover. Then standin' up, that's the first he saw me, I aimed my rifle an' shot him. Man, I was scared shitless, him bein' a lawman. I couldn't let 'im see th' girl though, 'cause she was hurt bad."

"I don't believe it," Joe said. "It'd be more like you dumb cruds to run like scared rabbits than shoot a man."

"I was scared, man. What we did to th' Keefover girl would've put us behind bars for a long time."

"What makes you think she won't tell and put you in jail anyway?" Joe asked.

"She don't have no idea who we are. Everyone always thinks it's Tommy Lee Hillberry when a girl's raped around these parts, anyway."

"I hear doin' time for murderin' a lawman is a lot harder than time for rapin' a girl," Joe said.

"Nobody knows we did it if'n ya keep your mouth shut."

Cliff and Randy, their guns drawn, slipped from the shadows into the circle of light.

"We know," Randy said.

"Looks to me like you guys are a direct result of Sheriff Moats' ignoring what's going on on the mountain," Cliff said, sorry that Jacob McCallister was not the one who had killed Paul Frank. If he had been, he would have definitely been out of their lives forever.

"Tell me," Randy asked, "did you kill Tommy Lee Hillberry?"

"Why would we kill him? He took the blame for most of our doin's."

It was obvious which boy had confessed to the murder of Paul Frank. He was huddled against the tunnel wall, where he had scampered when the two lawmen stepped into the light, with his head between his knees, shaking like a leaf.

"Get up, boy." Randy got him by the elbow and helped him to his feet.

"My pa's goin' to kill me," Robby sniveled.

"You should've thought of that before you raped a girl and killed a good man," Randy said.

"Your father won't be able to get to you in jail, son," Cliff said.

"But you'll wish he could before it's all over with," Randy put in.

"All he cares 'bout is his beer joint," Robby accused.

After taking Robby Rudd to the sheriff and informing Hump Rudd that his son was charged with murder, Cliff and Randy started home with heavy hearts. The loss of Paul Frank seemed even more tragic now that they knew he had died so needlessly at the hands of an unruly, thoughtless boy caught in the process of a foolish crime.

"I'm glad that Robby Rudd will be brought to Wheeling to be indicted and held for trial," Cliff said.

"Yeah, with Ozzie Moats in charge we'd get a horse and monkey show. Anyway, stopping the likes of him will make life much safer for the young girls in Winding Ridge and in the cabins on the mountain."

"Do you think that Robby Rudd killed Tommy Lee?" Cliff asked.

"No, absolutely not," Randy answered. "And I can't imagine Jacob McCallister killing him, to tell the truth. He had no reason, especially not while Tommy Lee sat in a jail cell. I mean if McCallister had been confronted by Tommy Lee, then I could see it."

40

"HERE THEY ARE!" WINTER ANN SKIPPED AROUND THE room.

Tuesday opened the door, surprised that the men were back so soon. *Did they know something already?*

"Am I happy to see you!" Cliff took Tuesday in his arms, hugging her close, with Winter Ann tugging at his pant leg. Releasing Tuesday, he reached down and swung Winter Ann high into the air, and with a flourish he kissed her on the forehead.

"Come on in, Randy," Tuesday said. "We can talk in the kitchen. I'm sure the two of you are hungry. I'll call Cora to come and take Winter Ann to play with Linda so we can talk."

After a lunch of chicken salad sandwiches and iced tea, Cora took Winter Ann back to her house. Cliff and Randy filled Tuesday and the girls in on everything, except the part about them going after McCallister that very night.

"I don't know what to think," Patty said. "I for one am not going to allow my father to ruin my life. What can he do, anyway? I'm not a child any longer. He can't just come in here and take me away. It's not me he wants anyway." She looked distressed. "I don't mean to minimize the cruelty he's capable of, but he wants Tuesday, not me. Cliff, you are always there to protect her, and I'm not going to live in fear of him. If I can get through Paul Frank's death, I can get through anything."

"I say bravo," Mary Lou added. "I'm not going to let what happened in the past rule my life either. When Frank Dillon gets out of jail, I'm going to be wary, but I'm not going to crouch in fear. I have a life to live too."

They talked for a few hours before Cliff decided it was time to announce that he and Randy were not finished with the matter just yet. They were going after McCallister, and they were leaving that night. With nothing else on which to go after McCallister, they had convinced Daisy to charge him with assault and attempted kidnapping. It had not been easy, but after making Daisy understand that she and her children were in danger if he remained on the loose, she relented.

"I know what you're up to." Tuesday took the news in stride, aware that it was the only thing Cliff could do in his role as the family's protector and provider. Although she and Patty had resolved not to allow Jacob to overshadow their lives any longer, they would live in mortal fear of him. At the same time, they refused to cower in fear, living as if they were about to be brought under Jacob McCallister's thumb at anytime.

"What's that?" Cliff's grin had a charm that lit up his handsome face.

"It's that ever-present hunch of yours." Tuesday put her hands on either side of his face and gazed into his eyes. "You think everything will fall into place, and you will discover Jacob's hidden purpose for using the 9/11 tragedy to fake his death."

As she continued to hold to his face, Cliff placed his large hands on Tuesday's forearms, making them look small and frail.

"I do," he said as he slid her arms around his neck and kissed her.

Ending the kiss, Tuesday whispered in his ear. "I'm afraid. Not only for myself, but for Patty too."

"I know." Cliff held her tighter, allowing her to hide her tears.

Cliff did have a strong hunch that there was more to all this than it appeared on the surface. So far it had been established that McCallister had not been responsible for Paul Frank's death, but they had not ruled him out for Tommy Lee's, nor had they charged him. The only thing that really tied McCallister to Tommy Lee's death was that he was in the immediate area at the time of the shooting. As far as Cliff was concerned, it was too bad McCallister could not be forced to stay in town while the investigation went on.

Randy left to pack, and Cliff packed his own things, with help from Tuesday. While they worked, Cliff updated her on other small details, telling her about the team who were now searching the tunnel for McCallister and then for evidence against McCallister or anyone else involved in the crimes. Also there was a lead on Jacob and Brandi Rose, who had booked a rental car on her credit card—a piece of evidence that had been deliberately kept out of the news report. They had picked up the car in Pittsburgh and dropped it off in Chicago. "We're going to try to pick up their trail. It's not obvious if they were being careless or trying to throw us off track. But they were foolish anyway, because it gave us a place to start."

"Where's that?" Tuesday asked.

"What?"

"The starting place. What do you mean?"

"First, how did they get to Pittsburgh to rent the car?" Cliff answered. "I'd say one obvious way was to charter a plane or take a commuter flight."

"I see. But maybe they drove in Jacob's truck."

"There's already an alert out for McCallister's truck. Her car was found in her garage."

"I don't like any of this," Tuesday said.

"No way I'm going to let McCallister get away this time."

"Away from what? We don't even know if he did anything. Tommy Lee and Ike Harris had Patty."

"He's involved, and like all criminals, he'll give himself away if pressure is put on him."

"You're right," Tuesday agreed. "More than anything I want him behind bars so I can feel safe again. I just want to wake up one day to find we're not living in Jacob's shadow."

"It will happen. Even if I have to take a leave from the FBI and track him down myself. In my opinion, even though Mc-Callister wasn't the one who pulled the trigger, he's responsible for Paul Frank's death. Had McCallister not kept pushing himself into our lives, Paul Frank would still be alive, working in Wheeling as a state policeman." Cliff shoved his fingers through his tousled hair. "And I'll be damned if I lose another loved one at McCallister's hand."

With his family on Cliff's mind, he and Randy continued the hunt for McCallister. The first stop on their list was the small airport on the outskirts of Wheeling. He and Randy found a parking space easily, as the next flight out was not scheduled for another two hours.

Cliff and Randy walked up to the lone ticket agent at the counter.

"Howdy," Cliff greeted the man, flashing his badge. "We're looking for this man and woman." He pushed a photo of Jacob McCallister and one of Brandi Rose across the counter. "Have you seen them?"

"Nah," the agent said, shaking his head, "but I'm not the only one working the ticket counter. Maybe one of the others can help ya."

"What are the shifts?" Cliff asked.

"Day, evening, and graveyard."

"When does the afternoon shift start?"

"My relief is Bobbie. She'll be in at three."

"We'll wait in the coffee shop over there."

"It's open till midnight, so go ahead."

After downing two cups of coffee each, Cliff and Randy made their way back to the counter, where a young woman was busy at the computer, her coworker apparently gone for the day.

Cliff once again flashed his badge, pushing the two photos across the counter to her. "Have you seen these two?"

The young woman picked up the photos and examined them closely. "What a handsome man," she said, smiling. "I can tell you that I haven't seen this one. Who could forget him? I remember this woman, though. She purchased two tickets, but"—she had been punching the keyboard rapidly as she talked, intently watching the screen—"they were not used." She looked up as she spoke. "I've found the name she purchased them in."

"What is it?"

"Victor Newman."

As they left the counter, Randy asked, "What was that all about?"

"I'd say they thought they would throw us off," Cliff said. "Apparently they didn't realize it would be so simple to find out that the tickets were not used, but they counted on us learning that they were purchased."

"Yeah, I can see where the average person would not even think of there being a record of a ticket going unused."

"Knowing that they didn't take that flight really doesn't help us much," Cliff mused.

"It was booked to Los Angles. I'd say that was to throw us off, too. That was where we already thought they might go. Brandi Rose's family lives there."

"Okay," Cliff held up his forefinger. "She bought airline tickets they did not use." Holding up a second finger, he said, "Her credit card shows she rented a car in Pittsburgh and dropped it off in Chicago. Third," he held up another finger, "he's using the same alias he used before he was sent to prison."

"Brandi Rose and McCallister traveled to Chicago in the rental car."

"Looks that way," Cliff said.

"But why run?" Randy asked. "It'd be next to impossible

to prove that he faked his own death in the 9/11 disaster. What's he running from?"

"Something big. That's what. McCallister's hiding something really big."

They notified the FBI in Chicago of the situation and sent the photos over the wire.

Three days later Cliff got word that McCallister and Brandi Rose were subleasing an apartment in Chicago. Cliff and Randy flew there immediately and met with the FBI agents assigned to the case. They were as anxious to get McCallister as Cliff and Randy were. Assuming that McCallister used the 9/11 tragedy to fake his death, it was, in their book, the lowest of crimes.

At five in the morning, Cliff, Randy, and two Chicago FBI agents were at the door to McCallister's apartment. After repeatedly knocking and shouting, "FBI. Open up!" they rammed the door open. The apartment was empty. Apparently no one had moved in during the five days since the lease had been signed.

Annabelle and Sara struggled to keep food on the table, although Joe continued to bring supplies to his Aunt Aggie, Frank Dillon's women, and to his mother and Sara. Without funds from his father, his paycheck didn't go very far. And with only one child to support instead of three, the Social Security payment had dropped considerably.

Seeing how hopeless it had become, Annabelle relented and allowed Sara to get a job. She felt very lucky to land a position at The General Store. With Daisy's twins gone, Annabelle found it easy to take care of one little girl while Sara worked, earning a very small paycheck. Unlike Daisy, Sara received no tips to compensate for her low wages. She did get a discount on the supplies she bought, though, and was able to provide most of what they needed after Joe made his less and less frequent visits, making it crystal clear that his only motivation in helping was fear.

With the help of the shelter for abused women, Daisy found a small, affordable apartment. She also found a job in a daycare center, where she was permitted to bring her twin boys. The woman from the shelter led her to agencies that helped low-income families with medical care, food stamps, and the like.

Daisy was happier than she had ever been, making friends, discovering the theater, dining out, and getting together with other families and friends. Being sought after by men introduced to her by neighbors and new acquaintances was fun and exciting.

Tuesday, Cliff, Patty, and Mary Lou went on with their lives, very slowly getting over Paul Frank's death.

Cliff kept up an intensive search for McCallister and Brandi Rose, realizing that after losing her usefulness, Brandi Rose may have been dumped by McCallister. Cliff would not rest until McCallister was dead or permanently behind bars.

Still living in fear of Jacob, Tuesday organized a foundation called "Winter Ann," intended to inform women of the dangers of trusting men whose background they had no first-hand knowledge of. The foundation advocated extreme caution: "Know his credentials and check them out."

Mary Lou continued her schooling and became closer to Patty and Jordan Hatfield. The three had a lot in common, including having grown up without a father figure in their lives, and each overcoming having been abused in their adolescence.

Patty became friends with Randy McCoy as together they moved her grandmother, Myrtle Landacre to Wheeling.

Hesitant to cross a line of impropriety, Randy did not allow himself to become more than a friend to Patty. He knew she needed time to truly get over Paul Frank and let go of her dreams of a life with him. The possibility of Patty and Randy getting together must be left to another day.

Aunt Aggie sat and rocked, dreaming of the day she would meet Winter Ann, who was her nephew Jacob's daughter by the only woman he had ever professed to love. In her mind, Aggie went over and over Jeb's life. She would tell Winter Ann all. She knew that as Patty had, Winter Ann, too, would travel to the mountain in search of her truth.

Purchase Autographed Copies

**The Cabin: Misery on the Mountain
Cabin II: Return to Winding Ridge
Cabin III: The Unlawful Assembly at Winding Ridge
Cabin IV: In Jacob's Shadow**

Name: _____

Address: _____

_____

_____ Copy(ies) of *The Cabin* $7.99 ea. $_____

_____ Copy(ies) of *Cabin II* $7.99 ea. $_____

_____ Copy(ies) of *Cabin III* $7.99 ea. $_____

_____ Copy(ies) of *Cabin IV* $7.99 ea. $_____

WV sales tax (if resident) 6% $_____

Shipping & handling (first book) $2.49 $_____

S&H (each additional book) $1.13 $_____

Total enclosed $_____

Method of Payment

☐ Check or money order enclosed.
   Make payable to: Michael Publishing Co.
                PO Box 778
                Fairmont, WV 26555-0778

☐ Charge it to:
   ☐ Master Card   ☐ Visa
   ☐ American Express   ☐ Discover

Card Number: _____

Expiration Date: _____

Signature: _____

Note: Canadian price is $9.99.
Ask for copies at your local bookstore.

Thank you for your order.

Watch for the next installment in The Cabin Series!